Di Morrissey is one of Australia's most successful writers. She began writing as a young woman, training and working as a journalist for Australian Consolidated Press in Sydney and Northcliffe Newspapers in London. She has worked in television in Australia and in the USA as a presenter, reporter, producer and actress. After her marriage to a US diplomat, Peter Morrissey, she lived in Singapore, Japan, Thailand, South America and Washington. Returning to Australia, Di continued to work in television before publishing her first novel in 1991.

Di has a daughter, Dr Gabrielle Hansen, and Di's son, Dr Nicolas Morrissey, is a lecturer in South East Asian Art History and Buddhist Studies at the University of Georgia, USA. Di has three beautiful grandchildren: Sonoma Grace, Everton Peter and William James Bodhi.

Di and her partner, Boris Janjic, live in the Manning Valley in New South Wales when not travelling to research her novels, which are all inspired by a particular landscape.

www.dimorrissey.com

Also by Di Morrissey
in order of publication

Heart of the Dreaming
The Last Rose of Summer
Follow the Morning Star
The Last Mile Home
Tears of the Moon
When the Singing Stops
The Songmaster
Scatter the Stars
Blaze
The Bay
Kimberley Sun
Barra Creek
The Reef
The Valley
Monsoon
The Islands
The Silent Country
The Plantation

Di Morrissey

The Opal Desert

Author's Note:

The method of treating snakebite as described in this book
was used in the 1930s but is never used today.

First published in Macmillan in 2011 by Pan Macmillan Australia Pty Limited
1 Market Street, Sydney

National Library of Australia
Cataloguing-in-Publication data:

Morrissey, Di

The opal desert / Di Morrissey.

ISBN 9781742610351 (pbk.)

A823.3

Internal illustrations by John Murray
Typeset in 12.5/15 pt Sabon by Post Pre-press Group
Printed in Australia by McPherson's Printing Group

The characters in this book are fictitious and any resemblance
to real persons, living or dead, is purely coincidental.

Papers used by Pan Macmillan Australia Pty Ltd are natural, recyclable products
made from wood grown in sustainable forests. The manufacturing processes
conform to the environmental regulations of the country of origin.

Prologue

THE DESERT. RED SOIL, white domed mullock heaps, a landscape scarred by acne eruptions of excavations, the excreta of miners' enthusiasm and despair. Among the green smudged hillocks, dwellings were burrowed into the hillside. Other barely discernible buildings looked temporary. What was permanent was hidden below.

In this lonely landscape a figure appeared, resolutely running through the clinging dust, searing sun and empty wasteland.

A slight figure, whose flying footsteps left no imprints in the red soil, she darted between the clumps of spiky desert plants and the fuzz of new, greener growth. Since the spring rains, the dry soil had exploded seemingly overnight as vigorous plants awakened from two years of somnolence.

This morning she varied her usual track, taking Sampson's Hill first before circling the quiet dugouts where rusting machinery waited for the return of the fossickers and the part-time miners. These itinerants always came back in the milder winter months to pursue a dream, a lifestyle and the special beauty of the outback. They left only when the searing summer heat became too much.

From the cool, dim interiors of their dugout homes, few saw or heard the girl pass. One bearded miner stood by the entrance to his simple dugout and dragged deeply on his cigarette as he watched her pass. She gave no acknowledgment of his presence. He ground out his cigarette and returned to his snug hole as Anna continued her morning run, circling the tiny hamlet of Opal Lake before heading back towards the town's sole hotel, where she worked.

Bev and Wayne, unmistakable Australian grey nomads, were seated outside the horseshoe entrance to the Shincracker Motel, watching a baby magpie hop from step to step up a long ladder that leant against a gum tree.

'Fell out of its nest and can't fly up that high,' explained Anna, pausing briefly to speak to the tourists, only faintly breathless, her skin glowing with moisture.

'Ingenious,' said Bev smiling. 'I just love magpies. How can you run like that when it's so hot?'

'Going to be a stinker,' agreed Wayne.

'I don't mind. I just like to run.' She glanced at their caravan. 'You setting off today?'

'Yep. This has been fascinating but we have to meet up with friends. We're heading to Darwin,' said Bev with some pride.

Anna glanced at the caravan with *Bev 'n' Wayne on the nomad trail* printed on the rear beside their CB radio call channel.

'I've never been there. Have you had a good time here?'

'Interesting place. We didn't find any opals, but. Reckon Sampson must've got the lot, eh?' Wayne smiled.

'Was there a Sampson?' asked Bev.

'I don't know. But if you want to buy some opals, Greg in the general store or Mick at the pub sells them. Excuse me, I've got to get cleaned up before the pub opens.'

Wayne watched her disappear around one of the low hills. 'What's a young girl like that doing working in a place way out here?' he wondered.

'She seems nice, very pretty, too. I suppose she's a backpacker. What we should've done when we were in our twenties,' said Bev.

'We're doing it now, love. Forty years later. These are going to be the best years of our life.' He glanced over to where the girl had disappeared, an early morning apparition that stirred memories. 'That girl can certainly run. Wonder why she does it out here? She's in good shape, though.'

'You noticed,' said his heavy-set wife. 'They say running clears the head; maybe she's got a lot of thinking to do.'

'Looks like hard work to me. Maybe she's just running to get away. Well, we're off now, so we'll never know. C'mon, let's get packed up and hit the road. New places for us to see. This is the life.'

Anna let herself into the pub. She knew that those tourists were curious about her. Most people were. She was very out of place here, but the locals, all forty-eight of them, hadn't asked questions, adhering to the unspoken rule of the opal fields where, for a hundred years, no man was asked his last name, where he was from or what he'd found. Anna liked that rule, and she realised that the time she had been at Opal Lake had been the most peaceful she'd known for a long time.

But she knew that she had to keep running.

3

I

As soon as the limousine cruised through the iron gates into a landscape of shorn green lawns and clipped ornamental bushes, where discreet signs planted in the grass pointed to the various chapels, memorial gardens and meditation rooms, Kerrie knew that her husband would have loathed a send-off like this.

People stood in dark clusters while journalists hovered on the periphery noting their names as photographers, some unusually wearing ties, snapped other arrivals. The formality, the sterility, the hushed reverence was not what either Kerrie or her late husband, Milton Faranisi, would have wanted.

'Too bad none of his works are on display. This is pretty boring,' muttered one reporter.

'Don't be stupid. Have you ever seen the size of some

of his stuff? You should go to the Museum of Contemporary Art. There are a couple of his big sculptures in the courtyard,' responded another.

'That's where his early work is. Google the Met in New York, the Getty in LA or the Tate in London – that's where his best pieces are,' added a photographer. 'And by the way, how'd he get the name Milton? He was Italian, wasn't he?'

'The story is that his mother liked English poets. His brother's name is Byron.'

'You're kidding. Is he an artist too?'

'Nah, apparently he's a computer nerd. Started back in the early eighties and made a fortune.'

Inside the large chapel, rows were filled save for the front pew. Kerrie Faranisi made her way silently to it, trying to avoid eye contact with the other mourners in case she started crying again. She sat alone, a slim figure in black linen, her head bowed as she studied her hands clasped in her lap, as though trying not to acknowledge the unadorned coffin that lay in front of her. In the row behind her sat two of Milton's daughters. Their expressions appeared to be eternally disapproving. There were conversations, carried on in hushed tones, and many a head leant forward to study the widow, ostracised to the front pew.

With a clatter, a late arrival rushed in, hair dishevelled, huge dark glasses obscuring her face as she glanced around, and, seeing her sisters, hurried forward. She paused, looked at the lone figure of the woman in the very front and deliberately sat immediately behind her, with her sisters, who greeted her with solemn nods of the head. If the young widow was aware of the arrival of her youngest stepdaughter she did not show it, but everyone else noted the deliberate snub and eyebrows were raised.

The widow straightened her back as the memorial service began.

Brief but sincere eulogies were delivered by the director of the Modern Art Gallery, the director of the International Sculpture Centre of Australasia, the governor of New South Wales and an esteemed artist who described the renowned late sculptor, Milton Faranisi, as a national treasure who had helped shape the form and standing of Australian sculptors internationally:

> Milton Faranisi built a formidable reputation and his body of work will live on for centuries, challenging our senses, our concepts of the interpretation of harmony, space and logistics while expanding our intellectual horizons, minds and hearts – as he did personally as well as professionally. Milton's legacy – in marble, bronze, stone, wood and paper – will continue to inspire. Milton had a talent that dwarfed his contemporaries'. This talent and love for life, equally majestic, sometimes threatened to swamp lesser mortals. In Milton's company you were in no doubt that you were in the presence of a genius who was happiest when he had a chisel and a hammer in his hand.
>
> He leaves behind a wonderful family of three lovely daughters and a devoted wife, but it is his intimidating, awesome sculptures that will continue to touch our hearts, minds and nerve endings and bring wonder to those who stand before them and ask, 'What kind of a man could create this?'
>
> Those here today were privileged to have known and loved him and we can all acknowledge that there will never be another Milton Faranisi.

The next speaker came not from the art world but from the world Milton had long left behind – an Italy not yet recovered from war. He spoke of Milton's parents who had come to Australia with their young sons and forged in them a desire for stability, permanence and

9

beauty. Partly as a result of their sacrifices and influence Milton's magnificent creations were displayed around the world as a beacon and a symbol of one man's steady footprint on the surface of an increasingly fragile and rocking planet.

A faint cultured accent of Northern Italy clung to his words and Kerrie smiled briefly at the elderly, courtly friend of her husband's parents, dressed in a vintage shiny dark suit that had seen better days and happier occasions.

The final eulogy came from Milton's youngest daughter. Alia walked to the podium, her face streaked with tears and reached for the microphone, bringing it closer.

'My father . . . was a great man. Everyone here knows him for his work, for being charismatic and . . . out there.' Her mouth twisted, whether in a grimace or a smile was hard to tell. 'But I, we, know he was a wonderful father, fun and loving. And that is how we will remember him, as the father who loved his little girls.' Her head moved and behind her dark glasses she gave the impression that she was looking at her stepmother before continuing, 'We had to share you, but we love you Daddy.'

She stepped down and as she returned to her seat, both her sisters reached across and briefly touched her hand.

From the front pew the widow stood and, holding a dramatic long-stemmed red heliconia, walked to the coffin, kissed the blood-red flower and placed it on the lid. As the congregation stood to sing the final hymn she walked from the chapel, through the snapping photographers, to the waiting limousine.

The driver sprang forward and opened the door. 'Where to, Mrs Faranisi?' he asked.

Kerrie took off her sunglasses and rubbed her eyes. 'Actually, I have no idea. I just couldn't stay in that poisonous atmosphere any longer.'

'Do just want me to drive a little while you gather your thoughts?' he suggested.

'Yes, thanks. Good idea.'

Kerrie leant back and closed her eyes as the car purred away from the chapel where Milton's daughters had insisted on holding their father's funeral. 'Milton, I'm sorry that was not the sort of send-off that you would have wanted. The formality. All those speeches. I'm sure you would have preferred an informal farewell, with a few celebratory drinks to remember the good times. But I'm afraid that this is what the girls wanted, and they won this round,' she apologised silently to her husband. She reflected that her entire married life had been one long battle with her stepdaughters. As hard as she'd tried to accommodate them, nothing pleased them. Now she felt too exhausted to fight any longer.

There was only one reason for the animosity. After the death of their mother, Milton had indulged and spoilt the girls, who, in spite of their father's subsequent brief associations with other women, had never felt threatened by any of these relationships. There had been brief liaisons with young girls and voluptuous movie actresses, minor European royalty and older women, including an artist known more for her bright red wig than for her art. But in spite of these reckless habits, the girls had always felt secure in the knowledge that he still loved them best. They never took these passing indulgences seriously; they sighed and teased their father about the women who drifted in and out of his bed and his life. They took it all in their stride – until he met Kerrie.

'We can go no further, Mrs Faranisi,' said the driver, stopping the car.

'Oh, I was daydreaming. You're right, we're at Watsons Bay.' She looked at the small historic lighthouse atop the craggy headland. Below it was the dramatic drop into the ocean.

'It's none of my business, but I thought you might like to go down to the beachfront. Perhaps have a glass of wine, some food.'

'Well, I could certainly stand a drink, even if I don't have anything to eat.'

The memory of the simple fish meals she and Milton had shared at the Watsons Bay restaurant on the edge of the water brought a sudden tear to her eye but now she also recognised that she was extremely hungry. Indeed, she couldn't recall eating a solid meal in the days since Milton's sudden heart attack.

She was shown to a shady table to one side of the main restaurant. She held the menu and watched a family enjoy their meal as their small children played on the sand in front of the outdoor tables. While the young waiter was attentive, and the owner came over to give his con-dolences, Kerrie sensed that even going to her favourite places was not going to be the same without Milton. She could see him sitting opposite her, silhouetted against the water, leaning back in his chair savouring the view and the ambience. Throughout their twenty-year marriage he had always been the most stimulating and interesting company. His conversation never dwelt on the mundane. Small talk was not part of his vocabulary. He discussed art and history and people he'd met, ideas for new works, food and childhood memories, family stories of Italy, the struggles of the past, and his dreams for the future. Milton, despite his enormous success, never considered he was at his peak. He had so much more to create and achieve.

When Kerrie opened the flood gates to her memories,

tears began to fall onto the menu she was holding. She quickly dabbed at her eyes and took a sip of iced water.

Twenty years earlier

The art school was at the bottom end of George Street in Sydney, so Kerrie caught the Manly ferry across to Circular Quay three days a week. Initially she'd found the detailed drawing classes frustrating, for she would have preferred to splash paint boldly over large canvases and have the freedom to express herself rather than be regimented and restricted by pencil and charcoal assignments. But gradually she learned the discipline of controlling her pencil and mastering the technicalities of form, shape, perspective and balance, which she conceded would give her the grounding she needed in creating the core of a painting. Her tutor explained that learning these basics allowed her the freedom to 'take off like a bird, control the flight and then land safely. It might look natural and effortless, but you are using your inherent knowledge of aerodynamics and physical talent, be it feathers or a pen, to achieve that freedom.'

Kerrie carried a small sketchbook and a sharpened pencil with her at all times and as a scene, a shape, a figure, an expression, caught her attention, she'd swiftly attempt to capture it on a page of her book. Often her tutor asked to see her workbook and would make a comment or a suggestion, always handing it back with a nod and the curt comment, 'Do more.'

When she could, Kerrie carried a box of watercolours with her and would do quick washes over a pen sketch or paint a scene in watercolours. Gradually she started to master the mercurial run of the paint on paper and even if a painting emerged that was not what she'd planned, she was often pleasantly surprised with the result.

She experimented with life drawing, portraiture, landscape and watercolours and took the compulsory short courses in sculpting and draughtsmanship. The students frequently visited museums and galleries and it was in her final year that her class was invited to an exhibition and a lecture by the famous sculptor Milton Faranisi.

The gallery where the exhibition was held was an airy white space with soaring ceilings opening onto a large courtyard where the sculptures glowed in the twilight. The Faranisi figures and dramatic works interpreting the theme of separation dwarfed the guests slowly circling the courtyard.

Kerrie was overwhelmed. Sculpture had never particularly attracted her or affected her emotionally. She'd thought the hard surfaces cold and found it difficult to connect with the artist's intent. But there was something about this work that nudged aside her previous feelings and preconceptions.

'This is quite an event, isn't it?' said Sam, a fellow classmate who had joined her. His glasses had slipped down his nose and his face shone with perspiration from the crush of people as he tried to juggle a cigarette, a glass of wine and a small spring roll.

'Fabulous setting,' agreed Kerrie. 'Imagine having a whole space like this to show your work.'

'Big art, big price tag,' said Sam.

'Faranisi is certainly a big talent,' said Kerrie. 'Not that I'm usually a fan of large works. These are impressive because of their scale but there's something else about them – a sensitivity, a lightness, it's incongruous, given their weightiness.'

'Form, shape, substance, it's all very solid, but using a hammer and chisel doesn't seem as artistic to me as controlling a brush. You'd have to have a lot of strength to be able to create something like this.'

Kerrie smiled at the slightly built art student beside her who looked as though he could barely lift any sort of hammer.

'You're right, Sam. I'd stick to painting, if I were you.'

More and more people arrived and what was once a zen-like space was now jammed, making it difficult for waiters to move through the throng with trays of drinks and food. Noting the growing enthusiasm of the crowd, the director of the gallery decided to introduce the sculptor right away.

Stephanie Oates, the respected director of the Gallery Museum of Modern Art, called for silence and announced, 'Ladies and gentlemen, Milton Faranisi.'

He came through a side door, politely shook the director's hand and then stood to one side, smiling broadly. It was not a flamboyant entrance but his presence dominated the room and held everyone's attention. While the gallery director extended her welcome, her acknowledgements and thanks to everyone involved in staging the exhibition, the creator of the show folded his arms and watched the crowd. As the director continued speaking, Kerrie studied Milton Faranisi from the sideline.

She wished she could sketch his firm profile, his thick dark hair and roman nose, and the slightly amused expression lurking at his mouth. He was tall and solid and seemed to bear out Sam's comments about the strength that was needed for sculpting. He wore a cream linen jacket over brown pants and a cream shirt and an unexciting tie. For someone with such a wild reputation, Kerrie was a little disappointed to see him so conservatively dressed. Then she noticed the expensive leather loafers, what seemed to be a designer belt and his classy watch.

As if sensing her scrutiny, he swung around and looked directly at her, his deep green eyes staring into her face, causing her to blush, but she did not look away. His eyes narrowed slightly and his lips curved into a brief smile and then he turned away leaving Kerrie feeling as though she'd been caught out in some childish prank.

Stephanie Oates was lauding the work of Faranisi:

... continuing the tradition of great European sculptors who have pushed the boundaries to embrace new mediums, new materials and new constructs, yet always communicating to an audience who invests the time and trouble to investigate these new sculptural forms. I predict that his work will be acquired by museums, galleries and corporations all over the world. And, as Faranisi's work is growing significantly in size as well as reputation, we are elated to have such a collection as wonderful as the magnificent pieces you see on display tonight. I'm sure you will agree the impact of them in one place is powerful.

There was a smattering of applause, most guests finding it tricky to clap while holding a drink, catalogue and canapé.

Stephanie concluded by commenting:

Milton Faranisi has studied science, drawing, architecture and engineering, and I'm sure he would have been an outstanding achiever in any field. His work incorporates these skills and you can see his knowledge flowering in the magnificent pieces on display tonight. We applaud his dedication to his art, and also his energy and enthusiasm, which is ours to share. Please welcome Milton Faranisi!

The sculptor spoke eloquently but briefly before thanking Stephanie, his friends, fellow artists and the arts administrators who had supported his work. After his speech he stepped to one side to pose for photographers and submit to the TV cameras.

'I'm looking forward to his lecture next week,' Kerrie said to Sam.

'I don't see the point, we're not doing sculpture.'

Kerrie shrugged. 'Stephanie Oates said Milton Faranisi studied drawing, architecture and engineering. He's not that narrow. We might learn things from him that can be of use to us.'

'I'm just not interested. Why are you? You always say that you only want to paint.'

'Perhaps I'll broaden my horizons! You never know. I'm going to take another look at his work in the court-yard. The place doesn't seem so full now.'

Kerrie drifted out to the garden. Most of the crowd were indoors, helping themselves to the complimentary wine, so she took her time, circling each of the exhibits, appreciating the changing surfaces of the three-dimensional forms. Pausing before one sculpture called 'Distant Future', she reached out and laid her hand on the cool stone, finding it solid and earthbound despite its delicacy and light-as-air appearance.

'Ah, you couldn't resist. What do you feel?'

Kerrie turned to see Milton Faranisi regarding her with an amused expression. Before she could move he placed his hand over hers.

'Oh. Sorry. It looks so delicate, almost translucent, I wanted to see if it was hollow,' Kerrie apologised.

'Can you feel the small groove marks from my tools and the strength in this stone? I'm pleased that you think this is light. The small sphere represents a distant planet that could drift away into the night at any moment. As a sculptor I've tried to utilise three-dimensional thinking and direct abstract thought into the physical, using my mind to guide my hand.' He continued to hold her hand. 'Are you an artist?'

Kerrie knew that the older man was flirting with her

and was secretly flattered, but she couldn't help being impressed by the description of how he worked. 'Not really. I'm an art student. At the Armitage School.'

He nodded. 'You get good formal training there. The discipline is good, but just going to classes there won't necessarily make you a great artist. I'm speaking to Armitage students in a few days. I hope to see you there.' He saw Stephanie Oates coming towards them. 'Excuse me, I must thank Stephanie for her kind words.' He let her hand go, after gently squeezing it.

The whiteboard beside the lectern was covered with sketches and outlines. The forty students in the lecture room looked slightly dazed as the torrent of information, demonstrations and anecdotes from Milton Faranisi continued nonstop.

Kerrie was impressed, not just by the insightful sculptor, but by how entertaining he was. Even Sam was taken by his eloquence and the ideas Milton used to illustrate the history of sculpture and the interrelationships between contemporary and classical sculpture:

> The key to your studies is to reach that moment of truth known as 'the breakthrough', where you discover you are working from instinct, you just know you are ready to create from your heart and mind as well as with your body. That is when you begin to trust yourself and create for yourself. The power and wisdom and spirit within you will let you flower and set you free to make your own art, your way. Don't get distracted, don't get seduced by profit, and don't get sidetracked by commercial middlemen seeking to milk your talent. Remain true to yourself, to your art.

'He's compelling, though I bet the art schools don't like him encouraging students to get out and go it alone,' commented Sam.

'He makes me want to try new things. I really do want to experiment,' said Kerrie.

'I think he remembers you from the exhibition. Notice how he keeps glancing at you?' teased Sam.

'Is he?' she replied innocently. But Kerrie had caught Milton's eye a few times and assumed that he had remembered her.

'Come on, Kerrie, let's see if he does remember you.' Sam rose as the lecture concluded and edged from their row to join other students clustering around the sculptor.

Milton Faranisi spoke to Kerrie as soon as she approached. 'You were at my exhibition the other night, weren't you?' When Kerrie nodded, he smiled. 'Did you enjoy my talk? Find it useful?'

'We all did. It was very inspiring.'

'And what is your name?'

'Kerrie. Kerrie Jackson.'

She didn't think more about her meeting with Milton Faranisi. He was far removed from her world. But when he turned up at the art school looking for her she found that she wasn't totally surprised.

He met her after class and took her to a wine bar, where they sat in a dark corner and talked, laughed and discussed art and life. She asked him questions about sculpting, trying to extract information from him, a kind of masterclass, while Milton obviously enjoyed the rapt attention of the pretty young woman. She was unsure why he had asked her out, and he gave no indication of wanting to take things any further. Nor did they discuss anything personal so she didn't know what his marital status was.

She resolved to check out his biography, but then chided herself. What would be the point? Why would this sophisticated man be interested in a young art student? But later she did look up his biography. She found that he was a widower, whose very wealthy Brazilian wife had died a few years earlier, leaving him three daughters to raise.

Two nights later he asked her to dinner. She was surprised but she accepted. As she got ready to go out she found that she had put on her lacey, sexy underwear. She stopped and laughed at herself. Had she decided to go to bed with the famous sculptor? She knew that she could offer him no more than her body and her attention, but his smile, the attentive warmth in his eyes, his stories and anecdotes, the plans he shared with her for future projects, made him wonderful company.

'I'll just take things as they come,' she told herself.

And, she had to admit as she sat across from him at a table in a small Italian restaurant, she was stirred by his physical presence. His dark T-shirt stretched across his muscular chest and shoulders and was tucked into jeans, which were belted across his taut stomach. His arms were tanned and he wore an expensive watch. His conversation was erudite and his manners polished. The hardened calluses on his hands were the only clue that this was a man who indulged in physical work. He asked about her plans after art school.

'I don't know,' Kerrie replied honestly. 'I don't know if I'm any good. And even if I have some talent, it's not easy to make a living as an artist.'

'You're right, it is very difficult to make it as an artist. You really have to believe in yourself, be prepared to make sacrifices and have a lot of luck. It won't be easy for you, even if you have talent, and maybe you don't. And maybe you'll never know. You can only persist because you cannot live without art. Do you feel that way? There is always a price to pay so you should weigh up the risks before saying I want to be an artist.'

Kerrie looked down at her plate of pasta feeling as though she had just wasted four years of her life. He reached over and covered her hand with his. 'Perhaps you need a benefactor, a patron, like in the old days, or you could marry a rich man and indulge yourself.'

'Yeah, right. And that's going to happen,' retorted Kerrie, her face hot with annoyance.

Milton removed his hand and shrugged. 'All things being equal – love, passion, sex – it could be a perfect arrangement.'

'Is that how you got started?' asked Kerrie crossly.

Milton leaned back and looked at Kerrie in amusement and lifted his glass of wine. 'Touché. You are right. I have been tactless.'

Kerrie sipped her wine and gave an enigmatic smile. 'Apology accepted. Anyway, what was your first job?'

As they ate their dessert Milton talked of living in Rome and being apprenticed to a renowned sculptor who had modelled himself on Rodin and liked to sculpt classical figures. 'I admire Rodin, but I didn't see the point in trying to cast myself as a poor Australian imitation. But an apprenticeship is valuable. I learned skills, then I rebelled and began to do my own thing, which is as it should be.'

'But those skills you learnt came in handy, didn't they? So I'm not wasting my time at art school.'

'Everything you learn you can use. It's surprising where it can be applied. But what you must ask yourself is: why do I want to be an artist? how important is it to me? why am I doing this? For ego? Or for money and acclaim? If you never sell a painting, never receive any true praise, would you persist?' He paused. 'Sorry if I'm haranguing you.'

Kerrie looked up from her plate and spoke firmly but quietly. 'I'll make it as an artist one day and I'll make it on my terms.'

He looked at her blazing eyes and smiled. 'Good for you. I hope you do. Now, more coffee? A liqueur?'

Kerrie shook her head. 'No, thanks. It's been a wonderful evening. You've made me think.'

'I have really enjoyed your company. No one listens to me.' He smiled. 'My daughters treat me like an old man and are really too young to understand my work.'

'Your daughters . . . are at school?' asked Kerrie. She had no idea about their ages but Milton looked barely forty so they couldn't be very old.

'The older ones are almost into their teens, but already they seem to be at that rebellious stage. I'm not around them as much as I should be. I always seem to be overseas now that I am starting to get commissions from other countries. Anyway, they think that I'm very uninteresting. Perhaps you can help me . . . "lighten up", as they keep telling me.' He smiled at Kerrie. 'Take pity on a man of forty-five and take him out dancing or clubbing or whatever it is you do to enjoy life, so that my daughters don't think I'm so boring.'

'I'm sure they don't think that at all,' said Kerrie quickly. 'I don't think you're boring.'

'Okay then, next time it's your turn. Come out with me again, but take me to your favourite place . . . a club, a bar? Unless you would be embarrassed to be seen out with me?'

'Of course not,' laughed Kerrie, 'but you mightn't enjoy it. Wild lights, loud music, crowded dance floor, overpriced cocktails. People passing around joints and stuff.' She rattled off a description of what she imagined he thought she enjoyed, the sort of evening her friends tried to persuade her to share, but which in all honesty didn't really appeal to her. Shouting all evening over loud music in order to be heard really wasn't her scene, but she tried to think of the places the other students talked about. She didn't think that he really wanted to do this but was rather chuffed that he wanted to spend more time with her on her terms.

'It sounds familiar, though it's been a few years. Ah, Positano. I'll tell you about it sometime. Shall we go?'

Kerrie gathered up her bag and pushed back her chair.

'I meant that, about the dancing, the wild night out,' he said, rising from his seat.

'If you really want to,' she said. 'I hope your daughters will be impressed.'

'I'm not doing it for them,' he said, contradicting himself. 'I'm going to do it for me. You pick the place. Thursday night okay with you?'

To their surprise, by the end of Thursday evening they both agreed that they'd had a brilliant time. Kerrie had asked her friends the best place to go dancing and their suggestion had been perfect. She felt strange going into a trendy club with a man old enough to be her father, even if a very young one. Initially dancing with Milton had been awkward, but as the floor space became more limited they had been forced to stay in one spot, wildly gyrating or clinging together, bodies sensuously rubbing together in time with Madonna's 'Vogue'.

In the heady atmosphere, combined with the music and the swift downing of drinks, Kerrie's inhibitions slipped, and she didn't care what anyone else thought about her date. Later, as they pushed their way through to the back bar, she noticed a sexy waitress flirting with Milton, who didn't seem to mind at all. Then, when he struck up a conversation with two girls drinking beside them at the bar, she felt a rush of jealousy. He was amusing and attractive to women, that was clear. Not that those girls would realise that he was famous. However, when a roving photographer spotted Milton and took a photo of him with his arm draped around Kerrie, one of the two girls later asked her, 'Who's your boyfriend then? Someone famous?'

'Just my favourite uncle,' Kerrie said airily, as the girls hooted at her in disbelief.

To Kerrie's disappointment when Milton took her home he kissed her ardently then pushed her gently away.

'Too much wine. Get some sleep. I'll call you soon.'

'Do you feel lighter?' she asked, nuzzling him. 'You're fun. Half the girls there had the hots for you.'

'Lucky for me I had you. G'night, Kerrie-cups,' he said as she walked into her house.

Two days later Kerrie found that she was the subject of some interest in class when the photograph of her and Milton appeared in the paper. Her friends teased her.

'Are you taking private classes?'

'Or modelling for the master, perhaps?'

She merely smiled and kept her head down. It was Sam who suggested that she should be careful. 'Watch yourself, Kerrie. Remember, you aren't the first and won't be the last.'

'Sam, you're not telling me anything I don't already know,' she retorted. 'Anyway, I'm learning a lot.'

'I bet you are.'

'It's not like that at all. And I certainly haven't slept with him if that's what you're hinting at.' said Kerrie. 'Not that it's your business, anyway.'

'Bet you do.'

Kerrie laughed. 'We'll see.'

Kerrie's mother was pleased that Kerrie was obviously in the throes of a new romance, but she was surprised when a friend at her bridge club showed her the photograph of Kerrie and Milton at the club.

'Kerrie, is this the man you're seeing?'

'It was just a date, Mum.'

'But when you said you were going out with a sculptor, I assumed it was someone from your art school. A student, not a teacher. You're only twenty-two and this man looks so much older. I'm not sure what your father would think.'

Kerrie waited for another comment about her late father, a man who had died when she was eleven, but whose presence was always in their lives as her mother had raised him to a level close to sainthood. Kerrie had warm memories of him but her mother had declared that no other man could measure up to her late husband. So she devoted herself to the home they had made together and raised their only child. Glynis Jackson had worked as a secretary in a small building firm, but her husband had left them comfortably off in their northern beaches home, near the good school where Kerrie had been sent.

Kerrie could not fault her mother's devotion and perhaps the only criticism she could make of her mother was the fact she kept so much to herself. Her mother's best friend was her late husband's sister whose two sons worked interstate and rarely visited, so Kerrie hadn't grown up with much family around. Even at Christmas the two of them had enjoyed the time by themselves, generally going to the beach for a picnic lunch. At other times of the year they might go to barbecues at neighbours' places. As a teenager Kerrie sometimes spent time with girlfriends' families, but never stayed away much more than a night.

'Well, I hope you know what you're doing, Kerrie. Older men can be very . . . casual. Don't get too serious. I don't want you getting hurt,' said her mother.

Kerrie was amused by her mother's advice. Glynis was a woman who'd always prided herself on the fact that she'd never gone out with any man other than Kerrie's father. 'You sound very worldly, Mum. Don't worry, we're just having fun.'

'No offence, darling, but why on earth would a man as sophisicated as Milton Faranisi be interested in you? I know you're young and pretty, but I think that you could be just an easy target.'

The remark was said quite innocently and Kerrie knew there was no deliberate malice, but the blatant comment made her laugh out loud. 'He says I make him feel young. He likes the fact I'm deeply interested in his work. I don't make any demands on him. His daughters are very immature, so they don't really provide him with stimulating company.'

'So he has a family? Have you met them yet?'

'Oh, Mum, lighten up.' Kerrie laughed. 'I'm happy, I'm having a good time, and there are no strings attached, I promise.'

'Well, I hope that you're right.'

'He's not a bad man, Mum. He's full of life, and he's kind and generous. I know he's famous in Australia, but he makes me feel important, too. He really does like talking with me,' said Kerrie with some heat.

'Talking!' snapped her mother. 'Well, I just hope you know what you're doing. Please be careful.'

'Mum, I'm just fine. You worry too much and there's no need.'

Not surprisingly, Kerrie and Milton did become lovers and Kerrie never felt more womanly or sensuous. Milton was unlike the boys she'd previously had sex with. At the time, she had thought that they were enamoured and deeply in love with her, but she now saw how shallow they'd been, merely satisfying themselves. Any time they subsequently spent with her seemed like an obligation for a sexual payoff.

Milton was different. He pleasured her, lingered over her body, played with her, teased her and satisfied her. Sometimes she skipped a class to while away an afternoon in his studio where he had a single bed and a long table littered with hand-painted bowls, empty pizza boxes, a wine decanter and sketchbooks. A shelf held some of his clothes. There was a small kitchen and in the garden was an open-air shower hooked to the roof. Its floor was merely wooden slats and the water ran underneath it and onto a garden that contained one of his bronze works rising from a small pond. A large cement square at the end of a driveway was specially constructed with scaffolding designed to hold weighty stones which could be lifted in place by a hoist. A shed was fitted out with a forge and also contained woodworking tools and more machinery and equipment for making moulds and casts than there were at the art school.

Kerrie loved Milton's studio, a large space in the inner city completely surrounded by a thick wall of bamboo. If it wasn't for the banging and the sound of the machinery Milton used when he worked, few would have known of this oasis.

Once or twice he'd taken her to the house where he lived with his daughters when they were at school. It was a large home in Rose Bay with panoramic views, a pool and an overgrown garden. When Kerrie peered into the girls' rooms, she saw that they were filled with stuffed toys, posters and piles of messy clothes.

The master bedroom was coolly white with a large black and white Brett Whitely drawing on one wall and little else. The bed faced double windows with an expansive view of the harbour. But the house, apart from the girls' rooms, seemed impersonal to Kerrie.

Curled up in Milton's arms, Kerrie asked, 'Why don't you have anything more personal here? This is like a hotel room.'

'I've never liked this house. My wife bought it. I prefer my studio. I also have a little place in Italy that I like.'

'Why don't you have a place here that you like, too? Isn't Australia your home?'

'Would you like to see my place in Italy?' he asked suddenly.

'Of course I would!' exclaimed Kerrie.

'I can go next week. Come with me.' He was matter of fact – as if this invitation presented no problems at all.

'Milton! I have art school. I have an assignment to do. What about your daughters? Will they be coming too?'

'No, they have school. The housekeeper will look after them. And they are used to me coming and going these days. They'll be fine. Kerrie, if you come with me to Italy, you'll learn more about art than a year of lectures at that school.'

'You said it was a good school,' protested Kerrie.

He nuzzled her hair with his lips. 'But my school is better. Come with me. I like having you around. You'll like Italy.'

Kerrie sensed that Milton's offer was not an idle one and if she didn't take it their relationship would founder. In an odd way it was a kind of test.

'You'll have to meet my mother first.'

'Mothers always like me,' he said simply and kissed her. The decision was made.

Not surprisingly, Glynis was dubious at first.

'I think that you're throwing away your career

prospects. You're in your final year. You should finish the course.'

'Mum, wait till you meet Milton. This is a fantastic opportunity. Just think what he'll show me. I'd be mad not to take up the offer.'

And Milton was right. Her mother was charmed. He persuaded her that he'd look after Kerrie like the precious treasure she was and, by taking her to the best galleries and museums in Italy, he'd give her a better education in art than she'd ever get in Australia.

'I know every statue, carving and painting in every gallery and street and piazza in all of Roma!' he proclaimed.

'I can see why you're smitten with him,' agreed Glynis later. 'I know that I should protest, but I also know that it wouldn't do any good.'

'Thanks, Mum. I'll bring you back a really good pressie,' said Kerrie, pleased to accept the olive branch.

Kerrie ignored her friends' digs about Milton and her impending trip to Italy. She knew that they were all wildly jealous and she took the whole thing in her stride. Sam told her that he thought that her *c'est la vie* approach to life made her a refreshing change for Milton, since he was probably used to more manipulative women who were after his money. But while Kerrie had no guile, she was not naive. She knew that Milton liked her directness and honesty and her ability to make him laugh. Moreover, the fact that she genuinely admired his work and was keen to learn from him flattered his ego.

They spent a month in Italy and Kerrie wished their time there would never end. She was thirsty to see as much as she could and because of Milton's growing reputation, they had entrees to private showings and meetings, and often dined with arts administrators, curators and other prominent artists. The two of them seemed so compatible that only once was Kerrie asked if she was Milton's daughter.

'I think that we've had enough art for the time being,' Milton announced one morning. 'How about we go down the coast so that I can show you my little villa?'

'Where is it?'

'Porto Ercole, a couple of hours south. I bought it years ago. One of the smartest things I've ever done. Back then Porto Ercole was a quaint fishing village, now it's a massive marina and tourist place but in the off season, like now, it's still a liveable place.'

Looking back, Kerrie always thought those days at Milton's very modest but delightful old villa with its views over the sweep of the bay and the town below were quite magical. Milton worked on sketches and ideas for a new work he had been commissioned to do, while Kerrie shopped in the small market and learnt to cook local dishes. She kept a diary in which she put small pen and ink sketches of people and scenes, as well as watercolours of the landscape and the buildings in the old quarter.

Milton didn't share his work ideas with her, nor ask to see what she was doing, although she did once catch him flipping through her sketchbook, then putting it to one side without commenting. However he was effusive and complimentary about her cooking of the regional dishes, and made her promise to make him an Italian meal at least once every week after they got home.

They took a break from the villa and Milton hired a convertible. Kerrie held her breath as he drove ridiculously fast and kept asking him why he had to drive like he was in a grand prix.

'Just keeping up with the traffic,' he assured her even when they'd left the *autostrade* and were driving along the spectacular coast road. Kerrie couldn't bear to look at the sea below them as they wound towards Amalfi but once they were cruising through the picturesque towns and villages, she was entranced. They stopped for coffee and then wound uphill to the town of Ravello where they had lunch with one of Milton's friends in a villa which had spectacular views across the valley to the sea.

Afterwards they wandered around the small square, dominated by the cathedral, and along the narrow lanes behind the walls of villas with their hidden gardens and stunning views. Kerrie was enchanted. Milton took her to see the magnificent gardens of the Villa Cimbrone and there, over lunch on the terrace, he gave her a beautiful gold filigree bracelet.

'It's from the jewellery store next to the duomo steps. You can change it if you don't like it,' he said. 'Put it on so I can see how it looks.'

'I love it. But Milton, it looks so . . . expensive,' she exclaimed. 'I'm not sure that I should accept it.'

'Nonsense. I am simply thanking you for your excellent company over the past few weeks. The bracelet suits you because it is not ornate. It's understated and tasteful. Like you. Actually, you do dress rather well,' Milton said, looking at her simple sundress. 'But I think that you could use some better sandals. While we're here, we'll shop for shoes for you.'

Kerrie lifted her foot and inspected her narrow brown foot and her basic, if somewhat worn, leather sandal.

'Thank you, Milton. But I don't like glitzy shoes,' she said. 'I don't want to accept any more presents from you. I owe you quite enough.'

'Rubbish. You owe me nothing. Your company has been my payment. But your shoes! I think that we should buy a pair of Italy's softest and finest leather sandals. You'll see. And your feet will thank me.' He blew a kiss towards her toes.

'I like being spoiled,' said Kerrie.

'Enjoy, *cara*. I want you to be happy. Remember times like these when I am deep in my work and you might feel neglected.'

Ten days later Milton announced that he was going to Holland about a commission for another work, so Kerrie had to make her own way back to Australia.

Glynis Jackson didn't ask too many questions about the sojourn in Italy and when Kerrie went back to art school, she refused to tell her classmates much about the trip at all, except to say that it had been educational.

A week later Milton turned up in a flurry of talk, plans and good humour, bearing gifts for Kerrie and her mother.

'I'm so over Dutch food. You can cook me something Italian,' he said to Kerrie.

'I'm glad my mother didn't hear you say that,' she replied.

'Why? Do I make you sound like my servant?' he asked, surprised.

'Well, she does think you boss me around.'

'I think if you love someone, you would want to cook for them. If you like, I could cook something for you then . . .'

'Please, don't. I've sampled your cooking and know why you buy so much takeaway pizza! All right then, I'll make us some pasta.'

'Perfect. And after dinner I'll show you my plans for the Dutch work. The formwork I can make in the studio in Australia and then ship it over and do the casting and finishing in Holland. We'll be away for several weeks, or longer.'

Kerrie stared at him. 'You expect me to go to Holland with you? For weeks, months? To cook?'

'Not as my cook, my darling. I can always hire some-one to do that for us.'

'Milton, be practical! I can't drop my life and go to Holland with you for however long you're there, even with a cook supplied,' laughed Kerrie.

'I enjoy having you around. You're good for me. Anyway, what plans did you have when you finish these art classes?'

Kerrie felt confused. 'I told you, if I'm good enough to support myself painting, then I will. If not, I guess I'll have to look into advertising, graphic design or something.'

'And that's what you want? You'll learn far more travelling with me than burying yourself here, in Australia. I am rescuing you, Kerrie!'

'From what? My life is happy. I have a passion I'm pursuing, I have friends . . .'

'You have a boring life. You still live with your mother, who is nice enough, but your home life isn't very excit-ing. Don't you want to spread your wings? Please, can't you make me the passion in your life?' He grabbed her shoulders and pulled her to him, forcing his lips to hers. Kerrie pulled away and stared at him, breathless and at a loss at this outburst. But he wasn't finished. 'We can do wonderful things together. I promise you that if you marry me, you will have a life you never imagined or dreamed.'

2

KERRIE'S LIFE WAS QUICKLY turned upside down. She had little time to herself. Milton wanted them to get married before he had to return to work in Holland.

'A three-month engagement doesn't seem very practical,' said her mother. 'We have a wedding to plan.'

'Milton doesn't want a big fancy affair, he likes things to be more casual, more fun, not formal,' said Kerrie. 'After all, he's been married before.'

'But you haven't!' exclaimed Glynis. 'You haven't even got an engagement ring.'

'Actually, I do. He gave me one last night,' said Kerrie holding out her hand to show her mother the diamond and emerald ring. 'He had it made.'

'It's very nice, Kerrie, lovely, in fact. But this decision seems rather sudden. Are you sure you're not being swept up in the glamour of this man and his life? What about his daughters? What do they think of this engagement?'

Kerrie sighed. 'They don't know yet. Milton is breaking the news to them and then we're having a family dinner. I've only met two of them, briefly, but I don't think they realised Milton was serious about me. Alia is the youngest, then Luisa, then Renata is the eldest. They're all very close to their father.'

'That's hardly surprising, since they have no mother. Who looks after them when their father's away?'

'He has a housekeeper. A nanny, I guess. She's been with them since their mother died. Wendy's her name and she's a former boarding house mistress. Strict with the girls, according to Milton, but very loving. Apparently the girls adore her.'

'How do you feel about a readymade family? How old are they? Thirteen, eleven and nine? They might still be children, but they're not much younger than you. You might find them a bit of a handful.'

'We haven't had a chance to get to know each other yet. I'm hoping I can relate to them in a different way, more of a big sister or young aunt and not a parental figure.'

Glynis didn't look convinced. 'I think you're being optimistic. Perhaps you should get to know them before the wedding is announced. They will feel threatened by you. It won't be easy for you in that situation.'

'He loves me, Mum. And I love him. The girls will get used to our marriage . . . eventually.'

But Kerrie's optimism was shattered when she encountered the hostility and coldness with which Milton's daughters greeted her. They were polite, shook her hand, but did not smile.

Renata said to Kerrie in a very cool voice, 'We give you our congratulations and hope you will make our father happy. Now we have to go and help Wendy in the kitchen.'

Alia stood, staring balefully at Kerrie. 'We don't want you as our mother.'

'Alia! Be nice to Kerrie,' said Milton. 'I told you Kerrie will be your friend.'

'Is she going to live here?'

'Of course. This is a large house,' said Milton affably, going to the sideboard and pouring two glasses of wine.

'I can never replace your mother, Alia,' said Kerrie. 'But I hope we can be friends and I can help you. I'm sure that we will all get along and make your father happy.'

'We have enough friends already. And we have Wendy.'

Kerrie didn't want to get into an argument with an angry nine year old. She glanced at Milton, hoping that he would say something to support her, but he just shrugged and handed her a glass of wine.

'Alia, come and sit on my lap and give me a hug. I've missed you,' he said.

He put his wine on a side table and sat in a chair, opening his arms, but Alia shook her head.

'I don't want to hug you, Father,' said the little girl coldly.

'Well, in that case you may go and help the others in the kitchen,' said Milton calmly as Alia stomped from the room.

'Milton, I feel badly about this. I so want the girls to like me,' said Kerrie miserably.

'Give them time. I've had other girlfriends, but the girls have never really had to share me seriously with anyone else before. I suppose I have indulged them to make up for my absences.'

'Do they remember their mother?'

'Of course the two older ones do, but Alia was only

a toddler when her mother died and she has only vague memories. My wife's death was a stressful time for us all.' He sipped his wine.

'Yes, that's why I want to try and get to know the girls really well. I'll do things with them,' said Kerrie. 'I'm an only child, I've no siblings, no one to really relate to, except my mother, but I'll work hard to make them like me.'

Milton leaned over and touched her arm. 'Give it time, *cara mia*. Don't rush. They will respect you more if you don't chase after them. Be yourself and once they know you, they won't be able to help liking you, you'll see.' He smiled.

Kerrie's mother was becoming very upset about the forthcoming wedding, and she confided in her sister-in-law.

'I can't believe Milton doesn't want a proper wedding. Kerrie's father and I used to talk about it from the time she was born. And those girls of his are going to be a handful. I thought that the youngest one might enjoy being a flower girl, but evidently none of them wants to be part of the wedding at all. Their father has put his foot down and told them that they have to be there, but we're going to see some sulky faces.'

'What does Kerrie think? Is she upset because she's not getting the big white wedding?'

'Well, no. She says that she agrees with Milton, that they should have one of these modern weddings where they stand under a tree or barefoot on the beach.'

'Well, if Kerrie's happy with that, let them get on with it. Invite who you want, and who comes, comes. So long as everyone enjoys the day, that's the main thing. Anyway, a more informal wedding will be cheaper for you.'

'Actually, Milton's offered to pay for some of the costs, but I think that it's the bride's family who should pay,' began Glynis.

'Rubbish. That sort of thinking went out with the ark! Last wedding I went to the kids did it all themselves. Let Milton do what he wants and you be happy that Kerrie's in love and found someone who's going to make her very comfortable.'

'I suppose you're right, but I just can't help feeling that . . . well, Kerrie is being bulldozed a bit into this marriage. She might look back and regret it.'

'It's her choice. I think that they'll be just fine with each other.'

In spite of Glynis Jackson's objections, Milton was very generous. He insisted on paying for the best food and wines, and for Kerrie's dress.

'I want you to look like a dreamy nymph of the sea or the forest. I see you in drifting chiffon, your hair flowing down to your waist, studded with flowers.' He went to his desk and picked up a pad and a pencil and made a sketch. 'You know those wonderful children's illustrators like Ida Outhwaite? My girls love her books.' Swiftly, using the side of the pencil lead, he shaded and filled in the surrounds. He studied his sketch, leaning closer to add a few more details, and then handed it to Kerrie. She stared at the delicate, romantic picture of a fairy standing beneath a willow tree, leaning over a pond to catch her reflection. The face was Kerrie's, smiling as her hand held back her long dark hair.

Kerrie caught her breath. 'Milton, it's beautiful. For someone who hammers and chips away at blocks of stone, you have a delicate touch. But I'd shock the guests if I appeared in a transparent dress made of flimsy cobwebs.' She laughed. She made light of his drawing but she was taken aback by Milton's fine pencilwork. She knew she didn't have such skill.

'I used to do drawings for the girls when they were very little as a way of getting them to go to bed. I still do, on occasion. But you get the idea. I hate those stiff-as-a-board wedding frocks. You're so svelte, you should wear something soft and flowing,' he said.

'I would have liked the girls to have been more involved,' began Kerrie, trying to broach her mother's ideas, but Milton cut her off.

'Don't even bother asking. Sorry, darling. I know they're a bit difficult at present, but they'll come round.'

'Milton, this is really hard. We all have to live together. Surely you can persuade them to make an effort. It's not like I've come in and usurped their mother. Or Wendy. You've been on your own a long time. They must see that getting married again is right for you.'

'Well, that's the crux of the matter, isn't it? The girls assumed that things would go on forever as they were, with Wendy and me being the centre of their universe. They don't understand that I don't want to go on living like that anymore. They should be grateful I have you and a new start. But they're still too young to see just how important you are to me. Things will settle down,' he added equably.

Kerrie stared at him. 'And in the meantime? Hostilities to prevail for the next few years? Alia is only nine!'

'It won't be that bad. I'm sure you'll manage to find a way to smooth things over. Wendy will help.'

'What if Wendy wasn't around? If she's not here, the girls would be forced to deal with me,' suggested Kerrie.

'What, and cramp our style? I have to travel,' said Milton. 'I have to take overseas commissions. It's the only way I'm going to make my name internationally, and I want you to be with me. I need Wendy here, to look after the girls.'

'Well, I suppose I could travel with you for the next few years, but what about when we have children? I wouldn't want to be separated from them, Milton. I'm not leaving my children behind to be raised by a nanny or housekeeper,' said Kerrie firmly.

Milton took her hands. 'Darling, it's too soon to be thinking about that. I want you all to myself for the time being. Anyway, I have a family already, and I don't need another one just yet. I have to work hard to make my name not just in Australia – I want my work to stand in the great galleries and museums all over the world! I need you to help me do that. You will be my inspiration.' He lifted her hands and kissed them.

The wedding went ahead as Milton wanted. And Kerrie was as happy as any bride could be. In spite of her mother's fretting, everything went smoothly, and the ceremony and the reception were held in a stunning garden overlooking the harbour. It was romantic and stylish. Milton and Kerrie exchanged vows beneath an archway of roses by the lushly landscaped pool.

The three Faranisi daughters sat with Wendy. Sam from Kerrie's art class tried to talk to the girls but they were aloof and reserved.

Kerrie asked some old school friends to her wedding but the intervening years had seen them go in different directions. Some were still at university and saving to travel overseas, some had jobs and they all found that they now had little in common. They all wondered at Kerrie's decision to marry an older man, even if he was famous, but when they met Milton and saw how attractive, sophisticated and attentive he was, some were impressed. What none of them envied was the responsibility of a relationship in which Kerrie had acquired three stepdaughters.

Kerrie's school friends struck up a conversation with Sam, probing him with questions, and Sam was all too pleased to show off his knowledge of Milton Faranisi.

'Is he really a famous sculptor?' asked one.

Sam lowered his voice conspiratorially. 'He has buckets of money partly because his first wife was very rich but mainly because he is very good at what he does and people pay loads to get one of his works. But he's really ambitious and wants to make an even bigger international name for himself as a sculptor.'

'I heard they have three houses or something. And they're going to live in Europe. Lucky Kerrie.'

'Is she still going to art school?' one of the girls asked.

'No, I think she'll be doing a lot of travelling. Anyway, she can always have private lessons from her husband!' said Sam. 'Personally, I can't see Kerrie having much time to paint after she's married,' he continued with unusual prescience.

Kerrie often thought that if they hadn't gone to Holland straight after the wedding for Milton's commission, she might have been able to bond with Milton's three daughters early in the marriage. But when they came back from Holland so pleased and buoyed by Milton's success, the girls felt left out, and they blamed Kerrie.

As time went on relations between Kerrie and the girls did not improve. They all lived together in the Rose Bay house, and Kerrie devoted herself to working on the administration of Milton's art projects – publicity, promotions, exhibitions and lectures – and dealing with the growing interest from overseas in his work, for Milton refused to trust anyone else. Wendy organised the day-to-day household routine and supervised the girls, while Kerrie juggled Milton's time at Rose Bay, at his studio, the annual trip to the villa in Italy and family skiing holidays with the girls.

In addition to the time she devoted to Milton's career,

Kerrie tried to involve herself with the girls, who had very demanding schedules. She attended school events, drove them to and from endless extracurricular activities and functions, took Luisa – who was horse mad – to pony club and drove the horse float to gymkhanas. She helped out at fundraising barbecues and attended school plays and eisteddfods, dragging Milton along whenever she could.

Milton was pleased with the effort that Kerrie was making to spend time with his girls, but there was little true warmth in their relationships. While they chatted with Kerrie about their friends and school, they never shared anything too personal or got too close to her.

Kerrie discovered that Renata often visited her father at his studio on the way home from school, when she had led Kerrie to believe that she had an extracurricular class, and Kerrie was quite hurt.

But Milton laughed it off. 'She wants to have a little time with her father, weasel a few bucks out of me, and see what I'm working on. Actually, I think she visits me because she's keen on one of my assistants.'

'But why keep it a secret?' asked Kerrie. 'It makes me feel as though she still doesn't trust me.'

As Milton's success grew, Kerrie became busier. When her mother asked her if she had any time to herself, Kerrie shrugged. 'I don't know where the time goes, Mum. Wendy's a treasure, but we seem to entertain a lot more than we did. And Milton relies on me to handle the business side of things now,' she added with some pride. 'It lets him stay focused and on track. It's a great partnership.'

'I hope you're enjoying it all. You certainly travel a lot.'

'Mum, we'd love you to come with us, I don't know why you won't come and stay at the villa.'

'Thanks for asking, but you know I don't like flying.

Anyway, you have enough on your plate without worrying about me.'

As Milton's creativity continued to flourish and his work was more and more in demand throughout the world, he made a decision that his daughters vehemently opposed.

'I have decided that the best thing for us all is that you girls start boarding at your school.'

His daughters wailed and protested.

'I bet this is Kerrie's idea. She wants to get rid of us,' said Renata.

'What about my horse?' Luisa started to cry.

'You hardly ride him any more,' snapped Alia. 'I won't like it. I'll be lonely.'

'Girls, I promise you that you'll enjoy it,' said their father. 'And you already have stacks of friends there. Besides, you can come home on the holidays. You'll only be gone in term time.'

'But why do we have to board? Why can't we stay at home?' demanded Renata.

'Because I think it will be easier for us all. Wendy says it will broaden your interests, give you greater stability and you'll learn to be independent,' said Milton.

'You and Kerrie don't want us around,' snapped Luisa. 'Next thing you'll be selling this house and going away with her.'

'Girls, I think you're overreacting. This will always be your home, but Kerrie and I are overseas so often these days and Wendy doesn't want to work fulltime anymore, although she'll always be here for your holidays if we're not. Now I have the opportunity to work in Paris for a while and, rather than disrupt your lives, I think that boarding school is the best solution. We will come back and forth, and you can come to Paris in the holidays. Let's at least try it for a year. It really is simpler all round.'

'It's a horrible idea,' said Alia, fighting back tears. 'Wendy would never agree to letting us board.'

'Well, that's where you're wrong. She knows what a top-notch education you'll get.'

'I've told the girls about boarding,' said Milton as Kerrie entered the room. 'It seems they aren't enthused.'

'It wasn't my idea,' began Kerrie, 'but I have to agree with your father and Wendy that this will be the best because it will be less disruptive.'

'Naturally,' said Renata spitefully. 'Well, I'm not going. I'm going to move in with my best friend. I'm sure her parents will agree.'

'You can't send us away!' Alia began to sob.

Milton stood up. 'There will not be any more discussion. You're all enrolled and the first term has been paid for.'

'You can still see your friends every day,' began Kerrie. 'There will be so many opportunities, Wendy says that you'll have more time to do drama, Luisa . . .'

'I don't care. You'll never come and see me in any plays, you'll be swanning round Europe,' yelled Luisa and strode from the room, followed by her sisters.

Kerrie sighed. 'I suppose it's a shock for them.'

'It's a logical and sensible idea. Wendy is right. If the girls are to get the best education, they need to have as much stability as possible.' He kissed Kerrie and added softly, 'Besides, it will be nice to have you all to myself. I love you, sweet girl.'

Kerrie loved Paris and for the first time in years she felt her creative juices flowing again. Everywhere she looked she saw pictures she wanted to paint. Cobbled streets, quaint bridges, street markets and interesting characters all excited her but when she told Milton he was dismissive.

'Tourist stuff. Sunday painters. Very unadventurous. You can think of better things to do than that. Start looking at modern ideas, abstracts. In the meantime, we have some entertaining to do. A big gallery curator and agent are in Paris from the Guggenheim. I have to impress them.'

And so it went. Kerrie was once again caught up in Milton's world, mixing with the corporate and society art set and any time she'd hoped to have for herself evaporated. But one day she found she had a few spare hours.

'You haven't had much time to yourself and I have to spend the morning at the studio workshop. Why don't you go shopping, darling?'

'You're on track with that piece, aren't you?'

'It's coming along, but I get a lot of interruptions what with artists calling in to talk to me and see what I'm doing,' he said.

Kerrie smiled. 'Don't tell me you don't enjoy that. But yes, darling, I think I will take a stroll. You never know what I might find.'

Kerrie decided against her initial idea of going to St Germain and went instead to explore other parts of the Left Bank. She made no conscious decision as to which crowded little street to follow but suddenly she found herself outside a fascinating-looking business that announced that it had been established in the late nineteenth century and seemed to have changed little since then. The minute Kerrie saw Sennelier Art Supplies, she knew she had to go in. She closed her eyes in joy as she inhaled the rich smell of oil paints. In utter delight she prowled past the old wooden cabinets filled with every variety of paint.

'This is an artist's wonderland,' she breathed aloud.

A woman wrapping a parcel smiled at her and spoke in thickly accented English. 'It is indeed. Artists have been coming here and falling in love with our colours for more than one hundred years. Cézanne, Picasso. And the

Sennelier family invented paints and pastels and water-colours especially for them.'

'Really? How amazing.' Kerrie studied one cabinet filled with acrylic paints. 'The depth of luminosity, the richness of the colours, I want to eat them.'

The shop assistant laughed. 'Yes, Gustav Sennelier started creating his own paints using raw pigments from minerals and plants and bones, binding them with honey, egg whites, tree gums, and because his colours were so vivid, it changed the way some of the impressionists painted. If an artist wanted a special colour and it didn't exist, Gustav created one.'

'What a clever man. It's a bit like our Australian Aborigines who use natural ochres and other bush materials.' Kerrie was entranced. Already she held several tubes of paint.

'The family also invented metal tubes for paint so that painters could work outdoors. And Henri, Gustav's son, invented the pastel oil stick for Picasso so he could put it straight on any surface.'

'And look at these watercolours . . . molten rainbows,' sighed Kerrie.

'Would you like a basket for your supplies?' asked the woman as she saw Kerrie selecting a range of colours and paper. 'You might find the brushes interesting; again, all handmade.'

Kerrie followed her in a daze, collecting art materials at will.

'What medium do you prefer?' asked the assistant, seeing the collection in Kerrie's basket.

'I've worked in all styles as a student. I'm still experimenting,' said Kerrie, suddenly feeling embarrassed that she hadn't progressed past being a student.

'Where are you studying? Les Beaux-Arts? It is near here.'

'Unfortunately, no. But my husband is a sculptor and he did give a lecture there recently.'

'Is that so? And you a painter. What a family. Who is your husband? Would I know of him?'

'Milton Faranisi. His family was from Italy but he . . .'

'Is Australian. Of course. I know of him. His work has become quite famous. You are privileged to be married to such a man. I hope you enjoy your time in Paris and work well with your Sennelier supplies.'

Kerrie hugged the large parcel as she walked back along the Seine, smiling at people who had set up easels and were painting the familiar scenes. One woman sat on the grass swiftly sketching a bridge as a baby lay on a rug beside her. Kerrie paused, sighed and walked on. When she passed a small store selling exquisitely embroidered lingerie, she went in. After looking at several beautiful garments, a tiny pink baby's dress, embroidered with roses and pale pink smocking with puffball sleeves and a satin sash, caught her eye. It was the sweetest thing she'd ever seen.

'You have the good eye, madame,' said the lady behind the counter. '*C'est magnifique, n'est pas?*'

'I'm afraid I don't have anyone to give it to,' said Kerrie.

'But this is an heirloom! A treasure,' exclaimed the woman. 'One day you will have the perfect little girl for this dress.'

Without really knowing why, Kerrie bought the little dress and paid more for it than several of the items of lingerie she bought for herself. Back in their apartment that afternoon, she laid the lingerie on the bed but tucked the baby dress and art supplies into a suitcase in the closet.

Milton was elated at the sight of the lingerie and demanded that she put it on for him right away.

It was dark before they left the bed and Milton was ravenous.

'Let's go to Pietro's to eat. What a wonderful day. I love Paris.'

Milton did not conquer just Paris. He was also acclaimed in Rome, London and New York as one of the world's foremost sculptors. He seemed to be forever working and the house at Rose Bay, at times, seemed more like a hotel than their home.

The girls were growing. Renata was at university, Luisa at fashion school. Alia was in her final years at high school. Wendy was still there for them at holiday time.

One afternoon as they shared a pot of coffee and Wendy's scones, Kerrie thanked her for the role she had played in the family.

'I appreciate what you do for all of us. I know it hasn't been easy for you these past few years. But I respect you for all you've done for the girls. You've provided a stability in the household that I don't think I could have managed to bring about.'

'Don't underestimate what you've done for those girls,' responded Wendy. 'I think the fact you didn't tell their father about the time Renata came home drunk and Luisa got into trouble with that awful boy earned you a few brownie points.' Wendy smiled.

'Well, I might have brownie points but I don't have their love. I don't think that I even have their respect.'

Wendy sighed. 'They put their mother on a pedestal where no one can ever touch her. But I often wonder how they would have got on with her if she hadn't died. She was a beautiful and wealthy woman, but somewhat self-absorbed. I'm not sure she would have done all those things for the girls that you did: looking after the horse, driving that wretched animal around, cooking sausages at the school fundraisers, sitting through all those school sports events.'

'Really?' said Kerrie. She felt pleased by Wendy's praise, but she also realised that no matter what she did for Milton's girls, she could never compete with their long-dead mother.

'Happy birthday, Kerrie.' Glynis Jackson gave her daughter a kiss and settled back in her armchair as Kerrie undid the carefully wrapped parcel.

She lifted out the pretty scarf and a framed cross-stitched picture of a flower arrangement. 'How lovely! This must have taken you ages, Mum. Thank you.'

Her mother looked pleased. 'My eyes aren't what they used to be but I have this wonderful contraption with a magnifying glass and a little light so I can sew while I watch TV in the evenings.'

'You sound lonely, Mum. I wish you'd spend more time with us. We've got plenty of room in the house now that two of the girls are out on their own. There's just Alia, when she's home on school holidays. She quite likes being the only one at home. Gets more of her father's attention.'

'Then she doesn't need me around.' Her mother lifted her shoulders and sighed. 'Of course, if you had a baby I'd be only too happy to be under your feet as much as possible.'

'Mum, we've discussed this before. Milton doesn't want another family, you know that. A baby would be nice, I suppose, but we have a busy life. We'll see,' Kerrie added vaguely, hoping to deflect more talk about grandchildren.

'Kerrie, you're in your thirties now. Don't leave it too late. Just do it. You devote your life to Milton, his work, his children . . . What about what you want? What about your dream to be an artist? Is that on hold too?'

'There's plenty of time, Mum,' said Kerrie lightly. 'Maybe when Alia leaves home . . .'

'Milton only wants to work and that seems to involve a lot of travel. He won't want to deal with a new baby, I bet. Just make sure that you won't have regrets, darling. I know how important children are. I don't know what I'd have done without you all these years. You've given me so much. You're my best friend as well as my daughter.'

Kerrie hugged her mother. 'Stop fretting. Let's just take things day by day. Now, where's that cake you said you made for me?'

Kerrie's mother didn't raise the subject of a baby again. Once she wondered if she should say anything to Milton but she knew it was not her business to interfere in her daughter's marriage. Kerrie seemed very happy and Milton certainly seemed to idolise her. But, thought Glynis, while some men in their fifties enjoyed starting a family, or a second family, Milton didn't seem to want to. His work was his obsession and his sculptures, his own creations, were his children.

While the older girls had moved out of the house, their lives still impacted on Kerrie and their father, though Kerrie felt she bore more of the brunt of their problems than Milton did. The girls visited frequently, and often brought their laundry home to be washed as well as helping themselves to the freezer, pantry and Milton's wine while they were there. Kerrie sometimes felt that they treated her like the maid, and so for once she put her foot down.

'You've moved out of home and your father pays you a very generous allowance, so you don't have to support yourselves. But you have to be responsible, and that means paying your bills, doing the shopping, looking after your-selves and not expecting us to do it for you.'

'Look, Kerrie, this is our home and we'll come and go as we please. You can't stop us.'

'I'm not trying to. I'm just suggesting that you stand on your own two feet.'

'You mean like you did? Where was your career? You've just sponged off Dad.'

'That's not right. I've worked very hard to further your father's career. And I've always tried to be supportive and helpful to you girls but you've always shut me out.' Kerrie turned on her heel and left the room, surprising the girls with her vehemence.

Several days later, when she went into the laundry, she found the girls' clothes still in the dryer. With a resigned sigh and a shrug of her shoulders she pulled out their washing and began folding it.

'Darling, what are you doing? I've been looking for you and here I find you being a laundress! I pay Mrs Anderson do the washing. Come on, the girls have pre-pared us a lovely lunch.'

Kerrie refrained from telling him that she had made the quiche and a fruit compote and had asked the girls just to do the salad. 'No, these clothes belong to the girls. I'm just getting them ready so they can take them with them later.'

'Why are you doing this? Don't they have a washing machine?'

'Actually, I don't know,' confessed Kerrie. 'They bring their gear here and sometimes Mrs Anderson does it, if she's around, but if she's not, I do it.'

'That's ridiculous. You're not their servant. They can look after themselves,' said Milton and went to confront his daughters as they sat down to lunch.

'You must stop treating Kerrie like your personal

maid! This is not a damned Chinese laundry! Why can't you do your own washing?'

'My machine is broken, it's so old,' started Renata. 'I need a new one.'

'Then take your stuff to a laundromat. Why can't you buy a new machine? What do you do with your allowance? What about the money you get from that boutique where you work?'

'She buys half their stock,' giggled Luisa.

Milton continued as though he hadn't heard her. 'If you must bring your things here to be washed, then do it yourself. You're old enough. It's not on, having my wife wash your dirty clothes. You're spoilt and selfish and bloody rude to Kerrie. I see how you treat her, you know. She's tried for years to be kind and helpful to you and you have never made an effort to try and meet her even halfway.'

The girls stared at their father in shock.

'Milton, it's all right,' said Kerrie as she came into the room.

'It's not all right. I'm ashamed of you girls. Come on, Kerrie, I'm taking you out to Watsons Bay for a fish lunch.' He looked back at the girls. 'And clean up after yourselves. This isn't a tavern for travellers passing through.'

'No, it's our mother's house,' said Renata spitefully.

Her father stared at her. 'Well, that does not give you the right to abuse its privileges.'

'I wish you hadn't made a scene,' sighed Kerrie as Milton poured her a glass of wine.

'I should have said something years ago. I don't always pay attention to what's happening under my nose. I apologise for my spoilt daughters. I know it hasn't been easy for you but you've been wonderful to them and very patient. I always hoped they'd come around.'

Kerrie thought that it was a bit late for Milton to be thinking about this now. Had he been firm with the girls from the moment they were married things may have been different. But she pushed the thought away. Milton was Milton and maybe she was also partly to blame for not standing up to them sooner. 'They'll settle down eventually, you'll see.'

Milton smiled and raised his glass. 'I'm glad you think so. Thank you, my darling. No matter what, we have each other. Are you going to have the John Dory?'

Kerrie lost track of the time between their lazy lunch at Watsons Bay and the time she called the Nightmare. Relations between her and the girls did not improve. Indeed, at times, Kerrie thought that they got worse. But as they had, by now, all left home, she did not have to see them so frequently. When they did meet, it was frosty. But if there were still problems with her stepdaughters, there were none with Milton. His reputation as an artist continued to grow, culminating with a retrospective at the Tate gallery in London. He had finally established himself.

On a summery morning some years later Milton made love to Kerrie, kissed her, showered, dressed, threw a change of clothes, some food, his newspaper and spectacles into a bag, and cheerfully headed off to the studio.

'I think I'll stay there tonight. As much as I need my assistants, sometimes I can get more done without them. Feel free to pop in and interrupt any time!' He grinned. 'There's cold wine in my fridge.'

'Thanks, darling, but I have to take my mother to the cardiologist again. She's getting so frail. She doesn't seem to eat anything at all, and she's always so short of breath. I'm very worried about her.'

'I know you're concerned, but her doctor is trying to do the best for her. If you want to, why don't you stay the night?'

They held each other tightly, then he kissed her quickly. 'Go back to sleep. I love you.'

'Love you, too, and I might just do that. I'll see,' said Kerrie, and pulled the sheet around her, deciding to try to return to sleep to block out the thought that she might lose her mother.

After taking Glynis to the doctor's where the news was not terribly optimistic, Kerrie spent the afternoon with her mother, cooking dinner for them both. She planned to have a nightcap with Milton on her way home but Glynis wanted to talk, as if she knew her days were limited, and Kerrie decided to take Milton's advice and stay the night. Her mother took Kerrie around the house pointing out photographs, a silver candlestick, ornaments and special books that had belonged to her parents.

'When I've gone, I want you to look after these things, Kerrie. I so wish I had grandchildren I could give them to. I know they're not valuable, but they mean so much to me, especially your father's medals from the Korean War. You will look after everything, won't you? Don't throw anything away, you know what I mean, dear?'

Kerrie put her arm around her mother, shocked again by her thinness. 'Mum, I'll treasure everything. I grew up with these things too, remember. Anyway, you're talking nonsense. You're going to be around to enjoy them for many years to come.'

In the morning they shared breakfast together on the sunny back patio and Kerrie was pleased when her mother managed to eat an egg as well as her usual solitary piece of toast and honey.

Back at home in Rose Bay, Kerrie showered and changed and rang Milton at the studio. She knew it was time to discuss her mother's future. Glynis needed someone to come in every day to help. Her mother was neglecting her hair and nails and didn't seem to notice that the top she was wearing had food spilled on it. Kerrie was shocked that the house, which had always been so spick and span, now looked decidedly grubby.

There was no answer from Milton. Kerrie left a message telling him that she was bringing his lunch over.

As soon as she walked into the courtyard in front of the studio she felt something wasn't right. Milton's car was there but everything was too quiet. He normally had a classical CD playing loudly, competing with the radio, while he banged his chisel extra hard when he disagreed with a point someone was making. But today there was no whistling, hammering, clanking of tools, no music. Kerrie walked faster, going around to the yard where he worked, calling out his name.

There was no answer.

She rushed inside, plausible scenarios racing through her mind: he'd wandered down the street for a coffee . . . One of the girls had come by and taken him out . . . A neighbour had asked for his help . . . She pushed from her thoughts the possibility that anything could be amiss. But nagging at the back of her mind was a vision of the tall ladders, the hoist and the scaffolding he used when he was working high above the studio floor.

Nothing seemed out of place. Then she noticed the lights were all on. She hurried towards the kitchenette and stopped, gasped and then caught her breath.

'No! No . . . No. Milton!'

He was lying face down, an arm stretched towards the refrigerator. He was wearing the shorts and T-shirt that he'd left the house in the morning before. He looked composed, with a slightly surprised expression on his face. Kerrie crouched beside him, tears running down her cheeks, her breath now came in long shuddering sobs. Slowly she reached out and touched his pale face. It was eerily cold, like the marble he sometimes sculpted.

She didn't know how long she sat there stroking his hand and letting thoughts of their time together come and go, floating through her mind like drifting shadows or bright flashes.

Eventually she picked up her mobile phone and rang Milton's doctor.

'I'll handle matters, Kerrie,' he said. 'This is terrible, a great shock.'

The doctor prescribed medication for Kerrie to keep her calm and help her sleep, but she refused to take it, preferring to be involved in all that was happening. She wished the doctor would give something to Milton's daughters who were hysterical and kept questioning Kerrie as to how this could have happened. The explanation Milton's doctor gave about a massive and unexpected heart attack, which could have happened at any time, didn't pacify them. There were veiled accusations and demands.

'Why wasn't he seeing a doctor for checkups?'

'He ate too much rich food and drank too much and you let him.'

'He didn't do enough exercise. How come no one checked on him yesterday?'

On and on it went. Kerrie dully plodded through the arrangements for the funeral, gradually relinquishing control of it to his daughters, who battled between themselves over every detail.

Even though Milton's daughters took over the organisation of the funeral, Kerrie found herself exhausted and emotionally drained each night when she fell into bed. Sometimes, when she reached out for Milton's comforting shape and found only a cool empty sheet, she cried. If she was lucky, she would eventually fall into a dreamless sleep.

There were bills to pay, documents to sign, arrangements to make. To Kerrie, watching as if through a fog, it was like a performance, a theatrical extravaganza, stroking the egos, calculating how much time each eulogy should have and listening to Milton's friends' and colleagues' reminiscences. Kerrie was patient, unfailingly polite and hospitable. But what she really wanted was to be left alone to deal with the dreadful shock of her husband's sudden death and the knowledge that her mother was dying.

And so here she was – lunching alone where she and Milton had shared so many happy, casual occasions at the waterfront at Watsons Bay, eating freshly caught fish. She glanced at her watch, a gift from Milton. She'd asked the driver to come back for her in an hour. She still had twenty minutes to spare. She went to the bathroom, removed her dark stockings, then paid the bill, thanked the maitre d' and the owner and, carrying her shoes, walked along the sand, letting the water wash over her feet.

Everywhere she looked she could see Milton: in the broadness of a stranger's shoulders, in the glimpse of a profile with a roman nose, in a shock of greying hair. Kerrie realised that being in surroundings that they'd shared and enjoyed was going to be too hard to bear.

But what was she to do now? she wondered. She knew there would be a lot of administrative work to attend to in connection with Milton's personal collection, which was on loan to various corporations and public buildings. Then there were the works he had completed for an exhibition as well as the last piece he was working on in his studio. What was she to do with these now? Already auction houses had been calling her, seeing if she wanted to sell any of his pieces. But until she knew what Milton's wishes were she felt that she could make no decision.

After the funeral Kerrie put everything else on hold, despite the demands of the girls who wanted the estate sorted out straight away. She told them that she had to spend time with her mother. They grudgingly conceded that she must, and offered to go through their father's things to save her the trouble.

'No,' said Kerrie firmly. 'Your father's solicitor is still away on holidays and his office has asked us to do nothing until he gets back. We'll just have to wait.'

Sitting by her mother's bedside was peaceful for Kerrie, which surprised her. Her mother lay with her hands clasped on her chest, a serene expression on her face, but her breathing was beginning to become raspy. Occasionally she would open her eyes and Kerrie would lean over and ask if she wanted a sip of water. Kerrie smoothed Glynis's hair and wiped a cloth scented with rosewater over her forehead. This action would bring a small smile and a slight nod in thanks. Once Glynis's fingers flickered and Kerrie took her mother's hand in her own, smoothing the veined skin.

'I love you, Mum. You've been the best mum in the world.'

Her mother surprised her by whispering, with great effort, 'Love you, Ker. Such a good . . . girl.'

They were the last words her mother spoke. Over the next forty-eight hours Glynis struggled, her breath coming in hoarse, laboured gurgles. Kerrie went into the kitchen, shakily trying to make a cup of tea. The palliative care nurse she'd hired when her mother had made it clear that she did not want to go to hospital quietly explained to Kerrie that her mother's body was closing down and that it wouldn't be long now. Kerrie burst into tears.

'Let me do that for you,' said the nurse softly. 'Stay

with your mother. These are precious moments. You're lucky she isn't in pain.'

'Does she know I'm here?'

'You know you are here, with her, and that will comfort you,' answered the nurse.

When the moment came, her mother suddenly tried to lift her head, her eyes snapping wide open as she looked towards . . . something.

Kerrie grabbed her feather-light frame in her arms, putting her face before her mother's eyes.

'Mum, it's Kerrie, I'm here, I'm with you. Be safe, be happy. You deserve it. Oh, Mum . . .' As the sounds in her mother's throat stopped, Kerrie lay her gently on the pillow and rested her head on her mother's chest, her tears spilling onto those frail hands.

'Stay with her as long as you like,' said the nurse as she watched Kerrie from the doorway.

The late afternoon light faded from her mother's bedroom, which was filled with the little things she loved. Kerrie sat there, feeling completely desolate. The nurse brought her a cup of tea.

'What do I do now?' asked Kerrie, a rhetorical question that she quickly amended to, 'I mean, about my mother . . .'

'I'll notify the doctor. If you let the funeral home know . . . Can I call someone to come and be with you?'

Kerrie shook her head. 'There's no one.'

'There will be some paperwork, but there won't be any red tape over the death certificate,' said the doctor, when he came. 'This must be hard for you. You've just lost your husband, haven't you?'

'Yes, I have. I just wanted to say thank you for all the care and attention you've given Mum . . .' Kerrie choked up and could say no more.

'She was a very sweet lady. I'm glad that you were here. That will give you some comfort in the future.'

Kerrie nodded tearfully. 'I just wish I'd been able to say goodbye to my husband . . .'

The doctor patted her hand, knowing there were no words he could say. He felt immeasurably sad for this still young woman who seemed so alone in the world.

Glynis Jackson's funeral was small and simple. Relatives, neighbours and friends, who'd known her for years, came along to say goodbye. Her mother had asked to be buried next to her husband and there were only a few from the funeral who came to the graveside. Milton's daughters sent flowers but did not attend. Kerrie stood bleakly as the small service concluded and she walked back to her car by herself.

Three weeks later she was contacted by Milton's solicitor to arrange an appointment to read Milton's will. Milton's brother Byron was the executor, but couldn't travel from his home in the USA due to complications from a knee replacement. The solicitor, Walker Smith, a family friend, had told Kerrie it wasn't necessary for Byron to be present anyway, as he had spoken to him on the phone.

Kerrie sat opposite Walker Smith. His hands were folded on top of a file. He smiled at Kerrie.

'How are you holding up?'

'All right, thanks, Walker. I've had two funerals to deal with.'

'I was sorry to hear about your mother. This is a hard time for you.'

Kerrie nodded. 'I'm coping. But it's a bit overwhelming with all the cards, emails, phone calls about Milton. It's going to take a long time to respond to so many.'

'Will the girls help you?'

'They could, but they won't.' She sighed. 'Now that Milton has gone they seem to have dropped all pretence of being cordial to me.'

'They're grieving, Kerrie. Like you. Let them do it their way. They're lucky they have each other. Who's looking after you? Helping you?'

'Oh, lots of our friends have called, invited me to come and be with them for meals, outings. But I find it too hard. I'm not ready to talk about Milton . . . the good times, reminiscing . . .' Her eyes welled up. 'I just want him back,' she said, her voice rising.

'I can understand that. Have you any close friends, particularly a girlfriend? My wife tells me that they are very useful at times like this,' said the solicitor kindly.

Tears rolled down Kerrie's face, and she shook her head as she searched in her handbag. 'None that I really want to talk to.'

The solicitor pushed a box of tissues towards her.

'Maybe you should take a short break, Kerrie. Get away from that house in Rose Bay with all its memories. Gather yourself and start to come to terms with your life now. Maybe away from everything you'll be able to deal with things better.'

'Where would I go? I couldn't face the villa in Italy. I don't think I'll ever go there again.'

'Have you thought about what you would like to do now, Kerrie? You've devoted yourself to Milton for twenty years.' He paused and asked delicately, 'Isn't there anything that you want to do for yourself?'

'Milton swept me off my feet and I haven't thought of anything but Milton, his wishes, our life together ever since.' She smiled softly. 'We have . . . We had a wonderful life. I've been very lucky.'

'So don't you think it's time to think about yourself now?' he persisted gently.

Kerrie was quiet for a moment, she looked down, avoiding Walker's gaze. 'I was an art student when I met Milton. I thought I was going to be an artist,' she said slowly. She looked up and gave the solicitor a rueful smile. 'I haven't picked up a brush in all this time. Milton was the gifted one.'

'Indeed he was. But as I understand it, when you have a talent, a dream, like your desire to be an artist, the passion is always there, it doesn't go away. Maybe it's time to let your own creativity flower.'

She stared at the kindly man in the dark suit and neat tie. In her head she suddenly saw a vision of Walker Smith as some kind of artist angel handing her a palette and a fan of paintbrushes. She smiled in amusement. 'Actually now that you've said that out loud, you've kind of made that fuzzy dream seem vaguely possible.'

'You'll never know if you don't try. But leave that for the present. What I'm advising, as a friend, is to just take a little time out for yourself. You'll think a lot more clearly about the future, then. Especially after we go through this.' He patted the file. 'Shall we?'

Kerrie nodded. 'Shouldn't the girls be here?'

'Byron is the executor and he is privy to the contents of Milton's will, and he has instructed me to act on his behalf to administer the estate according to Milton's wishes.'

Walker Smith opened the file, took out an envelope, removed a document from it and, in a professional voice, began reading the last will and testament of Milton Carlo Faranisi. The words washed over Kerrie and seemed to have little meaning as Walker intoned the legal jargon. There were some specifics about where certain pieces of his work were to go. His boat he left to one of his old friends, there was a bequest of certain pieces to Byron and a handsome bequest to Wendy. When Walker paused and glanced at her before clearing his throat and continuing, Kerrie sat up straight and tried to pay more attention.

'As my three daughters have been more than adequately

provided for from their mother's estate, I leave my entire estate, excepting those bequests aforementioned, to my wife, Kerrie Joy Faranisi, to administer as she sees fit. The disbursement of my work is to be her decision as is the distribution of my personal effects . . .'

Walker glanced up at Kerrie. 'The rest of this is pretty mundane. Milton did not want an ostentatious memorial plaque or statue erected. And obviously you will know which works he is referring to in this attached list of pieces he wants you to keep or dispose of to appropriate people, or places.'

As the solicitor paused, Kerrie shook her head. 'Walker, have I missed something? Does he say in effect that I am the sole beneficiary of the bulk of his estate? Surely that can't be right? What about his daughters?'

'He says quite clearly that they were provided for from their mother's estate.'

'But I know they'll be expecting something from their father!' exclaimed Kerrie.

'Possibly they are.'

'But this is terrible! They're going to think that I coerced Milton into making this will to benefit just me. What did Byron have to say?'

'That if that's what Milton wanted, then so be it.'

'Should I give them something?' asked Kerrie, feeling quite overcome.

Walker Smith looked at her. 'Listen to me. Milton had his reasons for doing this. He wanted you to be in control of his estate and decide, as you've always helped him decide, where his sculptures should end up. Maybe, down the track, when you have had time to think, you might want to do something, but this is not the right time for rushing into rash decisions,' advised the solicitor.

'I suppose I could do that.' Kerrie sighed.

'Milton has made you the custodian of his legacy.

You know his daughters are more than adequately provided for. He wanted to make sure you were looked after. Kerrie, when he did this will after he won that big art prize in Brussels, he told me that he owed so much of his success to you and that you had given up your dreams and made him your career. I can only agree.'

Kerrie sat quietly, digesting what Walker had said. She didn't know what to think or feel, knowing that Milton had acknowledged, if not to her then to his lawyer, the fact that she'd sacrificed her own dreams to support him. 'I didn't know Milton felt like that. I never considered him a selfish person, it's just how he was, so focused, so single-minded about what he was doing that he swept everyone along with him.'

'You're a generous and selfless person, Kerrie. A lot of us on the outside looking in considered Milton took more from you than he gave. The way you ran everything for him, tried so hard with those girls, and never seemed to argue or complain. Milton knew that you once wanted to be an artist and that you gave up your ambitions for him so maybe this is his way of thanking you.'

'I didn't give up being an artist,' said Kerrie quietly. 'I never even tried.'

'Then I rest my case,' said Walker. 'You are only in your early forties. You are beautiful and independent and now wealthy. So take time out just for you.'

'Where would I go? I've never been anywhere without Milton.'

'Do you like the outback?' asked Walker suddenly.

'I've never been. Milton preferred to travel overseas.'

'Then may I make a suggestion? I have a friend who happens to be an artist. Lives way out west. I can put you in touch with him if you like. He's a terrific character. I'm sure you'll like him maybe he can help you.'

'Thank you, Walker. I'll think about it.'

3

SHE WAS NOT ALONE in the car. Andrea Bocelli kept her company and Kerrie sang along with the Italian tenor, trying not to cry as memories of the times she and Milton had spent in Italy flooded over her. Porto Ercole and their villa, Rome, Ravello, would she ever go back?

The countryside through which she was driving could not have been more different from Italy. The landscape was flat. The arrow of bitumen in front of her pointed to the centre of the horizon where a smudge of hills seemed to float above the earth. Perhaps it was a mirage. She wouldn't know for some distance yet. Stretching away on either side of the highway were scrubby patches of grass and grey shrubs that looked barely anchored in the black soil plains.

A few times her car was observed by statuesque emus,

their soft feathers as dusty as the earth around them, their expressions imperious, heads held high on graceful long necks. But their eyes were beady and hard and Kerrie had no doubt that their beaks were sharp.

As she drove, so much of what she saw was familiar to her, even though she had never ventured past the city limits. Pictures she knew from books, calendars, magazines and movies, the familiar flora and fauna of Australia, seemed almost a cliché in reality. She wondered why she and Milton had never come out here.

Their life in Sydney was always so hectic, and when they got away it was for Milton's work or to places he loved, in Europe. And that's where most of their friends and acquaintances were, too. In Sydney, Kerrie realised she had no close friends who lived nearby.

Her mother had once tried to persuade Kerrie to take a little holiday just with Milton and had recommended Lord Howe Island where Glynis spent her honeymoon. Kerrie didn't even bother mentioning the idea to her husband, for she knew that it would not have appealed to him.

But now, out here, the openness, the light, the colours, so different from Europe, began to enchant her and she wished she and Milton had explored at least a little bit of the Australian bush.

The deaths of Milton and her mother had overwhelmed Kerrie. There was no time to grieve, she found that there was simply too much to do and so her feelings were put on hold.

Her mother's estate had to be finalised and her house emptied and sold. Sifting through her mother's possessions had been heartbreaking and as she sat alone in the house where she had grown up, surrounded by the things that her mother had loved, Kerrie realised just how much she had relied on her mother for support and companionship.

But however emotionally hard sorting her mother's effects had been, it paled in comparison with the difficulties Milton's estate had presented.

Kerrie had to make decisions about many of his sculptures, sorting through which of them were on loan, which were part of an unfinished commission, and which he owned. She also knew that Milton would have wanted some of his work not just sold but donated to favoured institutions.

But any determination she tried to make was immediately and violently opposed by his daughters. Although Milton's will had made it clear that all decisions regarding his works were Kerrie's sole preserve, the three girls had argued about them. They accused Kerrie of not doing enough to maintain their father's reputation and that she was getting rid of much of his work with indecent haste so that she could make money from it.

Their opinions became too much for Kerrie. She remembered Walker Smith's suggestion and so here she was on her own, escaping, at least for now, to an unresolved future.

She stopped for a break in the tiny township of Burren Junction and found a take-away shop where she had a mug of rather bad coffee and an excellent meat pie. As she drove through the town's outskirts she saw a large green and white sign and halfway down it was her destination: Lightning Ridge 160 kilometres.

The outback opal mining town was not what she'd expected. In her mind's eye she had a vision of corrugated-iron shanties, a couple of old-style pubs, a basic motel, an ageing supermarket, a few shops, places selling mining supplies and an old fossicker selling an opal or two. But as she drove down Morilla Street, she was amazed at what a vibrant tourist town Lightning Ridge appeared to be. Signs for mine tours, fossicking trips, an unusual underground sculpture gallery, events and shows seemed to be everywhere, but art galleries and souvenir shops were outnumbered by dozens of opal shops. There was a new supermarket. Kerrie saw signs for accommodation of all descriptions: caravan parks and motor home areas, B&Bs and renovated fossicker's cottages all vied with the staid sixties-style motels for customers.

She pulled up outside a trendy café that would look at home in Double Bay or Kings Cross. She ordered a cappuccino from the blackboard menu of vegetarian and health food specialities and sat at a small outdoor table. A man at the next table drained his coffee, folded his newspaper and handed it to Kerrie.

'Yesterday's *Herald*. Like to look at it?'

'No, thanks, I've read it already . . . yesterday. But thank you for asking.'

'Not all the papers get up here on time. You visiting, eh?'

'Just arrived.'

'Picked the best coffee in town. Sightseeing or fossicking?'

'Bit of both perhaps. Are you a local?'

'Yep. Though what qualifies you as a local is a bit elastic. Where're you staying?'

'I haven't found anywhere yet. I assumed I'd just find a room at a motel,' said Kerrie.

'Hmm. You can't stay at the Diggers. It burnt down. Again. The pub and motels could be booked out. There are buyers in town. But there's some good little B&Bs. And the caravan park of course. How long you staying? Mind if I sit with you?' He pulled out the other chair at the small wrought-iron table and waved to the girl at the counter for another coffee.

'I'm Billy. At your service.' He held out his hand.

Kerrie smiled as she shook Billy's hand, glancing

at his friendly blue eyes, the salt and pepper beard, the faded T-shirt and shorts and the bush hat he carried. An expensive mobile phone, she observed, was clipped to his belt. 'I'm Kerrie and actually I have no clear plans at the moment. I've come to meet a friend of a friend and just look around.'

Billy grinned. 'Lady friend? There's a lot of t'riffic women working up here now. On their own, too.'

'What sort of thing do they do on their own up here?' asked Kerrie.

'Lots. They mine, work in the shops and the local community, and in the hospitality industry, of course. Most of the opal stores are run, or owned, by women. Some are talented jewellery designers. One grew up here. Her grandfather and father mined and she learnt a lot from them. Some girls come to the Ridge for a couple of days and never leave. So who's your friend? I might know her.'

'It's Murray Evans. He's an artist.'

'Too bloody right he is. Lovely fellow, so's his wife, Fiona.'

'You know him?' said Kerrie.

'Sure do. Known John and Fee since they first came to the Ridge. Nearly twenty years ago. His gallery is down the end of the street but he works in his studio out at his camp. Fiona is nearly always in the gallery.'

'How long have you been in Lightning Ridge?' asked Kerrie. 'Sounds like a long time.'

'I was born around here in Mehi. Went away for a long time then came back. My missus died a while ago and so I moved out of town. You caught me on a town day. If I can help you, let me know. Murray has my number. I'll take you for a drive out to a mine or whatever, if you'd like.'

'Thanks, that's kind of you. Do you mine for opals?'

'That's the name of the game. The *raison d'être* for being at the Ridge. Yeah, I've got a claim or two round the place.'

'Do you find many opals?' asked Kerrie. 'I don't know much about them.'

'That's a question you never ask around here. No one ever talks about what they're digging – though word creeps around soon enough.'

'I'm sorry. I didn't mean to pry. Is it because someone else comes and pegs a claim next to you?' asked Kerrie.

'Nah. Because of ratters.'

'Ratters?'

'Bastards who sneak into your mine at night and rip out your opal. The night shift!' explained Billy.

'Can't you secure your mine at night?'

'These blokes have night-vision goggles and heavy artillery. Serious stuff.'

'It sounds like the wild west. Do the ratters get caught?'

'There's always been Ridge law to deal with ratters. Funny how some fellas get pissed and stumble down a fifty-foot mine shaft in the dark and break their neck.' Billy grinned. 'But now days, crims come in many guises. Some of the blokes who arrive in smart cars and fancy shoes are just as crooked as any ratter. The boys from the big end of town are creeping in.' Seeing Kerrie's startled look, he went on, 'We're facing the end of an era here. But that's not what visitors want to know. You should get a sense of how it was in the old days.'

Kerrie nodded. She was startled by Billy's tales of law-lessness and wasn't sure whether to take them seriously or not. 'Billy, you are a mine of information. Sorry about the pun,' said Kerrie.

'No worries,' said Billy. 'Ridge people are friendly on the whole. It's the spirit of the place. It's always been a pretty rugged lifestyle and if you don't help a mate in strife, well, don't count on getting help when you need it.'

'I suppose so,' said Kerrie. 'To tell you the truth I've never been this far outback before.'

'Out here you have to rely on other people for everything – social life, helping with a job, getting supplies, that sort of thing. Mind you, there are people out in the scrub who prefer to keep to themselves. Might go months without seeing another human being. But that's the way they like it.'

'Thanks, Billy. I have enjoyed talking with you. Let me pay for your coffee.'

'Thanks, but no thanks. It's on the tick. I have a running account here.' He waved to the girl behind the cash register who smiled and held up two fingers, then pulled out a tattered notebook and added two coffees to Billy's account.

Leaving the café Kerrie could feel the deep warmth of the sun even though it was, by local standards, a balmy spring day. 'It must get terribly hot here in the summer,' she said to Billy.

'Too right. Quietens down then, too. The tourists leave and so do the winter miners.'

'Who are they?' asked Kerrie.

'Lots of retired people come up for the winter and dig away at their claims. It's a lifestyle thing, though they get a kick out of picking up a few dollars here and there.'

'They don't make any big finds then?' said Kerrie as they strolled along the street.

'Nah. Most of them just pick through the old diggings. To work anything new now you need decent machinery. A jackhammer can be hard work for an old bloke. The real professionals use heavy-duty gear. Can be very expensive. But you can get lucky, and that's what everyone dreams of and why they keep pecking away. There could be opal an inch away. There's a story goes that one couple hit a patch of good-quality opal a few years back, and made several million bucks. And you know what? They're still here, living in their caravan, except that now it has a satellite dish.'

'Maybe in the summer they go to their new million-dollar home in the Bahamas,' said Kerrie.

Billy laughed. 'Who knows? Anyway, they're here because this's where they want to be.'

'Must be nice to feel like that, and doing something together that you enjoy. Maybe finding opals is just an excuse.'

'Might be. Some of them work like navvies, keeps them fit and they live together in little communal camps scattered round the place. But there are others who are deadly committed to finding opal. Opal mining gets to you. Opal is such hypnotic stuff. The men love it as much as the women.'

'Like gold?' asked Kerrie.

Billy nodded. 'I guess it can become an obsession. Now here's Murray's studio. I'll just pop in and say hello.' He pushed open the swinging saloon-style doors of the large gallery and shouted out, 'Murray? Fiona? You've got a visitor.'

Inside the gallery was a counter cluttered with post-cards, fridge magnets and brochures and on the wall behind it were two huge paintings of political leaders portrayed as animal caricatures. There was a small office to one side and Murray Evans came out to greet them.

'G'day, Billy.' The artist smiled at Kerrie.

'This is Kerrie, just arrived and says you have a mutual friend. So I'll leave you to it. Sold a few, have you, Murray?' enquired Billy as he glanced around at the gallery walls.

'Doing all right. Had a lot of visitors. See you, Billy.'

'Hooroo, Kerrie. I'll see you next time I'm in town, if you're still around.'

The artist came around the desk and shook Kerrie's hand. He looked to be in his fifties, his sandy hair was flecked with grey, and he radiated energy and good humour. 'So who's our mutual friend?'

'Walker Smith. He's my solicitor. My husband died recently and Walker suggested that I get away for a bit, take a trip out here and look you up.'

Murray nodded. 'Sounds like Walker. Sorry to hear about your husband. Walker and I went to uni together. I was supposed to be doing law but I dropped out. I knew a collar and tie job wasn't for me.'

Kerrie glanced around at the two large rooms. 'Your work is very strong. Do you paint in the field or take photos? Where are these places?'

She walked up to the wall hung with brilliant oil paintings of dramatic arid lonely landscapes. Some featured an uncoiling rusting wire fence or a rotten slab of wood that was once a small hut and was now a home to lizards. The remains of a half-buried old truck abandoned to the sand years ago caught her eye. In a small detail she noticed the tiny animal tracks in the sand, and a shadowy shape and a pair of wary eyes peering from beneath a splintered mudguard. 'Makes you wonder, who lived in the old hut, who drove the truck, and what happened to them. Now they're homes to little animals,' she said.

Murray looked at her with a half smile. 'Very observant. You paint?'

She shrugged. 'I studied art, wanted to be an artist, but didn't stick with it. I married an artist instead. A sculptor.'

'Who's that?' asked Murray. 'Would I know him?'

'Milton Faranisi.'

'Of course. I read that he died. All of a sudden wasn't it? I'm sorry about that. So Walker sent you to see me. You must come out to the camp, meet the wife and see what I'm doing. The stuff I really enjoy doing.' He pointed to the second showroom. 'That's what the tourists like. Not big works, they like the more fun stuff.'

'Quirky sense of humour!' said Kerrie, looking at his paintings of native animals and birds. 'You use them instead of people to make political statements.'

'Yes, I get away with bloody blue murder that way,' Murray said.

Kerrie smiled at three galahs that bore a striking resemblance to some well-known politicians. 'I think I like the picture with the kookaburra and the frog best. You really like living at the Ridge do you?'

'I leave as little as possible. Fiona goes to Sydney regularly, as our son is at uni. But the art scene in the city doesn't much like what I do. I'm not sophisticated or adventurous enough. That's fine by me. I enjoy my art and why try to be something you're not? I've been here almost twenty years and can't imagine living anywhere else. It's a great place. I love the air, the scenery, the people, the lifestyle.'

As they returned to the front of the gallery where several tourists were flipping through large colourful prints of his paintings, Murray added, 'Hasn't always been a piece of cake. Had a rough patch or two, but that can happen anywhere. I think staying here saved my life. But that's another story. Are you staying in the Ridge for a bit?'

'I thought I might stay a couple of days. Billy mentioned a few places . . .'

'I'd say come and stay with us, but the spare room is chockers with furniture – we're renovating. Building actually, adding a room and a deck. But can you come to dinner tonight?'

'Please, I don't want to be any trouble . . .'

'No trouble at all. I'll take you round to Denise's

place. She rents a very comfortable cottage and I'm pretty sure it's vacant.' He turned to the tourists who were now strolling round the gallery. 'I just have to duck out for a minute.'

'Okay,' said the man. 'But can you help my wife?'

'I'd like a couple of those fridge magnets, the frog and the galah,' said the woman, delving into her purse.

The sale was swiftly concluded, and when the tourists left Murray hung a sign that said 'Back in 5 mins' on the door and turned the key.

'Took me a long time to agree to those bloody fridge magnets but I tell you what, they keep turning over at five bucks a pop. Amazing. Not easy to spend five grand or even five hundred on a painting but five bucks? No worries.' He grinned. 'You'll like Denise, she's a real treasure.'

They strolled to the corner and turned down another road.

'Is this how it is everywhere out here? People being so friendly and helpful?' Kerrie asked.

'If they're not trying to kill you,' joked Murray. 'It's a small place, so you learn to rub along together. Even though the tourist industry is growing. But everything still rides on opal. It's the reason for our existence.'

'And the lifestyle? Would you stay here if there weren't tourists and opals?'

'That's a thought I'd rather not contemplate, but frankly I think there's still a lot more opal to be found. And everyone loves the lifestyle. This is Denise's place,' he said as he led Kerrie down a small lane behind a building housing a hardware and camping store and next to an empty block of overgrown land.

To Kerrie's surprise several flowering trees and shrubs protected a small fenced garden containing a little cottage with a bull-nosed verandah. A eucalyptus tree behind the cottage offered some shade and at the rear of the block stood a modern house with a small shop attached. A woman came out of the shop to meet them as they crossed the garden.

'Hey, Murray. What's new?'

'Cottage still vacant, Denise? This is Kerrie, she wants to stay a couple of days or so.'

'Nice to meet you. Yeah, last lot left last night. Haven't stocked the fridge yet, but it's all clean and tidy. Just you is it?'

Kerrie nodded. 'What a sweet little place.'

'Used to be an old miner's shack, must be eighty to a hundred years old. Been dolled up, and my old bloke added the patio and the barbecue. It's pretty quiet here, even though we're right in town. And if you need any-thing, you can just give us a shout.'

When Kerrie saw the spotless cottage, freshly painted in cheerful colours, she knew she'd like it far better than a motel.

'Looks like everything I need,' said Kerrie. 'I'll get a few supplies. My car is back by the café.'

'I'll leave you to it,' said Murray. 'How about I give you directions and you can come out to our camp and have a drink at sunset and meet Fiona.'

'Sounds great. I can't thank you enough, Murray. How about I give you my mobile number, in case I get lost.'

Settled in to her little cottage after a trip to the small supermarket, where she'd been shocked by the high price of the wilted vegetables and tired fruit, Kerrie poured her-self a cold mineral water. What on earth was she doing here? she wondered. This was so remote. She couldn't imagine Milton in such a place. She wished there was someone she could ring to tell them about this unusual town that had sprung up on the back of opals.

Perhaps she could call Walker and thank him for

the introduction to Murray, who seemed so nice. But she didn't know Walker well enough to chat about such inconsequential matters. Who else could she call? The three girls certainly wouldn't care about Lightning Ridge. Wendy? Kerrie was very fond of her, and their relationship had always been cordial, but there was no more to it than that.

Suddenly Kerrie realised that there was not a soul in the world, now that she no longer had Milton or her mother, who was the slightest bit interested in what she did or where she was. How could she not have any close friends? She knew the answer. Milton had absorbed her life to the exclusion of everyone else. Tears of loss and self-pity began to trickle down her face. Then she shook herself to stop this train of thought and, locking the cottage door, she set out to tour the streets of Lightning Ridge.

It was early afternoon and there was now a laziness to the place. Shops were empty of customers and sales assistants read their newspapers beneath slowly turning fans. Kerrie told them that she was just browsing as she went from opal shop to opal shop. Some were small jewellers, others just tourist souvenir shops displaying inexpensive opal pieces. One large store was designed as a cave filled with all manner of displays of uncut opal, great chunks of rock showing the opal seam within. There was lavish jewellery as well as polished opal ready to be set.

A cheerful man with a loud Slavic accent pounced. 'Lovely miss, are you looking for a special opal? Let me show you some pieces. You have a favourite opal? The fire? The green? The blue and red flash?'

Kerrie shook her head. 'I'm just looking. This is all quite dazzling and I need to take it in.'

'Ah. Here try this on, see it against your skin. This is a beauty.' He lifted a necklace featuring a huge pendant shot with hot flashes of colour against a turquoise background. 'This is a gem-quality harlequin. Very rare, very beautiful.'

'It is stunning,' admitted Kerrie. 'I hadn't realised the variety . . . This looks expensive,' she added, pointing to a large ring.

'Oh, yes, this piece is not for sale. Very unusual colour. Did you have something special in mind? A colour? A price? Set? Unset?'

Kerrie held up her hands. 'It's my first day here, I'm still looking.'

'How about a DVD about opals? We have a very interesting one here. Or what about a tour? We can take you to a mine and there is another display room. We have pieces you won't see anywhere else. And our opals are not just from Lightning Ridge. We have high-quality opal from Andamooka, Coober Pedy, other fields round here like the Grawin, plus Yowah nuts, White Cliffs pineapples and opal from Quilpie . . .'

'Enough. Too much information. Thanks. I'll just wander round a little more.' Kerrie found the man's enthusiasm overwhelming and she made a quick exit.

Just the same, she was quite bowled over by what she'd seen. Her knowledge of opals was very limited and she had always associated them with the gaudy, overlit pieces displayed in duty free stores. Now she felt as though she was in sensation overload with all the beautiful pieces she'd seen on her short walk. She wandered back towards her cottage, pausing outside a small restaurant where the window had posters for an extraordinary range of sightseeing events and places to go in the Ridge. There was a weird castle made from bottles, entertainment in a cave, a ghost tour, all manner of mine tours, cactus gardens, a fossil museum, lots of art galleries. At the end of Pandora Street was a hot artesian bore baths. Lightning Ridge, Kerrie thought, had a lot to offer.

When she arrived at Murray and Fiona's camp another surprise awaited her. From what Kerrie had seen, most of the local houses were simple boxes with shade cloth awnings, struggling gardens and sheds housing hardworking dust-covered trucks, four-wheel-drive vehicles and earthmoving machinery.

But Murray's place was quite different. He had built a quaint rustic home from wood, including pillars of dead trees and old wooden railway sleepers, as well as stone slabs, sheets of corrugated iron and even stained-glass windows. A pergola, draped in a grapevine, shaded a long wooden table with church-pew seats. Bright red geraniums grew in all manner of containers from old kerosene tins painted in bold designs to roughly made ceramic pots. In the kitchen, pots, pans and interesting jugs and teapots were suspended from the ceiling above the workbench. Everything was colourful and practical.

'Welcome to our camp,' said Murray. 'This is Fiona.'

Fiona smiled at Kerrie. 'I'm glad you came. Though this place is still a work in progress.'

'It's amazing. I can honestly say that I've never seen anything like this before. I love it!'

'Want to see my favourite bit?' asked Murray as he took Kerrie outside to the patio.

Kerrie shaded her eyes. 'What an enormous expanse of water. Is it a lake, part of river?' she exclaimed.

'Nope, it's my dam,' said Murray proudly. 'Looks a bit muddy at present, but she settles down. I stock it with yellowbelly so occasionally we can have a fish feed. When I first camped out here it was a massive natural hollow, and we got one of the miners to bring his earthmover and dig it out.'

'Find any opals?' asked Kerrie.

'No, wrong kind of rock. Found a lot of fossils though.'

'What a fun home!' exclaimed Kerrie as they went back inside.

'It's kind of grown like Topsy,' laughed Fiona, who was a warm, curly-haired woman with freckles and a big smile. 'Every time Murray wants to take on a new project he builds another room. You should see the new bathroom.' She led Kerrie through the kitchen and showed her an outdoor room, with a claw-foot bathtub open to the sky. 'Doesn't rain most of the year,' she explained. 'Though it's quite nice to sit out here when it does.'

'We kept the old shed, and it's now my studio,' said Murray. 'Come and see it. Can you pour us a drink, please, Fee?'

The old slab shed with its iron roof looked as though termites, spiders and possibly snakes could be in residence but when they stepped through the door Kerrie laughed.

'It's a real studio!'

The lined walls were painted white. There were no windows but it had large skylights and an air conditioning unit, which, Murray explained, was powered by their generator. Scattered around the studio were paints, canvases, jars of brushes, easels, bits of driftwood, a coil of rusting barbed wire and the flotsam and jetsam of an artist at work.

She drew a deep breath and closed her eyes to block the tears. 'This seems so familiar,' she whispered.

'If you want to use it any time, feel free. There's plenty of room,' said Murray. 'I'm working outdoors at present at various locations and trying different textures, adding the sand, soil, bits of scrubby bush, mixed in with the paint. You know the sort of thing.'

Kerrie drew breath to compose herself. 'Sounds interesting. Thanks for the offer. But I'm just here . . .' She paused before she finished, 'For a short time.'

'What brought you out here?' asked Murray as he led

her outside to the patio where Fiona had set out drinks with cheese and bread.

'White or red wine?' asked Fiona.

'A glass of white, please.'

Fiona poured herself a glass of red and handed Murray a long lemon squash. Passing the cheese platter, she said, 'Just break off a chunk of bread. The brie is quite runny.'

'Home-made bread,' said Murray. 'We have a wood-fired oven too.' He bit into the bread. 'Thanks, darling. I was asking Kerrie what she's doing out here.'

'Murray said that you're an artist. Do you plan on working out here? This is wonderful country to paint. Murray finds it endlessly inspiring, even though to city eyes it can look quite barren and uninteresting,' said Fiona.

'You know, I'm not sure why I'm here,' said Kerrie. 'Walker suggested it. Thought I could do with a change of scenery.'

'Great bloke, Walker. I had him do my will a few years back, when I was sick,' said Murray.

'You're one of the healthiest looking people I've seen,' said Kerrie. 'How sick were you?'

Murray grinned. 'Years of too much whisky, over-weight and a poisoned leg almost did me in. But the blood poisoning was probably the best thing that ever happened to me. Shook me up so I went on a fitness campaign and got myself back on track.' He leaned over and patted Fiona's arm. 'Couldn't leave my beautiful wife on her own with a half-finished camp, could I? Besides, she'd miss me too much, right?'

Fiona regarded him fondly. 'Yeah, right.' She grinned at Kerrie, 'Of course, like everything he does, he went over-board with the new lifestyle. Started running, bike riding, stopped drinking and even became a vegetarian for a while.'

'And never felt better. I even took up surfing again.'

'Surfing? Where?'

81

Murray laughed. 'Byron Bay, at first, though now we go to Indonesia for a month or so every year. Close up the gallery in the height of summer. Not much in the way of customers then, and Fee and I meet up with old friends from our wild youth and we go away and all pretend we're twenty again.'

Kerrie felt a pang as she watched the two of them smile, their casual interaction. 'Sounds great,' she said. 'You have the best of both worlds.'

'Many worlds. We have a nice lifestyle here,' said Fiona. 'Lots of friends, lots of visitors, the business does well. Murray gets asked all the time to work in Sydney or other cities. Even Darwin approached him. But we like it here. He's part of the scenery, aren't you, darling?'

'Yep. I might make more money elsewhere, but what would I do with the extra that I don't do now?'

'But this doesn't help you, Kerrie. Murray said your husband died recently? He must have been very young. That's hard.'

'He was a lot older than me but he was still young. He had so much more he wanted to do. And now, without him, I feel like the proverbial ship without a rudder,' said Kerrie.

'But you have your art. Why don't you throw yourself into that?' asked Murray.

'Are any of your friends painters too?' asked Fiona. 'You could come out here and do a painters' camp. Quite a few come through doing that.'

'I know a lot of artists, but just through my husband.'

Fiona and Murray exchanged a glance and Murray reached for more bread. 'Everybody paints up here. Soon as the tourist season dries up and it's too hot to work, out come the brushes. Everyone and their dog sells paintings. Stuffs them into a garage or a back room and calls it a gallery,' he added disparagingly.

'Murray, be nice. Not everyone is as brilliant an artist as you, darling. What sort of work do you do, Kerrie?'

'I like landscapes,' said Kerrie, surprising herself as she'd never thought about what she might actually paint if she did start again. 'But I haven't painted in twenty years. I wouldn't know where to start. I'm probably not much good anyway.'

'Let us take you around. Go for a bit of a drive and see if you feel inspired,' suggested Murray.

'I don't want to take you away from your work,' began Kerrie.

'Nonsense. Murray loves getting out to the wilderness,' laughed Fiona. 'We have a friend who can look after the gallery for a couple of days. I'd quite like a little escape too.'

'Do you paint, Fee?' asked Kerrie.

'Not at all. I cook and read. Do come, I think you'll enjoy it. Just a day or so.'

'You ever camped in the bush, Kerrie?' asked Murray.

Kerrie shook her head. 'I suppose I could do some sketching and maybe a watercolour,' she said dubiously.

'That's the idea. You could take home some sketches and see what you can do with them later.'

'Murray, don't rush Kerrie. She might have other plans. Do you have any family?' asked Fiona.

Kerrie shook her head. 'Not much. My mother died not long after my husband and my stepdaughters are grown up. I'm pretty well on my own,' she added with an attempt at a smile.

'That's hard,' said Fiona.

Kerrie spent the next day wandering around Lightning Ridge. She spent time in the little museum and historical society housed in an old miner's cottage looking at old photos of the opal fields. It all looked very exciting and busy. There she chatted to a charming museum volunteer who introduced herself as Holly and told Kerrie that she'd come to Lightning Ridge fifteen years before.

'How enterprising. Do you mine?' said Kerrie.

'My partner did. We went our separate ways years ago, but I stayed on and taught at the school as a casual and now I volunteer here in the museum. There're quite a few women like me in the Ridge. It's a great place for a single woman. Lots of social life.' She smiled. 'And I just love the history of the area. There're a lot of very interesting artists around here, too.'

'I've noticed. Do you live in town? I gather a lot of people have places out of town,' said Kerrie. 'It seems a bit rugged.'

'It can be. Some of the camps look pretty rough. Some people only come up here in the winter, for the opal season. Some of their temporary places have been here for thirty years,' she laughed. 'A couple of people converted a double-decker bus to a home and someone else made a very cute place out of disused railway carriages and even shipping containers. But that's another story. Are you enjoying yourself? Thinking of doing some camping? Be sure and get out to some of the camps and mines. Know anyone here? I'm happy to make introductions if you like.'

'Actually Murray and Fiona are looking after me.'

'Lucky you. A great couple. Renews your faith in marriage, those two. Most people here are on their own or onto their second or third partner.' Holly lifted an eyebrow. 'You just can't be too fussy. But I must say, under the opal dust, grime and working boots, some of the guys in the Ridge are decent enough and scrub up rather well.'

'I'm not actually looking . . .'

'Of course you're not, I didn't mean to be rude. You staying here long?'

'Not really. I'm thinking of taking up painting again.'

'You're a painter! Lots of people come here and paint for the first time. I think they're inspired by the scenery. Get Murray to take you to some of his secret locations – if you don't mind roughing it.'

'He's already volunteered to do that,' Kerrie replied.

Murray laughed when Kerrie later wandered into his gallery and told him what Holly had said. 'They're not secret places, they're just in the middle of nowhere and to some people there doesn't seem to be anything there but a lot of sand. And it is a bit remote, which is why I like it. I love our lost places – like the middle of the Birdsville Track, the Simpson Desert, outside Oodnadatta – quite haunting. Not that I'm taking you that far away.'

'He disappears for a month or more, sometimes by himself and sometimes with a mate,' said Fiona. 'I can't be away for that long, someone has to run the business. But I enjoy his short trips. You'll just love the bush. It's magnificent.'

Kerrie lifted her shoulders. 'What can I say? It sounds very exciting. Can I help at all? What will I need to bring? You're both so kind.'

'That's our pleasure and we'll travel light. Just take the truck and camping gear, some food, water and, of course, the painting equipment. That'll do us,' said Murray. 'Let people know that you'll be out of touch for a bit, and not to worry. We have a satellite phone for emergencies. Not that there'll be any, of course.' He smiled.

'No one's going to worry if I don't check in. I'm so excited. I hadn't considered going bush. I thought this town and the opal fields would be as remote as I'd get.

But I'm open to anything new right now.' Kerrie suddenly felt lightheaded. It wasn't the glass of wine that she'd had with her lunch but the idea of the possibilities, the adventures, and doing something utterly different from what she'd known. 'I can't wait for new horizons!'

'Since we're not leaving straight away, why don't you do a tour of a mine?' suggested Fiona.

So Kerrie drove out near the airstrip, surprised to see opal camps scattered so close to it, and took a group tour down one of the working mines. Wearing a hard hat, she climbed down a spiral staircase, discovering the cool and even temperature of the mine, its underground earthy mustiness, and was surprised by the dugout caverns they called ballrooms. In the tunnels small motorised vehicles carried men and machinery to the face of the mine, where the miners were gouging through the sandstone.

The mine tour leader explained, 'You never know when you're going to come on opal. There're a lot of stories of fellows blowing up gem opal worth millions and salvaging the remains worth only a few thousand because they were in a hurry or didn't know what they were doing. The more you know about the geology of the area, the better.' He told the group about looking for ironstone gravel on the surface, and then drilling through layers of silcrete and mudstone, which the miners call shincracker because if the hard rock hit you it could break your shin.

'What they're looking for is a band of sandstone, preferably without colour. Unfortunately, some sandstone can go down well over thirty metres. But when they hit clay, hopefully under that is opal. You can pick up nobbies like pigeon eggs if you're really lucky. Most of the mining here has either been underground shafts, or big open-cut mines. If you go up to the Three Mile, you'll see one of the massive old open-cut mines. It's closed now, but you can see what it was like in the old days.'

Kerrie was intrigued and wanted to know more, but the group was moved on, finally ending up at the mine's opal shop. The tour had given her an inkling of how relatively small-time opal mining was. Opal mining, she thought, was unlikely to ever become a huge and invasive industry like gas, oil and iron ore.

Later Kerrie told Murray and Fiona how intrigued she'd become with her outback experience.

'When you get home and get stuck into your sketches and paintings, you can digest things, look at your pictures and, you never know, perhaps you'll start planning your next trip,' said Murray.

'Do you think you might come back?' asked Fiona.

Kerrie shook her head. 'I don't know. I have to look after Milton's legacy, but at present I'm not in any hurry to get back to Sydney. It's so interesting out here. This scenery is so different. I wonder if it will inspire me to paint again.'

'Why don't you spend a bit more time out here? You could go to other places. You should definitely go to the Hill.'

'Broken Hill,' explained Fiona. 'You've heard about the Brushmen of the Bush? Pro Hart and Jack Absalom. Jack is still going strong and Pro's gallery is a great tribute to him and his art.'

'I've heard about them, of course, but I'm not too familiar with their work,' confessed Kerrie.

'Best go and have a look then. There were originally five artists who started going outback to paint for fun and to raise money for charity. As well as establishing a much-loved style of Australian art they raised more than a million dollars,' explained Fiona.

'I reckon they made outback art mainstream, not just in Australia, but overseas, too. Sometimes critics knock it as being kitsch,' said Murray. 'But I think that's because people in the city don't believe the colours they paint really exist.'

Kerrie nodded. Murray's work also had such a vibrancy that the heat seemed to shimmer off the canvas. 'I'm really fascinated by all this. I'll go to Broken Hill, then.'

Murray laughed. 'After you get there let us know what you think of it all. I want to keep tabs on you.'

'Sorry it's a bit late,' said Murray as they set off the next afternoon. 'It's only a couple of hours to the campsite, and it will be nice to get there and settle after the heat has died down. Even in winter the sun can be fierce. But dawn is the best time of day, I think.'

'I haven't been out and about to see too many dawns for quite some time,' said Kerrie. 'Milton was a night owl. Used to work in his studio at night till all hours, then he wanted to talk about it. He was always so exhilarated and exhausted at the same time.'

'Yes, I suppose that it's different for a sculptor,' agreed Murray. 'I like to paint by natural light so I tend to knock off at sunset and we go to bed early.'

'We can't get TV unless we use a satellite dish, so we haven't bothered. And radio's good enough to find out what's going on,' said Fiona.

'This is just lovely,' said Kerrie as the old truck drove along a dusty road. 'The softness of the light after the full sun, the birds, and seeing those wallabies and roos, ears pricked and then bounding away from us. It's magic.'

'You got to be quick to catch the morning light. It changes so fast,' said Murray. 'Tonight we'll get everything ready and then tomorrow morning we'll set off in the dark and be waiting, brushes poised, when the sun comes up.'

Kerrie discovered he wasn't joking. Fiona and Kerrie had small pup tents beside the campfire they'd made. A fold-up table and three collapsible chairs made up their kitchen, but they ate on their laps around the fire and Murray dragged in a large log for his seat.

'Fiona, you're amazing! How can you cook such delicious food in one pot and on a barbecue grate?' asked Kerrie. 'Why does something so simple taste so good?'

'Flavoured with gum leaves and the smoke from old wood, lit by stars and firelight. Can't beat it,' said Murray. 'I'm going to sleep like this log. Will you wake up when I start banging the billy around in the morning?'

'I'm sure I will,' said Kerrie.

'If you do that, I won't be able to sleep in and I'm making a late breakfast,' said Fiona.

It was the smell of the rekindled campfire more than Murray's soft whistling that woke Kerrie. She pulled on a light sweater, surprised by the morning's coolness, but she knew that it would get hot later in the day.

'Sleep okay on that blow-up mattress?' asked Murray.

'Fabulous. What smells so good?'

'Tea in the billy, I'll pour you a mug. Grab a banana and we'll be off as soon as you're ready. Throw your gear in the truck. I'll make up a thermos and we've got bottled water. When we get back in a couple of hours, Fee will have fresh damper and eggs ready.'

Murray drove across the dark landscape with assurance, the headlights shining on rocks and logs as he steered the truck along a gully, peering ahead. 'There's a beaut old tree not far from here . . . Got to watch for the wildlife. Shout if you see a roo. I've got a shoo roo on the front bumper but it doesn't always work.'

'As in shooing away roos?'

'Yep. It's a whistle, too high-pitched for our ears. There she is. We'll stop here.'

Beside the old tree in the early morning light, Murray stopped the truck, opened the rear and started pulling out their chairs, their art materials and an easel.

Kerrie took out a sketchbook, a board and some charcoal. 'I feel nervous,' she admitted.

'Got to start somewhere, sometime, Kerrie. Take this chair, get ready and just look around you.'

Murray sketched for a while and then took some photographs. He looked across at Kerrie, who had not yet made a mark on her sketchbook. 'I'm going for a bit of a stroll. I want to get some sand and some bark, and whatever else takes my fancy. I won't be far away. If you need me, just shout.'

Kerrie nodded, grateful that he was leaving her to work unobserved. It was silly to feel self-conscious, she admonished herself. But the knowledge she hadn't made a sketch or thought about painting seriously since her honeymoon weighed on her mind. How had she allowed herself to neglect it?

Milton had never told her not to paint, but neither had he encouraged her. She realised now that his immense talent had swallowed her up and swept her along. Her work was, she knew, in comparison, utterly insignificant. He appreciated her when she pulled off a meeting, or a successful show, or set up a big interview, but their life together was always about him. Kerrie had never minded that and understood why that had been so, but she now saw that her artistic confidence had been completely undermined.

She sat with her sketchbook open and, as Murray had instructed, began to look around. The silence, the openness, the immensity of where she was began to fill her mind and heart. Now the land seemed to be taking its first breath as a breeze stirred, and against the waning stars she saw the silhouette of a dead tree spiked against the lightening sky. It seemed as though this composition had been arranged specifically for her. Kerrie lifted a stick of charcoal and suddenly her urgent scratching on the pad was the only sound she could hear. She worked quickly, before the stars completely faded. Then, as the pearl light began to run with the first streaks of pale pink, she found her watercolours and a new page.

She was so absorbed, trying to work quickly to capture the sliding kaleidoscope of sunrise colours, that she forgot where she was and was startled by a movement beside her. On a thorny bush a tiny brightly jewelled bird was watching her, head cocked, eyes following her every move. Suddenly it darted to another branch, its movements like quicksilver. Finally it opened its beak and gave a short sharp whistle.

'Stay still, little bird,' she said softly as she tried to sketch its inquisitive expression. But then it was gone in a flash of red and black.

As the sun rose, the scene changed dramatically. She heard a crunch and saw Murray coming back carrying a branch and a bunch of grasses in his hand, his knapsack over his shoulder.

'Good hunting?' she asked.

'Yep. Not sure how I'm going to use all this.' He crouched down and began spreading seeds, grasses, bits of bark, twigs and small plastic bags of soil on the ground in front of him. He didn't look at Kerrie. Indeed, he didn't pay any attention to her as he sorted through his finds. Finally, he said, 'How'd you go?'

When Kerrie didn't answer, he sat back on his heels, regarding the expression on her face. Her eyes were closed and she looked close to tears.

'That good, eh?' said Murray.

Kerrie smiled, wiping her hand across her eyes. 'Yes. That good. I'd forgotten. Thank you, Murray.'

He nodded and resumed his sorting.

After a pause Kerrie spoke. 'I saw a bird. Sweet little thing. I tried to draw him but he was too quick.' She reached over and held out the sketch. 'I got his head a little, I think.'

Murray stood and peered at the small pencil sketch. 'Aw, it's a zebra finch. Funny little birds. They're very social. If they're on their own they'll call out, trying to find where their mates are.' He turned back to his collection, poured some deep red soil from one of the plastic bags into the palm of his hand, and went over to his canvas. 'Right, here we go. Finger painting, just like kindergarten.'

Three hours seemed to pass in minutes and when they drove back to the camping spot the smell of breakfast was tantalising.

Fiona smiled to herself as Kerrie and Murray talked and talked about styles, subjects, different mediums and how they worked. It was as if a rusty tap had been turned on and Kerrie had come to life.

While Murray had a nap and Fiona sprawled reading a book, Kerrie continued to work on her sketches, but in the late afternoon they set out again, this time heading in a different direction.

Murray stopped the truck and jumped out, flinging his arms to indicate the surrounding countryside. 'Pretty scratchy territory around here. Years back someone tried sheep, and there were a few mines, too. All gone now.' He kicked the dry surface. 'Y'know, Australia had about nine inches of topsoil before the whitefellas came and brought in hard-hooved animals – cattle, horses, sheep, pigs. Broke up the ground and then the wind and rain washed the top-soil away. We're down to about two inches now. It's hard to make a living out of such poor land.'

'You wouldn't even know that anyone had ever lived and worked here,' said Kerrie. 'How sad.'

'Might look like nothing was ever here, but if you walk around you see things. Little signs,' said Murray.

Driving on further, Murray pointed out a few buried bits of rotting wood that were once part of a fence line. 'Out here, closer to townships, there were a lot of camps.'

'Is that a car?' asked Fiona. 'Or a mirage?' She pointed to a rusty red wreck in the distance.

'That's an old Bedford truck. Don't make trucks like that anymore. Come on, let's take a walk.'

Past some spindly mulga trees, they came across the remains of a mine. A broken and rusting windlass lay on its side, and beside it was the skeleton of a bucket with no bottom, although a frayed rope was still attached. A sheet of old corrugated iron, pockmarked with rust, was covered with boulders. Rotting timbers that once might have held up a building lay in a tangle. Coils of old barbed wire spun uselessly from the shreds of a wooden post.

'It looks like a mine was burrowed down there,' said Kerrie. 'How deep would it have been, do you think?'

'Don't know. Maybe fifty feet or so,' said Murray. 'I love all this detritus. The wire, the windlass, they're testament to man's folly, or his optimism.'

'It's like the land just swallows everything back up,' said Kerrie. 'In years to come there won't be a sign that anyone was here.'

Murray leant down and pointed to the soft soil under the tin. 'Look, lizard prints. There's a bearded dragon under there. I like those.'

Kerrie and Fiona looked closer and saw the foot marks in the sand.

'Very geometric. I think I'll copy those and scratch them into the sand on the canvas,' said Murray. 'This place always excites me.'

While Fiona and Murray carefully peered under the iron looking for the lizard, Kerrie meandered into a clump of box trees and she-oaks growing in a dry river bed. Around her it was cool and quiet. The soft sighing of the wind through the sandlewood trees was hypnotic. As she was thinking what a lovely place this would be to put down a swag or swing in a hammock, she was startled to find behind the largest tree the remains of an old tent. Rotted sections of it had torn away. Blackened stones marked a campfire and rusted tins and old bottles lay in the congealed dirt. The sagging frame of a camp bed, the remains of a table and a chair that had been made from branches were infinitely sad, thought Kerrie.

'This was once someone's home, but how long ago? And where did they go?' she asked aloud. The swish of the leaves was her only answer. 'Well, whoever you were, you picked a perfect spot,' she added, and sat on a convenient tree stump to quickly sketch the scene.

That night the three of them shared laughter and a ratatouille made in the camp oven as they talked of art and life and love and dreams.

'This is such a magical, almost mysterious place,' said Kerrie.

'Yes, some of the old fellows who lived alone out here have some strange stories,' said Fee. 'Tell her about Earache.'

'Earache?' asked Kerrie. 'Why was he called that?'

'Earache was a miner and a retired geologist who bent everyone's ears with his stories,' began Murray. 'Also an amateur astronomer, interesting chap. He was getting on when he came into the gallery one day. He brought me a notebook of observations and some papers about an odd find he had. But he thought he'd had a bit of a heart turn and didn't want to cark it out in his camp and leave things there.'

'What sort of things?'

'Well, he asked me to look after them. They looked like rocks. But they were round, with a rough surface but perfectly circular ranging in size from a cricket ball to a bowling ball. Unbelievably heavy for their size. I know this is going to sound peculiar, but he told me they had unusual properties.'

'Did they fly?' asked Kerrie with a smile.

'Might have,' said Murray, seriously. 'I stuck them in the studio and discovered at certain times they glowed. Brilliant light came from inside them and pulsed. I saw it once. Gave me such a scare I chucked them out the back door. I didn't want to know.'

'Did you ever crack one open?' asked Kerrie.

'It was impossible. Earache said he'd tried and never could. Then a few weeks after leaving them with me, he came back and said he was going to take one of them down to Sydney. So he left his old cattle dog with me while he was gone. Old thing slept outside near the rocks. One night I heard a terrible howl. I went out and called the dog but it had gone but I hoped it'd come back in the morning.'

'And?'

'Next morning the dog was still gone. So were those rocks. I was a bit rattled and worried what I'd tell Earache.'

'What happened?' asked Kerrie, intrigued.

'It was all a bit weird. The dog was found the next day miles away. In the back blocks of Queensland. He had a tag on his collar and someone had turned him in, said the dog was traumatised but okay. No one could have even driven that far in such a short time.' Murray looked at Kerrie's incredulous expression and shrugged. 'I heard all kinds of stories from miners living out in the middle of nowhere in the desert who saw strange things. Low lights hovering and swooshing away faster than they could believe. Odd markings in the ground.'

Kerrie stared at Murray, not sure whether this was a joke or some delusion. 'What happened to the dog and Earache?'

'Earache died while in Sydney and the woman who found the dog kept him after I told her what had happened to Earache. I never mentioned the dog had disappeared that night. Everyone assumed he'd been wandering for weeks or had been picked up and dumped.'

'What a story!' said Kerrie laughing.

'There are dozens of stories like that out here,' said Fee.

'I feel like I've known you both all my life,' said Kerrie, shaking her head in amazement. 'It's such a strange feeling. Wonderful. But different.'

'Thank you for those kind words,' said Murray.

'I just hope we keep in touch. I can't thank you both enough. You don't know what you've given me,' said Kerrie.

'I think we do,' said Fiona, smiling. 'People fall in love with the Ridge. We've seen it before. I reckon you'll be back.'

That night Kerrie decided to pull her bed out of her tent and sleep under the stars, confessing to the others that she'd never done it before.

She snuggled down, wishing she had done something like this with Milton. But as she drifted to a sweet sleep, Kerrie realised that Milton wouldn't have enjoyed this at all. He loved his five-star existence and she'd enjoyed their luxurious lifestyle too but, for the first time, Kerrie could see that new, and different, possibilities awaited her.

She slept soundly.

4

THE FIRST THING THAT Kerrie noticed was the huge grey mound of soil next to the main mine, like a fortress between the town and the desert beyond. She drove into a petrol station, climbed out of her car, straightened her back and stretched her stiff legs. It had been a full day's drive between Lightning Ridge and Broken Hill and the car had covered nearly one thousand kilometres.

When she paid for her petrol she asked the woman serving her how Broken Hill got its name.

The woman slid Kerrie's credit card into the machine and answered, 'According to some Aboriginal story the hills out there used to look like a broken line of bones along a serpent's back, but they were flattened by the mining years ago.'

'I suppose the mines are everywhere,' said Kerrie.

'It's what made the town. We're the Silver City. And we do very well, too. Between the mines, the unions, the tourists, we have a bloody good standard of living.'

Kerrie drove through the town and noticed that the streets were named after various minerals, such as Oxide, Mica and Cobalt. Broken Hill's large solid nineteenth-century buildings had ornate metal columns and iron roofs. The elaborate Trades Hall, modern malls, churches and the mosque reflected the colourful and varied heritage of the town.

Even though Broken Hill was surrounded by the flat red plains of the desert, homes with flourishing gardens and lawns were dotted everywhere. She even noticed a few boats parked in driveways and garages. 'Water doesn't seem to be a problem,' she said to herself.

It also looked as if Broken Hill had an active social life. Aside from playing fields, the town pool, a cinema, game parlours and pubs, she saw that there were a lot of social clubs and sporting organisations. She wondered what the early miners who had come here to work in the lead, silver and zinc mines more than one hundred years ago would make of the place now.

She checked into the hotel she'd booked from Lightning Ridge and, over a cup of coffee, browsed through the brochures that sat on the table in her room. Tourism was obviously a big industry. There seemed to be a proliferation of art galleries and a great many town tours. There were also tours to the nearby tiny township of Silverton, famous as the location for many movies including the *Mad Max* series. Kerrie laughed when she saw an advertisement for a camel ride. 'Not for me,' she told herself.

Following the directions on one of the maps, she wandered through some of the smaller art galleries and then onto Pro Hart's studio and gallery. Here she had to smile at the late artist's humorous and colourful take on his subjects, and his vividly decorated Rolls Royce parked out the front.

'He was quite a character,' said the woman in the gallery. 'Larger than life, opinionated and did things his way. We certainly miss him in the Hill. So many of the other old boys are disappearing, too.'

But Jack Absalom welcomed Kerrie to his gallery with hearty enthusiasm.

'Come on in, come in. What're you interested in? Have a look around. Plenty to see, take your time. That's the wife, Mary, over there. She'll help you if you want something.'

He bustled away to greet a busload of visitors who had just arrived.

Kerrie strolled around the spacious main gallery looking at Jack's work depicting landscapes and characters in the life and history of outback Australia. She noticed several of the tour group buying signed prints of Jack's work as souvenirs of the places they'd visited on their outback trip. Others bought inexpensive opal jewellery and Jack quickly told them where each piece had come from. Then he showed them his prized collection of opal pieces he'd mined all over the country since he had first fallen in love with Australia's national gemstone.

'No, that one's not for sale. Dug that up meself when I was about twelve in South Australia. Out at Andamooka. Nobody wanted the stuff from there then. They only knew, and liked, the white fire opal. Same thing happened with Boulder opal – couldn't give it away. I love it. Look at that matrix, the colours . . . Worth thousands now.'

As Mary wrapped up the tourists' purchases and made suggestions of other places they could visit in Broken Hill, Jack went over and joined Kerrie as she stood before a large painting of a strange flat moonscape that was dotted with white mounds covered with scarlet flowers. As she looked more closely at the painting, she saw indentations on a hill, a slab of metal, the outline of a vehicle and a glint of glass. The horizon stretched beyond the lonely location, yet somehow the place didn't look desolate.

'Now that looks to be somewhere you can take a deep breath of fresh air,' commented Kerrie, more to herself than the old bush artist.

'White Cliffs,' said Jack. 'First place they commercially mined opal in Australia. Magic little spot. You should go there if you're into opals.'

'I'm more into painting,' said Kerrie. 'By the look of your paintings, you've certainly been around outback Australia.'

'Born and bred. Just love the place. I've made countless TV shows about our country. From cooking to survival, to talking about the future of the planet,' said Jack cheerfully. 'And if you want to paint, get out there, girl. Nothing like it anywhere else in the world.'

'I'm beginning to see that. How far is White Cliffs from here? If I drove there, is there anywhere to stay?'

'There's a motel and one of those B&B places. Both underground. It's not too far. You could take a day tour over there. You can see the whole place in a couple of hours. Not like here, you need a good week to do it properly!'

After she left Jack Absalom's gallery, Kerrie continued wandering around. She could see why tourists stayed a while in Broken Hill; there was a lot to see and do. But she was now less interested in restaurants, shops, galleries, mine tours and historical places. She longed to recapture the tranquillity and intense creative urge that she'd shared on her camping trip with Murray and Fiona in the isolation and strange beauty of the bush. It was unlike anything she'd experienced before.

She was on her way to the tourist information office to see about going to White Cliffs when a small tour bus parked outside the post office caught her eye. It was hard to miss. The minivan was covered with paintings of emus, gum trees, red rocks, strange carvings, mullock heaps and windmills. Across its side was painted 'Davo's Best Tours' and a list of locations was displayed underneath. But what caught Kerrie's attention was that the rough pictures were similar to Jack Absalom's painting of White Cliffs.

She pulled out her mobile and rang the number painted on the bus.

'Davo's Tours, Davo here.'

'Hi, I'm in Broken Hill and I was hoping to go to White Cliffs. I've seen your bus. Where do your tours go?'

'Depends. Do you want the whole box and dice camping under the stars, or just a day trip?'

'I think I just want to go to White Cliffs for the day, to start with.'

'Can do. I leave the Hill in the morning at eight, make a couple of stops, get to White Cliffs in time for lunch, spend an hour or so seeing the town, then back here around six. If there's enough interest I could run over to Opal Lake, but it makes for a long day. How many people do you want to book?'

'Just myself. I have a car but I think it's easier to go on a day tour. I haven't heard of Opal Lake. Is it a real lake?'

'Real enough, when it rains. But that's not often. Used to have water in it but it's dried up now. It's a couple of hours from White Cliffs.'

'Where's your office? I'll come around and pay you,' said Kerrie.

'The office is right behind you if you turn around.'

Kerrie turned around and saw a solidly built, tanned and bearded man wearing khaki shorts and a bush shirt, a battered bush hat and sturdy boots standing a hundred metres behind her. While he might have been trying to look like Crocodile Dundee, he reminded Kerrie more of an overweight football coach. He was holding a mobile phone to his ear and he grinned to acknowledge her, lifting his finger in a bit of a salute. She walked towards him. He held out his hand.

'Dave Best. I run Best Tours. Call me Davo.'

'I'm Kerrie. Kerrie Faranisi.'

'Visiting the Hill, eh? Where're you from?'

'Sydney, but I've just come from Lightning Ridge.'

'On the opal trail. Been out to any of the other opal fields, like Yowah?'

'No. I'm not an opal fossicker. I'm an artist looking for, well, inspiration, I suppose.' She smiled.

Davo took a small notebook and a stub of pencil out of his shirt pocket and flipped to a page. 'Umm, got six booked and you make seven, that's enough to make the tour worthwhile. Room for more, if they turn up. So, Kerrie. You're in. Where're you staying?'

She told him and he nodded. 'Right. See you at seven forty-five at the front door. You might have to organise an early breakfast. You paying cash?'

The next morning, Davo pulled up right on time at the hotel where Kerrie was staying. Kerrie was carrying her oversized hold-all and had packed her pencils and sketch-book. She thought it was unlikely she would have time to sketch, but put it in anyway, just in case. The other passengers were two widowed sisters, a retired couple and a Danish couple on their honeymoon.

As he drove along Davo infrequently pointed out things of interest, but mostly he chatted to the retired couple who were sitting closest to him. It took more than three hours to reach the small settlement of White Cliffs.

When it came into view, someone commented, 'Not much here. Looks like a ghost town.'

'It's all underground,' said Davo. 'The mines and the homes.'

Kerrie could see how the township got its name. The settlement atop the two main hills seemed to be propped up by white cliffs, which were, in fact, white soil tipped down the hillside from the diggings. Around the rise of the small hills spread a flat red plain smudged with the grey-green stubble of hardy desert plants.

The bus stopped outside the pub in the main street and everyone went inside for a cold drink. Kerrie walked around the bar, looking at the photos and memorabilia tacked to the walls. When they'd finished their drinks, they wandered back outside.

'Anything else to see?' one of the sisters asked Kerrie as they looked at the opal shop, the general store and a camping and hardware supplier.

'I think there are more buildings up there on the small rises,' she replied.

'Too hot to walk.'

'That's an interesting-looking house,' said Kerrie, noticing a round building with large glass windows. 'I wish we could go into one of the underground places Davo told us about. I'll go and ask him.'

She found Davo sitting at a table outside the pub talking to a man who had a selection of rocks spread out and a glass jar of coloured stones beside him.

As Kerrie approached, Davo lifted up the jar and spoke to her. 'Want to buy a jar of rough for a hundred bucks? Could get ten times that for them when they're cut and polished.'

'Thanks, but no. Actually some of us would like to go up the hill, or the one further over there. Is that where everyone lives? Do they mine for opals there, too?'

'Some do. There're a couple of underground motels, a decent B&B and a coffee shop over there. And some people have a bit of a shop or gallery attached to their places.'

'So they live and mine in the same place?'

'Some do, but most of the hills are dug out now, so serious miners are digging further away. I've got a camp meself, well out of Opal Lake.' He waved his hand expansively towards the red plains. 'But been some mighty opal come out of this little place. It's called gem crystal opal. Light with bright fire flashes. Brilliant stuff. The opal from here really put Australia on the map. You should go and look at the cemetery. Not far to walk. And the first experimental solar station is further along. It's closed now, but proved a point. Then you can go past the Blocks and Sullivans Hill to the fossicking field and, well, that's it, you've done White Cliffs.'

'I see. Well, after you've taken us to these places I'd like to see Opal Lake, too,' said Kerrie.

Davo lifted his shoulders. 'Dunno that anyone else wants to trek all the way out there. More of the same, 'cept smaller. Scenery much of a muchness, if you're looking for that.'

Kerrie could tell that he didn't want to go any further than White Cliffs and suddenly his attitude made her determined to go to Opal Lake.

'Look, Davo, you said that a visit to Opal Lake was an option. Well, I want to take that option.'

'Okay. I'll talk to the others. But they're not going to want to hang around out there, I reckon. It'll be just in and out.'

'Well, that might not be long enough for me. Is there somewhere to stay? If there is, you could just leave me there and pick me up next time you're on tour.'

He shrugged. 'Yep, there's a pub, a small motel and a B&B. Not as much as here.'

'That sounds fine. Could you give me details, please, and I'll call them.'

'Did I mention I won't be back for a week?' said Davo with a smugness that annoyed Kerrie.

'No. You didn't. But that's fine, too. Pick me up in a week then.'

'Cost you extra, if I have to make a special run out there.'

'I'll pay. Now, shall we get going?'

There were a couple of surprised looks in Kerrie's direction when Davo announced that there would be a detour to Opal Lake to drop her off. Most of the passengers seemed happy enough to have an extended trip, even if they weren't staying more than ten minutes.

'What's out there? It is an interesting place?' the Danish girl asked Kerrie.

Kerrie shrugged. 'I don't know. I've never been there. But I'm about to find out.'

The girl smiled. 'It sounds very romantic.'

Kerrie leant back in her seat, wondering about her sudden decision. What on earth was she doing? Had it just been Davo's complete lack of co-operation that had irritated her, or was she finally doing what Murray and Fiona had suggested – listening to her heart and following whim as it took her fancy? She pulled out her phone to ring the B&B and make a reservation only to discover that there was no mobile reception.

The ground was flat and red but occasionally it looked like sparks glinting in the afternoon light.

'It's the gypsum fragments,' said Davo when someone asked about the sparkles. He pointed out a dry gully lined with wild orange trees and for the first time expounded at length. 'They say trees are an indicator of opal because they grow where there's water along the fault lines. You seen the lines of trees along gullies and creeks. What's

105

called wild orange is more of a shrubby tree, has fruit kinda like a plum, generally full of ants. But it has a pretty orchidy sort of flower. Box trees, leopardwood, gidgee trees, every area has its speciality. 'Cept for Coober Pedy where there aren't any trees so they built one of steel.'

'Apart from the trees, how can you tell where you should dig for opal?' asked one of the Danes.

Davo gave a hard laugh. 'Opal is where you find it, mate. Miners all have their theories about why opal is in one spot and not over there a few yards away. It's anyone's guess. Opals are a mystery.'

'Sounds like they can be hard to find,' commented the retired man. 'Are you looking for opals?' he asked Kerrie.

His wife looked at Kerrie's casual but groomed appearance and manicured nails. 'Does she look like she's going to take up digging?' She smiled at Kerrie. 'I hear you're an artist.'

Kerrie returned the smile, adding, 'I have been known to get my hands dirty.'

'This looks similar to White Cliffs. But smaller,' said the Danish girl as they drove into the small town.

Davo pulled up in front of the Opal Lake Hotel, which Kerrie thought looked like every other pub she'd seen since she'd left Sydney.

'Time for a cold drink, use the toilets, pop into the souvenir shop or walk down the street. Fifteen minutes and we're off,' he said to the group. Then to Kerrie, 'Well, here we are. Opal Lake. See you in a week.'

One of the men sitting outside the pub said, 'You leaving her here? Give you a bit of trouble, did she, Davo?'

Davo shrugged. 'Her choice. Don't ask me what she'll do with herself here for a week. Not my problem.'

Kerrie heard the exchange but ignored it. The man behind the bar was polishing a glass with a torn cloth. 'Good afternoon. I've just arrived with the tour bus and —'

'What can I get you?'

'Actually I want to know where the B&B is. I'm staying in town for the week.'

'No car then? Hmm, probably the best place is the Golden Dome. Up on Sampson's Hill.' He pointed towards one of the small hills at the far end of the street.

'I hope they have a room, though it doesn't seem too busy around here.' Kerrie smiled, trying to sound cheerful.

'There are a few people around. Everything's underground so it's hard to tell how many tourists are about. A private plane came in yesterday with a party of four. The caravan park is fairly full, too. We've got rooms, but I don't think it would suit you. Not sure about the Shin-cracker. That's the motel.'

'Do you have the number for the Golden Dome?'

'Here, use my phone. Mobiles don't work too well around here unless you have a sat phone.' He pushed his phone towards her.

Kerrie was starting to regret her impetuous decision until she heard the woman's voice at the end of the phone. It was friendly and welcoming.

'Of course we can put you up. Do you want a double room or a large family double? No ensuites, plumbing is too difficult, but the bathrooms are central.'

'It's all underground, isn't it? Maybe I'd better have the big room. I don't think I get claustrophobia, but just in case,' said Kerrie.

'You'll be surprised! Just drive up Sampson's Hill and swing around to the right at the top . . .'

'Actually I don't have a car, I came on the tour bus and decided to stay on.'

'No worries, I'll pop down and get you. I have to pick up the mail anyway. You're at the pub, you said?'

Kerrie waved goodbye to the other tourists as they got back into Davo's small bus. Davo gave her a nod and a cocky grin as he closed the doors and the bus drove off, leaving her standing there with her carry-all slung over her shoulder and her sunglasses shading her eyes.

'Sit down, miss, if you like,' called out the publican. 'Pam will be along in a minute. She'll look after you.'

'I hope I don't look like I need too much looking after,' replied Kerrie.

'You'll like the Dome, and Pammie's a good sort. They've done a marvellous job on that place. Doug's done it all himself, too,' said one of the customers.

'Are you a local? Are you a miner?' asked Kerrie.

'I reckon everyone's a miner who comes to stay here,' said the publican. 'We all walk around with our eyes down, just in case we kick over a floater.' He grinned.

'And it's happened,' said another man. 'Mick here picked up a beauty in the creek behind town a few years back.'

'An opal?' asked Kerrie. 'A valuable one?'

'You bet. He gave it to one of the girls working behind the bar. She left town the following week. Silly dill.'

'Here's Pam.'

A small red car drew up and a woman got out. 'I'm Pamela James.' She smiled at Kerrie. 'How you going, fellas?' She nodded to the men sitting outside the pub. 'Where's your luggage?' She opened the passenger door for Kerrie.

'I decided to stay here on the spur of the moment, so I hope I'll be able to pick up a few necessities. Davo said he'll come for me next week,' said Kerrie as she got in beside Pam.

'No worries. How about you pop into the general store while I go to the post office and you can get a toothbrush at least.'

While Pam collected her mail, Kerrie looked around

the small general store. 'Well,' she thought. 'I've got myself here, so I'll just have to rough it.' With that she bought some toiletries and a couple of souvenir T-shirts with 'Opal Lake' embroidered across them.

As Pam drove up the hill to the Golden Dome, Kerrie was surprised at the expansive view of the flat country. There was the occasional tree and mounds of mullock, as well as mine shafts and machinery. A far line of hills broke the horizon and a cloud of dust trailing behind a vehicle seemed to follow a road scratched into the dirt.

Kerrie noticed that some places had vegetable gardens that were fenced and shaded. Some of the entrances to the underground dwellings were partially visible, while others were fully screened by slabs of corrugated iron and tarpaulins. In one garden rusting machinery and an old-fashioned caravan had been turned into garden ornaments, making it look messy and cluttered.

'Some places look a little abandoned. Is that because most of it is underground?' asked Kerrie.

'No, not entirely. A lot are empty. People might only come here for a couple of months a year. But Doug and me hardly ever get away. It's good to be busy. This is us.'

Kerrie was pleasantly surprised when Pam drove through two red rock pillars with stone frogs sitting on top. She parked the car in a rough clearing near clumps of red flowering bushes. Behind the parking area was a shady outdoor spot containing tables and chairs. Pam opened a green doorway into a bright foyer filled with lush potted palms. The domed roof above them disappeared into the orange stony earth of the hillside.

'How lovely,' said Kerrie.

'Have to pick your time to sit out here. Cool evenings are best, but you have to use insect spray. Sometimes the midges and mosquitoes are bad.'

Steps descended from the entrance foyer, and Kerrie

realised that she was walking into the hillside beneath the dome. The walls were bright with white limewash, which was painted over the rough surfaces where the rooms had been dug out. While electric lights blazed, wherever possible skylights had been set into the curved ceiling to let in even more light. Some skylights seemed to double as air vents.

'It's so bright, so light. And so cool.'

'The underground stays around twenty-three degrees all year round. Bit like living in a wine cellar,' said Pam. 'This is the reception area. I'll get you a form to fill in. There's a bar off the kitchen if you want to help yourself to iced water or juice. There's a lounge area, reading room, dining room and laundry down there. That corridor leads to the bedrooms and the bathrooms are just up on that level near the laundry so you won't have far to walk.'

Kerrie's room was a cave scooped out of the earth. It was white and clean and, although there were no windows, it didn't feel at all claustrophobic. 'This is so homey. It's amazing. Did your husband build all this?'

'These hills have been cleaned out of opal, so people made homes up here. Doug still has tunnels running back into the hillside and every time we want to expand, he digs out another room.' She laughed. 'The original mine is still back there if you want to have a look. We run tours for visitors, but they won't disturb you.'

'I'd like to have a look around.'

'Wait till we show you the route. You could get lost in the old maze. Now get settled in. At sunset we like to gather outside for a glass of wine and you can meet the other guests. Dinner is in the dining room at seven, or if you'd prefer there's the pub grub or Molly's Café. Bit hard to get to at night without a car, though. There are books and a bit of memorabilia in the reading room. TV in the lounge works pretty well and there are plenty of DVDs. But most people don't bother too much. They find they go to bed early out here.'

'I'll be fine,' said Kerrie. 'Your place is wonderful. I'm glad I decided to stay. I'd never have experienced this on Davo's lightning tour.'

'Davo's a bit of a loose cannon for a tour guide. He either gives you a full-on tour, camping out, the works, or else races people around like he can't get rid of them fast enough. He does a bit of gouging, opal digging, on the side at his camp out in the backblocks.'

'Pam, I've just realised that I haven't let the hotel in Broken Hill know what I'm doing. Could I ring them?'

'I'll do it for you, if you like. Just tell me which hotel you're staying at.'

'That's very kind of you, Pam. Is everyone here this friendly?'

'Well, maybe not everyone in Opal Lake, but most are.'

'Is there an opal lake? Can you tell me about it?'

'Actually it's pretty interesting, especially during the rare times when there's enough rain to fill it up. It's very shallow and thousands of birds appear out of nowhere and it looks like an inland sea, except most of the birds are standing not floating. Talking of inland seas years and years ago this whole area from White Cliffs as far across as Lightning Ridge was under the sea. Sometimes miners dig up fossils of shells and sea creatures, even dinosaurs. Shirley knows all about that.'

'Shirley? Is she a geologist?'

Pam laughed. 'No, Shirley's just Shirley, but she knows a bit about everything. She's our local historian, sort of. Lovely, lovely lady. I'll take you over to meet her if you like, she loves visitors because she rarely goes out.'

'If she doesn't mind. I'd really like to know more

111

about this place. But don't people get cabin fever if they stay here all the time? In Lightning Ridge, my friends were telling me that they like to get away for a break.'

'In Shirley's case it's her choice. She's been here for years, although it's a lot harder for her to get about now, even if she wanted to. Poor darling, she's nearly crippled from arthritis and her eyesight isn't too good. She is nearly eighty. But so independent. Lives by herself in her dugout, doing her research and writing.'

'You mean she's living in a cave? At eighty? That's just amazing. I'd love to meet her,' said Kerrie.

'Righto, we'll pop up tomorrow. Now, I'd better go and see to dinner.'

'Can I help?' offered Kerrie.

'Not at all, you're a guest. Go and sit outside and Doug will introduce himself and bring you a wine or anything you'd like.'

Kerrie found that there were two other couples staying at the Golden Dome, a pair of married lawyers, and a banker and his wife. Over dinner they told Kerrie about the trip they were making, flying across the inland on a chartered jet to Broome on the north-west coast.

'It's the holiday we've promised ourselves for years. No children, no rushed overseas trip, but a month going to places in our own country,' said one of the lawyers.

'Places we know virtually nothing about,' added the banker.

'And it's been the best holiday we've ever had,' said his wife. 'Our pilot's staying at the motel. He said that he didn't want to be tempted by the nice wine at the Golden Dome,' she added. 'We're all leaving early in the morning, so we hope we don't disturb you.'

Kerrie had enjoyed the other travellers' company and she slept well that night, but found it confusing when she woke up to find no light coming into the room. When she went into the bathroom, which had a skylight, she was surprised to see bright daylight. She showered and dressed and went to the dining room.

'What time is it?' she asked as Pam put a fresh pot of coffee on the table.

'Only seven, but the others you met last night have already had breakfast and gone. They wanted to be airborne by six. Hope they didn't disturb you.'

'No, not at all. These walls seem very thick. I vaguely remember hearing a noise when I was falling asleep, but I might have imagined it,' said Kerrie.

'You might have heard Doug. He goes into the back tunnel and has a bit of a dig some nights after dinner. He's enlarging a space for an office for himself and a wine cellar. He doesn't use the jackhammer, just the pickaxe, to keep the noise down. Sorry if it woke you.'

'I might take my mug of coffee outside and sniff the morning air. See what kind of a day it's going to be,' said Kerrie.

'Same as yesterday,' said Pam. 'Would you like scrambled eggs or pancakes, or both, for breakfast?'

'Just eggs, please.'

The morning was crisply cool. The light around the Golden Dome was brilliantly clear and the distant low hills hazy soft. There was no movement in the town. Suddenly Kerrie had an urge to sketch the scene and hurried inside to get the sketchbook she'd brought with her in her hold-all. Looking around, she realised that Murray had turned on a passion inside her that could not be extinguished. Everywhere she looked she saw subjects to paint. Now she had the desire and the will to sketch and plan paintings, collections of subjects, and she found that she had hazy, yet-to-be-explored ideas for other mediums and styles.

She'd completely lost track of the time when Doug

appeared and looked over her shoulder at her little sketch of the township.

'Breakfast is getting cold. Say, that's good. You've captured the feel of the place with just a few lines. Will this be the basis for a bigger picture?'

Kerrie straightened up and looked at the sketchpad. 'I haven't decided.'

'Lots to paint around here, I could show you a few places if you like. Old mines, historic huts, a pretty gully, the Opal Lake, of course. I don't mind taking you for a drive.'

'That's so nice of you, Doug. I feel so silly coming here on the spur of the moment and without a car. But I'm glad I came. You and Pam are being very kind.'

'Our pleasure. Come and have breakfast. Pam said she was taking you up to see Shirley later.'

After breakfast and before it got too hot Kerrie walked around the loop road at the top of the hill. There she found a small hidden community. Letterboxes and front gates were replaced by names painted on a large red boulder: 'Ian and Trish', 'The Ballards'. In one place a rusty piece of machinery had been turned into a sculpture with a number hanging from it. There were a few attempts at creating gardens, but most front yards were littered with vehicles, machinery, or a storage shed reached by a steep rubble-strewn path. A few places had a garden or tank on top of their roofs. It was a strange rabbit-like existence, thought Kerrie. Practical, but odd looking and certainly private. No inquisitive neighbours peeking through their windows here. She wondered what Shirley's dugout would be like.

Towards the end of the loop, one garden in particular grabbed her attention. A dry-stone wall of local red-gold rocks surrounded a garden filled with vegetables and fruit trees. Several grapevines were trained along a professional-looking trellis. On a raised terrace was a stone table with

114

chairs facing the view to the north. Shells, stones and pebbles marked the path and to one side of it was a wooden building containing tinted glass windows and shaded by an overhanging corrugated-iron roof. On the other side of the path was a greenhouse made from shade cloth, which sheltered an assortment of pots and plants. The place had a look of permanence and peace, and a rakish air. The entrance to the underground house was faced with flagstone slabs set in blood-red mud and Kerrie immediately thought of the hippy homes she'd seen in the south-west of the USA. The place struck her as being rather creative and she spotted a sculpture of a giant bird, and several other works, roughly hewn from weathered desert tree trunks. Maybe an artist lived here.

Shirley lived on Old Tom's Hill. Pam drove down into the town, past the pub, and circled around the road leading to the cemetery. 'Worth a visit,' she said. 'Lots of pioneers' graves in it, if you like that sort of thing.' The second hill was slightly steeper and higher than Sampson's Hill and, to Kerrie, it seemed an older, rougher area, as if spurned by those who had made money.

'What's the difference between Sampson's Hill and Old Tom's?' she asked Pam. 'Is it like the right and wrong side of the tracks?'

Pam smiled. 'No, it's not, despite how it looks. It's just that we like to think we make a bit more of an effort on Sampson's. We're the newcomers.'

'City people?'

'Mostly. Old Tom's Hill is named after an early prospector who mined here in the 1890s and made some of the first big finds. The original mines were here, but they're finished now. Mind you, someone digging their garden a few years back found a beautiful nobby, so you never know.'

Pam drove up a packed-earth driveway, past gas bottles, drums of diesel, stacks of firewood, some potted plants and two large garbage bins. She parked the car and they walked past a small corrugated-iron shed and onto a stone patio. The old wooden doorway at the entrance was made of thick gnarled tree trunks, while the walls beside it were rock slabs, hand cut and set together.

Pam went inside calling out, 'Shirley . . .'

'Come in.'

Kerrie followed Pam inside, glancing around as best she could in the dimness of the rooms. This felt like a cave. The walls were not limewashed as Pam's were and it smelled musty. Earthy. It reminded her of the mine she'd been in at Lightning Ridge. It appeared to Kerrie that this room was where its occupant ate, slept, worked and watched television.

Shirley was seated at a long wooden table that was smothered in files and paperwork. A large box-like computer and its cumbersome hard drive took up one end of the table. It was the oldest computer Kerrie had ever seen. Two walking sticks leant against the table. A large woman smiled at them both and made no attempt to get up.

'Pammie! And you've brought a visitor for me. Wonderful!'

'This is Kerrie. She's staying with us for the week. She's from Sydney and she's an artist.'

'Lovely. Plenty of nice scenery to paint out here. And the diggings, of course. Pam, put the kettle on and make us some tea, would you mind? How long have you been an artist? I suppose that's a silly question, isn't it?' said Shirley, waving Kerrie to a chair at the table. Pam bustled into the small kitchen alcove.

Kerrie warmed to Shirley instantly. She was large, overflowing from her striped cotton shirt and baggy slacks, her wispy grey hair knotted on top of her head.

Her blue eyes peered at Kerrie through her glasses and Kerrie sensed that Shirley missed nothing.

'To tell you the truth, Shirley, I've hardly been an artist at all. I studied art then I got married and now that I'm on my own I'm trying to remember how to do it again,' said Kerrie.

'Are you divorced?' asked Shirley.

'No, my husband died – not very long ago.'

'That's very sad. You're young to be widowed . . . I hope you're making up for lost time with your painting.'

'I'm trying,' said Kerrie, not really wanting to talk about herself. 'How long have you lived here?' she asked. 'Pam said you were the local historian.'

'I suppose I am. I moved back here years ago when life took an unexpected turn and then I began to be interested in the old stories. This place holds some of my happiest memories from when I was a little girl.'

'Really? You lived here when you were a girl?' asked Kerrie.

'I did. Before the war my father used to mine at Lightning Ridge, but then ended up here. This was his mine.'

'Did he find opals?'

Shirley nodded. 'Yes, he did, but not enough to make his fortune. Not many people do.'

Kerrie looked at the files on the table. 'What are you researching, Shirley? Are you writing the early history of this area?'

'Yes, but not in the way you think. People have written about the pioneering days and many of them are totally wrong. I'm trying to correct a lot of the myths and misconceptions.'

'You sound like a detective,' said Kerrie. 'But you haven't always lived here, have you?'

'Heavens, no. I used to be a nurse in Sydney. You

know, my skills have proved to be very useful out here,' she said.

'Shirley is always stitching up some miner. She's great for emergencies. Serious medical help is hours away in Broken Hill, and Dubbo Base Hospital's even further, so Shirley's talents are certainly useful to us here in Opal Lake,' said Pam.

'Tell me, what have you seen since you've been here, Kerrie?' asked Shirley.

'You're the first port of call,' said Pam. 'Kerrie doesn't have her car. She came on a whim with Davo. He's picking her up next week.'

'I feel a bit silly coming here without a car, or anything at all really, but Pam is being wonderful,' said Kerrie.

'Don't need much out here. Good lord, I haven't driven a car for years, and I get all my supplies from the general store. I give them a list and they deliver the goods. Easy. I've got everything I want,' said Shirley. 'But if you want a car to drive around here, my old bomb is out the back in the shed. If someone can get it going, you're welcome to it.'

'Really? How long since it's been driven?'

'Can't remember. Didn't Doug turn the engine over a few months ago?' Shirley asked Pam.

'That's right. I'll ask Doug to come and have a look at it,' said Pam.

'I don't want to put you to any trouble,' began Kerrie.

'It's no trouble at all. I wouldn't take the old car too far, but if you're keen on painting the area you have to get out and have a look around,' said Shirley. 'There are some interesting places fairly close by. I've always thought it would be great to capture them before they disappear. Barney's Well, the Dutchman's camp. The gully – and the lake of course. Pretty dry at the moment, though.'

'How long since you've been out to these places?' asked Kerrie.

'Me? Oh, not for years. But I doubt they've changed much.'

'If Doug can get the car started, why not come with me and show me where they are?' said Kerrie.

'Not me,' said Shirley. 'I don't like to leave my dugout. But ask Pam. You'd like to go, wouldn't you, Pammie?'

'I'm happy to go,' said Pam. 'But how long since you've been out for a jaunt, Shirley?'

'Oh, who's counting? You know I'm happy here in my little hole but I can tell Kerrie the best places to go.'

'Right,' said Pam, 'then let's make sure that car is working.'

Shirley drained her tea and held it out to Pam for a refill. 'That's settled then. What else are you doing? Has this girl met Ingrid?'

'On my list.' Pam turned to Kerrie. 'Ingrid is a very talented jeweller. A true artisan. She's made some stunning pieces with opal, very contemporary.'

'And controversial,' added Shirley. 'Even if you don't enjoy her work, Kerrie, you'll find it memorable.'

'It sounds intriguing. In a small place like this there are so many fascinating people!'

Pam and Shirley both laughed.

'Ah, you don't know the half of it!'

The teapot was empty by the time Pam and Kerrie rose to leave Shirley's dugout.

'I'll send Doug over later on to look at your car, Shirley,' promised Pam. Once they were outside, she turned to Kerrie and added, 'It's a shame Shirley won't go out.'

'She doesn't seem very agile,' Kerrie said tactfully.

'Poor old Shirley. She is a bit of a mess, physically. Vicious circle. She's got poor circulation, and arthritis in her feet, so she never likes to move, so then she puts on weight. She doesn't go out and she likes to live in the past,

119

I mean, with all her research into the old days. But she loves company, as you can see.'

'She's very warm, very intelligent. I liked her enormously,' said Kerrie.

'She's a good old stick. Very dry acerbic wit, too.'

'Where does Ingrid live?' asked Kerrie as they drove away.

'Ingrid lives around the back of this hill, but it's best if I call and ask if I can bring you to visit.'

'Of course.'

'She has a lot of security around the place, because of her opal collection. Sometimes when she's working on something she doesn't like to be disturbed. You'd understand the creative process,' said Pam.

'Sure do. My husband totally lost all track of time, and whether it was day or night, when he was working on a sculpture.'

Pam glanced at Kerrie. 'Doug said that you do, too. He said that you were immersed in your sketching this morning.'

Kerrie gave a slight shrug. 'That's the idea, but I haven't had much chance to do a lot of immersing in the last few years.'

'Then this is the place for you to be,' said Pam. 'Why don't you come and stay for a while? We could find you a place to rent, nominal charge. People are always coming and going. Give yourself some breathing space.'

Kerrie looked at Pam as she drove down the bumpy dirt road to the flat. 'I don't know what to say. My friends in Lightning Ridge made much the same suggestion. I feel so . . . comfortable out here. So welcome. Thank you, Pam,' said Kerrie, wondering if she was so hospitable and helpful to all her guests.

*

Ingrid agreed to meet Kerrie the following day.

'She says she's not working at present, but she's very happy to see us,' said Pam, looking rather pleased.

The view from the other side of Old Tom's Hill was quite different from Shirley's outlook. Shirley faced the town and gully but Ingrid looked out across a moonscape of creamy white mullock heaps that seemed like an empty honeycomb.

'That's the old area that was mined out years ago,' said Pam.

'The mines are so close together. People must have had claims lying cheek by jowl.'

'In the big rush they did. Can you imagine being underground and seeing your neighbour in the dull light, and he finds opal and you don't? Apparently that's how it went. Lot of luck involved.'

Pam swung the car up a steep driveway where Kerrie was surprised to see trees and shrubs. As they reached the top of the driveway she caught her breath. 'Heavens! How amazing. This is some garden.'

'Give anything enough water and it goes mad in this climate. Ingrid has a massive tank and a drip system so the water doesn't evaporate. Plants just love it.'

'I see what you mean about the security,' said Kerrie as she looked at the chain and padlock fastening the gate of the wire fence that surrounded the garden. Beyond the cultivated garden, on the other side of the fence, Kerrie could see the untouched bare red earth.

A tall fair-haired woman, straw hat on her head, straightened up from among the plants and waved. She smiled as she let the two women in. 'Welcome, welcome. Pamela. So good to see you. And this is your friend – hello, I am Ingrid.' She spoke with a strong Scandinavian accent.

Kerrie shook her hand and they gave each other a frank, appraising look.

Ingrid was slender, tanned and very Nordic looking. Kerrie guessed she was probably about sixty and
would have been stunning in her youth for she was still
beautiful.

'Thank you, Ingrid. I hope we're not imposing. I'm
so keen to see some of your work. Pam made it sound so
interesting.'

'These days I don't make as much jewellery as I used
to. My garden has become my passion. Look at the pro-
duce, Pamela! You must take some with you.' She led them
through the garden and pointed to a small raised terrace
with a vine-covered pergola. An iron table and chairs sat
in the shade beneath the pergola facing the view. 'I sit out
here and have a glass of wine to watch the sunset and pretend I am in Portofino.'

'Or Ravello,' said Kerrie, suddenly thinking of the
wonderful time she'd had with Milton when he'd first
taken her to Italy.

'Ah, you know it! I adore Ravello.'

Pamela followed Kerrie and Ingrid into the dugout,
and Kerrie paused to admire a small sculpture by the front
door.

'This is lovely. Who did it?' She touched the rough
surface of the clay figure of a child carrying a bird.

'It's an experiment. I'm using the local clay. I've started
making pottery, too.'

'You're always making something, Ingrid. Are you
going to sell them?'

'You have a gallery?' asked Kerrie.

'Did have. I've closed it. It was too hard to keep up
with the work. It started to become a job and I became too
commercial, so I stopped. It was not what I wanted . . .
You know what I mean?'

Kerrie nodded. 'But you still make jewellery?'

'Only when I want to and when I have some suitable

opals. I'm making some exhibition pieces.' She smiled. 'They're a bit wild.'

The women followed Ingrid into a vestibule lit by a skylight and then, following Ingrid's lead, slipped off their shoes. The floor had been laid with cool slate tiles, some of them handpainted with unusual patterns.

'I love your tiles,' said Kerrie. 'I suppose you did the artwork, Ingrid.'

The rooms in Ingrid's dugout were domed, circular and painted pale blue. Everywhere pictures, carvings, wall hangings, books, rugs and ceramics were displayed. Through a beaded curtain, which Ingrid lifted, lay her workshop. Benches and tables were covered with tools, pots, paint and lumps of clay under plastic wrap, which lay next to boxes containing a jumble of not easily identified odds and ends.

'I do a lot of gold and silver work, but the pottery is interesting me more at the moment,' she said.

'You're so talented, Ingrid,' said Pam. 'I wish I had some creative outlet. You and Kerrie have a lot in common. Kerrie's an artist, too.'

'I'm just trying to be a painter. Ingrid has many skills. I'd like to see some of your work, if that's all right?'

'Look in the cabinets.' Pam nudged Kerrie.

'I'll make us some coffee.' Ingrid and Pam went to the kitchen as Kerrie stood, awestruck, in front of the glass cabinets.

The cabinets held a display of jewellery unlike anything she'd ever seen before. Strange one-eyed creatures clasped dazzling pieces of opal between their teeth. A necklace was made up of a shining crystal opal held between two dainty paws and suspended from lengths of gold. Bones, fossils, chunks of rocks, leaves, wood and other objects were studded with various coloured opals, some cut and polished, some just glittering from their bed of potch, exactly as they had been dug up. There were solid gold and silver figures, weird-shaped boxes and decorative pieces.

Pam joined her. 'Pretty stunning stuff, isn't it.'

'How does she make these? I love that necklace of golden balls, their texture, and they're not perfect spheres,' said Kerrie.

'Kangaroo droppings. Dipped in eighteen-carat gold,' said Pam.

'What? So they are!' Kerrie laughed aloud. 'And the little paws holding the opal?'

'Mice. She uses lizards, frogs, beetles, any wildlife that curls up its toes in her garden.'

Ingrid came back with a pot of coffee and three colourful handmade mugs on a tray. She smiled at Kerrie. 'My work is amusing, do you think?'

'That's a very dramatic necklace,' said Kerrie, pointing to large circles of opal encased in heavy gold.

'They're from a fossilised worm, the inside of which was opalised. So I sliced it into rings of opal. I love fossils. Some of these have come from this area. Have you been to the lake? You must go there.'

'We've arranged that. I'm going with her,' said Pam.

'That's wonderful. You'll love that. Such a dramatic landscape,' said Ingrid.

'Have you met Shirley yet?'

'Yes, yesterday.'

'I wonder if she will tell you about Stefan. She tells most people,' said Ingrid.

'Stefan was Shirley's partner,' explained Pam. 'It's a strange, sad story.'

'What happened?' asked Kerrie.

'It would be better if she tells you,' said Ingrid.

'I don't want to pry,' said Kerrie.

'Shirley has a lot of interesting stories to tell. Especially

124

about the early days,' said Ingrid. 'She was so kind to me when I first came here.'

'She's a special lady all right,' agreed Pam. 'She might be nearly eighty, but she's got the energy, humour and smarts of someone much younger.'

'I'm looking forward to going out to see Opal Lake,' said Kerrie.

'Some visitors see only a dried-up lake bed – unless we've had unusual rain,' said Ingrid. 'But if you see it through an artist's eyes, a very different world will open up.' Ingrid smiled at Kerrie as if sharing a secret.

5

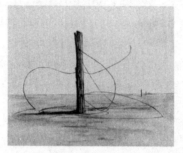

THE MORNING SUN HAD yet to warm the ground, cold from the winter's night. Kerrie climbed the small hill to Shirley's dugout, enjoying the walk and relishing the crisp clean air and a horizon that stretched for miles. She was looking forward to seeing again this woman who was so warm, humorous and intelligent. How quickly one seemed to make friends out here, she thought. She circled the top road. What an eyrie it was up here, almost fortress like.

As she approached the dugout she heard Shirley call out, 'Good morning, Kerrie. If you've come about the car, Doug's still looking at it. Would you like to join me for a cup of tea while you wait?' Shirley, who was sitting by the entrance to the dugout, indicated the chair next to her.

'Thanks, that would be good. Can I get it?'

'No, thanks, Kerrie. Enjoy the view. My joints are good this morning, so I'm getting about just fine.'

Kerrie sat back in the sun and looked around her. The town of Opal Lake was essentially flat but there were some small hills, and Shirley's place, on Old Tom's Hill, was high up. From her perch she could see all of the little township below. A blue car came into view, stopping outside the hotel.

When Shirley brought their mugs of tea, she too noticed the blue car down below.

'That's Carl, in for his weekly heart starter and to pick up his messages. He mines out past the lake and comes in every Wednesday for a few supplies, his rum and updates from his stockbroker.'

'Really?' laughed Kerrie.

'He worked in a bank for years, took early retirement and invested his super. He's one of the few people who seems to make money out here. Sells a bit of opal, too.'

'Does he do well with his opal?'

'Who's to say? If he does, he certainly doesn't spend it on himself. Lives like a bloody bat in a cave, comes out to forage and then retreats. Doesn't like to socialise, that's why he comes into town early. A pity he's such a loner, he's well educated and we've had a few deep discussions over the years. Mainly comes to see me so that he can borrow a few books.'

They drank their tea.

'What a great spot this is,' mused Kerrie. 'If you sat here all day, you could pretty much see what everyone else in Opal Lake is doing.'

'Only when they're on the surface,' said Shirley with a smile. 'I don't leave my place, but in the morning I love to sit out here, look around and think. It's always so peaceful.'

Kerrie glanced at her. 'Memories, too. I suppose you must have a lot of them.'

Shirley was thoughtful for a moment, then she said, 'When I was a little girl and came here with my father, I thought that this was a wonderland. When I came to the opal fields as an adult, I thought I'd landed in a war zone. All those holes and craters in a barren desolate landscape. All the hardship, all those failed dreams.'

'You see the world differently when you're a kid. I suppose everyone sees it from a new perspective at every stage of one's life. The world certainly looks different to me now,' said Kerrie.

'It's funny how I don't feel any different on the inside, even though I know time has moved on. I'm still the energetic, passionate young woman I once was, although that person is trapped inside a failing body. Very annoying,' said Shirley cheerfully. 'The best I can do to deal with these changes is not to have any mirrors in my dugout.'

'What were you like as a little girl?' asked Kerrie. 'I bet you were a happy child, cheerful and polite, and everybody liked you.'

'I think I was a bit of a horror. My mother was always very glad to pack me off with my father to the opal fields, Lightning Ridge and, later, out here.'

'What an adventure that must have been,' said Kerrie, but before she could ask Shirley more about her childhood, the older woman turned to her.

'But how about you? You've told me that you recently lost your husband. That must have been a terrible thing. Can I ask what happened?'

Kerrie suddenly felt herself choke and she couldn't speak. Her vision became blurred by tears. When Shirley reached out and took her hand and squeezed it, she couldn't hold back an uncontrollable sob.

'It's all right, Kerrie. It's good to cry. You don't have to tell me anything if you don't want to.'

'Oh, Shirley, I've had to be strong for everyone else,

128

do everything. There's been nobody I could talk to . . .' Her crying stopped her words. And then, suddenly, she began pouring her heart out to Shirley. 'I loved Milton so much. I miss him so much. I keep going into his studio, expecting to see him. I can't believe he's not coming back. We didn't have long enough together . . . He was so wonderful. I just don't feel that I want to go on without him. Everything is so . . . empty.'

Shirley nodded and handed Kerrie a tissue from her pocket. 'There's an enormous hole in your life now, and you need family and friends who love you, care about you, to help you through this.'

Kerrie dabbed at her eyes, feeling calmer. 'There isn't anyone. I'll just have to move on with my life by myself. But it's hard. I'm so lonely. I never really realised how much my life revolved around Milton.'

'It happens. One person can dominate your life forever, even if they are only around for what seems too short a time. I can sympathise, because I also lost the man I loved far too soon.'

'Did you?' asked Kerrie, feeling more in control and not at all embarrassed about her sudden breakdown in front of Shirley.

'We met when I was nursing in Sydney. It's a long story. Sad and hurtful. But for another time, perhaps.'

Kerrie instantly felt guilty that she had caused Shirley pain. 'Oh, I'm sorry if I've brought back unhappy memories.'

'They're always there, below the surface. The hurt, the loss. But it was a long time ago now. Tell me, do you have any children?'

'No,' said Kerrie. 'I don't.'

Shirley looked at her. 'I'm sorry. I thought you would.'

'Milton already had a family from his first marriage and he didn't want any more. I have three stepdaughters.

But they're a challenge. They've never accepted me. The smallish age gap between us hasn't helped,' said Kerrie candidly, surprising herself. 'They're really not that much younger than I am.'

'So Milton must have been a lot older than you? Why did you marry an older man? Surely you had lots of handsome young men chasing you.'

'Milton was more than twenty years older than me. He was so much more mature and sophisticated than all those other young men, who seemed gauche in comparison.'

'You'll be a target for them now, I bet. Young, beautiful and available,' said Shirley with a smile.

'I'm not looking for a relationship,' began Kerrie.

'No, you're not. Do you have close friends?'

Kerrie shook her head 'Not really, our friends were more Milton's friends. I had my mother, but she died not long after Milton's heart attack. I was always so busy with Milton, his career and his girls that I didn't need anyone else. Oh, Shirley, he was so talented. All the world knew what a wonderful artist he was and I loved being part of that, too. It was such a privilege.'

'But no time for you, huh?'

Kerrie's tension subsided. She smiled. 'That didn't matter when I had Milton. He was amazing. You would have enjoyed him, Shirley. He was such a powerful personality, he just swept you along, made you laugh, got you excited about his ideas. He had enthusiasm for everything, from a building to a plate of food. He was generous and loving and passionate about everything. There were no half measures in his life.'

'He sounds exhausting. Exhilarating maybe, but overwhelming, too,' said Shirley. 'But this is the old, wise Shirley talking. The young Shirley would have totally enjoyed being with him. No wonder there's a big gap in your life, now.'

'Yes. I'm not sure how to fill it,' said Kerrie slowly. 'I hope that taking up my art again might help. If I'm good enough.'

'It's not a matter of being good enough,' said Shirley briskly. 'It's doing something you enjoy, and which fulfils you. So tell me more about these stepdaughters. What happened to their mother? Is she around as well?'

'No. She died when they were quite young. Alia was still a toddler. Milton had a housekeeper for years and she stayed on, even after we were married, because Milton and I travelled so much. He took on commissions all over the world.'

'So really you're the only mother that Alia's ever known? I would have thought that would make the two of you close. But I'm no expert. I've never had children – mine, or anyone else's.'

'Alia was attached to Wendy, our housekeeper, but she was also influenced by the older girls who didn't like me coming along . . .'

'And taking their father's attention. They stopped being the centre of his world,' finished Shirley.

'I did try hard. I tried to find the balance between laying down rules and being authoritarian and being their friend, but it was very difficult. And I'm afraid they were spoiled by Milton.'

'And now?'

'It seems even harder. None of us has Milton to turn to and all of Milton's estate was left to me, and the girls really resent that, even though they have a lot of money from their mother. And it's been a mammoth and sad job going through his studio and sorting out his work – some of it has been on loan to galleries throughout the world. I also have to decide which pieces to sell if the galleries want to retain them, and what the fair price should be. I'm getting conflicting advice from dealers, auction houses and curators. It's all very confusing, which is why I wanted to get away for a couple of weeks.'

'I see. Are his girls involved in any of this?' asked Shirley.

'No. They were very possessive of his work, and they liked the attention, the openings and the money it generated, but they didn't really understand it. Milton knew that.'

'But you did, and you appreciated it,' said Shirley quietly.

'I thought he was a genius. Still do. And I was happy to be his administrator, social secretary, wife, you name it,' said Kerrie. 'While I had Milton I didn't care that I didn't have time for my own art.'

Shirley nodded. 'But you have time now. And the independence, too, by the sound of it. So go for it.' Shirley glanced at Kerrie. 'Just tell me if I'm being a nosey old lady.'

'No, not at all,' said Kerrie quickly. 'Actually it's nice to talk to someone who's interested in what I'm doing, and what I feel.'

Shirley reached over and patted her arm. 'Come and spend some time here in Opal Lake. I think you'll find a few kindred spirits, as well as an opportunity to work.'

Kerrie felt a sudden rush of gratitude to Shirley with her motherly tone. 'I just might do that. I like it out here. So many people want me to come again. I feel as though I've been drawn here for some reason.'

'It's how a lot of things happen in life, sweetie. By accident. Always follow your instincts.'

'Is that what you did? Tell me your story, Shirley.'

'Time enough for that. Look, here's Doug. Well, what's the verdict?'

'I wouldn't want to drive it to Broken Hill, but it'll do for around here. Where were you thinking of going, Kerrie?' asked Doug.

'Out to the lake,' said Kerrie. 'It's really the reason I wanted to stay. Pam said she'd come with me. But would the car be all right to get there?'

'Tell you what,' said Doug, 'how about you go in Pammie's car. Much more reliable and she can take the satellite phone and if there's any problems she can ring.'

Barely an hour later Kerrie and Pam were on their way. They soon settled into the rhythm of the journey. Pam was happy for Kerrie to drive and Kerrie, who hadn't driven a four-wheel-drive for a long time, found she was enjoying the experience. The dirt road was relatively smooth if she followed the tyre tracks of other vehicles. Red rocks had been pushed to either side of it, and signs of past rains were etched in the dried mud. Beyond the road tufts of grey-green shrubs and small red and purple flowers spread across the baked landscape.

'I'm so pleased that you could get away, Pam. It's nice to have company. I thought that Shirley might join us, too.'

'Not a chance. Shirley doesn't like to leave her dugout at all, not even to go for a drive. She says she likes to stay close to home.'

'I see,' said Kerrie. 'Has she always been like that? I mean, she does own a car. Doesn't she ever use it?'

'Virtually not at all now.'

'What does she do with herself then?'

'You've seen the place. She takes an interest in almost everything. Loves that old computer. Says she's writing a history of Opal Lake. Living in a cave doesn't seem to worry her. Did she tell you her story? I think that has a lot to do with the way she is.'

'No, she didn't. What happened?'

'I think that it's up to Shirley to tell you. Enough to

say that she came here to hide away from what had happened, but really she has only hidden away from herself.'

'You mean that she has avoided reality?'

'That's probably a little harsh. But people often come out here to hide or run away from something and some people never do face their fears. There are people down a hole, buried out here in more than one sense. Look, we're here. See that rise over there? Swing around to the left, there's a track through to the upper end of the lake, away from the main part where the tourist buses go.'

The distant edges of the dry lake quivered in the shimmering heat on the horizon. The lake spread out into the distance, a shallow indentation on the silvery surface of the flat land, as far as Kerrie could see. She parked the car beneath a grove of spindly trees.

'You might be thinking that there isn't much to see here,' said Pam as Kerrie turned off the engine and they sat looking at the dry lake.

'It's sort of eerie, but also delicate, ephemeral almost, and very dry and empty. Is it safe to walk across?'

'It's fine, if you don't go too far. The lake's wider than it seems, and you could lose your sense of direction as there are so few landmarks to get your bearings. But in the years when we have proper rain this place is a miracle. Full of sparkling water, thousands of birds and plants bursting to life, fish and frogs seeming to come from nowhere.'

'Must be quite something. But this is wonderful too . . . The space, the immensity of the desert and the sky. Shall we get out? There's a little bit of shade under the trees there,' said Kerrie, keen to stretch her legs.

'I put an umbrella in the back, and two fold-up chairs. If you want to, you could explore a little. I'll watch out for you, then we can have our picnic lunch.'

With Pam settled in a canvas chair with a book,

shaded by a large golf umbrella, Kerrie pulled on her hat and took her camera and a bottle of water to go for a short walk. She didn't want to go far as she found the desolate lake rather intimidating.

The lake bed was rippled red and around the edges the soft dirt rolled into waves as though a storm had whipped across its surface. Other patches looked crusty dry and Kerrie felt that if she stood on them she would crash below the surface, although she knew such an idea was nonsense. While the air was still, all around her looked as though it could be turbulent and dangerous.

She moved cautiously onto the dry lake, stepping over partially buried driftwood and the occasional pile of stones. Her gaze was drawn to the centre of the lake, a wavering silver expanse where a mirage floated, a vision of trees and shining water. She could understand how such an image could draw wanderers, lost in the desert, to their deaths. She glanced back at her visual anchor, a small leaning tree, where, under her bold umbrella, Pam sat in the hazy bright glare of the sun.

Kerrie decided to turn around and leave the edge of the dry lake. She stepped up onto the higher ground that sloped from the lake in small sand dunes. The whole place looked as if it had been vacuumed by the winds that swept over it. There was not a mark on the ground anywhere that she could see. 'I feel like the first person to walk here since the dinosaurs,' she thought.

Kerrie reached a rise and trudged through the immaculately cleaned loose soil. She idly kicked the sand to disturb its perfection and something flew out of it. She bent down and brushed the sand away from the object and saw that it was a ring. It looked as though the ring had been in the sand dune forever. The stone in it was so dirty and blackened that it was impossible to tell what it was. Kerry rubbed the band, which was black as well, and she could feel that the setting was quite delicate filigree work.

She hurried back to Pam to show her the ring.

'It's pretty dirty,' Pam said. 'It looks as though it's been out here for a long time.'

'Do you think it's valuable?'

'Probably not, by the look of it. It's black from being exposed to the elements, so you'd have to get it cleaned to find out. Would it be worth it?'

'When I get back to Sydney, I might just do something about it.'

'Before you get too carried away, how about we sit down and relax, and eat our lunch? Then we can drive back in comfort. Thank heavens for air conditioning. It's starting to get pretty hot now,' said Pam.

Pam delved into the basket and handed Kerrie a sandwich. They ate in silence, staring at the empty lake.

'This is really a forsaken place,' said Kerrie as she finished her sandwich and picked up a piece of fruit.

'It's magic after the wet when it's brimming with wildlife I'm told. Now it looks barren, but I think that it's still beautiful. It's the light I love, mostly at sunset, when the sky turns red. And at night the stars hang just above your head, like Christmas lights. I'm glad you got to see all this.'

'Pam, before we drive back, would you mind if I did some sketching, in case I don't get back here again?' asked Kerrie.

'Of course not. I'll just go on with my book. I'm quite happy to stay here for a bit more, as long as you don't think it's getting too hot.'

Kerrie took out her sketchbook and pencils and sat in one of the folding chairs. She looked around her and tried to imagine what the place would look like full of bird life. Then she began to sketch just what she could see now, the emptiness and the desolation. The landscape seemed so featureless and yet the dried lake was, in a strange, even haunting, way, very beautiful. As she began to draw, she became more and more enthusiastic. Even without the wildlife, this place seemed to be magical.

Eventually Pam spoke. 'I hate to be a spoilsport, but we'll have to start back soon. I've guests coming and meals to prepare.'

'Pam, I didn't mean to hold you up, but this has been such an experience for me. Sketching is becoming easier and so enjoyable. I guess it's the subject. Now, I wonder if I can turn some of these into paintings.'

'Great. So when are you coming back to stay with us?'

'I'm not sure, I mean, about making plans. Staying at Opal Lake wasn't on my agenda in the first place.'

'Well, you have friends in the Ridge and now us. Seems pretty easy.'

'Pam, that's nice of you, but as much as I would love to drop everything, I still have demands on my time. I can't walk away from Milton's estate and nor do I want to. I expect that there will always be exhibitions of his work that I will have to arrange, but I will think about your idea.'

'Ah, you'll get back to the city and think that Opal Lake was just a wild and crazy dream. But promise me you'll do something with the sketches you've made here.'

'Okay. I promise. Now let's make a move. Do you want to drive, or will I?' asked Kerrie.

'I'm happy to. And, by the way, I've enjoyed getting out for the day, so thank you.'

Kerrie rolled the blackened ring into a paper napkin and tucked it into the picnic basket. 'Pretty extraordinary to find a piece of jewellery in such an isolated place.'

'You'll have a story to tell your Sydney friends, won't you?'

But, thought Kerry, who would take an interest in her old ring found on a dried-up lake? People she knew might make polite noises, but they wouldn't really be interested in Opal Lake. The girls probably wouldn't even want to see the ring since it had no value.

'Well, I'll have a good story to tell Doug tonight,' said Kerrie.

Dinner was indeed stimulating. Pam had asked the owners of the motel, Sue and Darren, to join them, as well as another couple, Helen and Gustav, from Canberra. They owned a dugout in the backblocks and came to Opal Lake for a few months each year. They all sat chatting under the pergola as the night fell.

'Gustav's a lecturer at the Australian National University. So we come here partly for a holiday and partly for field research so he can stay here longer with a clear conscience,' said Helen.

'When did you first come out here?' asked Kerrie, as Doug poured wine.

'Quite a few years ago, now. Gustav is a palaeontologist, but I'm just an amateur, having fun,' said Helen.

'Not any more,' countered Pam, 'Helen knows an awful lot about opalised fossils, too.'

'Gustav and Helen have made some highly significant discoveries,' added Doug.

'And they've made the mining fraternity aware of the value of opalised fossils,' added Darren.

'You mean like some of the specimens Ingrid showed me in her collection?' said Kerrie. 'Wonderful coloured teeth and small bones all made of beautiful opal?'

'That's the kind of thing,' said Helen. 'I know that Ingrid makes some stunning jewellery, but even her use of common fossils is what we'd like to stop. The early

138

miners weren't terribly interested in fossils, either. Opal was what they were after, so who knows what treasures and knowledge have been lost when they broke up the opal fossils just to sell as gemstones? Anyway, even if museums and universities had the chance to buy them, they couldn't afford to because the price of gem opal made them too expensive. But we've been trying to raise awareness about opalised fossils and how they are a really important part of the geological history of Australia,' said Helen enthusiastically.

'Pam told me that the opal fields were all part of a great inland sea,' said Kerrie.

'That's right,' said Gustav. 'About one hundred and ten million years ago, Australia was part of the super continent, called Gondwana. As the huge continent started to break up, a vast inland sea was formed and it covered about a third of what is now Australia.'

'So this area was part of that?'

'It was. And the climate was different, too. It was much warmer and there were forests of ferns and pines and dinosaurs roamed the wilderness. Creatures like plesiosaurs and ichthyosaurs swam in this inland sea as well.'

'Do people find fossils of them?' asked Kerrie, thinking how fascinating this geological history was.

'Yes, their teeth and bones,' replied Helen. 'And we've found lots of invertebrate fossils, too. Brachiopods and gastropods, which are snails, and beautiful crinoids, or sea lilies, which are related to modern brittle stars and starfish. Do you realise that Australia is the only place in the world which has opalised animal fossils? They're not only beautiful, but important scientifically.'

I hope I'm not annoying you with my questions,' said Kerrie. 'But you're so knowledgeable.'

'Not at all,' said Gustav. 'It's nice to have someone

interested in opal who doesn't just want to know about its commercial value. Opal fossils are formed when an animal part is buried in sediment, which later becomes rock. If silica fills up the empty spaces left by the animal, sort of like filling up a jelly mould, then the fossil eventually becomes opalised.'

'So all the fossils in the different opal fields would be the same?'

'Actually, no. They are similar in White Cliffs, here in Opal Lake, Andamooka and even Coober Pedy. But the fossils in Lightning Ridge are unique and diverse. It's a very important scientific site. In that period in Australia, mammals were tiny and delicate, not at all like the dominant dinosaurs, so mammal fossils are virtually unknown, except at Lightning Ridge. That area was on the edge of the sea rather than in it, so the fauna living around it were different and included early mammals. So opalised remains of them have been found.'

'Yes,' added Helen, 'the most famous fossil found in Lightning Ridge was the jaw of an ancestor of the platypus. I have to say that things have changed in recent years. Now palaeontologists like my husband talk to miners and explain to them what they should be looking out for. Some of them are really co-operative and interested so without their help many important discoveries would have gone unnoticed.'

'Some miners have terrific collections,' added Pam.

'Unfortunately, the lure of opal will generally outweigh the value of the fossilised bones of an ancient creature. But the interest is growing and there are some very passionate collectors,' said Doug.

Kerrie shook her head. 'It's incredible. I had no idea. What a fascinating place this is.'

'It's not always sunshine and glittering opals,' said Pam as she began passing a platter of food.

'Ah, the dark underbelly of the opal fields!' said Doug. 'Murders, mystery, ratters and ratbags. That's us.'

'Don't frighten Kerrie away,' chided Pam.

'No, this is a wonderful place,' said Gustav. 'As an artist, I expect that you can appreciate its wild beauty. And where else in the world can a man go to work in the morning with the backside falling out of his pants and come home in the afternoon a millionaire?'

'Well, that's the theory,' said Doug. 'But it doesn't happen very often, I can tell you.'

Later, after dinner, they all sat in the cosy curved loungeroom. The sparkling whitewashed sandstone walls looked to Kerrie like a pristine snowdrift.

'This is like being in an igloo,' she said.

'True, but no ice and no smoking seal fat,' laughed Helen. 'So when are you returning to Sydney?'

'Davo comes back for me on Saturday. Sydney's going to seem a different world after being here.'

'Do come back. You have friends here now. And it's obvious that you appreciate the area.'

'Everyone is asking me to come back. I want to work on some of the sketches I've made of this country and if they work out I might return and do some more.'

By the time Saturday morning arrived, Kerrie was in such a routine that she felt she'd been in Opal Lake for a month rather than a week. She returned Shirley's car and thanked the older woman as she hugged her goodbye.

'You've been wonderful. I've enjoyed our daily chats so much. You are such a good listener, Shirley, I'm going to miss you.' Kerrie felt awkward, not sure how to explain how much, since the death of her mother, she'd missed having another woman's company.

'I've loved your visits, too. Keep in touch. Call me

occasionally, or at least email me. And get going with your art, my girl. I'm anxious to hear – and see – what you're doing. Remember, find some time for yourself.'

Kerrie nodded. 'I just don't know how to thank you for everything.'

'You don't have to. It's worked both ways. But there is a favour you can do for me, if it's not too much trouble.'

'Anything. Love to,' said Kerrie.

Shirley opened her desk drawer and pulled out a small leather bag. 'I'd like you to take this to a friend of mine in Sydney.'

'Of course. Write down the address, phone number, or whatever I have to do.'

'I'll tell you what it is. Just between us,' said Shirley.

'You don't have to do that. I don't need to know anything.'

'No, I'd like you to know. There're uncut opals in here. Old stones. I have a bit of a stash left from my Lightning Ridge days. It's sort of my superannuation.' She smiled. 'I have an old friend, a reputable jeweller and buyer, Roth Cameron, who buys them,' she added. 'He's a lovely man. He's semi-retired now and his son runs the business. Here's Roth's card.'

Kerrie took the small bag, surprised by how heavy it was. 'I'll look after it very carefully and keep it in my safe at home till I meet him.'

'Thank you, Kerrie. The stones aren't cut or polished, just snipped on each corner to get an idea of their quality. The stones are good so every now and again I cash them in.'

Kerrie zipped the pouch into her shoulder bag just as there was a call at the door.

'Where are you, Shirl? It's me, Davo.'

'In here. Saying goodbye to your passenger.'

'Ah, you found Shirley, my favourite girl, the gem of Opal Lake,' said Davo as he came in, carrying some grocery bags. 'How's it going?' he asked her. 'I've brought you the goodies you ordered from the store. They had everything on the list.'

'You're a good man, Davo, thanks. Dump them in the kitchen and put the coffee on, will you?'

'Can't stay for coffee. We need to hit the road. But I'll catch up with you in a couple of days when I bring some campers out to the lake. You ready?' he asked Kerrie.

'I was born ready,' she retorted, and turned to Shirley who gave her a smile and a wink.

'We'll talk soon.' She hugged Shirley and kissed her surprisingly smooth cheek.

'Drive carefully, Davo,' said Shirley firmly.

'Hey, you know me, Shirl. Solid as rock. Steady as a tightrope walker. Promise I'll make more time next visit. Line up some wood chopping or any odd jobs.'

'Thank you, Davo.' Shirley gave Kerrie a final wave and settled herself back in her chair.

'Poor old duck. Doesn't get around much anymore,' said Davo as Kerrie opened her door and got into the van.

'Maybe,' said Kerrie. 'But she's a very smart lady. Lovely person.'

'Yeah, not a lot gets past Shirley. Knows where all the skeletons are buried.'

Davo started the engine and they drove out of Opal Lake.

When they got back to Broken Hill, Kerrie paid Davo the money she owed him for picking her up and collected her car. It seemed ages since she'd left it and impetuously taken the tour to White Cliffs and Opal Lake. As she drove back to Sydney she thought about the last few days. In some way that she couldn't yet define, she felt she'd jumped a hurdle and her life had changed.

But when she went into the Rose Bay house and knew Milton would never come smiling through the door to meet her and was greeted, instead, by the scattered possessions of the girls who'd obviously visited and not tidied up, Kerrie came to a decision. Things were going to change around here. She wasn't sure how, but for one thing she was going to start painting seriously.

After she'd been home for a week, she called Roth Cameron and made a time to meet him at his store in Pitt Street to give him Shirley's parcel. Kerrie took out the ring she'd found and looked at it again. Would it be worthwhile cleaning it up? She decided to take it with her and see what Roth could do with it. Perhaps he could even identify the stone.

Cameron's was one of Sydney's older jewellers, the type that were now gradually being replaced by international designer storefronts of tubular steel, expensive carpets and spectacular lighting. Kerrie liked the cosy, old-fashioned store, with its antique display cases of jewellery, china and crystal. Comfortable leather chairs, mirrors, a vase of flowers and subdued carpet gave it a special feel. In one corner a young couple were intently studying a tray of engagement rings.

A woman around Kerrie's age smiled at her as she entered. 'Good afternoon. Can I help you with something or do you just want to browse?'

'I have an appointment with Mr Cameron. I'm Kerrie Faranisi.'

'Roth's in his office. I'll just buzz him.' She leant over and pressed a small button under the counter.

'Thank you.' Kerrie sat in one of the chairs to wait, glancing at the sparkling gems in a cabinet.

Roth Cameron appeared almost immediately. A smiling, white-haired man, he had courtly manners and Kerrie liked him instantly.

'Shirley sends her best wishes.'

'Thank you, thank you. How is she doing? I do worry about her in such an isolated place.'

'She seems fine and as sharp as a tack. I enjoyed her company immensely. We had a great time together.'

Roth ushered Kerrie into his small office, which held a desk, two chairs and shelves of books, along with jars of stones, old-fashioned weighing scales and a large oyster shell, complete with pearl blisters, containing paperclips and rubber bands.

Kerrie opened her handbag and took out the old leather pouch. 'This is from Shirley.'

'Some more of her collection. She lets them go when she needs some money. Have you seen them?'

Kerrie shook her head. 'No, not at all. She told me that these are opals that she found.'

'From quite a few years back, now. Lovely pieces. Sometimes they're from Opal Lake and sometimes from Lightning Ridge. She's a bit cagey, sells them off gradually. A sort of life insurance, I suppose.'

He spread the rough opal stones across the blotter on his desk. Initially they looked unprepossessing. But then as Roth picked up each one and examined it, Kerrie saw that a small section had been rubbed off the back and polished, showing the glittering quality of the stone.

'Gem crystal. Beautiful. These will cut into lovely stones,' said Roth. He picked up his magnifier and peered more closely at each piece of opal. 'Hmm. I remember the mine these came from. Shirley and her partner abandoned it, convinced that the seam was finished. Years later the place was open-cut and another good patch of opal showed up. You just can't tell with opal finds, so much luck involved.'

'Will you turn these into jewellery or sell the stones?' asked Kerrie, amazed at the vibrancy of the shifting patterns of colour.

'Both. I just make the occasional piece now. My son runs our businesses and he has a lot of young modern designers, but he gets me to make pieces for some of our older clients. Those who can afford custom-made jewellery.' He picked up another stone and began separating them into piles.

'You say "businesses" – you have more than this shop?' asked Kerrie.

Roth put down the eyepiece. 'I've had a few offers to sell, take part in joint ventures or set up franchises of this business. But since I'm semi-retired, my son, Timothy, runs with the expansion.' He smiled and lifted an eyebrow. 'He's made quite a decent fist of it. You've heard of Diamond Rose Jewellers?'

'Of course. Their shops are everywhere. They're a more affordable chain of jewellery shops, aren't they? Not as exclusive as this one?'

'That's how Tim describes it. He wanted to bring real gems to new customers. There's always a place for costume jewellery but there's nothing like owning a genuine stone, and he's tried to make them more affordable for more people. Australia has some remarkable natural gemstones, of which opal, of course, is queen.'

'I love Broome pearls, too,' confessed Kerrie. 'And Kimberley diamonds.'

'Well, that's the high end of the market! There are a lot of wonderful gemstones that aren't so expensive, but they tend to go in and out of fashion. The coloured topaz for example.' He lifted up one of the opals. 'But nothing beats opal. They've made synthetic ones, but you can spot them straight away. Real opals are so alive. The movement and play of colour is different every time you look at it.'

Kerrie smiled at the enthusiasm in his voice. 'I love the way everyone's so passionate about opals. I'm beginning to understand the attraction. Talking of unusual stones, I found a ring out at the lake and it has intrigued me. I'm wondering if you can tell me anything about it and if it would be worthwhile having it restored.'

'Of course. Be delighted to give you my opinion.'

Kerrie took the ring from her handbag and handed it to Roth. 'It must have been buried a long time because it certainly needs cleaning.'

Roth studied the setting, wiped the surface of the stone and peered at it closely through his magnifier. Kerrie watched his expression change as he turned to her.

'It's an opal. But damaged, although the few scratches might polish out.'

'It's an opal?' said Kerrie. 'I suppose that makes sense, considering where I found it.'

'Yes, though we won't know how good an opal it is till I have a go at polishing it.' He turned it over. 'It's a solid stone, not sliced and layered. And an interesting setting. Looks like it could have been made in the 1920s.'

'Do you think it's been out there all that time? Surely not,' said Kerrie. 'I wonder who owned it.'

'Let's wait and see how it comes up and then we'll have a better idea of how old it is,' said Roth. 'I'll be in touch when I get it done, if you like. And thank you for delivering Shirley's parcel. I'll send her an email as soon as I know what's here and I can give her a price.'

'It's been lovely talking to you, Roth.'

'I'm sure we'll meet again.' They shook hands and he escorted her out of the shop and watched her walk down Pitt Street. In their short meeting he was struck by what an intelligent woman Kerrie was, although he detected a sad air beneath her friendliness. He could see why she and Shirley would get on so well in spite of the age difference.

*

Kerrie felt different since her return from her outback trip, and others noticed it. The girls, who rarely paid much attention to her, commented to each other that their step-mother seemed to have changed a bit.

'Probably looking forward to spending all of our father's money,' said Renata cattily.

They still came and went from the Rose Bay house, which they continued to treat as an open house. They invited friends to the house and sat by the pool without bothering to ask or even consult Kerrie. Eventually Kerrie decided to leave them to their own devices, and didn't bother to supply food and drinks for their parties.

Late one afternoon, when she was alone emptying out some cupboards and playing her favourite music, the phone rang and a pleasant voice introduced himself as Tim Cameron.

'You saw my father, Roth. As I was coming past your house this afternoon, he asked me if I could drop a small package in for you.'

'Of course. My ring. You don't need to make a special trip. I didn't expect that. It's just a little curiosity . . .' began Kerrie.

'I have to visit one of our shops in Double Bay, so I'm actually quite close to your place. I'll be happy to pop in and give it to you. The ring cleaned up really well. I'd like to show it to you.'

'Great!' Kerrie ran a hand through her hair. 'I've been doing a bit of spring cleaning. If you'll give me a few minutes . . .'

'Of course. I won't hold you up. My father said you'd just come back from Opal Lake with some opal from Shirley. He's sending a bottle of wine over with me to say thank you for that. How is Shirley?'

'Terrific. Amazing woman. I'll find some cheese and biscuits to go with the wine. See you in what, ten minutes?'

'Make it fifteen. I think you'll like the ring,' he said. 'See you shortly.'

Kerrie brushed her hair, put on some lipstick and perfume, and threw on a clean top over her jeans. How nice the Camerons seemed, to have gone to so much trouble for her. Perhaps they were being this kind because she was a friend of Shirley's. Not that it mattered. Tim sounded pleasant, like his father, and after two days of being alone in the house and not seeing anyone the idea of a social drink was appealing.

Timothy Cameron shook her hand, smiling broadly. 'I hope this isn't an intrusion. Dad sends his best and said that he enjoyed chatting with you. He's down on his farm this week, which is why he asked me to return your ring.'

'Come in. Really, there was no rush about the ring, but thank you for bringing it.'

Tim followed Kerrie down the hallway, pausing to admire a small bronze statue on a pedestal in the hallway. 'Beautiful. It's one of your late husband's, I presume? I've seen his work. Brilliant sculptor. I'm sorry about his sudden death. You must miss him.'

'Yes, I do.' Kerrie glanced at the sculpture. 'It's called "Centaur with Pipes". He did a larger version in polychrome wood. It's in the Tate gallery.' She led him to the terrace where she'd set out glasses and a platter with cheese, olives and bread rolls. 'Very basic fare, but I'm peckish. I was busy and forgot to stop for lunch. It seems rather decadent to have such a lovely wine with such rustic food,' said Kerrie rather apologetically as she glanced at the wine label. 'Please thank your father.'

Tim put a small velvet bag with 'Cameron's' in gold printed on it, onto the table.

'I'll get an ice bucket.'

'I'll pour the wine.'

'Saluté,' Tim said when Kerrie returned. 'Hmm.

I needed that. It's nice to have a bit of a break before I head back to the office.'

'You must be busy if you have to get back so late in the day.'

'We have a big promotion coming up in the chain-stores, so there'll be a lot of long hours for a while.'

'Yes, your father told me about your shops. Sounds very enterprising. I suppose people like to buy jewellery.'

'Yes. People buy jewellery for presents and for them-selves. Hence our marketing campaign. Jewellery fashion tends to be a bit faddy, but once something catches on everyone wants the same thing. It's been an interesting challenge.'

'Yes. I have three stepdaughters and I know that when one of them gets something fashionable, the others will want it, too.'

'Aren't you going to look at your ring? Dad was very pleased with the job he did.'

'How lovely of him. How much do I owe him?'

'Oh, he won't have a bar of that. He enjoyed doing it. And you are a friend of Shirley's. If you like, I can tell you something about the ring, although Dad could tell you more.'

Kerrie loosened the tie on the little velvet bag and tipped out the ring, staring at it in amazement.

'Pretty good, huh?' said Tim with a smile.

'Is it real? I mean, the stone was black and it had scratches and now it looks like new,' gasped Kerrie.

The ring glowed and sparkled as she turned it around in the late afternoon sunlight. It had a deep blue back-ground and was shot with iridescent green but, even more stunningly, across the centre was a brilliant red-gold flash that seemed to burn as it moved with the light.

'That's a pretty rare stone. You don't see a pattern like that very often,' said Tim.

'How awful that someone lost it, Tim. It must have cost a fortune.' She looked at Tim, who nodded.

'It's certainly a collector's piece. It's so unusual that it's hard to put a price on it. It's black opal, so it didn't come from Opal Lake. It's from Lightning Ridge. And, looking at the setting, it's probably post First World War. It's ornate but the gold isn't thin like that used in later rings, when gold was scarcer. Interestingly, the ring was originally rose gold, but it has been plated over with yellow gold. Dad suspects that it could have been done in the flapper era – when those wild girls liked jazzy, stylish jewellery.'

'So the rose gold was covered? I love rose gold myself.' Kerrie studied the ring.

'In the twenties it was considered old-fashioned, so I think that the original ring might have been made earlier. Also, because of the straight edges to the stone, I'd say the opal was cut and polished by the man who found it. It could have been put in this setting some time later.'

'You can tell all that?' asked Kerrie.

Tim smiled at her and topped up her glass. 'Dad is the expert. We had a long discussion about this ring.'

'What am I going to do with it?' Kerrie was overwhelmed by the magnificent ring. 'Should I keep it?'

'Wear it. After all, you found it,' he suggested. 'It would be very hard to find the original owner after all this time.'

Kerrie stared at the transformed ring in her hand. 'I can't believe that strange black stone has turned into this.'

'Put it on.' Tim slipped the ring on to her right hand.

Kerrie glanced at the simple gold wedding band on her other hand, which she'd worn since the day she married Milton. He'd given her a lot of elaborate and expensive jewellery but she thought even Milton would be knocked out by this ring. 'It's pretty dramatic, isn't it?'

'Suits you. You need to dress up and go out to show it off.'

Kerrie shook her head. 'I don't know. It doesn't feel right to keep it. What if I put it out there, on the net, to see if anyone knows about it, and can prove it was theirs?'

'You'll be flooded with con men, believe me.'

Kerrie put the ring on the table. 'It's the size of an olive!'

Tim laughed. 'It's got such a fire in it, it looks hot, doesn't it? I can study opal for hours. By the way, Dad wanted to know if you are going back out to Opal Lake.'

'Me? Gosh, I've just got back. I'm still thinking about all I saw, and the people I met. I haven't even had a chance to look through the sketches I made,' said Kerrie.

'Are you an artist? Great place for inspiration, out there, I'd think.'

'Yes, it is, which is why I made a lot of sketches. Since I got home, I've been setting up a studio for myself so that I can try and turn some of them into paintings.'

'Good on you. Be sure and send me an invitation to your exhibition,' said Tim.

Kerrie smiled. 'I'll be happy if I can complete a few canvases that I'm relatively happy with.'

'I like going out to the opal fields. Special people out there, too, don't you think?' Before she could answer, he went on, 'There're some gems like Shirley, some oddballs, some creative types and those with opal fever. It's a place that affects everyone. I always feel that one's a slightly different person out there.'

Kerrie nodded. 'I know what you mean. Do you get a chance to get out there much, or does your business keep you tied down? Do you have a family?' she asked suddenly.

He nodded. 'An eight-year-old son. And he has two stepsisters, so he's spoilt rotten. After my wife and I divorced she married a man with two daughters.'

'It's not always easy being the stepmother,' said Kerrie.

Tim nodded. 'So I'm told. But we seem to have a fairly lucky arrangement. I'm very involved with my son, and I liaise with my ex-wife and her husband to make sure the little terror's not playing us all off against each other,' he said cheerfully.

'That all sounds very civilised. I'm afraid I haven't had it so easy with my husband's three girls.'

Noncommittally, Tim commented, 'Families are always complicated, aren't they? But I don't mind the challenges of a blended family.' He finished the piece of bread and cheese on his plate. 'I'd better be going. Tell me, did you meet Ingrid and see her strange jewellery?'

Kerrie smiled and nodded. 'Yes. I did. I can honestly say that I've never seen anything quite like it. Please thank your father for me. In fact, I'll phone him and thank him myself.'

'He'd like that.' Tim held out his hand. 'Really lovely to meet you. And enjoy that ring. I think it's meant to be yours.'

'Thank you for delivering it, and thank your father again for the wine.'

'Our pleasure. I'm sure we'll meet again.'

'That would be nice.' Kerrie opened the front door, just as Luisa arrived on the doorstep. 'Tim, this is one of Milton's girls, Luisa. Luisa, this is Timothy Cameron.'

'Lovely to meet you, Luisa.'

Tim took her hand and Luisa murmured a perfunctory 'Nice-to-meet-you', and disappeared indoors.

Tim gave Kerrie a smile and a wink and headed to where his car was parked.

Kerrie closed the door and went back out to the terrace to finish the last of her drink. The sun had set and it was getting cool. She picked up the ring, slipped it into the velvet pouch and put it in her pocket.

At that moment Luisa exploded through the glass doors to the terrace. 'What is going on, Kerrie? Who was that?'

'What do you mean? He just brought me something of mine as he was in the neighbourhood.'

'Some delivery boy who brings posh wine!' Luisa picked up the bottle and waved it at Kerrie. 'What was he delivering?'

'Luisa, I don't like your attitude.'

'Well, I don't like yours. My father's barely dead and you've already got your new boyfriend here. I bet he only likes you for your money. Boy, are you a snake.'

'Luisa, I think you're overreacting. I had never met Tim until this afternoon.'

'No, I'm not. Not only have you got yourself a new boyfriend – wait till the others find out about that – but what I also want to know is what gives you the right to throw me out of my own room! How dare you.'

'Ah.' Kerrie caught her breath. 'Well, I was going to tell you.'

Before she could go on, Luisa broke in. 'You want us out so that your new boyfriend can move in.'

'For goodness' sake, it's not like that at all. Tim's father repaired something for me and Tim was delivering it. And as for your room – as you've moved out, I've decided to make a few changes.'

'Changes! My room is empty!'

'You girls know you are always welcome to stay here, but you do have places of your own. I need the space. I've decided to turn the upstairs loft into a spare bedroom. It's huge and airy, and I was going to ask you to help design it so we could perhaps partition it off . . .'

'Why do you need my bedroom? Boyfriend moving in?'

'I'll ignore that silly comment. I'm going to use it as a

studio. It has good light and it's on the ground floor so it's easier to move canvases and materials in and out.' Kerrie headed for the kitchen.

'Studio? For what? What do you need a studio for?'

Kerrie's annoyance suddenly subsided and she felt strangely calm. 'I'm taking up painting again and I need a suitable space, so I chose the most practical room, which happened to be the one you lived in as a child. You don't live in it now.'

'But it's mine! I always knew you hated me. You're so selfish.'

Kerrie tried not to laugh. 'Luisa, don't be silly. You've moved out and you have your own place – with your own utilities,' she added pointedly, 'And you told me, quite emphatically, that you didn't want to be around here any-more.' Kerrie put the plates and glasses in the dishwasher.

Kerrie's calmness unnerved Luisa. Normally she could easily bully Kerrie, but this time her belligerent attitude wasn't working. 'I don't know why you're bothering to go to so much trouble. It's a waste of time. You've never painted because you can't. I don't know what makes you think anyone would be interested in anything you'd try to do.'

'I'm not doing it for other people. I'm doing it for me,' she said quietly to Luisa, who stomped from the room. Moments later, Kerrie heard the front door slam.

'Round one to me,' Kerrie told herself later as she took a long relaxing bath. 'For once I didn't shout and I didn't get rattled. And I am going to start painting.'

After she dried herself, she took out the extraordinary opal ring and stared at the shifting colours in its stone. A crystal gem, Tim had told her. Well, she wished it was a crystal ball and she could see her future in its flaming heart. Slowly she slipped the ring on her finger.

SHIRLEY

6

THE TINSEL DRAPED OVER the faded gold star was thread-
bare and wilted by the heat. Inside the hotel fly-spotted,
vintage crepe-paper streamers drooped around the bar.
But the small crowd gulping icy beers was in a festive
mood.

'I'm only opening for an hour, just for ice, you blokes,'
Mick announced to his customers.

'So the drinks are on you, are they, Mick? Merry
Christmas!'

'Yeah, right,' said the grinning perspiring owner of
the Opal Lake Hotel. 'Hey, Doug, how're things? Give my
best wishes to Pam. And thanks for the invite, I'll catch up
with you before New Year. Want a beer?'

'Bit early in the day for me, thanks, Mick. Just came
in to stock up on ice for us and Shirley. We have a couple

for Christmas dinner. Backpackers. They're here in the middle of summer, would you believe? Germans love the heat, that's for sure. And Pam tells me there's someone else turning up. I remember when there was hardly anyone around at this time of year.' Doug turned to the man beside him. 'Good to see you in town, Carl. You staying around for the day?'

'Nah. Got a joint in the camp oven roasting nicely. Lamb, potatoes, carrots. I'm just popping in to give Shirley the compliments of the season, return some of her books and get some rosemary for my lamb, and then I'll be off. Want me to drop in Shirley's ice?'

'Sure, thanks, Carl, if you're going that way.'

'Did you do the red suit thing last night, Doug?' asked Mick.

'Over at the hall, for the Christmas party. The kids had a ball. They still enjoy Santa's visit, even though they know it's me. Well, I'd better be off. Ho, ho, ho and all that.'

Back at the Golden Dome, Doug began unloading the bags of ice into the coldroom.

'This should see us through, Pam. You're still not telling me who else is coming for Christmas dinner?'

'It's a surprise.'

'Not your aunt. Please.'

'Of course not. You know that she wouldn't come out here at the height of summer.'

'All right. Well, I hope whoever it is realises they're coming at a quiet time of year. Are they staying with us?'

Pam shook her head, suppressing a smile. 'No.'

'So you've persuaded one of the blokes from the backblocks to come in for a decent meal? Good on you.'

It was getting dark when the doorbell chimed.

'That's perfect timing. Dinner's almost ready,' said Pam. 'I'll get the door.'

She came back into the lounge room leading a beaming Kerrie who was carrying a stack of Christmas parcels.

Doug leapt to his feet. 'Kerrie! What a wonderful surprise! What a great Christmas present you are.' He gave her a hug.

'She's only in town for a fortnight, Doug. But it's good to see you here, Kerrie, even if it is as hot as a furnace,' exclaimed Pam.

'You're staying with us, of course,' said Doug as Kerrie placed the parcels under the plastic Christmas tree.

'We'll tell you about the arrangements in a minute, Doug,' said Pam. 'First, I'd like to introduce Kerrie to our other guests, Andrea and Peter.'

The German backpackers, looking flushed and shining from their exertion and the weather, shook Kerrie's hand.

'We have been walking about the little town. Even at night, it is still very hot,' said Andrea. 'Excuse us while we freshen up.'

'I hope I haven't held you up, Pam,' said Kerrie. 'The drive took me a bit longer than I thought. This is certainly a different place in the summer, isn't it? The heat must send you into a stupor. Is there anyone else left in town, or have they all fled?'

Pam handed her a glass of wine. 'No, there are still a few people about. Sit down and relax for a moment. I've been excited all day – so looking forward to seeing you.'

'And I've been looking forward to this, too. Are the arrangements okay with Ingrid?'

'Sure are. Here's her key.' Pam turned to Doug. 'Kerrie's spending tonight here, so we can have a good old catch up, and then she's staying at Ingrid's place while she's away.'

'Talk about secret women's business,' said Doug. 'Who else knows you're here?'

'No one. I want to surprise Shirley,' said Kerrie. 'Is she coming here for Christmas?'

'We invite her every year but of course she never comes,' sighed Pam. 'Not that she'll be on her own. Davo generally drops in to share it with her. But you'll be our surprise present.'

Christmas dinner in the dining room of the dugout was a merry meal. Pam had baked a ham and cooked a traditional Christmas pudding. Andrea and Peter sang a duet in German, and Pam introduced a silly pass the parcel game. There was lots of food, wine and laughter, and all the guests helped serve and then clear the dishes and stack the dishwasher. Kerrie found the warmth and informality so different from the Christmas meals she'd shared with Milton, his girls and friends. Kerrie had often spent days lavishly decorating the house, and then she and Wendy would prepare a rich and extravagant meal that was never fully eaten. The final leftovers were thrown out of the refrigerator a week later. There always seemed to be arguments between the girls over the unfairness or unsuitability of their presents until they made their escape to laze by the pool while Kerrie cleaned up.

Here Kerrie felt immediately relaxed, and she could tell that the young German couple also felt at home and included on this festive occasion. In the satisfied, over-indulged, post-dinner torpor, Andrea and Peter returned to their room, Doug watched television, and Kerrie and Pam stretched out on the two lounges to catch up.

'Any thoughts about what you want to do while you're here?' asked Pam.

'Paint, definitely. It's too hot to go out to the opal lake again, but I have my sketches. And it's nice to know it's close by. It's an intriguing place,' said Kerrie.

'What happened with that ring you found? Did you ever do anything with it?' asked Pam.

'Oh, heavens, yes! The ring is actually quite stunning. I took it to a jeweller friend of Shirley's, Roth Cameron, and he went to a lot of trouble with it and did a great job cleaning it up. His son, Tim, dropped it back to me. He's a nice man. I've seen him once or twice since. He pops in for a drink occasionally when he's in the area on business.'

'I know the Camerons. They're a lovely family. Roth still comes out a bit. But I understand Tim's taking the business in a new direction. I don't know that Tim has the same romantic passion for opals that his father has,' said Pam.

'I'm not sure. But he did tell me quite a bit about them. Evidently I possess a rather rare and unusual stone, so I'm a lot more intrigued by opals than I was,' said Kerrie. 'I should have brought the ring to show you, but I didn't think about it.'

'Never mind. But you're right, every opal is unique, that's part of their charm. Each one is a total original. Doug is still obsessed with them. He started digging a new tunnel. Says it's for a wine cellar but I think it's a way of exploring in case there're opals there!' Pam laughed.

'Handy you can add another room just like that,' said Kerrie, gazing around at the whitewashed sandstone walls. 'Why doesn't Shirley spruce up her dugout? It's so dark and quite cramped. I'm sure there'd be people willing to help her.'

'Of course. But the old darling likes it the way it's always been since she first moved in there with her father. She's not big on housekeeping, and with all her papers and books she'd just mushroom out to fill up any extra space.'

'Is she still writing the history of the area?' asked Kerrie.

'That's what she tells me. She has a lot of material and notes and taped interviews with some of the old miners. And a lot of the old characters have talked to her. Some

163

of them took their possessions to her to look after in case they died in their camps and their things were taken or lost. She's got quite a treasure trove tucked away in that cavern of hers.'

'I'm looking forward to seeing her again,' said Kerrie.

Even though the temperature was already above thirty degrees, Shirley had settled herself with her breakfast toast and tea outside the dugout to enjoy the early morning sun. There was no movement in the town. The store was closed, but Mick would open the hotel later.

She closed her eyes, hoping the sun would loosen her stiff joints. The sound of a car coming up the hill caught her attention. She looked at it but didn't recognise it. Slowly she rose and went inside to top up her tea.

The voice at her door a few minutes later caused her to cry out in delight.

'Kerrie? How wonderful. This is certainly a surprise.'

'It's your Christmas present,' called Pam. 'She's come to see what Christmas in Opal Lake is all about.'

'Well, it's not very exciting, but this is a joy indeed.' Shirley hugged Kerrie and kissed Pam. 'Happy Christmas. I hope you and Doug are enjoying it.'

'Of course. And we had a couple of German backpackers and Kerrie to help us. Couldn't have been better. Is there any tea left?'

'Make a fresh pot, will you? There's a dear.' Shirley smiled at Kerrie and took her hand. 'I think this is a terrific idea of yours to have Christmas here. You'll see a very different town. No tourists, except for Pam's German backpackers. It's all very quiet. How long are you staying with Pam and Doug?'

'Actually, I'm staying at Ingrid's dugout for two weeks while she's away.'

'Great idea. It will be a lovely break for you. Are you planning to work?' she added as they sat down.

'Yes, I thought it would be interesting to experience a different time of year out here. I'm sure the colours of the landscape will look different, too.' Kerrie settled herself in the chair beside Shirley. 'Truthfully, though, I couldn't face Christmas in Sydney without Milton. I didn't see the point in being a hypocrite and pretending we're all one happy family when we're not. And the girls had made their own plans and hinted that I wasn't included, and I certainly didn't want to be part of something where I wasn't welcome.'

'Good. You're learning,' said Shirley.

Half an hour later, Doug called by to collect Pam and they set off to visit other friends, leaving Kerrie and Shirley at the kitchen table.

Kerrie leant back. 'It's unbelievable how cool and comfortable it is in here, when it's so hot outside. The temperature must be heading to well over forty.'

'That's the beauty of a dugout. A moderate temperature all year round,' said Shirley. 'But I sit outside first thing in the morning to get a bit of fresh air. It might be a dry heat, but it's certainly hot. It's been fifty degrees on occasion.'

'And here was I thinking I'd do a little open-air work! I think my paints would start to boil if I took them outside in this.'

'That's why Ingrid's studio is such a good idea. I'm told she has skylights and shafts angled to get the best light because she works in there all day. If you wanted to work outside, you could do it early, at first light. Start before dawn and enjoy the sunrise and then come back and work in the dugout,' suggested Shirley.

'It sounds good. I'll try it.'

'Have you done much painting these past months?'

Kerrie shook her head. 'A little. I know what I want to do. I studied the sketches I made here and at Lightning Ridge for hours. I know I can draw. But the painting, I don't feel so confident about what I've done.'

'Well, you have had other distractions,' Shirley reminded her. 'You're not the first woman to put her talent and dreams on hold for her family. You really don't know what you can do until you persist.'

'I watched Milton. I've seen other artists who push on no matter what. I know that nothing would have held them back.'

'They've got wives, for heaven's sake, helping them and boosting their egos!' interjected Shirley. 'That's why.'

Kerrie smiled at her outburst. 'Sometimes, that's true. But living with a world-famous artist was daunting. He once told me that talent takes you to the bottom of the mountain, but it's something special that drives you to climb to the peak. And that's the difference between those who put off trying, or dabble part-time, and those who tackle the climb.'

'You made Milton happy, remember that. And you told me that he made you happy. Perhaps you're still finding excuses not to try and make that climb?'

'I suppose so. But really, in these last few months, when I thought that I could start painting, I've had to deal with Milton's estate. There were pieces on loan, sculptures about which there were ownership disputes, others being held for possible acquisition and several commissioned works that he'd stored at a foundry. It all meant another round of disbursements and negotiations, which were time consuming.' She sighed. 'Milton is going to be something of an ongoing project. There's even talk of a retrospective in New York next year.'

'But I'm sure you're pleased that his work, his name and his creations live on,' said Shirley.

'Yes. I am. There are also some pieces put aside for his daughters, but at the moment they take no interest.'

'You mean they'd just as soon sell them?' said Shirley.

'I'm not sure. I certainly hope not, but it's up to them,' said Kerrie. 'Anyway, I have a bit of breathing space and I got a bit emotional about what to do with myself over Christmas, so here I am.'

Shirley patted her hand. 'And very glad I am to see you. But you know what, Kerrie? I just want you to damn well start painting. Pick up that brush and face the blank page. Canvas. No procrastination. Just take the first step up the mountain.'

Kerrie nodded. 'I know. You're right. I'm nervous. Suppose I won't be any good?'

'What's good? Who decides that? Don't be so hard on yourself. Anyway, who cares, but you? At least get something under your belt. See what you can do,' said Shirley.

Kerrie nodded. 'Like Pam said, there's nowhere to hide from yourself, is there? Not even in a dugout.'

'So go out early, put in your working hours, and then come and have a sundowner and dinner with me, every day. Promise?'

'It's a deal. I'll cook, too,' said Kerrie, putting down her tea mug.

'That would be nice, but you don't have to. We'll just keep it simple. Salads. Sandwiches.'

'No, Shirley, I enjoy cooking. Let me make you some nice Italian dishes. I'm sure I can find some suitable ingredients.'

'Well, that would be a bit of a treat,' said Shirley with a smile.

Their routine was quickly established and each looked forward to their time together.

Kerrie found she enjoyed the solitude of Ingrid's quiet dugout. She set out her paints, brushes, canvases and sketchpad in the studio. She made herself cups of tea but quickly ran out of distractions and excuses. Then she looked at the bursts of creativity that filled Ingrid's glass display cabinets and, finally, began preparing her paint. 'I put myself here. Okay. Let's see what happens.'

There was nothing else to do inside Ingrid's womb-like work space. Kerrie heard nothing of the outside world, and other than the evening light fading through the skylights, she had no indication of the time of day. She lost herself in the focus and concentration of her painting. And, as she pored over her reference sketches, she felt as if she was standing there in the bright light experiencing once again the incredible sensation she'd had when first exposed to the space and air and light of the bush with Murray Evans. Slowly Kerrie's hesitation and nervousness dissipated. She stopped pausing to judge what she was doing and simply lost herself in the process.

Shirley could tell Kerrie was making progress, but she didn't ask questions. Sometimes Kerrie arrived late at Shirley's dugout, where a glass of chilled white wine waited. Often she was still in paint-smeared working clothes, having stopped only to wash her hands and face. Sometimes they sat outside the dugout to watch the sun-set, even though the furnace heat of the day had yet to diminish, and Kerrie would talk about her work and Shirley would listen approvingly.

Sometimes Kerrie cooked dinner for them both, a task she enjoyed, while they listened to the news on the radio. Over their meal they discussed world events, politics and their views on national issues. Kerrie quickly appreciated that Shirley's knowledge and opinions were wide ranging, and, in comparison, she realised how out of touch she'd become in the months since Milton's death.

Sometimes they played a game of Scrabble or watched a DVD, but mainly they just sat and talked before Kerrie drove the few minutes back to Ingrid's dugout. Occasionally, late in the evening, they would have a nightcap in the dark on Shirley's small porch, looking at the carpet of stars above, and the few yellow pinpricks of lights below, and in the distant sky above the horizon, silent flashes of lightning would flicker.

'Wait till you experience a summer thunderstorm,' said Shirley. 'In Lightning Ridge it's said that the ironstone ridges attract the lightning.'

'Is that how it got its name?' asked Kerrie.

'Yes. The story goes that a shepherd and several hundred sheep were all struck and killed by a lightning strike. The thunderstorms are frightening and dangerous out here. I saw one at the lake once . . .' Shirley shuddered. 'A storm can be a spectacular sight just as long as you're not out in it.'

One evening, feeling mellow after a good dinner and the best part of a bottle of wine and grateful to this supportive and spunky woman beside her, Kerrie said, 'Shirley, you've become such a good friend. I feel I've dumped all my problems on you. You've always listened and given me such good advice. And I thank you so much for that. You know more about me than anyone else, I think. But you know, I hardly know a thing about you, your background, your life. I've been so selfish and wrapped up in my own issues that I haven't bothered to ask about you.'

Kerrie was expecting Shirley to brush her comment away or make a light-hearted remark about it, so she was surprised when Shirley looked suddenly thoughtful and was silent for a moment or two.

Finally Kerrie said quietly, 'Sorry, I didn't mean to pry.'

Shirley looked at Kerrie. 'People always say that I'm happy to tell them all about myself, if they just ask, but only a few people really know the true story of why I came here and why I stay. And sometimes I wonder myself.'

'Shirley, you don't have to tell me a thing if you don't want to,' said Kerrie quickly.

Shirley smiled at Kerrie. 'But you're right. I do know a lot about your life, and I'm happy to listen. Occasionally you can get close to someone you haven't known very long, but out here that doesn't often happen. Perhaps it's the isolation, the overwhelming enveloping sense of space and landscape, and the fact that many people come here to escape, so no one talks about their past.'

'I'm sorry. I've broken a cardinal rule.'

'Nonsense. You and I are different. Sometimes there's a connection between women that's spontaneous.'

'Yes. I've been thinking that, too,' said Kerrie. 'Although I haven't really experienced such a bond before, except with my mother. I was never a coffee-with-the-girls type.'

'Your Milton took front and centre in your life.'

Kerrie nodded. 'I don't regret the fact he was, but it's left me unprepared to face the future alone.'

'You mightn't be alone forever. But I won't lay platitudes on you because I can't talk. I stayed alone.'

'Here?'

She nodded. 'When you have a great and overwhelming love in your life you can't believe it won't be there forever. And when you're hurt by that person . . . I suppose we all deal with these things differently.'

'Were you hurt badly?' asked Kerrie softly.

Shirley shook her head. 'I've always been a very practical person.' She smiled. 'I was a career woman and thought my time for love had passed.'

'Did you get swept away?' asked Kerrie and, as Shirley nodded, she added, 'Don't you think to have known a great love is better than never having experienced such feelings?'

'If I'd known what was to come, I might have exercised some restraint,' said Shirley briskly. Then her voice softened. 'Actually, I would like to tell you what happened. But I suppose it's a bit like painting a portrait. You need to know the background and the life experiences to capture what's inside a person. When you get to my age, they say that your life story is written on your face, in your eyes. As an artist, perhaps you can see that landscape of the soul. To understand my story you have to understand about opals, and the effect they can have on people.'

'Like here, in Opal Lake?' asked Kerrie. She realised that Shirley might be slowly opening a door that had long been bolted.

'And Lightning Ridge. The opal fields. I've lived through a lot of changes.'

'And you wouldn't live anywhere else?'

'No, I wouldn't,' said Shirley. 'Well, that's how I see it. Others might have acted differently.' She straightened and resettled herself in her chair. 'Top up our drinks, and I'll start at the beginning.' The hesitancy had gone, and her voice became stronger, almost enthusiastic.

Lightning Ridge, 1939

The young girl bounced beside her father, taking three steps to each one of his strides. She skipped and hopped and occasionally spun in a circle, dancing to a tune she hummed, and then she ran to catch him up.

'You'll spend a lot of energy and walk twice as far as I do hopping around like that,' said Albert Mason. 'Slow down. You'll wear yourself out in this heat.'

'Where are we going today, Daddy?'

'Hmm. Where do you think? We're going to go down deeper into the mine shaft.'

'Are we getting close to the opals? When will we find some?'

'I don't know. It's the luck of the draw, sweet pea. There're a lot of hardworking fellows who never strike it rich and then some lucky chap comes along and finds opal in five minutes. Well, almost.'

'Are we lucky?'

'Sure we are, Shirley. Aren't we lucky to be out here with the birds and the animals, stars above us at night, food to eat, and a billy of tea by the fire?'

'But we're here to find opals! You told Mummy that you'd bring back opals.'

'Well, let's hope today is our lucky day.' He took her hand and they swung their arms as she skipped beside him.

'If we find an opal, will we be the first people to ever, ever see it?' asked Shirley.

'We will. It takes millions of years to form one, but opals have been treasured since ancient times. There's a story that a Mughal ruler wore an opal in his turban. And Napoleon gave the Empress Josephine the most beautiful opal in the world. It was called the Burning of Troy because it had wonderful flames of fire in it.'

'Where is it now? Can we see it?'

'It's sad, but after Josephine died, no one knows what happened to the opal. It might reappear one day, you never know. In Roman times, Mark Antony tried to buy a magnificent opal ring from an old senator to give to Cleopatra, the queen of Egypt. But the old senator refused to sell it even though he was threatened with all kinds of punishments.'

'Did he keep the ring?'

'Yes, he did. He escaped and lived as a poor man in another country rather than part with his opal ring.'

Shirley mulled over these stories. Her father dispensed

172

information in stories, anecdotes and sometimes poetry, all the time. The names he mentioned were not familiar to her but she knew that if she listened to her father she would learn things.

They came over the small rise studded with what her father called wild orange trees, which offered welcome shade to the diggings. They stopped and Albert contemplated the pockmarks in the white clay spread before them. The soft mounds of stark cream-coloured mullock heaps, which stood beside the mostly abandoned shafts, looked like the night foragings of giant bandicoots.

Albert smiled to himself. 'Well, lass, it seems as though everyone is hard at work, unless they've moved on to the new field out at Pig Tree Hill.'

'Will I go and see where everyone is?' asked the girl.

'You know the rules. You don't go near shafts or run around without me. There could be a mine that's not easy to see and if you fell down it, what would I do then? Come on, you and I have work to do.'

'Yes, Daddy.'

The little girl helped Albert pull the sheet of iron, branches and stones from the top of their shaft. Underneath was a roughly cut hole, two and a half foot square, disappearing into darkness below. Together they pulled the tattered canvas cover from their simple metal windlass, its green cowhide bucket attached to the rope. Albert slung the ladder, which he'd made from rough pieces of wood and wire, down the shaft, checking that it was secure, for the shaft was now fifteen feet deep. Initially he'd simply dug footholds into the sides of the mine with a tomahawk, but when Shirley had slipped and fallen, he had built the rough ladder, which they now used. Once he was at the bottom, Albert called for his daughter and helped her down.

Nimble and swift, her feet half slid down the ladder.

As she jumped lightly to the floor of the shaft, her father admonished her.

'Take it easy, kiddo. Wait till your eyes adjust to the light, and look around before you move. You never know what might be down here.'

It was easy to trip over the tools and piles of dirt and rocks that lay around the bottom of the shaft, and in the tunnel that angled away into darkness. Using his torch, Albert found their spider, the metal-ring candle holder that was stuck into the wall, and lit the wick of the candle. The pale yellow glow cast shadows onto the gouged earth walls.

He had started a small drive to the left, just high enough for him to sit reasonably comfortably and use his pick to bite into the packed-earth face of the mine. As the piles of dirt fell around him, his daughter scooped them up with a trowel and dropped them into the hide bucket. Her father smiled at her efforts. After he had been digging for some time, he stopped and helped Shirley fill the bucket. When it was full, Albert climbed back up the ladder and raised the bucket using the windlass, tipping it out beside the mine shaft.

Shirley scrambled out and stood beside him, ready to start picking through the dirt tailings as Albert had taught her to do. She had a keen eye and was quick to pick any stones that showed a discolouration that might indicate potential opal-bearing dirt.

After her father had sent up three or so buckets, he lit a small campfire and, hanging the billy over it to boil, he told Shirley that it was smoko time. While they drank their mugs of tea, they sorted through the bucketloads, putting any possibilities to one side. Occasionally Albert used his cutters to snip a corner off a promising-looking stone, searching for colour.

After they finished, he threw the dregs of their cold

tea onto the fire and with his boot scraped dirt onto the flame to smother it. 'Back to work, young lady.' Albert returned to the shaft and Shirley carefully continued to look through the mullock heap. She examined the dust-coated jelly-like lumps of rock, which her father had told her was called rubbish potch. He had also told her that, if she looked hard enough, sometimes these unprepossessing stones held the trapped fire of precious gem opal.

When she thought that she had looked long enough, she returned to her father at the bottom of the shaft. He gave her a small pick and let her chip away at the rock face with it.

'Listen very carefully to the sound of the metal on the earth,' he told her. 'If you hear a clinking noise, like you've hit glass, stop and take it slowly. You might just be on to something,' he said.

'Like opal?' asked Shirley.

'It could be. The colours will tell us if it's precious opal. No mistaking it,' said her father. 'You know when you've got gold, there's a nugget shining at you from the pan. But diamonds, even rubies and sapphires, look like very dull and uninteresting little pebbles when you dig them up. Not like opal . . . the moment it's uncovered it's flashing every brilliant colour of the rainbow. Like it's alive. You just have to look.'

'Like the opal in Mummy's ring?'

'Just like that.'

'Is that why we come out here? To find another opal for Mummy?'

'I doubt we'll ever find another one like that. Perhaps it was beginner's luck. But we can certainly try.'

'I wish Mummy could have come with us.'

'When your baby brother is older we'll bring your mother and Geoffrey out here to Lightning Ridge. But now is a special time, just for you and me.'

Shirley nodded. Her father had often gone to Lightning Ridge in the school holidays, but this was the first time that he had brought her to this strange underground world, so far from the bustle of Sydney. She loved having her father all to herself. She loved his stories. He knew so much about the whole world, which was why he was a schoolteacher, she thought. 'Maybe we can find an opal for baby Geoffrey in here,' said Shirley.

'Perhaps there's a pretty little stone or two sleeping away in the rock underground that will be a necklace or a ring for you.'

'Daddy, if we find an opal, do we have to sell it? That's what everyone says.'

Her father sighed. 'Yes, I know. For some people these are very hard times, but we're not as badly off as some of the fellows around here who've lost their jobs and are doing it tough. Everyone is hoping an opal find will change their fortunes overnight.'

They'd been working through the afternoon in the cool quiet tunnel, and Albert was considering packing up early and getting his gun to shoot a rabbit for dinner.

'Daddy. Stop. That's one,' cried Shirley and crawled up the drive to its face to tug at her father.

'What's up, kiddo?'

'The noise. The clink sound.' The girl began rubbing her hands over the rough surface of the solid clay. 'I heard it.'

'Did you? Best we have a good look then.' Albert continued chipping away with his small gouging pick by the soft light of the candle. This time he, too, heard the metallic clink. 'Bring the candle closer, Shirley, and be careful of the hot wax. It might be just potch.'

Using feather-light strokes, he began paring away the hard clay. There it was again, the slight grating noise. Using the point of his pick he began gently trying to feel for the size and shape of the rock buried in the clay. Slowly he began prising the egg-sized rock from its nest.

'You got it,' whispered Shirley. 'Is it one? Is it an opal?' She held the candle closer to the black lump.

'Hard to tell. Could be just a black potch nobby.' Her father carefully began to scratch away some of the caked clay surrounding the lump.

'Crack it open, see what's inside,' said Shirley, barely able to contain her excitement.

'And break it in half? Let's see here, first.' Her father pulled his snips from his pocket and carefully snipped off a protruding edge.

They stared at the sudden glimpse of colour. Hardly daring to hope, Albert pulled out his handkerchief, spat on it and then rubbed at the surface.

When the film of dirt was cleaned away a bright glittering array of colours winked up at them. They both caught their breath.

'It's an opal, Daddy! It's so pretty.'

'Hold it carefully, sweet pea, and let's see if this fellow has any brothers and sisters.'

While Shirley sat and held the stone tightly, her father continued to probe in the clay.

'How long has this one been in the ground, Daddy?'

'Millions of years. Ever since the dinosaurs.'

The two of them lost track of time as Albert exposed a channel across the mine face where, in a deeper pocket, nestled four more nobbies, which Shirley called 'opal eggs'.

'Are there any more, Daddy?'

'Not in this little nest, sweet pea. But there could be a patch of opal in this area, if it's good bearing dirt. But first we need to know just what we have in these little treasures. Don't get too excited. They might not all have opal,' he cautioned.

'Can we go up?' asked Shirley. 'We can see better.'

'Now, you know the rules. No jumping around, no squealing, and absolutely no telling. This is our secret. All right, let's clean up and call it a day.' Carefully he wrapped the nobbies in a rag and put them in his pocket. Together they packed the loose clay into the bucket, climbed the shaft and Albert hauled the bucket to the top, tipping the clay onto their growing heap. By now the sun was low on the horizon.

'Are you still going to hunt something for dinner, Daddy?'

'I don't think so. We'll just open a tin of soup, make a damper and put a couple of spuds in the fire. Sound all right to you?'

'Yep. I could eat a horse,' replied Shirley. Then she lowered her voice and whispered to her father, 'I'm excited.'

After securing the sheet of iron across the entrance to the shaft, they casually sauntered back through the trees to the tents that made up the rough camp of the makeshift community. A couple of fires were burning. Some people moved about, others sat contemplatively in front of their flickering campfires. The smell of woodsmoke mingled with the scent of billy tea.

Albert exchanged a nod or a subdued, murmured greeting with some of the other miners. Most of the men were friendly enough but, while the claims were close together, in this camp it was every man for himself.

Albert, called the Professor by the locals, had chosen to sink his claim further away from the main camp. He'd first come out to the opal fields of Lightning Ridge as a young man with an interest in geology and palaeontology not long after the Great War had ended, and had been intrigued by the landscape, the history and the wondrous black opal. He was bitten by the opal bug and had regis-tered a claim, which he visited as often as he could in the school holidays. At first his wife had come with him, but she had quickly lost interest in the harshness of the opal fields and had stopped coming altogether as soon as they started a family. It was clear to Albert now that his six-year-old daughter regarded her first visit to the opal fields as a big adventure.

As they neared their small tent, Albert said, 'Let's get the fire going, Shirley. Start dinner and get settled. You know the drill.'

Shirley was about to open her mouth to ask about the rocks nestled in her father's deep pocket in his baggy work pants, but Albert put his finger to his lips, so she nodded and, adopting her father's weary and casual demeanour, set about her chores.

After their dinner had been eaten from enamel plates by the fire and they'd cleaned up, her father sat down to enjoy a smoke by the dying embers. In the gathering darkness other figures could be seen moving about as men settled into the swags under their bough-and-canvas shelters and, at the bottom of the rise, a lantern shone from the primitive shack where Mr and Mrs MacKenzie lived. Even though she was getting tired, Shirley was finding it hard to control her impatience to discuss the excitement of the day. Albert tapped out his pipe on his boot, stowed his leather tobacco pouch back into his pocket and gave her a slight nod. They retreated into their small tent. It held two narrow camp stretchers, a tin trunk that they used for storage and a table where their kerosene lantern stood. Her father lit its wick and adjusted the flame inside the smoky chimney.

'Close the flap of the tent, sweet pea,' he said.

Sitting side by side, Albert spread the opal nobbies onto a rough army blanket. One by one he washed the stones in their old billy can and then carefully snipped and rubbed back a small portion of each. Together they slowly turned them over, examining them in the pale yellow light of the lamp.

Neither spoke, for Albert had again cautioned Shirley, but they were both mesmerised by the extraordinary brilliance of the stones that glittered with blazing red, gold and green fire.

'It's like they have a light inside them,' whispered Shirley.

'They're extremely good opal,' agreed her father quietly. 'Very good. We'll have our work cut out for us now. A lot of digging to do before we go back to school.'

'Do we have to go back to school? Can't we stay here? If we find lots more opal, we'll be rich and then you won't have to work anymore.'

'Your mother wouldn't agree to that and neither do I! Everyone has to go to school. It's how the world runs. If you don't get an education and look after yourself and your family, you can't expect everyone else to help you out. Now, let's get to bed. We have to start digging above that ledge tomorrow.'

'I'll say a special thank you in my prayers tonight,' said Shirley.

'That's a good girl. And don't forget your mother and little brother. Sleep tight.'

Anyone watching from across the field might have observed the silhouette of a man hunched over in the lamplight, head bowed, seemingly studying what he held in his hands, turning something over and over.

Several days later, they went into town in Albert's old truck to top up their supplies. The Ridge seemed as busy as it had been on their earlier visit. Men standing outside the Imperial Hotel watched these arrivals from the diggings.

Mrs Campbell at the small general store greeted Shirley and her father warmly. 'How're you two doing? Still enjoying yourselves, eh? Not too bored, love?'

'Not at all, thank you,' said Shirley. 'I help my father.'

'She's a hard worker. Good company, too,' said Albert.

'So you don't get lonely. Long days working down a shaft with little to show for it, eh?'

'My father tells me stories and teaches me things,' said Shirley rather primly in an effort to be polite but not divulge any information.

'Well, bless you. Help yourself to a couple of lollies from the big jar on the counter. And what do you need, Mr Mason?'

After Albert had loaded their flour, dried milk, sugar and potatoes into the truck, he and Shirley wandered a little way along the dusty street of ramshackle buildings made of rough corrugated iron and wood, that made up Lightning Ridge. A man, pushing a wheelbarrow with his possessions tied up in a sugar bag and a pickaxe and tools lying on top of it, trudged past them.

Past the end of Morilla Street, Albert caught sight of his old friend Ahmed with two of his camels.

'Come and meet a special friend of mine,' he said to his daughter.

Albert had first met Ahmed years before when the Afghan cameleer had made one of his infrequent visits to the Ridge, using his camels to transport goods to the scattered mining districts during the dry season.

'Hello, Ahmed,' called Albert. 'How are Afra and Malika?' He patted one of the camels. 'This is my daughter, Shirley.'

Ahmed's leathery face broke into a large smile. 'Missy, how you be? We are good, good. And you, sir, how are you?'

'Very well, thank you. Where have you been? What have you seen?' said Albert with a smile. It was always their greeting.

'I have seen many moons over the desert. There is a

promising new field in Queensland. Only a few men, but it is far from water.'

'Are there opals out there?'

'Yes, but it is not a place for you and your fine daughter. How goes your luck?'

'We like Lightning Ridge, don't we, Shirley, but maybe we might move further away one day. Perhaps Opal Lake. I hear that there's been some good finds there.'

'It is even more remote than White Cliffs. A very poetic place. Perhaps that would be beneficial. But are you planning to return to the city and to work? Especially if there are troubled times ahead in the world.'

'Yes, I have to get back to my school and to the rest of my family. This is just a short holiday for Shirley and me, but you are right about the troubles. I hope they won't affect us in Australia.'

'They are a long way from here. Perhaps there will be a war in Europe. Let us pray that is not so. Now, I must go fetch the water cans we are carrying to the dusty opal men.'

'What happened to your other camels?' asked Albert, remembering that previously Ahmed had had six or eight camels linked together by their mulgawood nose pegs.

'Things are changing. The days of cameleers are fading, like my eyes.' The Afghan smiled. 'So I released my old friends into the wild and they will make their own way in the desert.'

'What will happen to you?' asked Albert, suddenly seeing a bleak future for the old man frequently shunned by people in the community.

Ahmed shrugged. 'Only Allah knows. I have no means to return to my country.'

'Ahmed, if you found an opal you could go home,' said Shirley, thinking that if they found more opals she could give one to Ahmed.

'Thank you, little missy, for your generous thoughts, but I have come to love this desert where the sky and the billabong are my mosque. This is my land, now,' he said. '*Ensha Allah, salam aleikom.*' He inclined his head and, tucking the end of his ragged turban under his chin, he smiled at Shirley and Albert. Then, clicking his tongue, he and his camels walked away.

The two worked quietly but steadily for the next few days, carefully digging through the layer where they'd found the nobbies. Shirley still cheerfully examined the tailings that were tipped from the bucket to the side of the windlass. Albert helped her look, making sure that they didn't miss a thing. They had a growing collection of potch with good colour, which they put to one side. Albert knew that this could indicate they were getting close to gem opal, but there was no guarantee. When they were not working on the mullock heap, it was always covered with a piece of tarpaulin, in case it attracted unwanted attention.

Sitting by their campfire one evening, Albert said quietly, 'School holidays are nearly over and we'll have to make tracks back home. No more opal, but we've done well enough. I'll take the opal nobbies to a man I know in Sydney. We can be pleased with what we have. You've been a splendid assistant miner.'

'I think tomorrow is our lucky day,' said Shirley firmly and her father smiled as he puffed on his pipe.

'Well, keep that to yourself. Here comes a fellow from down the hill.'

Albert had heard that this man had been around the opal fields for several years, having first had a strike in South Australia at Coober Pedy before moving on to White Cliffs, then Opal Lake and now Lightning Ridge. He was holding an enamel mug and greeted them cheerily.

'Hello, cobbers. I'm down on me rations and in need

of a bit of sweeten' up. Would you have a bit of sugar to spare for me tea?'

'I expect I can find some,' said Albert. 'Shirley take Mr Gordon's cup and fill it up from the bag inside.'

'I very much appreciate it. Many thanks. A man is starved for those special things that sweeten the palate after a simple supper.'

'Well, sultana pudding in the camp oven, or damper and golden syrup is as fine a dessert as a man could wish for out here,' said Albert.

The man crouched, drew out his 'baccy tin and took out the makings of a roll-your-own. 'Smoke?'

'Thank you, no. I have my pipe,' said Albert affably.

Gordon lit up as Albert puffed on his pipe. 'The best time of day, no matter what trouble and toil we've had.'

'Indeed,' agreed Albert.

They smoked for a few more moments, until Shirley ducked out of the tent and handed the man his cup filled with sugar.

'Many thanks. I shall return the favour.'

Albert drew on his pipe, slowly exhaling a thin blue plume of smoke into the crisp night air. 'That's not necessary. It has been our pleasure.'

'Weather's cooling down. The winter will be upon us before we know it,' said the miner.

Despite the casual exchange of trivialities, Albert knew that Gordon's eyes were darting about their camp, taking in details, looking for any clue that might suggest success. But there was no untoward sign of serious activity.

'So, lass, you enjoy it out here? Bit of a lonely time for a little girl like yourself,' Gordon continued.

'I like it,' said Shirley. 'I like looking at the stars, and being here with my father.'

'Well, that'd be right. He's a smart man. The Professor, that's what they call him.'

'I'm sure your wealth of local knowledge is equal to mine,' said Albert. 'You've been around the diggings for quite a while, I understand.'

'Have you found lots of opals?' asked Shirley suddenly. If he was an old opal miner, he was sure to be rich.

Gordon straightened up. He couldn't resist a small boast. 'In my time, lass. Yes, I've had a find or two.' But he quickly added, 'It's hard out here when you're stuck in shincracker and the bloke beside you is knee deep in black opal.'

'Luck of the draw, eh?' commented Albert. 'I'm afraid we'll be heading east soon. School for both of us.'

'It's been a lovely holiday,' sighed Shirley.

The man opposite nodded. 'Not for the likes of some of us. No job waiting and an uncertain future. Well, I thank you for the sugar. I'll repay it in due course.'

'As I said before, don't bother,' said Albert. 'We have enough to see us through.'

Gordon finished his smoke and threw the end into the campfire. 'Well, I'll be off. Good luck to you.'

'And to you, Mr Gordon,' replied Albert. He watched the man wander back towards the other tents with his mug of sugar.

'I don't like him,' said Shirley.

'I should say that you shouldn't judge a book by its cover, or a man for being down on his luck,' said Albert. 'But, my girl, I have to agree with you. As your mother would say, he's got shifty eyes.'

Shirley lowered her voice. 'Do you think he knows what we found?'

Albert shook his head. 'No, he was just nosing around. Anyway, we'll be gone in a couple of days. But you were a good girl not to say anything. Best we keep our finds a secret.'

At mid morning the following day, Albert called

Shirley to come down the shaft. There was something in the tone of her father's voice that made her hurry and she slid down the ladder, her feet barely touching the rungs. She stumbled towards the candlelight which was shining against the rock face at the end of the drive.

'What is it, Daddy?'

'There, look there. What do you see?'

Shirley squinted, her eyes adjusting from the bright sunlight outside. Then, in the wavering, pale candle beam, she caught the flash of colour. It was only a few inches wide, but it was the length of her hair ribbon, a shimmering, sparkling blue-green strip of opal. 'Ooh, how pretty. How do you get it out, Daddy?'

'It's a seam. I have no idea how much is there. We'll just have to follow it carefully. Can you hold the light for me?'

Time stopped for the father and daughter as Albert used the small gouging stick to gently chip along the dazzling rainbow of solid opal. Chunks came away, embedded in the flow of clay and they carefully lowered the pieces into the worn leather bucket.

'We'll have to put the dirt at the far end of the tunnel in case there's opal in it. We don't want anyone scratching through it while our back is turned, do we?' said Albert.

'I'll use the shovel, Daddy.'

'I think you might be better with the trowel. Don't hurt yourself. I'll take a rest for a minute and then I'll give you a hand.' Albert was breathless from exertion and excitement.

But a sudden cry and squeal from Shirley had him dashing to the recess at the end of the shaft.

'Shirley, what is it?'

The little girl was crying and Albert grabbed the candle and lifted it high to see what had happened. Shirley was pressed against the wall of the mine, cradling her ankle. She pointed to a ledge a few inches above the ground.

Albert's heart constricted when he saw the shape of a dark snake, its head lifted in anger.

'Dear God! Did it bite you? Let me see.'

'Daddy, kill it!'

Albert picked up the shovel and lunged towards the snake, severing its head from its body.

'Did it bite you?'

'I think so.'

'Let me see.' He pulled the kerchief from his neck and swiftly bound it above the red mark on her leg. 'Sit still. Take deep breaths. It will be all right.' He spoke as calmly as he could. Shirley tried to stop shaking and take breaths as her father directed, but they came out in short, strangled gasps. Albert pulled his shirt off, ripped off a sleeve and tied a tourniquet tightly at the top of her leg. Shirley cried out in pain.

'Shirley, you'll be right. I know that the tourniquet hurts, but it's meant to. It's so the venom doesn't spread. I'll get you to the nurse as soon as I can. It won't take long. Just keep as still and quiet as you can. I'm going to pop you in the bucket and wind you up to the top.' Gently he lifted her and carried her back to the bottom of the shaft, tipped the dirt from the bucket and eased his daughter into it, folding her legs to one side. Then he scrambled to the top of the ladder and began winching up the bucket as swiftly as he could, praying that his daughter would be all right. He carried her over to the tent and gently laid her on the camp stretcher.

'Sweetie, I'm going to have to get the venom out of your leg and it's going to hurt you, but as soon as I've done that, I'll drive you into Lightning Ridge.'

Albert took out the sharp kitchen knife from the

storage box. He lit one of the spare candles and held the blade of the knife over its flame. When he thought that it had been there long enough, he took it out and held on to Shirley's ankle.

'Be a very brave girl for me.' With that, he cut into her leg as quickly as he could. Shirley couldn't help but scream out, but her father held her steady. Then he lowered his head over the wound and sucked her blood, spitting the poisonous venom onto the ground.

'My poor baby,' he said as Shirley sobbed in his arms. He lay her on the front seat of his old truck and drove as fast as he could past the trees and onto the dirt track that led into town.

'I'll be all right, won't I, Daddy,' said Shirley, sounding weak. Albert hoped that this was from shock rather than anything else.

The drive into town seemed interminable, although it could not have been more than thirty minutes, but at last he came to a halt outside a small shack with a corrugated-iron roof and wooden walls, where the bush nurse was based. Carrying Shirley in his arms he dashed inside.

'Nurse! Please help me.'

'Here I am, now what's happened here? Hello, young lady,' she said as Albert brought his pale daughter into the room that served as a clinic.

'Snake bite,' said Albert.

'Here, on her ankle?'

'Yes, it happened in a mine shaft. It was dark.'

'Hmm.' The nurse unrolled the cloth bandage which was now soaked in blood. She swabbed the wound to reveal the angry red bite.

'We'll give her what we've got and hope it's the right thing. We don't know for sure it was a poisonous snake, do we, dear?' she said cheerfully to Shirley.

Albert shook his head, smoothing Shirley's perspiring

face. 'I killed it. I should have brought it in. Then we'd know.'

Albert sat by Shirley's side as she slept fitfully. Hours passed. The nurse brought him a mug of tea and regularly checked Shirley's pulse and temperature.

'Do you want some sleep?' she asked Albert, who just shook his head. There was no way he would leave his daughter's side.

In the early hours of the morning, Shirley seemed better. Her breathing seemed more normal, and her fever less. At last Albert closed his eyes and slept. With a jolt he awakened as the nurse bustled in. Bright light shone in the street outside the window. He leant across and touched Shirley's forehead, relieved to find it cool and normal.

'She's come through it just fine,' said the nurse quietly. 'Obviously she didn't get much venom or it wasn't a very poisonous snake. Go and get yourself some breakfast at the café. I'll watch her. Bring her back something to eat. She'll be hungry when she wakes up.'

When Albert returned with a sandwich and some milk for his daughter, he was overjoyed to see her sitting up in the bed, chatting to the nurse and a man with his arm in a sling.

'Ah, Mr Mason,' smiled the nurse. 'Shirley was just telling us all about what happened. I would say that she's had a lucky escape, thanks to your prompt action.'

'How are you feeling?' Albert asked Shirley.

'I'm fine, Daddy. But my ankle's sore. This is Mr Price. He's injured his wrist,' she told her father.

The nurse looked at Shirley. 'Probably best that you stay until this afternoon. Just to keep an eye on you. But I'm confident that everything's fine.'

Albert looked relieved. 'I don't know how to thank you, nurse. I was so worried. If anything happened to Shirley, I would never forgive myself.'

The nurse smiled. 'Well, nothing did happen. Now you just give that food to Shirley. I bet she's very hungry.'

It was late afternoon when they drove back into the camp. They saw that several campfires had been lit as the miners started to prepare their evening meal. But others would work much later, until tiredness and cold drove them back to their camp. Everything looked normal and Albert breathed a sigh of relief as he patted Shirley's knee.

'Now, where were we?'

She smiled. 'Digging up opal, Daddy.'

'You stay here in the tent and have a bit of a rest. I'll go back down the mine and tidy up.'

'No. I want to come.'

'All right,' said Albert, realising that the little girl didn't want to be left by herself. 'Let's drive over to it and save ourselves the walk.'

So instead of walking the few hundred yards from their tent to their claim, Albert drove across the rough patch of ground, the truck bouncing over ruts and holes.

At the entrance to their shaft he stopped and put his hand on Shirley's shoulder. 'You wait up here. I won't be long.' He pulled a new candle from his pocket, made sure he had his matches and climbed down the ladder.

Shirley waited and when Albert seemed to have been gone a long time, she called out, 'I'm coming down, Daddy.'

'No! Stay there, Shirley,' shouted her father. 'I'm coming up.'

Shirley was shocked by the harsh-sounding command and stood back as she saw her father's hat and broad shoulders appear at the top of the shaft. He climbed out and immediately slumped to the ground.

'Daddy! What's the matter? Another snake . . . ?'

Her father dropped his face in his hands and his shoulders shook. She flung herself at him. 'Daddy? What's wrong?'

Finally Albert lifted his head and stared at her. 'It's gone. They've taken the lot.'

'What?' Then the little girl realised. 'Our opals? All the opals? Are they gone?'

He nodded. 'Ratters. I've told you about them, how men sneak into mines and steal other people's opal. I suppose that it was an open invitation to them, leaving everything unsecured. We left in a bit of a rush.' He tried to smile and his expression squeezed Shirley's heart so tight she felt like she couldn't breathe.

'Oh, Daddy. I'm sorry. The snake . . . I'm sorry.' Tears ran down her cheeks.

Albert reached out and took her hand. 'Heavens, it's not your fault, sweet pea. You're far more important than opals and we had to get you into town.'

Shirley jumped to her feet, blazing with anger. 'They are bad men, bad. Let's find them. Let's go over there. Maybe Mr Gordon saw the bad men . . .'

Albert tried to soothe her. 'Not right now. I can guarantee no one saw or heard anything,' he said in a resigned voice.

'But how did they take it away? All the rocks? What about the ones we found, Daddy, that were in the bucket?'

'Gone. They've taken the bucket, too. Would've been handy,' he said bitterly. 'Most of my tools are gone, too.'

'Can we find some more opal?'

'I doubt it. I can see where the seam ran out. They've worked through the night and cleaned out the run.'

'We still have our eggs, Daddy?'

He tapped the pocket of his work pants. 'Yes. We'll take them home and get them cleaned up.'

'Maybe something is left here . . .' She bent down and picked up a piece of clay from the top of the mullock heap.

'Leave it, Shirley.'

Albert drove the truck back over the rock-strewn terrain to where many of the miners had their camp. He jumped from the truck and strode towards one of the campfires.

'You stay in the truck,' he told Shirley.

The men around the fire looked at him, their faces non-committal. Gordon tipped his hat back on his head.

'Evening. Care for a mug of brew?'

'No, thank you, Mr Gordon.'

'How's the little girl? We heard she was bitten by a snake. I seen a big 'un down a mine once,' said the man squatting next to Gordon.

'My daughter is all right, but when I had to leave for town in a hurry, I didn't have time to secure my mine. When we got back, it had been ratted,' said Albert bluntly.

'You bottomed on opal then?' queried Gordon.

'A decent patch. Now it's cleaned out.'

The men shook their heads. 'Dunno how that happened. Didn't see anyone around here,' said the man next to Gordon.

'Did any strangers come through? Did you hear anything? There's less than a quarter of a mile between here and my mine,' said Albert. 'You must have seen or heard something.'

'I hope you're not accusing us?' said Gordon, his face starting to redden.

'I'm simply asking if anyone knows anything before I report the theft to the police,' said Albert, turning as Shirley crept forward, putting her little hand into his. Albert glanced down at her. 'I thought I told you to stay in the truck.' But his voice was gentle, so Shirley stayed.

'Better ask Harry over there. His place is nearest yours,' said Gordon. He gave a shrill whistle. 'Harry! Smoko!'

'Did you see the bad men who stole our opals?' Shirley asked Gordon.

'Sorry, girlie. If anyone was in your mine last night, I don't know about it.'

Harry, known on the field as Hopeless, stuck his head out of his tent. 'What's up?'

'The Professor has a question for you,' said Gordon.

Harry clambered out of his tent and ambled across to them. 'Heard you had to hurry into town yesterday. Snake, eh?'

'Seems news gets around. Did you also hear that I'd been ratted?' asked Albert.

'Ratted, eh? Bastards. So you were on opal?' He glanced towards Albert's mine.

'See anyone? Hear anything?' asked Gordon.

'If I did, I wouldn't tangle with them,' said Harry. 'Could be dangerous buggers.'

'But if you heard something, surely you would have raised the alarm?' said Albert grimly.

'Dunno. It wasn't till this morning I was told you and the girlie had gone to town. I thought you were working last night.'

'Last night? You heard working in my mine? I never work at night,' said Albert.

Harry shrugged. 'Gordon said you were heading back east soon. Thought you were having a last go.'

'Did you see anyone, a vehicle?' demanded Albert.

'Heard a truck. Thought you were coming back and working. None of my business,' said Harry.

Albert stared at the tightly closed faces of the men. 'I see. I hope that if any of you get ratted, your mates will be as helpful as you have been to me. Come on, Shirley.'

193

Shirley and her father climbed back into the truck and Albert drove towards their tent.

'Did those men steal our opals, Daddy?'

'I don't know. But they knew it was going on.'

'Are we going to tell a policeman?' asked Shirley.

'I'll report it, but it won't do much good. I'll speak to some of the fellows in town who buy rough and nubs, just in case. But I don't think our opals will be offered around here. Never mind, we'll just have to make the best of it.'

Shirley heard the frustration in his voice and said sadly, 'I'm sorry, Daddy. 'Bout the snake.'

'Oh, sweet pea, I've told you before. It wasn't your fault. These things just can't be helped. Main thing is, you're all right.' He paused. 'I know one thing for sure, though. As soon as we leave the camp, there'll be a bunch of new claims pegged near our mine.'

'What are we going to do, Daddy?'

'We're going home to see Mummy and baby Geoffrey and sell those nobbies and start somewhere else next holidays. That's what we'll do.'

'Will we find more opals in our new mine?' asked Shirley dubiously.

'You know, I think we might try a new place. I've heard about another spot, Opal Lake. Tucked away, past White Cliffs. Might try our luck out there, eh? We both have to work hard at school and then we'll be off. We'll start over, Shirley. If you get knocked down, you get up and start again.'

They packed up their tent and loaded their things into the back of the old truck. As they left, Shirley bent down and picked up a stone and put it into her pocket. It was valueless but it would remain with her for years as a talisman and a reminder that life was not always fair and just.

On the long drive back to the city, Shirley fingered the five beautiful nobbies. Her father told her opals were like a fire that spread and ate you up. Once seen, never forgotten. Like a warm fire on a cold winter's night, they drew you to their fierce and alluring flame. Maybe in this place called Opal Lake they would find more of them.

7

IN THE MOONLIGHT THE two figures, etched black against the silver stretch of the still lake, stood transfixed.

'Remember tonight, Shirley. It might be a long time before you see it like this again,' said Albert softly to his daughter.

'It's like a picture from my fairytale book,' said the little girl, holding her father's hand.

'The big rain this winter finally reached Opal Lake. I don't expect it's been like this for a long time.'

'But it is a lake, so it should have water in it,' said Shirley.

'Out here, in the west, it's very dry and the water only flows after massive rains. It's not often that it gets as far as this lake.'

'Can we stay here till the morning? I want to see it in the daytime.'

'You bet. We can throw down our sleeping bags and I'll fetch some wood and light a little campfire.'

Shirley sighed. 'I'm so glad we came here, Daddy. This is much nicer than that camp at Lightning Ridge.' She stopped, sorry that she'd reminded her father of their ratted mine. Her father had promised he'd find a new place to mine. She hoped these holidays would be better than the last ones. Shirley had worried that her mother wouldn't let them come away again after the episode with the snake, but her mother had been pleased with the beautiful nobbies they'd found, and whatever her father had told her had appeased her enough that she agreed to their coming on another trip.

'I'll get my bag. Are we going to live out here?' asked Shirley, heading for their truck.

'Not here at the lake. Tomorrow we'll head into town and get our claim organised.'

Together they sat at the edge of the shimmering lake, the light from their campfire dancing on the surface of the shallow water.

'It looks really deep. Could there be a huge monster down below, like a dinosaur?'

'Not any more, sweetie. They were here a long time ago.'

'I'd love to see one,' sighed Shirley.

'Well, in the morning we'll have a good look at the lake and see what's out there. Now you snuggle down. It will get chilly later, so I'll put another log on the fire. When we wake up, we'll watch the sun rise. How special will that be?'

'It'll be good, Daddy. Night, night.'

'Sleep tight, sweet pea.'

Shirley wriggled into the kapok padded bag and curled up like a fat caterpillar beside her father. He lowered a log into the embers of the fire and together they

197

watched its small red sparks flare into the sky, matching the stars for brilliance. Sleepily Shirley watched these red jewels sparkle and disappear. They reminded her of the red fire that danced in the heart of opals. She hoped this new place would lead them to more beautiful opals. But for Shirley it was also very, very special to be so far away from home, alone with her father in such a magic spot. She knew she'd always remember this time.

The smell of the fire and the crackling of wood woke her. It was still dark, but the sky was tinged a deep indigo, so she knew that daylight was not too far away. From the warmth of her cocoon she watched her father throw tea leaves into the bubbling billycan. Seeing she was awake Albert smiled at her and lifted the billycan with a thick rag. With an extended arm, he swung the pot of brew around in a circle.

'That'll settle the tea leaves,' he said.

Shirley laughed. 'Do it again, Daddy.' She loved it when her father did one of his campfire tricks.

They toasted thick chunks of bread on a stick and smeared them with golden syrup.

'Here they come, the bridesmaids dancing attendance on the queen, leading her towards her throne in the sky,' said Albert, pointing to the horizon. 'First the ladies in lilac, then rosebud pink and then pale gold.'

Shirley watched the sun rise, its colours running together more quickly, as a cloud of deep scarlet began staining the low sky. 'There it is,' she cried excitedly as the first gold rim of the day glinted over the horizon.

Hugging their mugs of tea, father and daughter sat, dwarfed by the enormity of the pageant marching across the sky. But they were not the only audience. Seemingly from nowhere, thousands of birds began to awaken.

'How do they know about the lake?' whispered Shirley as small birds flitted, others screeched and called, and – presiding over them all – pelicans glided and then splashed to a skidding halt in the shallows. The sky had suddenly come alive with darting birds, and the shining surface of the lake was ruffled as they jostled to find their own stretch of glistening water.

'Unbelievable,' sighed Albert. 'What a magnificent sight. They must have come from miles away. They know, they just know about the water. I don't know how, but it's wonderful.'

After breakfast, as the novelty of the scene wore off, Shirley raced through the shallow water, laughing joyously as flocks of birds rose and resettled. She waded far out into the lake, heeding the warnings of her father to watch out for submerged logs.

'It's so clear, Daddy. I can see everything on the bottom. There's little funny fish in here, too. And tadpoles.'

Eventually Shirley was persuaded that it was time to leave and push on to the tiny township of Opal Lake to find somewhere to stay, get supplies and then take up their claim.

'I've only seen markings on a map, so I don't know what to expect,' Albert told Shirley as the old truck churned through the soft soil towards the faint tracks through the scrub.

The sun was high and hot by the time they saw the small hills and cluster of buildings that marked the little town. Beside one rise they saw what they realised was a deep mine because of its large mullock heaps. On the hills they could see diggings that signified a rabbit warren of mines burrowed into the hillside.

'Looks a bit different from the Ridge.'

'I don't see many camps,' said Shirley. 'And that windlass has two handles.'

'I think that the people here live in their mines rather than in camps,' explained her father.

'Do we have to live in our mine as well?' asked Shirley dubiously.

'We'll be all right in our tent for a bit, but who knows? We might dig out a house in no time at all,' said Albert.

'What if there are opals?' asked Shirley. Then with her eyes alight she added, 'Could we have a house with the roof and all the walls and floor made of opal?'

Her father laughed. 'And anytime you needed money you could just polish the floor by scraping off a layer of gemstone. That's a nice fairytale.'

They stopped at the hotel and introduced themselves. Albert was pointed to the general store where the miners' licences were checked and lodged, and he was given a rough map and a lot of advice.

'How many miners working out here?' he asked.

'Aw, thirty or so,' answered the storekeeper. 'If you're after lodgings, there's a boarding house out at the open-cut. It's basic underground accommodation. Looks a bit like a Roman bath house.' He grinned. 'But it's comfortable enough and Mrs O'Brien cooks for those that want some tucker. We're a good little community. Some are just passing through, but most miners have been here a decent while, times being what they are. We look out for one another.' And he added, 'Troublemakers aren't welcome.'

'I'm pleased to hear it,' said Albert. 'We plan on camping on our claim eventually but maybe for a night or two we'll try the boarding house.'

Shirley was entranced by the doors leading beneath the now abandoned open-cut mine. The boarding house was a basic place. Hollowed-out caverns were turned into rooms, each with a bed, table and shelves. It was relatively clean, if a little dusty and smelling of earth. Mrs O'Brien cooked outside under an iron-roofed shelter and most people ate at the roughly made wooden table.

They spent two days there and while Shirley was

itching to get to their claim and set up their tent, Albert found the time at the underground lodging useful. People were friendly and forthcoming about recent strikes, shared rumours about new fields and the merits of the various buyers who came to Opal Lake. Mrs O'Brien spoilt Shirley with biscuits and one of the men gave her a small light stone that had a decent bit of colour in it. Shirley was polite and thanked him, but she knew that it could not be compared with the black opal her father had found at Lightning Ridge and asked Albert why this opal looked different.

'That's because it was formed in a different sort of rock,' explained her father. 'In Lightning Ridge, the rock is mostly sandstone and the opals are sandwiched between its layers, so that's the only place we find the black opals with the brilliant dark colours and red fire flash in them. Out here, the rock is limestone and it contains a lot of a mineral called calcium. So here, at Opal Lake, we get the light crystal opal, sometimes with lovely colours.'

'Blue and green and gold,' said Shirley.

'But no fire in the stones. The other wonderful thing about calcium deposits is that they can contain lots of fossils, which might become opalised.'

'Are there bones here too?' asked Shirley, thinking of long-dead dinosaurs.

'You never know,' said Albert with a smile.

'Well, I like all opals,' said Shirley firmly.

They set up their tent and campsite on their allotted square, which was a decent-sized claim. What they both also liked about it was the fact that it was on top of the hill with a view all around. Albert immediately levelled the area and started digging straight into the hillside, working back towards the centre of the hill, as others near him had done. A large burly man with a bushy beard and a heavy foreign accent came over and announced that he was Ivan, their neighbour, and offered to show them around his mine.

'I have been here two years,' he said. 'From Russia. I lost my family in the revolution and so I came here. This land is good to me.'

'Have you found any opals?' asked Shirley.

'Shirley, you know that it's rude to ask such questions,' remonstrated her father.

Ivan smiled. 'I have a few. Enough to keep me going. But perhaps I do not explain myself well. This land is good to me because it is a healing place. It is good for my soul. But you are right, little one. We all hope for a big strike so we keep digging. I have made a room as big as a ballroom in the palace in Leningrad.' He chuckled. 'Do you plan to live out here?' he asked Albert, glancing at Shirley.

'Only in the school holidays. I'm a schoolteacher. But if Opal Lake is as nice as it seems, we'll come as often as we can whether we find opal or not.'

'And if we make it really nice, Mummy and Geoffrey can come too,' added Shirley.

'If you need any help, I am at your service,' said the big Russian.

'That's very kind of you,' said Albert.

The other locals were equally hospitable, without being intrusive. Indeed, Albert and his daughter felt part of this small community in a very short time, sharing with the other inhabitants the privations and pleasures of life in a remote dot of landscape, united by their dreams of finding the precious gem.

So when Albert hit a small patch of relatively good opal, everyone was pleased for them. Although the seam petered out quickly, the burst of excitement created by his find raised everyone's hopes.

'When we sell the opal what will we do with the money?' Shirley asked her father.

'Not everything we find is going to end up being sold. The buyer only offers us a price based on what he thinks can be cut from our rough. He has to take a bit of a punt. But he'll make a fair offer for the bulk of our parcel,' said Albert confidently, and resumed swinging his pick.

The limestone was firm and solid and the mine didn't need wooden supports or a pillar in the central area to hold up the roof. But one day, as he tunnelled towards the west of the mine, Albert's pickaxe hit a point that was fragile and a seam suddenly split and opened up, rocks, clay and debris spilling into the drive.

He jumped back as Shirley cried out in alarm, 'Run, Daddy!'

'I'm all right, possum.' He headed back into the small cavern where Shirley had been filling a bucket. 'But I don't think we'll work down in that direction anymore. There seems to be a problem along there that we'd be better off not digging into.'

Albert and Shirley had decided on a plan for their dugout. Essentially it was a simple design with a main central room and a couple of smaller basic ones on the eastern side, with a bit of terrace out in the front from which to survey their view. They decided that if an opal find led in another direction, they would just have to build an additional drive.

The nights were cold so, when the mine was big enough, Albert dragged their sleeping bags into the entrance. There they were warmer and could still look out at the deserted landscape below, stark in the starlight. Occasionally a dingo howled. Sometimes in the morning, they found the footprints of a goanna that had been prowling for any scraps in their camp. In spite of her encounter with the snake, Shirley was unafraid of the lizards that roamed the arid country around them. Some of them were dainty, little bright-eyed ones, but others were larger, like the bearded dragons.

Ivan told Shirley the story of a reclusive old Scotsman who'd had a mine in the area many years before and was too mean to buy food and used to cook goannas over the fire like the Aborigines did.

'Oh, the poor things. What happened to the man? Did he find opals and buy proper food?' asked Shirley.

'If he found opals, he never sold them. He had a wild old horse and he used to ride him at night. People thought that he was out hiding his opals, but he died all alone and no one ever found them.'

'You hear a lot of stories of men not wanting to part with their opals,' said Albert.

Ivan touched his head. 'I think some of them went a bit crazy. Opal fever can do that, eh?'

The days passed too quickly, but it was time enough for Shirley and Albert to feel they had found a second home. Rugged up by the fire they talked about the future and how they could work the mine as long as it was fruitful and then turn their dugout into a home base and work another claim.

'I'll just keep this claim registered as our mine until the day comes when we can buy it outright,' said Albert.

'Could we, Daddy? Then I would feel even better when I come out here. I so wish Mummy would come. Maybe one day we can make the cave like a real house. Then she'll come,' said Shirley.

'Yes, perhaps, and baby Geoffrey. But until then, you and I will just have to come when we can.' He winked at her. 'Even if we don't find much in the way of opal, Opal Lake's a pretty good place to be, eh?'

Shirley nodded conspiratorially. 'Yes. But it's still nice to find opal!'

*

Kerrie gazed around Shirley's cosy, if cluttered, dugout. 'So this is the mine you started with your father?'

Shirley smiled. 'Indeed it is. I can say I've had a hand in building my home. Every mark on every wall in that front section was made by my father. Later, when I moved out here permanently, I had some help to extend it a bit.'

'How long have you been living here, Shirley?'

'I've been here for more than thirty years and before that I lived in Lightning Ridge. My father sold the opals we found when we first came here and he put the money aside to continue paying for the lease on this place. When he died I wasn't surprised to find that he'd bequeathed it to me. I had a good job so I continued making payments on it, but I didn't come back out here for many years.'

'Why didn't you come out here earlier?'

'I had my own life and career, and I was so close to my father and we had shared such a special time together. We only had that one trip out here. I knew it just wouldn't be the same here without him. But eventually I came.'

'Did your father ever come back here?' asked Kerrie. 'He obviously loved it as much as you did.'

'No. He didn't. The war came along, Mother had another baby, and within a few years he was made headmaster of his school. Then there were the twins. He always said that he wanted to return to Opal Lake, but there just never seemed to be the opportunity. I think it was in my father's mind that when he retired and all his children were independent he would then have the freedom to reopen the mine.'

'It never happened?' asked Kerrie gently.

'My father passed away just before he retired. It seemed so unfair.'

'Oh, I see. And you were working?'

'I had a pretty demanding job. As you know, I trained as a nurse. I was very dedicated to my profession and I

moved up the ranks to become the ward sister in the orthopedic unit of one of the top teaching hospitals in Sydney.
My work had long hours and a lot of responsibility.'

'I suppose that didn't leave much time for a social
life,' said Kerrie.

'I had a few flings, but no one ever really caught my
fancy. I liked a young doctor once, but to him I was just a
good nurse – I don't think the idea of asking me out would
have occurred to him. Actually, most of the doctors I worked
with for years didn't know a single thing about my personal
life, and absolutely nothing about me,' said Shirley.

'I suppose patients were hung up in those traction
contraptions for ages in orthopedic wards in those days,'
said Kerrie. 'Not like now, when they have you walking
around as soon as possible.'

Shirley smiled. 'That's right. I've seen a lot of changes
in my profession. I still keep in touch with some of my old
nursing friends with emails through my great whacking
box of a computer,' she said. 'It's pretty ancient. No one
seems to use floppy discs anymore.'

'Shirley! You have to update!' laughed Kerrie. 'Let me
help you.'

'That would be kind of you. I tend to handwrite a
lot of notes and my diaries and letters, and I'm still going
through research material, but I know that eventually I'll
have to type it all up into some sort of order.'

'Tell me, Shirley, why did you came back here?' asked
Kerrie.

Shirley gazed into the distance. Kerrie had the impression this was a time deep in her memory, and that Shirley
was recalling the place, the weather and the moment when
she returned to Opal Lake.

'I thought it was the start of a new life,' she said
wistfully.

'Why was that?'

'Because I thought that I had finally found the person that I would spend the rest of my life with.'

Kerrie looked at Shirley, startled by the vehemence of her words.

'I met him when he was a patient in my ward. Badly crushed legs and broken ribs. He was there for several months.'

'I suppose you get to know people well under those circumstances,' said Kerrie. And waited.

Finally Shirley nodded. 'Initially I was a bit bothered by the ethics of it – my profession being a nurse – and yet I was drawn to a man with whom I had something in common.'

'Why was that? Can you tell me about him? What was his name?' asked Kerrie.

If Shirley had been reluctant to speak initially, words now tumbled out.

'His name was Stefan. He was Croatian. He migrated from Yugoslavia during Tito's regime and, sadly, left his parents behind. I think he always felt guilty about that, even though they had insisted that he leave. Stefan was educated at the university in Zagreb. He was an engineer. He came to Australia as a refugee. No family support, no money and very poor English initially. He didn't feel that he fitted in.'

'So you met him in your hospital ward? What was he like?'

'When I first saw him he was not a pretty picture,' said Shirley.

Sydney, early 1970s

His eyes were squeezed tightly shut in pain. But sensing her presence, he opened one of them, struggled to focus, and then greeted her.

'Good morning, sister.'

'And to you, Mr Doric.' She stood beside his bed, checking the tension of the apparatus supporting his right leg. As he winced, she said, 'It won't be long now and you'll be out of this.'

'That will be a relief.' He tried to smile. 'It will be good to get out of this bed. My back is so sore.'

'It must be lonely for you, all these weeks in traction. You never seem to have any visitors.'

'I have acquaintances but they are not living in Sydney. I have received a few messages from them.'

'Checking up on you? That you're still alive and kicking?' asked Shirley with a smile.

He looked at her in surprise at this bald statement and then smiled. 'Ah, the Australian sense of humour. I suppose that might be true.'

'Would you like some books?' asked Shirley suddenly. 'Do you enjoy reading? I'd be happy to lend you some, if you like. Tell me what you enjoy, and what your interests are. I'm a big reader,' she added enthusiastically.

'You would do that for me?'

Shirley nodded. 'Of course. I'll make a selection for you and drop them by. You can choose which ones you'd like.'

'You are very kind. Thank you.'

'That is my pleasure. But you need to get out in the fresh air. I don't think that you'll be in traction much longer,' said Shirley, glancing at the notes that hung at the foot of the bed. 'And then I'll see if one of the nurses can take you into the grounds in a wheelchair.'

He closed his eyes and sighed. 'That sounds wonderful. Thank you, sister.'

It was several days, however, before he was freed of the weights and pulleys that had kept him bedridden. He lay there, staring at one of his legs which was still plastered. He was surprised when Shirley arrived wearing an attractive skirt and blouse, and pushing a wheelchair.

'We're very short on staff, so here I am.'

Stefan was shocked. 'I did not expect this. I don't want you to go to any trouble for me.'

'Since I'm off duty, I thought that a bit of exercise would do me good. I've brought you some books, too.' She pulled them from her basket and put them beside his bed.

With professional expertise she helped him from his bed into the wheelchair, his plastered leg stretched out in front of him. She put a light blanket over him and placed her basket on his lap.

'Hang on to that. It's got a few snacks in it.'

The grounds of the hospital were quiet and leafy despite being surrounded by offices and old homes. As they trundled along the broad path they heard only the squeak of the wheelchair and the chatter of birds in the spreading trees above them. Shirley turned off the path and bumped over the gravel to a sheltered spot hidden from view by their thick trunks. Sitting in the dappled sunlight beneath the branches were a bench and table.

'This is one of my secret spots. I often bring my lunch here. It's always restful,' said Shirley. 'Are you comfortable?'

He lifted his face to the sunlight and took a deep breath. 'Indescribable. Wonderful.' He turned to Shirley. 'I cannot thank you enough. I thought that I would never feel the sun again.'

'Don't mention it. It's pleasant for me too.'

'You do seem to work long hours. You are always in the ward,' commented Stefan. 'I hear your voice even if I don't see you.'

'Barking orders? I try not to crack the whip too hard, but some of the nurses are too timid or too slow and they have so much to learn. Still, their hearts are in the right place, so I shouldn't whinge.'

'Whinge. That is a new word. It means to . . . complain?' guessed Stefan.

Shirley laughed. 'Yes. In the Aussie vernacular. Now, cup of coffee? I brought a thermos. Hope you like it strong.'

'Yes, I do. When I first came to this country, it was difficult to get proper coffee. But I won't whinge,' said Stefan.

Shirley laughed as she handed him the coffee. 'Good. And I grabbed a couple of sandwiches from the cafeteria. Ham or corned beef?'

They sipped their coffee and sat in contemplative silence. Stefan threw crumbs to several pigeons on the ground beside them. Shirley felt comfortable with Stefan. She didn't feel the need to make superficial conversation for he was so obviously enjoying the simplicity of the fresh air and sunshine. They finished their sandwiches and Shirley scrunched up the greaseproof paper and packed up the basket.

'What books did you bring for me?' asked Stefan. 'I am looking forward to reading them.'

'A mixture. Donald Horne's book about Australia, called *The Lucky Country*. A very funny book written a few years ago by John O'Grady about the life of an Italian migrant. And then there's *I, the Aboriginal*, by Douglas Lockwood.'

'So has an Aboriginal written his autobiography?' asked Stefan.

Shirley smiled. 'Not exactly, he told it to Douglas Lockwood. It's about an Aboriginal man who crossed from his traditional culture to the white man's world in the 1950s. Reading his story will give you a wider knowledge of what is happening to Aborigines in Australia, if you're interested in that sort of thing.'

'I don't have a lot of knowledge about Aboriginal people. It is very hard to meet them. I hear conflicting stories,' he added diplomatically. 'So I would like to read more.'

'Indeed. Maybe we can talk more about it later, when you've read the book.'

'You have been very kind to me.' Stefan hesitated. 'Do I call you Sister Mason?'

'No, of course not. I'm Shirley.'

He studied her. 'You are very clever, very kind. Why are you helping me?' he said. 'I am nobody.'

'Don't say that. I know a lot about you, and it seems that we have something in common.' She smiled at his raised eyebrow. 'I gather, from your records, that you were in a mining accident in Lightning Ridge.' He nodded and she went on. 'I am very fond of Lightning Ridge and the opal fields. I went there with my father when I was a little girl.'

Stefan's face broke into a huge smile. 'Is that so? Were you mining for opals?'

'Indeed. We found some beautiful opals but our mine was ratted. My father was really angry.'

Stefan shook his head. 'Terrible, terrible thing. It still goes on. In fact, the ratters are quite organised now. How long since you have been back to the Ridge?'

'Too long. It was my father's dream that when he retired he would take up opal mining again. Actually, after the ratting incident, we moved to Opal Lake. He took up a lease there and we always planned to go back, but, well, life gets in the way. The war, family, work, and then my father died before he retired, so he never had the chance to fulfil his dreams, but I've sort of inherited them.'

'You would go back to the opal fields? To mine? To live?' asked Stefan in surprise.

'I've got a good job here at the hospital, a lot of

responsibility,' said Shirley. 'But I still have the lease on my father's mine and sometimes I think about going back. Finding opal was very exciting.'

'Oh, I know that very well. Even though this accident was terrible, I can't wait to return.'

'I've read the report of the accident, but it's a bit sketchy. What happened exactly?' asked Shirley.

Stefan picked up his mug of coffee and curled his hands around it, looked thoughtful, then drew a breath and began to speak as if it was a great relief to tell his story. 'I was living in Sydney, working for another Yugoslav as a builder's labourer, but I started to hear about people heading to the outback, looking for minerals and finding a fortune. I thought my engineering background might help me.'

'Did you make any big mineral discoveries?'

He shook his head. 'No. I didn't even get very far out west because I heard about some big opal fields that were doing well, so I went to Lightning Ridge. It is an extraordinary place and I liked it. I found an Australian partner. It made the work faster and easier. We were working in an old, large mine that had been abandoned, but we were sure that it hadn't been worked out. It was a pretty big excavation, and we had some machinery so my partner wanted to tunnel in further, but I was concerned about the weight bearings. I told him that we needed to put in wooden supports.'

Shirley nodded. 'Yes, yes. I know what you mean.'

'I went to get some timber, but when I came back my partner was going crazy, digging at the stone pillar that was holding up the roof. He said that he'd found some colour and he knew that he was going to find good opal.'

'I can see it.'

Stefan held up his hands in a gesture of dismay. 'I shouted out, "What do you think you're doing?" And he said there was good opal. And the next minute I heard a crack, like a groan, a sigh from the earth, and I realised what was going to happen. I dropped the timber and ran, calling to him to get out, too.'

'And the pillar broke?'

Stefan's face grimaced at the memory. 'I will never forget that sound. The roof collapsed and, although I ran as fast as I could, the edge of the cave-in landed on me.' He paused. 'They dug me out with a crushed leg, but my partner . . . well, he died with his opals.'

Shirley was quiet a moment. 'Men cheat and thieve and die for opals. For some it is a passion, an obsession, that never goes away. And so you will go back.'

Stefan smiled at her. 'I see that you understand. And you already know the answer.'

Shirley smiled at Kerrie as she reminisced.

They had finished the wine, so Kerrie put the kettle on for a cup of tea. While she was waiting for it to boil, she pulled her sketchpad from her bag. 'May I sketch you, Shirley?'

'Me? Goodness. Whatever for? But go ahead.'

Kerrie was fascinated by the changing expressions on Shirley's weatherworn face. While Shirley talked, Kerrie made a pencil drawing of her face, which softened as she continued her story, strands of grey hair escaping from the twisted knot on top of her head.

'That was how it started,' said Shirley. 'We found we had so much to talk about. I was keen to hear how Lightning Ridge had changed, the new fields and finds that had happened. I told him about Opal Lake, and the little dugout that my father had made, which now belonged to me. We talked and talked over the next few weeks as he recovered from the mining accident, and I found that I had a lot to think about.'

'What happened when Stefan left hospital?' asked Kerrie.

Shirley smiled.

'Well, that looks to be it, Mr Doric. When you've seen the bursar downstairs to settle your account, you're free to go. I bet you'll be pleased to see the end of us. If you want to, you can get a taxi from the front of the main building.'

'Thank you, Nurse. I'll take Mr Doric downstairs as I'm headed that way,' said Shirley as she appeared in the doorway of the ward.

'Yes, sister. Goodbye, Mr Doric, good luck.' The nurse hurried out the door, giving Shirley an odd look.

Shirley smiled. 'I couldn't let you leave my ward without a final goodbye.'

Stefan had plaster on his ankle but was moving about quite well on crutches, although he was having some trouble holding his small bag. He looked at Shirley. 'So this is where we re-enter our own worlds.'

'That's one way of putting it . . . If you like, we could continue our friendship. You'll be in Sydney for a bit longer and I could see you again,' said Shirley bluntly. 'To continue our book discussions. I've enjoyed them.'

Relief swept over Stefan's face. 'I would enjoy that, too. Is it always part of your job to be so nice to patients?'

Shirley smiled. 'No, Stefan, I can't think of another patient I've paid this much attention to.'

'Shirley, this is very important to me. We have enjoyed talking and spending time together. When I am able, would you allow me to take you out somewhere? I can manage the crutches quite well, so I want to take you somewhere that's my idea.'

'So you don't feel like an invalid,' said Shirley gently. 'Yes, Stefan, I'd like that.'

Shirley was glad she was in her starched uniform, for it gave her a sense of normality when, in fact, her heart was racing, and she felt flushed and distracted. It had taken some time for her to admit how she felt about Stefan and how much she enjoyed spending time with the gentle and intelligent Croatian. At first the attraction had simply been based on the link with her past, and their shared knowledge of the lure of the opal fields, but their conversations had expanded and taken them into territory as diverse as history, astronomy, zoology and music. They found that, while they had many things in common, their differences seemed an invitation to learn more about each other.

As Shirley walked slowly with him towards the lift, he said, 'Would dinner one evening suit you? Tell me when you are free.'

Shirley concentrated on the lift button, glad that he couldn't see her face. 'How ridiculous I am,' she thought. 'I feel like a sixteen year old.'

She had given up the idea of ever finding a man who attracted her. At forty she'd resigned herself to not finding anyone to whom she could relate but here was Stefan, the same age as she was, single, extremely good looking and clearly interested in her.

And so began the courtship of Shirley Mason. The nurses on her ward watched her transformation in some astonishment. She now seemed softer, happier. She was no longer available to work long, late, extra shifts, as she'd done before.

'Do you really think she has a man?' asked one.

'I think that she's been picky and scared men off. Mind you, I've seen her out of uniform and she's attractive, if she gets her hair done,' commented another. 'But I bet she'll fall heavily since she's left her run so late.'

'I wonder who he is?'

'I heard she was a bit keen on that Yugoslav fellow that had the mining accident. I never thought she'd fall for a patient. She's always been so professional and kept her distance.'

'Ooh, he was handsome. But I'm not sure about these foreigners.'

If Shirley suspected she was being gossiped about, she ignored it. Away from work she felt like a young woman, for the relationship between her and Stefan had grown into a full-blown romance. They went to the movies and out to dinner, Shirley gently helping him to walk as the strength in his legs returned. They talked easily and at length about everything under the sun. But as soon as he was walking with greater confidence, he began to plan his return to Lightning Ridge.

When Stefan discussed leaving, Shirley was shocked by her sense of loss and the passionate feelings he had aroused in her. She had fallen deeply in love.

'I'll miss you,' she finally confessed. 'Stefan, I've never felt like this before. Am I being silly?' She turned to him and he kissed her with equal longing.

'If I find a large parcel of opals . . . would you come and join me?' he asked hesitantly.

'Yes. I would,' said Shirley firmly. And suddenly she knew that that was what she wanted to do.

She could take long-service leave. She could resign. She could start a new life. She knew she had to grasp this opportunity with both hands as fast and as hard as she could.

Her whole world seemed changed. The settled life she'd imagined herself leading until she retired was now shaken and stirred. She'd never seen herself with a partner and had assumed that she'd missed the boat. But now she couldn't believe what had happened to her, how her feelings for Stefan continued to grow and almost overwhelm

216

her. Never, ever, did she believe that she would fall so utterly, totally, blindly in love. Things like this didn't happen to her. Had never happened. She felt like a silly adolescent.

She couldn't stop smiling. When she woke each morning, instead of leaping straight out of bed to head to work, she rolled over and hugged her pillow as the foggy, erotic dreams of Stefan cleared and she knew that she hadn't imagined him, that he was real flesh and blood. How had this wonderful, handsome, sexy man fallen into her life? She knew that he loved her back with equal passion and tenderness.

She moved through the days at the hospital as if by rote, years of training setting her on autopilot, while she relived every moment of the last time she'd been with Stefan. She savoured the smallest details, the expression in his eyes, the touch of his hands, his lips, the gentle caresses, how he softly sang a Croatian love song to her. If this was love, then it had all been worth waiting for.

As she soaped her body in the shower, she eyed herself critically. She had good legs, firm large breasts and a nicely defined waistline. She'd never considered herself beautiful or even pretty like some of the young nurses that she had worked with, and she'd never fussed over the latest hairdos or fashions, for there had been no one to impress. But Stefan told her that he liked her healthy naturalness and assured her that she was extremely attractive.

Nonetheless when they weren't together she felt as though she was only existing, marking time, until she was with Stefan, reassured by his presence that he was real and that he loved her. Shirley sometimes wondered if she was going crazy and whether she would eventually come back down to earth, even though she never wanted these intense and unfamiliar, but wonderful, emotions to leave her.

One Sunday afternoon after they'd been to see a French film, where she discovered that Stefan spoke French quite well, they made love back at Shirley's place.

Afterwards as he stubbed out his cigarette, he said, 'I have to leave, I will call you and see you soon. I promised Miro I would help him.'

'Your builder friend? The one you used to work for?'

'Yes. He used to be an architect in the old country, but now he makes cheap houses that he despises. But it is a living.' He kissed her long and ardently, finally pulling away with a slight smile. 'Ah, Shirley, Shirley. If I don't leave now you'll tempt me again.'

She watched him walk down the path to the front gate, so straight and tall, although he still moved a little stiffly. His shoulders were broad, stretching the fabric of his flannel shirt, but his back tapered to a narrow waist and slim hips. His long legs, in faded jeans, ended in the soft leather loafers that he favoured. While he dressed casually, he had an air, a style about him. The way he carried himself suggested that he was unaware of his own good looks.

She could picture his light blue-green eyes, his chestnut hair, and feel his smooth olive skin that a short time before had excited her as she'd clutched his naked body to her own. As though he could sense her eyes burning into him, Stefan turned, blew her a kiss and flashed her a wide smile.

She hated to see him leave. Shirley wondered what he was doing every moment he was away from her. Wrapping her cotton robe around her bare skin she went back to the table where two wineglasses stood beside the remains of a meal. She picked up the cigarette he hadn't finished and, even though she didn't smoke, placed it between her lips, trying to retrieve his kiss.

'I'm going crazy,' she thought. 'I can't go on like this. I'll have to go with him.'

*

218

'You are sure you wish to come away with me?' Stefan asked Shirley for the umpteenth time. 'You know the accommodation and lifestyle is very rough in Lightning Ridge, although we can stay in a shack belonging to another of my countrymen who has gone to South Australia to try his luck there.' Stefan held Shirley's hands and gazed into her eyes, making her tremble.

She didn't care what the conditions were like at Lightning Ridge. All she wanted was to be with him twenty-four hours a day. She hoped he wasn't having second thoughts. 'Stefan, I do remember what it's like out there. And it doesn't matter. So long as we are together.'

He smiled. 'I agree. But you are a beautiful, talented lady of good standing. Not like some of the women who come out to the Ridge. I mean, they have good hearts and are hard workers, but they aren't like my Shirley.'

'I have never forgotten how much I loved the opal fields. Not just the hunt for opals, but the lifestyle, the space and beauty. Why do you think I kept up the payments on my father's lease for so long? Because one day I knew I'd return,' she said. 'And I can't think of anything more romantic than to be out there with you.'

'Everyone will be very surprised when I come back with someone as lovely as you.'

Shirley tilted her head and studied him. 'Stefan, why me? Why haven't you found someone else before now?'

He shrugged. 'Who is to say how these things happen? Perhaps if I were still in my own country, I might have settled down. But in Australia I like the freedom that prospecting gives me. I am not an office person. And you say, why you? Because, my Shirley, you are warm and kind and loving. You are intelligent and educated, so we can talk and you make me laugh.' He leant over and kissed her lightly. 'And, you are like me.'

'You think so?' She looked at him quizzically.

'Yes. I think so. We might come from different backgrounds but I think we enjoy the same things, we have similar beliefs and desires, we enjoy each other's company and we love opals, so perhaps that is why I will give up my independence for you.'

'Oh, well, that clinches it, doesn't it!' laughed Shirley.

Shirley followed Stefan out to the opal fields a month after he left. As each kilometre disappeared beneath the car tyres, Shirley's excitement, and anxiety, grew. But as soon as she drove into Lightning Ridge she felt a huge sense of relief and calm. And as she pulled up to the Hidden Opal Café, where they'd arranged to meet, Shirley saw Stefan sitting at a small table outside, reading a newspaper, his long legs stretched in front of him. This was the man who was waiting for her to join him to start a new adventure together. Tears sprang to her eyes and she pulled the car up to the kerb behind a lorry so he couldn't see her.

Composing herself, she slid from behind the wheel and strolled to where Stefan was immersed in his paper. Shirley was almost at the table before he glanced up. He immediately jumped to his feet and in two strides had his arms around her, holding her tightly.

'You are late. I was getting worried that something had happened to you, or that you had changed your mind.' Before she could answer, he kissed her, and then kissed her again with such intensity that she felt as though he was drawing her into him.

Shirley was shaking. 'I'm sorry, but there was a truck that lost its load of sheep. Held me up. As if I wouldn't come,' she said breathlessly.

'Come and sit down, have a cup of coffee. Where's the car? You must be tired after such a long drive.'

She nodded, suddenly feeling shy, though she knew that was ridiculous.

He ordered coffee and sat back, holding her hand across the table. 'How do you feel?'

'Nervous. Silly, I know.' She gave a small smile. 'But I've never run away with a man before.'

'Not any man. This is me, Stefan.' He squeezed her hand.

Shirley shook her head. On the drive out, she'd wondered if she'd made him up, whether he really was too good to be true. Yet here he was, impossibly handsome, strong, gentle and with an expression of joy as he looked at her. As the coffee and a sandwich were placed before her, she realised how hungry she was.

'I'm starving. I was so anxious to get here, I left at dawn and I didn't stop for lunch. And now here I am.'

She sipped the coffee, took a bite of the sandwich and looked around the town. 'There are a lot more buildings than I remember when I was here before as a little girl. I'm looking forward to exploring the place. Where are you living?'

'Where are *we* living,' he corrected her. 'Two streets away. It's a pleasant walk. I hope you'll be comfortable. It's a simple house, but I think it's better than living out on the diggings.'

'I'm sure it will be fine,' said Shirley. 'How's the mine going?'

'I've cleared out the rubble. Got things working again, and it's all propped up, so it's safe. I've had a bit of a scratch around, but I have found nothing, yet. I'm waiting for my lucky girl to be with me.'

'I hope I am lucky,' said Shirley. 'Dad always thought I was.'

'Well, shall we go home?'

The words made Shirley feel excited again. 'I hope

I settle down and get used to this,' she chided herself, as Stefan took her hand.

It was a small house with a dusty front yard filled with Stefan's mining equipment and an old truck. Inside, the one-bedroom cottage was spotless, and Shirley was touched when she saw a vase filled with sprigs of gum leaves and flowering wattle.

'I think we will be comfortable here,' said Stefan. 'We can go to the bowling club for dinner tonight, if you're not too tired.'

'I'm just fine . . . now.' Shirley held out her arms and they embraced, then he picked her up and carried her into the bedroom.

Within a week, Shirley couldn't imagine her life being any better than it was now. It was as if everything that had gone before had just been waiting for her real life to start. To wake each morning and find herself cuddled up to Stefan, to hear the music of a butcher bird in the tree outside, to feel the warmth of the sun and know the day was theirs to fill as they wished was bliss beyond her imaginings.

Before they went to the mine, Stefan tidied the house while Shirley walked to the shops. She was now on nodding acquaintance with the people who seemed to be always seated on their small front verandahs watching the world go by. The woman who ran the little supermarket had quickly accepted her as Shirl, Stefan's lady friend from Sydney.

'People are friendly,' she said to Stefan.

'Perhaps for someone like you, but for a migrant like me people are not always so friendly.'

'You don't feel you belong here?' she asked.

They were sitting on the bank of the Narran River, fishing, having driven out to the small township of Angledool for the afternoon.

Stefan cast his line and sat down. 'In Australia? Or Lightning Ridge?'

'Both I suppose,' said Shirley slowly. 'I've never really thought about what it must be like to have left your family and your country. Surely it doesn't mean that when you come to a place like this, that's peaceful and friendly, and where you have a future, that you can't embrace it?'

'I know people who have married and started their own family in Australia. But it's not always easy. You want to share your culture, your faith, your family and your childhood friends with people who have similar ties. The people who know who you are.' He suddenly leant over and put his arm around Shirley's shoulders. 'That's not to say I can't share my life with you,' he added quickly. 'Since being here at the Ridge I've found we are a community, but of strangers. Maybe it has something to do with the landscape. It is so enormous. This space can be frightening. At home people know each other's family history but here friendships seem more superficial. We prefer to drink beer together, laugh and slap each other on the back and talk about the weather and call everyone mate.'

'You're making me feel sad that I can't give you the depth of friendship you're looking for,' said Shirley.

'But you do! You have filled my life, my new life. I have never been so happy.'

'Stefan, why don't you tell me more about your life in Croatia? Everything you can remember, your family, your grandparents, stories your mother told you, what you did at school, your first job. Everything. Then I'll know you better and will understand you better, too.'

He smiled. 'And I also want to know everything about you.'

'I'm really boring. I haven't escaped from an oppressive communist regime or had the adventures you've had. I've told you about my father and me coming out here.

223

Really, mining for opals with my father when I was a little girl seems to have made the biggest impact. When you are the first to see an opal after it has been buried for millions of years it's a defining moment. You must know what I mean.'

'I do, and in spite of what I have said, I do like this place. I love the space and freedom,' said Stefan.

'And the fish!' cried Shirley as her fishing rod suddenly bent and she concentrated on reeling in a good-sized yellowbelly.

'Good girl! Now we have something for our dinner!'

'I was hoping to catch one of those big old elusive cods. But this will do nicely,' said Shirley.

Late in the afternoon, they lit a campfire and Shirley cooked the fish while Stefan tied a tarpaulin between the side of the truck and two poles, to act as a shelter over their sleeping bags. Both found that they liked sleeping outdoors, and it amused Shirley to think that although they lived in a shack, they preferred to be under the stars.

The mine was a fifteen-minute drive from their house. Shirley enjoyed the familiarity that swept over her the minute she climbed down the shaft to the cool quiet chamber where Stefan was digging. The huge underground area was now safely supported by wooden props, and Stefan had started a new drive. Shirley enjoyed working with him, labouring as hard as any man.

'You don't have to work so hard,' Stefan told her as he kissed her dusty face.

'I know that. But I love being here with you. Shall we have a bet on who finds colour first?'

'You Australians love to gamble! You're on!' he laughed.

After a few weeks, Shirley felt she'd been with Stefan for years. They worked together from early morning into the evening, often losing track of time. They shared the cooking and household routine and rarely saw anyone else. They could work in different sections of the mine, because Stefan had rigged up an automatic self-tipping hoist. After the bucket was filled, the cable that pulled the bucket up the ladder onto the framework at the top of the mine could be tripped, so that the dirt was tipped to one side while the bucket fell back into the mine.

'When I think of the number of times my father had to climb up and down the mine ladder to get rid of the dirt, he would have loved a contraption like this,' said Shirley.

And then Shirley won their bet.

'Stef! Come here!' As he hurriedly joined her, she pointed her small pick at the face. 'See, colour! Beautiful colour.'

'Clever, darling. Go slowly. It's good blue-green,' he said. 'Let's hope there's more of it.'

After the initial show there was nothing till Stefan found a narrow seam of black opal above the sandstone layer. It took them an hour or more to gently dig out the small channel of opal.

'I think we both win the bet,' said Shirley. 'I suppose it's hard for you to tell how good it's going to be till it's cut.'

'Let's keep going,' said Stefan.

For the rest of the day, and lying together in bed that evening, with the rough opals carefully hidden, they talked and talked. They discussed cutting and selling and the what ifs.

'If we find a big patch do we travel? Buy a house, buy shares? What do you want?' Stefan asked Shirley.

'Buy better equipment. A digger and a front-end loader,' said Shirley briskly.

Stefan laughed.

They told no one about their find, but to celebrate

they decided to go to the bowling club the following night for dinner. There they were stopped by Bosko, the self-styled leader of the Yugoslav community. Stefan had pointed him out to Shirley on an earlier occasion and told her how much he disliked the loud and aggressive Serb.

'So this is why you have been keeping away from us,' exclaimed Bosko, shaking Stefan's hand while looking Shirley up and down.

'I'm just working. I have to go slowly since my accident,' replied Stefan.

'But not so slow that you don't have a woman working with you?' Bosko chortled heartily.

'This is my friend Shirley. She is a nursing sister.'

'You now have your own private nurse to look after you! Lucky man, looks like she is doing a good job, eh?'

Shirley held out her hand. 'Good evening. I'm working with Stefan. We are partners.'

Shirley's cool demeanour and tone of voice momentarily silenced the big man. He shook her hand, then, dismissing her with a curt nod, immediately turned back to Stefan.

'Why do you not come to the baths? We are all missing you. Come tomorrow. Just because you have a woman you shouldn't turn away from your friends. Your compadres, eh?'

Stefan felt Shirley stiffen with annoyance, so he said, non-committally, 'I might do that. *Dovidenja*, goodbye.'

As soon as they were out of earshot he said grimly to Shirley, 'This is a man's town, and he thinks he is king. Bosko's always going on about how hard migrants work while Australians are lazy but in fact Bosko is – what is your expression – a sponger?'

'You mean he lets other people do the hard work and he takes the credit and, I bet, the spoils?'

'There are a lot of rumours, but no one says anything

openly. Anyway, ignore him and don't let him spoil our dinner.'

'Are you really going to the bore baths tomorrow?' asked Shirley.

'If you don't mind, I might. It's a tradition and although I rarely go, I don't want to alienate all my countrymen; some of them are good people. And I might find out news from the old country.'

'If you think you should go, then of course, go.'

Shirley had heard about the open-air artesian hot-water baths. Locals congregated there to ease their aches and pains, gossip and get spruced up as many working in the bush camps had little access to water.

'I would invite you but when all the Yugo men are there together they tend to take over. The baths are a bit like the pub bar. Everyone boasts and talks too much. Probably that's because people live and work in isolation when they're mining,' said Stefan. 'There are more philosophers, poets and politicians out here than anywhere else I've been.'

'What do you all talk about in the baths?' asked Shirley.

He shrugged. 'It's a chance for them all to speak their language and that way no one else understands what's being said. I like it when someone reports recent news from home but they all just want to rehash the old days. They sing the old songs and talk about the old country. They have no curiosity about Australia or interest in its history or culture.'

'It takes more than buildings and a succession of wars to make a country,' said Shirley. 'They might be surprised if they opened their eyes and their minds. Our history comes from the continent itself, the landscape, and the opportunities for people to carve their own paths, using their skills and knowledge. Surely working out here they'd see that,' she said tartly.

'Exactly. Australia has taken them in, given them opportunities that they can't get back in Yugoslavia. Yet here they stick together as a group with their old prejudices and disputes, the same hates and grievances and, I am ashamed to say, I don't trust some of them, either.'

'But you don't want to alienate them,' said Shirley.

'No. So I suffer their criticisms of Australia as being a cultural desert, while they elaborate on the greatness of Europe and forget that many of them came from peasant villages.'

'It must be stultifying being lumbered with thousands of years of history,' said Shirley. 'Here, in Australia, you have the opportunity to be creative and original without the burden of the past. This country is like a clean slate and I'll tell that to Bosko if he starts to criticise Australia to me.'

Stefan smiled at her. 'You are clever, and I love you, but please, never argue with that man. He's not only arrogant, he's dangerous. Now let's forget about him and go and order dinner.'

Shirley sighed. 'Opals brought us together, and . . . well, that's the end of the story.' Her expression hardened, her mellow look was gone in a flash.

Kerrie flipped a page and began sketching the change in Shirley's face. 'That's the end of the story? Surely not. You and Stefan were in love, working together in Lightning Ridge. What happened?'

Shirley didn't answer for a moment and turned away, staring at the wall where a map of Opal Lake hung. 'I wish I knew. I really wish I knew.'

8

SHIRLEY AND STEFAN SAT beside their shaft in the sunshine, bent over the bucketful of 'possibles' they'd washed in their puddler, which was an old cement mixer. Filled with water, it tumbled the dirt from the stones so that any colour in them was more noticeable. While a lot of the stones were just potch, worthless colour with no gemquality opal, Shirley still found it fascinating to turn each one over and examine it closely.

The two of them were so deeply involved in what they were doing, the sun warm on their backs, birdsong in the distance, that they didn't hear Bosko coming across a mullock heap until he greeted them. Shirley dropped a cloth over the top of the bucket to cover the roughs. Even after five years she still didn't like the loud Yugoslav and remained suspicious of him.

'Where have you sprung from?' she asked.

'Just doing the rounds. Greetings, Stefan.'

'Hello, Bosko. How're things?' Stefan stood up and stretched, reaching for a cigarette pack in his pocket.

'Depends on what you mean,' he answered. 'Here or there.' He turned away from Shirley and said briskly, 'I want to talk to you, Stefan.'

Shirley shrugged. 'I'm not going anywhere.'

'There's something I want to discuss just with you, Stefan,' said the big Serbian.

Shirley watched them stroll a short distance away and light up their cigarettes. Although Stefan's back was to her, she could tell that Stefan wasn't pleased with what he was being told. Several times he shook his head and folded his arms across his chest as if to ward off Bosko's flow of words.

After a while the two men turned and retraced their steps, but they were speaking Yugoslav so Shirley did not know what they were saying. Finally, Bosko slapped Stefan on the back.

'So, I will see you at the bowling club or the baths, yes? We must stick together out here.' He glanced at Shirley but didn't bother to say goodbye. Giving Stefan a meaningful look, he walked away.

Shirley watched him weave between the mullock heaps to his parked car. 'What was all that about, Stefan? What's he after?'

'It's all to do with the old country. I'm not sure how much to believe. He's such a big talker.'

'You don't look very happy. Is it bad news?'

'Back home? There's agitation in Yugoslavia among many of the Croats, Serbs and Macedonians, so Yugoslav Intelligence is getting more ruthless. Bosko tells me that there is a big push by many people opposed to Tito's dictatorship, both in and out of Yugoslavia.'

'Support? You mean Yugoslavs here in Australia are supposed to help fight against Tito?'

Stefan nodded and sat back down. 'That's the idea. People like Bosko think that Yugoslavian loyalty should always be to the old country, whether we live there or not.'

Shirley looked hard at Stefan. 'I gather you don't feel quite like that. I mean, what does he expect? Does he want you to rally the troops and go back to Yugoslavia and help?'

'Bosko says that he is part of a group prepared to fight in Yugoslavia. He expects the rest of us here to help them by giving money or opals.'

'You're kidding. Bosko is certainly taking a lot upon himself, and even if people give him their hard-earned cash how do these fighters use it?'

'Bosko likes to be important. He says that he is sending money back to Yugoslavia to the right people, but I suspect he takes a fee for doing so.'

'Is that how he gets his money?' asked Shirley. 'He said he mines for opal, but I've never seen him work. He always just appears to be part of a group.'

'According to him, he owns some big claims and he says he has people working for him, but I don't think that's true. He makes demands and I think people are afraid of him and they pay up.'

'That's called being a standover merchant,' said Shirley. 'He's a bully. Don't you give him a penny and not a single stone we've worked hard to mine. There must be other ways to send help back to Yugoslavia, if you want to.'

'Shirley, it's very complicated. Yugoslavia is made up of so many different nationalities, and many want to go their own way. Maybe, if I knew for sure that the money Bosko collects could be effective, I might help a little, but I don't trust Bosko. Whenever any of the Slavs hit opal, Bosko is always there to put pressure on them to share their finds, but there is really no way of knowing who's doing the sharing.'

'All the more reason we keep any finds to ourselves,' said Shirley. 'I certainly don't want to share our opal with that Bosko.'

'But, my darling, if we do find some good pieces we have to go to a buyer to sell them and then everyone finds out.'

'Yes, I know, but that doesn't mean that we have to share them with Bosko and his fights. I think that charity should begin at home,' said Shirley briskly. 'If we have good opal, we should take it to Sydney. My father knew a firm of jewellers there who were trustworthy. I know that the buyers on the field are pretty fair but my instinct tells me to avoid the middleman, especially as he is liable to talk in town.'

Stefan smiled. 'Shirley, you are a very smart lady. And brave. Let's hope we have the chance to test your idea.'

'Back to work. There might be a gem at the bottom of the bucket!'

Stefan and Shirley were absorbed in their own deepening relationship. Their routine seldom altered. Long days at the mine were interspersed with the odd morning in town or an overnight fishing break. They didn't socialise much, though they enjoyed stopping briefly to chat with the people in the street or their neighbours out in the field. But they didn't need the company of other people. They laughed and shared experiences and memories, disappointments as well as achievements. Their lovemaking was passionate and tender, and although each gave the other space and time to be alone, they could also sit together in companionable silence, fulfilled and content.

Shirley sometimes caught herself wondering at the

amazing and glorious turn her life had taken. As well as love and friendship, she felt she shared a trust with Stefan that she would never have allowed herself to feel with anyone else. She knew, without any doubt, that Stefan was the centre of her life. And while her friends and colleagues might have been shocked to see their simple and basic lifestyle, Shirley loved it. She never imagined that she could be so happy. There was no thought in her mind of returning to Sydney and resuming her previous life. She planned a permanent life with Stefan. She sensed and hoped that he felt the same.

Ideas and future plans came naturally into the conversation as they talked about moving on from this mine to another, when the time would come that they felt this one had been fully explored. She hoped they'd get to that point soon, because knowing that Stefan's partner had been killed in this mine always made her feel slightly uncomfortable. But the two of them knew the uncanny luck of opal mines. One could swear there was no opal left and leave a mine only for someone else to come along, dig for a day and make a massive find.

One evening, as they were sitting down to dinner in their shack, there was a shout at the front door.

'My friends! It is me, Viktor.'

'Come in. Are you okay?' asked Shirley, who couldn't tell if their friend from the fields was upset or excited. 'Have you eaten?'

'No. I have been to the pub, celebrating.'

'Sit down and have some of our dinner. If you've been celebrating, does that mean that you're on opal?' asked Stefan.

'Yes. I've found gem stuff. Good-colour crystal. I've been scratching along for years and I've finally made a find, so I want to share my news with all my friends.'

'I hope you didn't make too much of a noise at the

pub,' said Shirley. 'Someone could be heading out to your mine right now.'

'She's right, you know, Viktor. Where have you left your opals? Did you get them all, or are there still more to dig out?' said Stefan.

Viktor flung open the long army greatcoat he was wearing to reveal layers of pockets inside. He put his hand into one of them and pulled out a handful of glittering nobbies, laying them on the table between the plates of food. 'Good enough to eat, eh! Aren't they beauties?'

Stefan picked up a stone and turned it over. Even as a rough, the colour burned through in flashing lights of blue, green and yellow. 'These are first quality opals, for sure. Congratulations. This deserves a toast.'

'I have the drink.' Viktor reached into another of the voluminous pockets and held aloft a bottle of brandy. From another pocket he produced a bottle of vodka. 'We drink the vodka with a little dash of brandy. It is a wonderful drink. Please, you too, Shirley.'

'It sounds a bit lethal to me, I'll just have one,' she answered as she got out three glasses.

Viktor measured out the vodka and added a splash of brandy. Lifting his glass he gave a short bow. 'To my friends, my mining neighbours, may the same luck shine upon you. May the sleeping opals awaken to the ring of your pick. *Zivio!*'

He threw back his drink in one gulp and Stefan followed suit. Shirley swallowed the strong liquid, gasped and smiled at Viktor's infectious delight.

Shirley put a plate of food in front of him, but it was waved away as his stories tumbled out. Time and again he refilled the glasses, which he and Stefan quickly emptied. Shirley busied herself tidying away the dinner dishes and making up sandwiches for the next day as the two men sat at the table and talked.

Stefan was obviously enjoying himself, telling stories of fishing in the ice as a boy, travelling across a snow-bound landscape in an antiquated train. Viktor in turn talked of the fights and challenges he'd won and lost, and how he missed hunting and the life he'd known as a teenager.

Shirley noticed that the drinks were getting larger and that the pale gold drink was now a deep honey colour as the quantity of brandy they contained increased. She'd never seen Stefan so relaxed and talkative, and she was glad to see him enjoying himself, but she was concerned for Viktor. If he had been like this in the pub he might not be totally safe.

Eventually she interrupted, 'Stefan, why don't you take Viktor back to his mine, just to be sure that everything's all right. And be careful. It's dangerous walking around at night with those open shafts and mullock heaps.'

'Viktor, Shirley's right. I think you should let me help,' offered Stefan. 'If we work in the mine tonight, we could move a fair bit of dirt and that would give you a head start for tomorrow.'

Viktor slapped Stefan on the back. 'You are a good man. No, don't come. You have to work tomorrow, too. I shall dig for a bit, then I can sleep in my mine. Thank you, Shirley. Now before I go, we drink one last time!'

With that he poured nearly a full glass of brandy, topped with a little vodka. He lifted his glass of deep brown liquid and tapped it heavily against Stefan's, spilling some of the liquor. Then he drank and after he'd finished, his beard was sprinkled with drops of the fiery drink that he'd spilt.

'Are you sure you will be all right to drive?' asked Shirley, thinking of the dirt track to his mine, barely lit by moonlight, that wound through trees, mullock heaps, abandoned claims and half-finished shafts. 'Why don't you get some sleep first in your tent, before you go down your shaft, Viktor?'

'This is a good woman. You are a lucky man, Stefan.' Unsteadily Viktor got to his feet. 'I will be all right.' He patted the pockets where his opals nestled and gave them both a broad grin. 'Yes, everything is all right. In one day, in a moment, how your life can change.'

'I'll see you to your truck,' said Stefan.

When he came back inside, Stefan put his arms around Shirley. 'He'll be okay. He drove down the street in almost a straight line. Viktor can certainly drink.'

'You did pretty well yourself,' said Shirley. 'I'm so pleased for him. He's been here quite a while and hasn't found much.' She leant into Stefan as he held her. 'I hope our turn is coming.'

Stefan held her tightly. 'You must have faith, but no matter what happens, good or bad, we will always have each other.' He lifted her face towards his and looked into her eyes. 'I will always look after you, Shirley. I never want us to be apart.'

As they kissed, Shirley knew that Stefan truly loved her. Any remaining barrier between them had fallen away. Perhaps the effect of the strong alcohol, Viktor's joy or reminiscing about his homeland that he thought he'd never see again had put things in perspective for Stefan. The words hung in the air between them and Shirley knew a pact had been made. She was as committed to him as he was to her. He turned off the light and, taking her by the hand, led her into their tiny bedroom.

Stefan's head was a bit woolly the next morning and, as he drank two mugs of strong black coffee, he said humbly, 'But this won't affect my work.'

'I wonder how Viktor is,' said Shirley. 'I bet he didn't swing a pick last night. I expect that he just slept off his little party.'

'We'll look in on him before we start work,' he said.

Stefan sang softly as he drove out to the diggings. His musical voice always entranced Shirley. She loved it when he played his flute, which he did occasionally. She came to realise that when he picked it up, it was generally when he needed to be by himself. When he played, he closed his eyes and he seemed to be in another place. She learnt simply to appreciate those moments and enjoy the music while leaving him with his thoughts. But at other times he'd whistle as he dug, or sing, as he was doing now, and Shirley knew that he was feeling happy.

There was no movement around the tents at the camp as their truck pulled up. Shirley assumed that everyone was either working in their mines or still sleeping.

'Stefan, before we get started, we'd better give Viktor a hoy. I'll go over and look in his tent.'

'Hang on. I'll check down his mine shaft first. He's probably asleep with his opals. Last night's vodka and brandy combination was pretty lethal.'

Stefan whistled as he trudged across the no man's land to Viktor's mine. The cover was off, the bucket was at the bottom of the shaft and a spade lay to one side. Stefan shouted down the narrow opening, but got no response. He was about to turn away but thought better of it and instead climbed into the mine, his feet feeling for the rungs of the iron ladder.

'Viktor? Wake up! Are you in here?' He couldn't hear any noise or see any light, so he switched on his torch and glanced at the mine's two drives. He chose the narrower one and, hunched down under the low roof, he headed along it, stepping over rubble and a cable strung along the length of the tunnel which conducted power from the generator for the jackhammer. Seeing nothing, Stefan retraced his steps to the wider drive.

The entrance into this tunnel was jammed with earth

and rubble, allowing only a small gap into the drive. Viktor must have been in a frenzy of digging once he found the initial opals, thought Stefan. But as he waved his torch along the rough walls, he sensed that something was not right. There was too much chaos. It looked as though Viktor had spent an entire night smashing through as much rock as possible. 'Well,' said Stefan to himself, 'If he's done that, he'll have crashed and be asleep in his tent.'

Stefan was about to retrace his steps when a pile of rocks caught his eye. A piece of coloured cloth was caught between some of the rocks. On his knees, Stefan inched forward and found that the rocks were placed like a wall in front of a cavity. He hastily pulled the top layer of rocks down and shone his torch over it, his head bumping against the low roof. As the torch beam waved against the gouged wall, Stefan could see a dark mound. He shone the torch onto it to get a better look.

He had to look twice before he could accept what he was seeing in the pale torchlight. The huddled shape of Viktor was crumpled against the wall. This was not the curled figure of a man sleeping, but the distorted limbs of a body that had been flung here. And as Stefan ran the torchlight over the pile of rocks, he gagged, for he saw that Viktor's throat had been cut.

Stefan flung himself backwards in horror, scrambling out of the tunnel, suddenly feeling fearful and claustrophobic. At the top of the shaft, in the warm sunshine, he collapsed onto the ground, his head in his hands, the nightmare of what he'd just seen too awful to contemplate. Pulling himself up, he hastily ran to Shirley, who was at their mine, ready to descend. Shirley saw Stefan stumbling as he ran towards her and she knew instantly something was badly wrong.

'Stefan, what is it?' She met him and he clung to her,

his breath coming to him in gasps, making it impossible for him to speak. 'Take it slowly, darling. Catch your breath. What on earth has happened?'

Stefan shook his head. He stared at Shirley and, after a moment, took a deep breath and said, 'He's dead.'

'What happened? Was there an accident?'

'No!' shouted Stefan, startling Shirley. 'There hasn't been an accident. He's been killed! Murdered!'

'No! Are you sure he's dead?' Shirley shook Stefan slightly. 'I'll go and check on him. Come on, quickly. How do you know he's been murdered? Dear God, what a tragedy.' She was already running towards Viktor's mine.

'Shirley! His throat has been cut!'

Shirley faltered and turned back to Stefan. 'Oh no. How horrible.' Her hand went to her mouth. 'The opals. I suppose they killed him for his opals.'

As they both hurried towards Viktor's mine, Stefan said, 'I didn't touch him. We should go straight to town and get the police.'

'Yes. I know, but first let me see him. Maybe I can do something.'

Stefan looked at Shirley and said, 'It's not a pretty sight.'

Holding the torch high so that she could see as she scrambled over the rocks piled in front of Viktor, Stefan watched Shirley put a hand to her mouth in horror as she crouched beside his body. She lifted his wrist and put a finger below his ear where the ugly gash had almost severed Viktor's head, which was now lolling at an unnatural angle.

'You're right, Stefan, there is nothing I can do. He's been dead for a few hours. Poor Viktor. They've taken his opals. I wonder if they dug any more out? What's the rest of the mine like?'

'A mess. If there was any more opal, they've probably got it.'

'There's nothing left in his army coat,' said Shirley angrily. 'He carried everything that was precious to him in those pockets.' She was close to tears.

'Shirley, come on, we have to get the police.' Stefan leant over and held out his hand to help her scramble back through the small gap.

In silence they went back to the ladder and Shirley looked back into the darkness of the mine. 'Poor Viktor. He was so happy and he said that he had such plans. This is just terrible,' she said angrily.

'He told me that he'd like to have enough money to move on. He was sick of being hounded and a good find would be his ticket away from Lightning Ridge,' said Stefan.

'Hounded? By whom? What's that mean?'

'When I asked him, he just made a joke of it. He said that women were after his money. I didn't believe him.'

Shirley straightened up. 'Well, no one deserves to die like that. Come on, we'd better get the police and let everyone else know that there's not just a ratter on the loose but a murderer.'

The murder caused a furore in Lightning Ridge, but the police were unable to find any clues. As Shirley suspected, the other miners at the campsite were totally unco-operative and all swore that they had seen and heard nothing that night.

Viktor's funeral was well attended, and afterwards Shirley and Stefan went back to work but they both felt uneasy. Among Bosko's group at the bore baths there was speculation that Viktor had been involved with anti-Tito sabotage, but no one really knew. Other rumours suggested that he was working with the Yugoslav government. Stefan told Shirley that it was just gossip, although Bosko seemed quite definite that Viktor was involved in something underhanded.

'Where does Bosko get all this information? Or does he make it up?' demanded Shirley.

Stefan shrugged. 'He certainly seems to have good links back to the old country, but I'm just never sure which cause or which group he's supporting. All I know is that he's always pressuring us to give money to support them.'

'Yes, the Help Bosko Get Rich Fund,' snapped Shirley. 'I not only don't trust him, I don't believe him. I don't think he's working for anyone but himself. I just wish when people come to our country they'd leave all their wars and intrigues behind them and start afresh.'

'That's not easy to do when you have family left behind,' said Stefan. 'I know that many immigrants do bring their prejudices, affiliations and loyalties with them in their suitcases, and it is not always possible to sever the links completely. Unless you are a little child, it is hard to let go of the way you were brought up, and just discard your culture and beliefs.'

'Do you feel the same? Your parents are still back there. I know that you say you're happy you've made a new life here, but do you ever want to go back? Would you go back to get involved in Yugoslavian politics?'

Stefan heard the strain in Shirley's voice and saw the uncertainty in her eyes. He put his arms around her. 'Of course not. You are my life now. I prefer to leave the ethnic tensions of Yugoslavia behind. The country might hold together under Tito's rule, and some people think of him as a great leader, but who knows what will happen when he dies? I suspect that there will be a parting of the ways between different interests.'

'It sounds a bit of a shambles. I suppose it takes a strong personality to bring together so many different people and ethnic groups under one flag.'

'Yes, and a very ruthless leader,' said Stefan. He hesitated and took Shirley's hand. 'I have made a happy life here, and I sometimes worry about my parents who sacrificed so much for me, but I have you and I've made my choice. I don't want to be involved with Bosko and his little patriot games.'

Shirley shook her head. 'This is all so foreign to me. I have lived in a city, worked with people from all walks of life, gone about my business, gone to the beach, the pictures, enjoyed myself. I really had no idea that this sort of thing went on.'

'Shirley, I suspect that there is a lot going on that Australians generally don't know about. I have been told that there are camps set up out in the Australian bush by the UDBa – the Yugoslav intelligence organisation – to train Yugoslavs to fight the elements hostile to Tito, both here and back in Yugoslavia.'

Shirley shook her head. 'You are joking. Here in Australia? Surely the authorities would do something about it, if it were true? This is too ridiculous for me to take in.' She looked into Stefan's eyes, trying to find the simple good man she thought she knew. 'You're not involved in this, are you?'

'That's the point, Shirley darling, I am not, and I don't want to be involved. I don't see it as my fight anymore.'

'And Viktor? Was he mixed up in this?'

Stefan shrugged. 'I really don't know. I told you all I know about opals being sold and the money being sent away, but I don't know for certain if Viktor was part of it, or if he was simply robbed and killed for his opals and nothing more.'

'Well, I want to know that we aren't slaving away here to help fund a cause on the other side of the world!' declared Shirley. 'I want to work for our future, not someone else's!'

He put his arms around her. 'We are! You can look after our opals. You sell them, you decide how we divide the profits and spend the money. You are not just my business partner, you are my love, you are my life! Shirley, this is what I want you to know.'

He held her and she felt her fears melting, and the vehemence of his words convinced her they would be all right.

'I know that you must have torn feelings when you are uprooted from your country. But I want you to be happy here. To love Australia like I do and then we'll be just fine,' Shirley said.

Stefan held her at arm's length, smiled and smoothed her hair. 'I love you, Shirley. You are the most important person in my life. Please believe that.'

As he leant close to kiss her she murmured, 'I just don't want anything to happen to us.'

A day or so later, while the two of them were shopping in town, they ran into Bosko.

'Don't talk to him,' Shirley begged Stefan. 'I think we should just leave him alone and have nothing to do with him.'

'Darling, I can't do that, but I won't talk to him for long.'

Stefan walked over to Bosko and Shirley heard him politely ask how Bosko was.

'Still devastated by the death of our dear friend Viktor, and it was all so unnecessary,' Bosko replied.

'How do you mean?' asked Stefan.

'Perhaps if he had made less noise about his discovery and asked his friends to help him look after his opal, then things might have been different.'

At this, Shirley came over and interrupted. 'How would you have helped Viktor? By taking part of his find and using it for yourself?'

'Shirley, please, don't say such things,' Stefan implored her, but Shirley was too angry to take any notice of him. She could only remember her own father's experience all those years ago, when no one had helped them.

'I'm not surprised that no one has heard anything or seen anything,' she said. 'All very convenient.'

'I have no idea what your girlfriend is talking about, Stefan, but I think that such a wild conversation is not a good thing. People might think that I know things that I am keeping from the police.'

'And maybe not just the police,' retorted Shirley. 'Maybe there are other authorities who would be interested in some of your activities. It makes me so mad that someone as sweet as Viktor can be killed and there will be no justice for him.'

Bosko gave Stefan a hard look. 'You must explain to your girlfriend that what she is saying is not helpful to either of you if you want to stay safe in Lightning Ridge.' With that he walked away.

'Shirley, you shouldn't have said those things. I told you before that Bosko's not a man to make an enemy of.'

'I'm sorry, but I'm sure that in some way Bosko knows something about Viktor's murder. Do you think we should tell the police what we think?'

'What do we think? We don't know anything, Shirley. You are not to say anything more to anyone. It's too dangerous.'

Later, when they were working, Stefan asked Shirley if she would like to go away for a little holiday. He knew that she was shocked and angry that Viktor's murder remained unsolved.

Shirley leant on the handle of the shovel she'd been using and said, 'You know, that's a good idea. I could do with a break away from here.'

'Where would you like to go? To Sydney? To the beach and see your friends?'

Shirley shook her head. 'After being out here, I don't want to go back to Sydney. That's my old life.' She suddenly smiled. 'I know just where I want to go. A place I want you to see.'

'And that is . . . ?'

'Opal Lake. Dad's old mine. I've been thinking about it lately. We can camp there, but I want to take you out to the lake, too. It's a magical place. There won't be any water there but once, as a child, I saw it full and I've never forgotten it.'

'A lake with no water. You mean it's a desert lake?'

She shook her head. 'Well, yes, but no. It's an opal lake. Anyway, that's how I think of it. It's where the rainbow ends, in melting colours. It's just special. Let's go, Stefan! Get away from this sinister place where such awful things happen.'

'Okay, we will. Opal Lake sounds lovely.' He kissed her. 'And you're right. It was a terrible thing that happened to Viktor. But we might be wrong, looking for conspiracies around Viktor's death. His murder might just have been done by greedy ratters looking for the main chance. Anyway, I think it's time that we made some decisions. Should we sell some of the roughs so we have a bit of a nest egg?'

'Yes, but the good firsts of black opal we'll take to Roth Cameron, later,' said Shirley firmly.

Shirley didn't talk much as they drove towards Opal Lake. Stefan hummed quietly, occasionally breaking into song. After a while he glanced at Shirley and reached over and squeezed her knee.

'You look nostalgic. Are you thinking about your father?'

'Yes, I was,' said Shirley quietly. 'It was a happy time, coming out here.'

'Opal Lake will be happy for us, too,' said Stefan.

Shirley truly believed that to be so.

They set up a tent by the edge of the lake and camped there. Both felt that they had come to rest in a very different, gentle and magical world.

As the sun set on the second evening, Shirley lifted her face to the crimson sky and sighed. 'I needed this. Soul balm. It's good to know there's a place you can come where it will be soothing and special.'

Stefan gazed at her lovely face, washed in the warm rosy glow of the sunset. 'I'm glad you've shown me this peaceful place. We can come here again if you like.'

'Hmm. That's nice. Nice to have someone to make plans with,' murmured Shirley. Then, after a moment, she asked, 'Just what are our plans?'

'Shirley, stop thinking ahead for a bit and enjoy this sunset. Tell me what it was like when you were here with your father.'

'It was wonderful. When I first saw this lake, it was filled with shallow water and covered in birds. Just a wonderland. My dad showed me the constellations, and taught me a bit about geological history and of course I was swept away with the idea that once there were ancient forests and dinosaurs here.'

'Hard to imagine. And no opals under the lake?'

'No, wrong sort of rock. So hardly anyone comes here, which is how I like it.'

The sky was molten red as the full silver moon rose over them.

The few days she and Stefan spent at the lake were forever cemented in Shirley's memory. Not only had she returned to the place she'd visited with her father all those years ago, but she'd done so with the man she loved, and it all seemed exquisitely appropriate. Now, out here, alone together, there was a poignancy to their passion, and an uninhibited and childish freedom. This was a place where they could run and laugh naked in the moonlight, calling out to the stars in ecstasy. Stefan sang to the lake, his tenor voice reaching across its empty surface, while Shirley imagined that his beautiful notes would sink into the silver sand, to be there always and if, in years to come, she dug into the lake, she would retrieve the sound of his voice. Oh, yes, these days would forever be in her heart.

One day they drove into the town of Opal Lake. Shirley wanted to see her mine, while Stefan wanted to visit the little township, which he found intriguing. He stood at the mouth of Albert's mine atop the hill and gazed at the few dwellings and buildings below, and the empty russet and olive landscape melting into the horizon.

'You would always feel safe here. It's as though the last survivors of a catastrophe could shelter in their mines and when the disaster was over they would quietly emerge from their holes in the ground and start over.'

'What nonsense. You talk like the end of the world is imminent. Don't be so depressing.'

'Slavs are known for the black dog. Woe is me!' said Stefan cheerfully.

'Don't you go getting mournful and negative on me,' said Shirley. 'I like happy people.'

'That's me. You make me happy. Come on, show me round inside.'

Stefan took Shirley's hand as she showed him the dug-out, pointing out what her father had done. 'He made it big enough so we could shelter inside, but we cooked outside. Dad and I always dreamed of making this mine into a decent living area.'

'And staying here?'

'Originally it was just for holidays in the winter season. But things didn't work out and we were only here the once . . . So here it sits.'

'We could make it liveable.' Stefan glanced around. 'There could still be opal in here. I mean, your father must have thought so, or he wouldn't have claimed it. What's that pile of rubble in that drive down there?'

'There was a fall-in. Dad decided to leave that section where the ground slopes away because he said that it was unstable.'

'We have better machinery now. Maybe we could dig it out and prop it up.'

'So this would be our holiday home?' Shirley laughed. 'We work in your mine and then come over here and work in my mine. When do we get a break?'

'When we go to Sydney to sell our fabulous collection of opals.'

'I wonder when that will be,' said Shirley. 'But it's the search, the living in hope, and the enjoyment of what we do that keeps us going. Right?'

'Never give up, Shirley, on anything or anyone. That's what I believe.'

After they returned to Lightning Ridge, Shirley remembered their stay at Opal Lake as the most romantic time she had ever experienced. But she couldn't help an occasional niggle about the future. She didn't want to push Stefan but, in her practical forthright way, she hoped that they might formalise their relationship. Moreover, it worried her that the mine at the Ridge was not proving as fruitful as it had been.

'Stefan, do you think it's time that we moved on from here?' she asked while they were taking a tea break after a very unproductive morning.

'There have been some big finds on the new field at Grawin,' said Stefan. 'The opal's light green and good quality. I wouldn't mind staking a claim there.'

'And selling this claim? How do we find a buyer?'

'Spread the word. Notify the miners. There're more people coming here all the time.'

'What about Opal Lake?'

'I think that we'll need more money to set us up for that, Shirley. We would have to fix up the dugout before we can get down to serious mining, and that will cost us. Unless we hit a seam while digging out the bedroom.' He laughed.

'I've got a bit of money saved and I'm never going back to Sydney to live, so I could use it for the Opal Lake mine,' said Shirley.

He kissed her. 'People will say you're a crazy woman. Maybe that's why I love you. Let's give it two more weeks here and then we move.'

Perhaps because they were both thinking about moving on, their efforts to clear out the final section of the mine were somewhat distracted. Shirley still felt uneasy in Stefan's mine because Stefan's partner had been killed in it. While the opal they had found had been welcome, it did no more than pay for their living expenses. It was not a payoff for their hard work. And ever since the murder of Viktor, Shirley felt slightly claustrophobic and apprehensive underground, and she was glad that Stefan was close by.

'I can't wait to have our claim together, away from here,' she said.

Stefan, working further down the drive, merely hummed and nodded.

Shortly afterwards, Shirley shouted to him over the noise of his small jackhammer. 'Stef! Come and look at this.'

He peered over Shirley's shoulder as she gently crumbled the clay away from where she'd been digging. She was rubbing dirt and clay from a small piece of oddly shaped rock.

'What is it?' she said. 'It's not like a regular nobby at all and it's quite an unusual shape.'

'Let's try and clean it up,' suggested Stefan.

He carefully began to remove the outside dirt and Shirley cried out. 'It's a piece of vertebra. I know one when I see one. It's an opalised vertebra. That's just amazing.'

'Let's see if there are any more.'

With their small gouging picks, they both gently scratched into the soft sandstone and clay, and found another odd-shaped piece of rock. Stefan cleaned it up and it, too, proved to be another small piece of a backbone.

'Have you any idea what this could be from?' asked Stefan.

'No, not really. Hold the light on it.' Shirley held the fossil against the light beam and they both saw the surface translucent with a faint hint of rainbow colours like a water slick on oil.

'Since it's a fossil it must be very old. Maybe there's more of whatever it is.'

'I've heard miners talk about finds like these but even if they have good colour, they won't cut into gems, so they're worthless, Shirley. Just little pieces of curiosity, and I'm not convinced that we should be wasting time searching for opalised fossils.'

'Stefan, I am really very curious. Dad used to tell me about the ancient animals that roamed this part of Australia millions of years ago, and these vertebrae are obviously the remains of one of them. I think finding fossils is very exciting.'

'Speculate away, darling, but they're not worth anything unless you can cut jewellery from them.'

Not dissuaded, Shirley was enchanted by her finds. The stories miners told around the fire when she was little came back to her: tales of weird creatures, their bones burning with opal fire and empty eye sockets filled with glittering gems, unearthed from their ancient sleep. Yet most fossils were deemed worthless and were smashed by uncaring miners just to get to the more valuable opal. As she looked at the wild and dazzling patterns of opal that had replaced the living tissue of a long dead creature, Shirley thought that these fossils were magical.

Shirley tried to explain how she felt about them to Stefan. 'Opal is a piece of silica that is transformed beyond beauty. But when something that was *alive* becomes an opal . . .' She lifted her arms, her eyes shining. 'It's just something else again.'

He turned one of the small gleaming vertebra over in his palm. 'I understand, I think. They're part of another world. Animals and plants frozen in time.'

'And shells, and fish from an inland sea, which is now an ocean of billowing dust,' added Shirley.

Stefan stared at her, then leant over and gave her a kiss. 'Shirley, you have changed my world,' he said softly. 'I thought opals were the most beautiful gem in the world. But you are the most precious.' He dropped the shining vertebra into her hand and curled her fingers over them. 'Because they are so important to you, we will keep these opalised fossils and never sell them.'

'Thank you, my darling. Anyway, as you have pointed out, we haven't found anything that is of great value. We should be so lucky. But I just love that we found these little fossils.'

Call it luck, or fate, but they did find another rare and beautiful object. Later on that day they unearthed part of an even more brilliant opalised fossil.

'Look at this,' said Stefan. 'I've found something. It's

251

solid opal, and I think that it could be part of an animal that's a lot bigger than the other ones we've found.'

Shirley looked to where he was pointing and there, embedded in the wall of the mine, was part of a large opalised fossil.

Her heart began thumping and she couldn't speak. She knew this was a stupendous find. Something she could never have imagined. 'I think it's a bit of a femur, the thigh bone,' whispered Shirley. 'It's amazing. Can we get it out?'

They carefully cut the block of clay from the wall and lay it on the floor of the drive. In the light they studied their find, gingerly reaching out a finger to stroke the exposed blue-green opal fossil shot with waves of red and gold lights.

'This is the best opal I've ever seen,' whispered Stefan.

'Can we get the fossilised bone out of the clay without destroying it?' asked Shirley.

'I think so, if we're really careful. Do you know what it came from?' asked Stefan in wonder.

Shirley touched it delicately. 'From what I remember my father saying, it must be part of a dinosaur. I'm sure it's a femur and it's far too big to be part of any mammal that was around at that time. Mammals were really tiny when these rocks were laid down. Oh, Stefan, as a little girl I always wanted to find a dinosaur, and now we have.'

'It's beautiful all right. I think that when we get it out of the rock, it will be worth quite a lot of money because it's such a big solid piece of opal. It's the pot of gold we've been talking about. The money we can use to reopen your mine.'

'No!' said Shirley vehemently. 'Stefan, I want to keep it. You promised that we wouldn't sell any fossils and this is really important to me.' She couldn't explain it, she'd never felt so possessive, so deeply attached to an object

252

before. She felt as though some incomprehensibly lovely gift had just been given to her.

Stefan looked at her, thinking of the immense value of the opal and how anyone else would sell it for a fortune. Then he laughed.

'Well, my darling, when I made that promise, I never imagined that we would find something that could change our whole lives, but if you want to keep it rather than sell it, I will stick to my part of the bargain. Of course, when we are living in discomfort at Opal Lake, I might just remind you that things could have been different.' He tenderly kissed the tip of her nose. 'Shall we give it a name?' he said suddenly.

'That's a lovely idea. Yes. Something that's just between us,' said Shirley.

Stefan thought for a moment. 'Tajna. Croatian for a secret, something that is concealed from others. Something that is mysterious, inexplicable, beyond understanding.'

'I'd say that sums up our fossil,' said Shirley with satisfaction. 'Now we have to keep Taj a secret from everyone else.'

*

Shirley straightened her back in the old chair. 'You know, Kerrie, later that day we found some good opals further along in the band, which normally would have made us jump for joy. But after finding the fossil, everything paled in comparison.'

'How fascinating,' said Kerrie. 'Do you mind if I ask what happened to Tajna?'

'We took it with us when we moved to Opal Lake. I thought it was a lucky omen. We were so happy out here. It was a smaller community than Lightning Ridge, but helpful and friendly, the same as now. We worked on making our dugout liveable, and it's pretty much as you see it now. I've only made a few changes.'

Kerrie nodded. 'Did you make a living from opal?'

'We did indeed. I had my payout from work, plus a little nest egg from my father. But Stefan and I did very well with opal finds. Some years we would try our luck on the new fields. Stefan went off for a few weeks to try the Coocoran and we both spent a lovely month at Yowah. There's a kind of fever that hits and spreads when new finds are made and everybody rushes out and pegs claims. People came from everywhere.'

'It sounds like an idyllic existence. Did you ever do anything with Tajna?'

'No. I won't say we forgot about Tajna. But I found a safe home for it so that even if we were ratted no one could have found it.'

'Did you ever try to have Tajna identified? You're such a researcher and so curious,' said Kerrie.

Shirley smiled. 'Tajna was so special to us. I knew enough to know it was a femur and that it could only have come from some sort of dinosaur. Being the size it was and solid gem-quality opal, we knew it would be worth a lot of money. Stefan had agreed that we shouldn't cash it in and let it be broken up. He said it would be our little secret. It became very special to us.'

'Where is it now?' asked Kerrie.

Shirley smiled. 'Would you like to see it?'

'You still have it here?' exclaimed Kerrie.

'Where else would it be? It will take me a little while to fetch it. Put the kettle on, would you?'

Kerrie nodded, thinking what an Australian habit it was in moments of stress or jubilation, or when pondering a problem, that the kettle was inevitably put on to boil for tea.

She was busy putting biscuits on a plate when Shirley

returned holding something wrapped in a towel. Gently she laid it on the kitchen table and unfurled the towel to reveal the fossil.

Kerrie gasped. The opalised fossil was the size of a baguette, and even she could see that it was obviously a leg bone. But it was the dazzling colours that mesmerised her. Even though the fossil was an inanimate object, it glittered and glowed as if it were alive. The wide, rounded ball of the joint was intense blue, shot with green peacock feathers and studded with crimson. The remainder of the shaft was filled with iridescent orange and gold bands that shimmered in the electric light.

'Shirley! How much must this be worth in solid opal?' breathed Kerrie. 'It's spectacular!'

'Today? Lordy, I have no idea, maybe thousands of dollars a carat but an awful lot, not just for its opal, but because it's such a fabulous fossil, I suppose.'

'I remember Gustav and Helen, the palaeontologists that I met at Pam's, telling me that although miners used to ignore fossils, now they recognise their intrinsic value. This one's in near-perfect condition, and it's such stunning solid opal. There can be no question that it's valuable as a scientific object as well as a gem,' said Kerrie.

'You left out the most important reason why I would never sell it,' said Shirley. 'And that's its symbolism. It's something between Stefan and me. Ever since I was a little girl, mining with my father, I'd wanted a dinosaur fossil. And even though we sometimes needed money, Stefan agreed that we wouldn't sell this one because it meant so much to me. So this fossilised bone showed me how much he loved me. And funnily enough, once we made the decision to keep it, we seemed to manage anyway.'

'Would you ever sell it?' asked Kerrie gently.

'Never.' Shirley shook her head vehemently. 'The fossils are all I have left to remind me of Stefan.'

Kerrie felt that she should try and talk sense to Shirley. She thought that keeping such a valuable fossil in the dugout was not a very wise thing to do, but obviously it was important to Shirley to have the fossil with her, so Kerrie took a different tack. 'Shirley, who else knows you have this fossil in here? I mean, I don't think that it's safe for you to have something worth so much in your dugout.'

'You mean someone could burst in and bash me over the head for this?' said Shirley with a surprising degree of cheerfulness. 'Could happen, but I doubt it. Besides, I've hardly shown it to anyone. You're one of the very few who's seen it.'

'Shirley, I'm honoured that you trust me,' said Kerrie in surprise. 'But really, I'm not convinced that it's a clever thing to do, keeping it here. Have you ever thought of taking it to a museum and having it properly identified?'

'And then what?' said Shirley. 'I'd be under pressure to donate it or put it on exhibition. I already know that it's a dinosaur femur and I'm not going to part with it anyway. No, it stays with me in the dugout.'

Kerrie was quite surprised by Shirley's attitude. 'What about Gustav and Helen? Couldn't you ask them?'

'No, they'll only want to put it into a museum. I just wanted to show you this fossil because it was important to Stefan and me, and I've probably told you more about Stefan than I've told almost anyone else. It must be these late-night chats.'

Shirley's bright demeanour had suddenly crumpled. Kerrie saw the frail and lonely older woman who'd been desperately hurt in some terrible way, and now had trusted and liked another woman enough to share her story. She stood up and went over to hug Shirley.

'Shirley, all I can say is that I'm your friend and so I'll respect your wishes, even if I'm not sure that it's the right thing to do.' She squeezed Shirley's hand. 'Now, how about I pour that cup of tea?'

The glittering fossil lay among the teapot and cups on the table. After a short interlude and a cup of tea, Shirley seemed to be herself again, so Kerrie gently asked,

'Do you want to share what really happened between you and Stefan?'

Shirley looked steadily at Kerrie. 'I can never let myself believe that Stefan stopped loving me, but he left me and I don't understand why.'

'What happened?' Kerrie knew that Shirley was hauling up memories she had probably suppressed for many years.

9

SHIRLEY PLACED A TUB containing a small cumquat tree by the freshly painted door to the dugout. 'It's for good luck. And the fruit is delicious,' she told Stefan, who nodded and then lifted a jackhammer to split one of the large boulders they'd dragged from the side of the hill. Shirley wanted Stefan to use it to build the rockery she was creating, which she planned to fill with desert shrubs and flowers.

She watched Stefan wield the jackhammer with ease. She marvelled at his physicality. Watching him work, his lean, firm body and tanned arms, made her long to hold him.

'I'm a lucky girl,' she said aloud when he turned off the jackhammer and surveyed the large pieces of red and gold rock he had just broken up.

'To have your personal slave?' he laughed.

'Builder, miner, good cook, pretty damned good in bed . . . Yep, I reckon I'm doing all right.' She smiled.

'So what does the boss think about the entrance to the SS *Dugout*?' he asked.

Shirley looked at the new entry to her father's old dugout. 'Shirley and Stefan will be very comfortable and happy here.'

'There's a bit of tidying up to do. We have to finish the limewash inside and we're done. Then we can get back to work.'

'I was hoping you might strike it lucky digging out our bedroom,' said Shirley.

After they'd found the fossil, they'd wasted no time leaving the mine at the Ridge to move to Opal Lake.

'I'm pretty sure this mine is worked out,' Stefan had told Shirley.

'I agree. It just feels . . . empty.' She was glad he felt that way as she was ready to move on.

They spent several evenings discussing their plans.

'Not so much social life in Opal Lake. No bore baths, clubs and all that sort of thing,' said Shirley.

Stefan merely raised an eyebrow. 'Come on, Shirley. As if I am the club type, and you know I only go to the baths as a social courtesy to the other Yugoslavs working here.'

'I think we'll be better off in Opal Lake,' said Shirley.

'You know that I care only about you. We don't need other people, anyway,' said Stefan. 'We'll do well at your father's mine.'

And he was right. The move to Opal Lake was propitious.

Shirley spread the opals on the table. She began to sort them into firsts, seconds and thirds, according to quality.

'I think Roth will take the firsts, and maybe pick through some of the seconds. What do you think?'

'You're right, but Tony Genovese will probably take the rest of these, or the Japanese buyer will,' said Stefan. He stood behind Shirley as she leant over the table, examining the opals they'd found in the last twelve months. 'Not a bad lot. Though I think that we've done better.'

'We've done all right. Holding our own, which is more than most can say,' said Shirley. She still found it amazing and wonderful that she and Stefan had continued to support themselves through their opal finds for the past years.

Wrapping his arms around her, Stefan kissed her ear. 'Instead of just racing in and out, why don't we spend some time over there at the Ridge? We haven't had a break away from here for quite some time.'

'You're bored with me,' teased Shirley.

'Never. What about you? Want to see some of your old friends?'

'Not really. They're more your friends than mine. But I think a break would be good. Okay, we'll secure our place and drive over to the Ridge. And one thing I'd like to do is to visit Roy and Eileen Lanyon on their property out near Hebel. Dad and I used to go there and camp sometimes. Roy's father and Dad were old mates and he used to let people go and fossick round the old mine shafts.'

'Does anyone mine there now?'

'They let a few regulars come and mine in the paddocks in the winter months. Hebel used to be a thriving township in the old days. Roy has been collecting artefacts from when, if the mines petered out, people just walked away and left most of their things behind. So he's got a massive shed full of broken sulkies, handmade machinery for milking and farming, antique coloured bottles and china, you name it. It sounds fascinating. The last time I heard, there were plans to protect those early mine shafts, too.'

'Rusty machinery, old shafts and mullock heaps? It doesn't sound very interesting,' said Stefan. 'Wouldn't it be dangerous?'

'I would think they'd have enough sense to make everything safe. I know it's not an ancient cathedral or a museum or an opera house like in Europe, but the slab shacks and stone cottages of the pioneers show the spirit of people who stuck it out in the isolation and hardship of the outback and made a life there,' said Shirley.

'Like we're doing.' He nuzzled her neck. 'One day we will go to Europe together and see the old world. I wish I could show you Dubrovnik, and the Dalmatian coast is wonderful.'

'Sounds pretty good and I would like to go, but when we've finished travelling, we'll come back here,' said Shirley. 'This is our home. Even if it is a hole in the ground.'

Stefan laughed. 'It would be hard to explain a dug-out to my family. Living in an underground cave would certainly be difficult for them to visualise.' But he straightened up and, looking serious, he said, 'The last I heard, many people back in Yugoslavia are struggling and living in poor conditions, so perhaps our underground cave would look good to them.'

'What have you heard from your family in the letter that's just arrived? How's your mother?' asked Shirley.

Stefan lifted his shoulders. 'As you know, after my father died, my mother went to live in a flat in Zagreb to be near her old friends. But my cousins tell me that she is getting old and sometimes she gets confused, I think.'

'That's sad,' said Shirley. 'Maybe your mother appreciates that you are happy and doing well in Australia, even if it is so far away.'

'The trouble is that the times I've phoned her, I'm not sure that she hears what I tell her. But enough of this sad conversation. Come on, let's go for a walk. The sunset calls.'

The steam from the hot water in the artesian bore baths at Lightning Ridge billowed into the night air. Stefan inched into the baths, gasping at the intense heat, which was such a contrast to the cold air.

The other Yugoslavs watched him gingerly settle and a few made joking comments about his timidity.

Stefan laughed along with them, acknowledging that he was out of practice with the very hot water. He turned to the man next to him. 'Where is Bosko?'

'He'll be here. He'll bring us news from home.'

'So what intrigues, battles and conflicts have erupted this week?'

'You won't be laughing when you hear what's going on in Yugoslavia.'

'All these problems seem so far away. So removed from what we're doing here,' said Stefan. He suddenly realised that he was tired of the way these men still devoured the Yugoslav newspapers they were sent, and discussed and debated every piece of news and rumour that came to them via relatives and friends. So he only half listened as the talk about the death of Tito and the growing unrest in Kosovo swirled around him.

As Bosko approached, the group fell silent. Stefan tried to talk to the others about local matters and the price of opal, but all eyes were on the large Serbian as he eased himself into the bore baths.

'So. There is more trouble in the south.'

'There's always trouble in Yugoslavia,' said Stefan.

'Now there is unrest everywhere. No province is safe.

262

If these nationalists get their way and create many little countries, Yugoslavia will no longer be strong and our families and friends will be in trouble,' said Bosko.

'Why are we continuing to talk about the problems in Yugoslavia when we can peacefully live together here? This is Australia, not the old country. There's no need for this,' said Stefan.

'I say it because I know what is happening. I haven't turned my back on my homeland like some,' retorted Bosko.

Stefan stepped from the baths. 'I'm overcooked. I will be going.'

'Our talk does not interest you, Stefan?' taunted Bosko. 'But I think that you cannot dismiss what is happing in Yugoslavia. You will be involved whether you like it or not.' Bosko stepped from the baths.

Stefan ignored the comment. 'I have to meet Shirley for dinner.'

Bosko's expression hardened. 'That woman is a problem.'

'And why is that?' asked Stefan.

'She is stirring trouble. She always says bad things about me.'

'Maybe she knows more than you think. She is a good judge of people.'

Bosko picked up his towel and jacket and took a menacing step towards Stefan, glaring at him. 'She knows nothing. She thinks she is a smart Australian woman, and too clever for us. Why don't you find a woman who knows her place and keeps to the old ways and lets the man be on top.' He took a step closer and lifted his fist. 'She needs a man to fuck her and show her who's boss. You are too soft.'

Bosko made an obscene gesture as the others roared with laughter.

Stefan suddenly moved forward and swung his arm.

He landed a punch on the Serb's cheekbone. Bosko was caught completely off guard but quickly retaliated with wild, swinging punches, one of which grazed Stefan's temple, as the mob in the baths began shouting and several scrambled from the searing water to encourage Bosko. He rushed at Stefan and tried headbutting him.

Stefan could smell the liquor on Bosko's breath and, realising that the Serb was unsteady on his feet, took another swing. This time his punch hit Bosko's jaw and, as Bosko staggered and fell to the ground, Stefan turned and walked swiftly away, ignoring the shouts that followed him.

Shirley reacted quickly when she saw Stefan walk into the small house they'd rented for their stay at the Ridge. 'What has happened to you? You look as though you've been in a fight. Sit down and let me see to that head.'

'I've had a bit of a run-in with Bosko down at the baths. The man is a dangerous fool, and I knocked him down.'

'Why?'

Stefan rubbed his face. 'He said unkind things about you and I won't stand for that, not from anyone.'

'I hope no one saw you hit him,' said Shirley grimly.

'Only about a dozen of his mates.'

'Stefan, I really appreciate your sticking up for me, and I won't ask what Bosko said, because it must have been pretty bad for you to react in that way, but in front of his friends . . . You've said yourself that Bosko is a dangerous person and now you've humiliated him in public. Do you think that was a good idea?'

'So now he knows I have his number . . . I promise I'll keep out of his way in future. Just as well we don't live in Lightning Ridge anymore.'

Shirley could only agree that Opal Lake seemed a lot safer.

*

A plump man in tight shorts carried a tray set with a metal pot of tea, cold toast in a paper bag, and a saucer smeared with Vegemite and a bit of marmalade across the parking lot and rapped on the door of room six, at the far end of the motel. A young girl followed him with a second tray of dishes under metal lids and she knocked on the door of number four. The men standing about in the street leaning against their vehicles watched the progress of the breakfast delivery to the visiting opal buyers.

The men were a ragtag group. Some looked as though they'd walked straight out of their mines, covered in dust and still wearing their workboots. Others had spruced themselves up, while many wore the local uniform of thongs, shorts and T-shirts sporting rude slogans. One man had a newspaper rolled under his arm, trying to conceal the jar of opal he was carrying. Others kept their hands in their pockets, probably curled around the stones they hoped would be the payoff for their hard labour.

The runners, who were selling for others, looked more relaxed. These men came and went to the buying room throughout the day. The buyers were swift to assess the quality of the opal, which the miners would spread out on the small desk in the compact motel room. Some men left disappointed, others satisfied, and one man was unable to suppress an elated smirk.

Shirley and Stefan were the last to visit room six.

Roth Cameron rose and embraced Shirley, and shook Stefan's hand. 'So good to see you both.'

'You too, Roth. How's the family?' Shirley sat on the single chair in front of the desk and Stefan sat on the spare bed.

'Excellent. Tim wants to come up with me next visit. He might be just a lad, but he's already showing an interest in the business.'

'That's nice for you. I'd love to meet him. I'm sure he's a lovely boy.' Shirley spread their stones on the table. 'These are the firsts.'

Roth picked up two stones and his magnifier, and studied them. 'Lovely. Hmm. These are good. We can do something with these.' He rifled through the stones, quickly putting half a dozen to one side. 'The Japanese market is very strong at the moment, so I'll take these. They'll do very well. Now show me your seconds, I might be able to place them.'

Stefan pulled a bag from his pocket and put them on the table. 'I haven't spent time on these ones.'

'You've done a good job cutting and polishing,' said Roth. 'Both of us know what you have here all right.'

'No nasty surprises, either,' added Shirley.

'These might be your seconds, Stefan, but some would call them firsts. That claim of yours certainly produces high-quality opal. Exceptional colour.' He wrote some figures on a paper and pushed it across the table. 'Does this suit you both?'

Shirley glanced at Stefan who nodded. 'Thank you, Roth.'

The jeweller leant back and folded his arms behind his head. 'How long are you staying over here at the Ridge?'

'Not long. Nice change to come and see it. But we love living in Opal Lake,' said Shirley.

'I could do with some good black opal, in case you have a bit of a noodle around or plan on pegging another claim out here. Do you think you might? There've been some good rushes further out,' said Roth.

'We're happy on our claim. We've sometimes looked at other places but we don't want to go to the expense of starting up somewhere else,' said Shirley.

Roth looked at Stefan. 'I'm told there's a couple chucking it in, out on the Grawin field. He's done his back in. They're open to someone taking over their claim completely, or going sixty-forty.'

'Wouldn't hurt to have a look,' said Stefan.

'That would mean moving back here for a spell,' said Shirley.

'Maybe I could just check it out. I could work it for a few weeks and you could stay at Opal Lake. It could be a good move. You know how opal could be an inch away from where they gave up.'

'Of course, that's always the argument, isn't it? But I don't want us to be apart, Stefan. We do things together or not at all.'

Roth looked at Stefan, surprised by the tone of Shirley's voice. He'd always assumed her to be a practical person and this was a good opportunity. 'It was just a suggestion. You two are doing very well where you are, so why should you move?'

'Thanks for the suggestion, Roth.' Shirley stood up. 'Please come over and see us when you have a chance. See what we've done to the place at Opal Lake. We're very comfortable. Stefan has even planted fruit trees!'

'Love to.' He shook Stefan's hand warmly, and kissed Shirley's cheek. 'Happy hunting.'

Hand in hand Stefan and Shirley strolled down the street in the fading light.

'Shall we go to the club or the pub for one drink to celebrate?' asked Shirley.

'We should have asked Roth to have a drink with us,' said Stefan. 'He is a true friend.'

'Yes, he is. I think he gives us a good price.'

'Does he?'

'I know he's a businessman, but he's scrupulously honest and I trust him implicitly.'

'We should show him Tajna,' said Stefan. 'He would appreciate something that beautiful and valuable.'

'Yes, he would. And he wouldn't rest till he'd either acquired it or persuaded me to sell it or exhibit it or put it in a bank vault or something,' said Shirley. 'So there would be absolutely no point.'

'All right, Shirley. I know how much it means to you. But if the day ever comes, just say, if one of us gets sick, or we have no money, Roth is where you'd turn.'

'Yes, you're right. But we're hanging on to that fossil.'

Stefan put his arm around her shoulder. 'Very well. Let's go to the pub and get a drink and listen to everyone boasting about the spectacular prices they got for their opal today!'

Shirley knew that Stefan was itching to get out and look at the mine Roth had told them about.

'I don't mind hanging around a few more days, if you really want to look at that mine. Just out of interest, mind you,' said Shirley.

He kissed her. 'Well, it doesn't hurt just to look. If you don't want to come, you can stay here if you like.'

'I'm not staying in town by myself after your fight with Bosko. He and his mates give me the creeps.'

'We could always camp out. It will be fun.'

'Yes, I like that idea. I think we have enough gear in the truck to make that work.'

There'd been recent rain and they drove through a magical blur of pink and purple groundcover, budding wattle and a dozen shades of green as the earth and trees burst forth in fecund growth. They passed a snake sunning itself on the side of the rough dirt road and Shirley remembered the snake in her father's mine. She took Stefan's hand.

'This is amazing country,' said Stefan. 'It seems so barren, so tough, but it has a soft heart when there's rain.'

'I could never live in the city again,' agreed Shirley.

That night they lay in each other's arms, watching the

mantle of stars, making wishes on shooting ones, counting the seconds as the glow from a satellite made its stately arc across the velvet backdrop. The mullock mounds around them gleamed like milky breasts in the moonlight. Yellow lights from fires, lanterns plus the gentle throb of diesel generators, swinging light bulbs in makeshift shacks, caravans and camps made them aware that they were part of a small community and everyone was here for the same reason. And whether they had nothing but a sleeping bag and pick, or a digger, a bogger, a blower or a hoist, they shared the common ground of opal miners, united in fanciful dreams of firey opal. Shirley knew that each day these people would disappear into the earth, hoping that today some dark rocky womb would deliver a breathtaking, shining gem, freed into the light after aeons of imprisonment.

They introduced themselves to the other miners as speculators who were thinking about taking over the Cornwells' mine because they didn't want to be thought of as squatters. Most of the miners were friendly and chatted about inconsequential matters and seemed unconcerned by their presence, making them feel very comfortable. But the couple in a tent near to the Cornwells' shaft touched Shirley's heart. Stefan noticed them, too. Their tired faces, etched with dispirited worry, spoke of disillusionment. It seemed as though desperation had driven them here and now there was no other place to go.

They nodded briefly to Shirley, who wished them luck.

When Shirley woke in the middle of one night she thought that an animal was disturbing the silence. But she quickly realised that the growling she could hear was the sound of anger, desperation and drunken rage. She lifted her head. The camp was dark, no light or movement hinted at anyone still awake at midnight.

Stefan stirred and reached for her. 'What is happening?'

'The couple in the tent seem to be arguing. He sounds as though he's been drinking.'

'He certainly does. I don't think they've had any luck. I wonder if this is their last chance. I suppose he drinks to escape.'

'It won't help,' said Shirley.

They pulled their sleeping bags around their ears, trying to drift back to sleep, but a wail, so wrenchingly unhappy, made Shirley sit up and grope for the torch.

'Shirley! What are you doing? You can't go over there,' mumbled Stefan.

The silhouettes of trees were charcoal grey against the watery dark sky and pale stars. Into the still landscape exploded the figure of a woman, hair wild, arms flailing, running blindly. Even in the wan night light, Shirley could see the woman's pain, and her hopelessness and anger was like a burst dam. Shirley got out of her sleeping bag and stood up.

The woman fell against a tree and began pummelling and hitting its sturdy trunk. Shirley went over to her and wrapped her arms around her.

The distraught woman's words seemed to choke her. 'There's no hope for us. It's over. There is no opal, no nothing in this Godforsaken place. I want my family. I want a home. I want to live properly, not like this. God, is it too much to ask for a bit of a chance? A bit of luck?' She screamed and tore herself from Shirley's grasp and began to rip shards of bark and small branches from the tree. Her screams became an unholy shriek as she vented all she'd lost and all that would never be.

Shirley knew how this hard life of searching for elusive opal could break even the most optimistic soul. 'Please,' she begged the woman, 'go back to your tent. Things will be better in the morning, I'm sure. They always are.'

The woman gave Shirley a curious look, as though

she had just noticed Shirley's presence, and then ran off into the night.

Shirley put her fist to her mouth to stop calling out after her. Every nurturing fibre in her, every practical medical skill she knew, were of no use to this woman.

Stefan came and stood beside her in the darkness. He put his arms about her, turning her to his chest, sheltering her. 'Let her be. I feel so sorry for that woman but I don't think you can do anything for her. We'll never be like that. Never, ever.'

The next day they returned to Lightning Ridge. Shirley stopped for a coffee while Stefan filled their truck with petrol. The coffee shop owner brought Shirley her coffee and asked her where she'd been. Shirley explained that she and her partner had been looking at a mine, but had decided not to take it because they already had a mine at Opal Lake.

'Fair enough, you know what's best for you.'

Shirley nodded. 'It is a good life over there, especially when you've got a decent partner, and find enough to get by on, that little bit of colour, now and then. But things could get you down if your luck is out and you get dealt a duffer of a mine.'

The woman nodded. 'There's a couple I know of out at Grawin, down on their luck but always hoping. I believe he's not much of a worker. Drinks. Anyway, it's all over town this morning, she fell down a mine shaft last night and got killed. Everyone reckons it was deliberate, and it wouldn't surprise me at all. She was pretty desperate, I'm told.'

Shirley stared at her in horror. 'Oh, no. We were out there. She was hysterical and I tried to help her!'

'Nothing you or anyone on this earth could have done would have helped her, from what I know, but it was good of you to try. You get on your way and don't worry about it.'

Shirley sipped her coffee in sad silence, waiting for Stefan. She was about to tell him about the woman at Grawin when he joined her, but he looked so very concerned that she asked if there was a problem. 'You look worried. Is there something wrong with the truck?'

'I just saw Bosko and some of the others.'

'I told you to ignore him.' She paused. 'Did he say anything to you?'

'It wasn't Bosko, it was Zoran.' Stefan looked at Shirley with stricken eyes. 'He said that while we were out looking at the Cornwells' mine, my cousin Franko in Split was trying to reach me. There's a problem with my mother. She's very ill.'

'Oh, darling. That's just awful. You'll have to phone Franko as soon as we get back to Opal Lake. How come Zoran knows about your mother?' she asked.

'Franko is married to Zoran's sister.'

'Is there someone looking after your mother?'

Stefan shook his head. 'Franko's mother in Zagreb. But she's old too. Look, I really want to get back to Opal Lake. I don't feel as though I can find out what is wrong with my mother if Bosko and his cronies are hanging about. Would you be really sorry if we don't go to Hebel to look at the old farm equipment?'

'Don't be silly. Of course not, we can always do it some other time.'

Shirley was glad to return to the peace of Opal Lake.

Stefan rang his cousin Franko straight away and was shocked to learn that his mother was dying.

'There must be something I can do,' he said miserably.

'But what can you do from here? You said she always said you had to leave and make a new life, so don't feel guilty about that,' said Shirley. But as Stefan nodded miserably, she said, 'Perhaps you should go back if you think it's safe enough.'

'I know there's unrest in the south with the Kosovo Albanians wanting independence and the government sending in troops to stop the unrest, but my mother's in Zagreb, and I'm not involved in any political activities here or back there, as you well know, so I'll be fine.'

'Stefan, you're always telling me about how fierce the Croatians, Serbs, Slovenians and Macedonians are about keeping their culture, customs and language alive, and that so many of them want to break up with the central government and go their own ways. You promise me that if you go back, you won't get involved with any of that.'

'Of course I won't. You know my feelings about Australia. This is my home now and I'll let others battle over the future of Yugoslavia. I know I told you about the UDBa operating in Australia, but that has nothing to do with me.'

'I'm not very happy about your going back and I'll worry about you, but it *is* your mother and if you don't see her because I don't want you to go, well, I couldn't live with that.'

'Thank you, darling, I do love my mother. I know that my parents both wanted me to leave and start a new life here, but I know that in her heart of hearts my mother always hoped that things in Yugoslavia would settle down and I would come back, marry a nice girl and care for her in her old age.'

Shirley looked at him. 'Really? How come you've never mentioned this before?'

'I never think about it.'

'But was that idea always in the back of your mind, that you were just staying here in Australia till things were calm in your country and then you'd go back and get married?' Shirley's voice quavered.

'I told you, I never thought about it.'

'Until now.'

'I am just thinking about my mother.'

'I appreciate that, but you obviously aren't thinking about me, and our future here. *We* could get married, you know!' Shirley herself was shocked at the vehemence she felt.

He looked surprised and then bemused, which irritated her even more. 'Marriage? Why would we? We're happy just the way we are.'

'I can't believe we're having this conversation. It's demeaning. You'd marry a Yugoslavian girl, but not an Australian one. Is that what you mean?' Shirley turned away. 'Just go home to your mother. But if you come back to me, we'll need to settle this.' She swung back to him, her eyes filled with tears. She was suddenly very rattled. Her sense of stability and permanence, and her future with Stefan that underpinned every day of her life had been rocked.

'Shirley, you are being utterly ridiculous. I thought we understood each other. We are really happy with each other. Perhaps I was wrong. Perhaps I don't understand Australian women at all.' He walked away from her.

'Stop acting like an arrogant Yugo!' shouted Shirley, furious with him, but also feeling unnerved by how this row had suddenly flared.

Neither mentioned their spat. Things seemed to return to normal. If Shirley sensed an undercurrent of strain, she put it down to Stefan's uncertainty about his mother and what he'd find when he returned to Yugoslavia.

As she watched him pack a small suitcase and put his passport and wallet in his jacket pocket she said, 'Maybe when you get back, you might get an Australian passport. Do you have enough money for the trip?'

He shrugged. 'I'll manage. I might need some bribe money. Wheels still need to be greased if you want anything done in a hurry, or done at all. I might need to pay for special medical care for my mother.'

'If you're worried, why not take some of our opals? You could see Roth Cameron in Sydney and sell them before you fly out.'

He nodded. 'That's a good idea. But I put you in charge of opals. Do you mind if I sell them for this?'

'Stefan, they're our opals. We worked together for them, so of course I don't mind.'

Shirley drove him to Broken Hill, where he caught the train to Sydney. At the station there was a group of Japanese tourists who were running late and in the confusion surrounding them, there was no time for lingering.

Stefan held Shirley briefly, murmuring, 'You are so very special to me, Shirley.' He kissed her swiftly, stepped on to the train and took his seat. As the train pulled away, she couldn't see him for the craning faces of the tourists, but she waved furiously anyway, tears running down her face.

Four weeks passed and there was no letter, phone call or any message from Stefan. Shirley finally called his cousin Franko in Split but his English was virtually nonexistent and she wasn't sure that he understood who she was or what she wanted. All she managed to get from him was an insistent message that, 'Stefan, no here.'

To keep herself from going crazy with worry and concern, she went back to their mine, despite promising Stefan she wouldn't work it alone. But she found the work calming and distracting and better than doing nothing.

They had been following a small faultline in the second drive, so she continued to chip away at it instead of powering through the main drive with the jackhammer. She was delighted when she found a small channel of good opal. She dug it out and washed the roughs outside and then took them back to the dugout. After snipping a chip off each one she decided they were good enough to put in the safe with the rest of their collection. But her pleasure in the find was tempered by the fact that she couldn't share it with Stefan.

When she opened the safe, she was surprised that Stefan had taken quite a few more of the firsts than she'd anticipated. She just hoped he'd got a good price for them and the money would serve its purpose and solve things for him in Yugoslavia.

As she locked the safe another thought struck her. Was her precious fossil safe? She pushed the thought away. She had always refused to keep the fossil in the safe, telling Stefan that, 'It doesn't feel right to lock such a beautiful thing away in the dark, when it's already been hidden in the dark for millions of years. And besides, if we were ratted, they'd take the safe.'

Stefan had laughed indulgently and never asked where she put the fossil gem.

But now, after her initial suspicion, she couldn't stop worrying about her precious fossil. At first she refused to go and check on Tajna as she felt that by even considering that he might have taken it she was being disloyal to Stefan. But as the silence from Stefan lengthened, she couldn't stand it any longer.

She went to the area they'd opened up as a work space and office. The room wasn't finished and smelt musty and dusty, with rubble still piled at the base of the back wall, but it was already cluttered with a filing cabinet, overflowing bookcases and a small desk. Photographs, a map and a calendar were tacked to the wall. Loose electric cables were looped so that a portable light could be rigged up to illuminate the unlined earth tunnel that led from the kitchen and ended at a wall. This wall was still to be removed so that the office would be linked with the main part of the dugout. In the meantime, the room had a separate entrance near where their car was parked.

Shirley reached up and removed the spotlight from its metal holder on the wall, which made the passage much darker. Then she slid back the metal brace that hung from a single bolt in the wall. She reached into the exposed cavity behind it and felt a surge of relief as her hand touched the cloth wrapped around the opal fossil. She drew Tajna out and, putting the light on the dirt floor, crouched down to examine her prize. She unwrapped the fossil and its dazzling colours leapt out at her. Slowly she caressed its surface, lifted it to her lips and kissed it. Then she held it to her chest, longing not for the precious cold relic of another life from another time, but for the warmth of Stefan.

Shirley lost track of the days as she stayed in the dugout and worked in the mine, sometimes emerging into darkness, unaware it was night. Finally she could bear Stefan's silence no longer. She had to find out if Zoran had any news of Stefan, or at least if he could find something out for her, so she drove to Lightning Ridge, checked into the motel and slept fitfully until morning. She sought out Zoran, who told her that he would make inquiries and would come to her motel later that day.

Shirley sat on a plastic chair outside her room pretending to read a book, but behind her dark glasses she watched the passing traffic. She knew some of the locals by name or by sight, and the few tourists she saw were obviously just sightseeing. She felt desperately alone. Now she wished she'd stayed in Opal Lake. Fear suddenly grabbed her. What if Stefan was trying to reach her and she wasn't at their dugout? Would he try to contact her again?

She jumped to her feet, deciding to drive back to Opal Lake right away, but just then Zoran appeared, walking towards her across the carpark accompanied by Bosko, who had a slight smirk on his face.

'So. I heard you were in town. You wanted to have a word with Zoran.' Before Shirley could speak Bosko continued, 'You want to know about that Croat boy-friend, eh?'

Shirley tried to adopt the same insolent and arrogant tone. 'If you know something, I'd like to know it, too. I have plans to make.'

'I hope you're not planning a little holiday on the Dalmatian coast.' He chuckled. 'Could be awkward.'

She stared at him and Zoran. 'Zoran, what do you know about Stefan? Where is he? Is he all right?'

Zoran opened his mouth to speak, but Bosko silenced him.

'I will tell Shirley the news. You can forget about your boyfriend. He won't be coming back.'

'Why? Why do you say that? What do you know?'

'I heard he got married. His Australian holiday is over. You'd better find yourself a new mining partner.'

'I don't believe you. Why would he do that?' Shirley struggled to take in what Bosko had told her. 'Zoran, is this true?'

Zoran looked at his boots, as though too ashamed to tell Shirley what had happened, but Bosko was not at all reticent.

'He has taken my advice and married a good Yugoslav girl. You Australian women think that you're so good, much better than our women, but you're not. Stefan will be much happier living with a good woman and in a better country than this.' He burst out laughing.

'But he never wanted to go back! He only went back to see his mother. He hated the fighting, the troubles. He loves Australia. *He loves me.*'

'He should never have turned his back on his real country. Forget him. You won't hear from him again. He's had his fun with you. Now you'd better find yourself a new man before you get too old to dig opals on your own. Come on, Zoran, we have better places to be.'

Bosko turned and strolled away. He didn't bother to look back at the shattered woman standing by the motel-room door.

Shirley drove back to Opal Lake on autopilot, her mind racing, her heart thumping. Images, memories, the sound of Stefan singing crowded into her mind. Above all she kept asking herself, 'Why? Why?' Surely he wouldn't have just slunk back to his previous life without a word to her. There had to be some reason. Had his dying mother really insisted that he marry some local girl and he'd agreed to do it just to appease her?

Then she thought of the disagreement they'd had just before he'd left. It was a silly argument. How stupid she'd been, to put pressure on him about formalising their relationship. She was happy as they were. She really hadn't cared about whether she was married to him or not. Or had she? Guilt began nagging at her. Was all this her fault? Had she frightened him away?

Shirley began to analyse their relationship. Had she been too aggressive and taken control of their lives by wanting to move to Opal Lake to her father's mine? Perhaps the move had put Stefan in the position of appearing to be dependent on her. She knew she'd made a lot of decisions for them both, because Stefan had insisted that she look after the business side of their venture. Had she undermined him?

He always said that she was a good businesswoman, but had she shut Stefan out of that area of their life? She had simply wanted everything to be perfect for them, so she had always contacted the buyer and decided what they'd sell and what they'd keep. Was it only in their close personal and private time that she asked for his opinions as they made their plans?

Had she been horribly wrong when she insisted that they keep the Tajna fossil? Stefan had wanted to sell it so that they could be well set up for the future, but she had wanted to keep it for entirely sentimental and illogical reasons. Was that the wrong decision?

She tortured herself with questions and castigated herself. She thought back over their discussions and tried to fathom how many of their decisions had been mutual ones and how many she bulldozed him into. Had she taken advantage of his sweet nature and been thoughtlessly selfish?

He was such a gentle, easygoing man, his anger reserved only for the likes of Bosko. She thought of his passion and his tender touch and their uninhibited lovemaking, and she cried out aloud in pain. Bosko's words, 'He's had his fun with you', kept repeating in her head.

Shirley stared at the road, and everything that was familiar to her suddenly looked foreign and ugly. Her world had changed. How could she return to their dugout where everywhere she looked at was a reminder of all they'd created and shared?

There had to be another explanation. Surely it could not be true that once Stefan was back in Yugoslavia he'd found that he still cared for it, and loved its familiarity, and realised that Australia had merely been an interlude. Had he simply used her as Bosko hinted?

Shirley was confused, hurt, bewildered, but she had no one to talk to and nowhere to turn.

Back in Opal Lake, she was embarrassed by Stefan's abrupt departure and just wanted to hide and never come out of her dugout. She felt such a fool. Everyone knew that she loved Stefan, and now they'd know that he had run off and married someone else. It was so humiliating. So she sat in her cave and tried to ignore the outside world.

Two weeks after her return, there came a soft call at her door. 'You there, Shirley?'

Shirley lifted her head, tried to smooth her hair and

came out to the entrance where Jock, a local miner, was standing, holding his old hat in his hands.

'Hello, Jock. What can I do for you?' If Shirley was surprised at the sight of a somewhat dishevelled old man standing outside her dugout, she didn't let him know.

'Sorry to bother you, Shirley, but Toby down at the store said you might be able to help me out with the loan of a bit of equipment. Me generator and jack have packed up and I reckon I'm bottoming on good opal. Toby suggested I might be able to borrow some of your gear . . . er, seeing you're not digging at present.' He paused and as Shirley didn't answer, he added, 'Hate to leave that opal just sitting there. The suspense is killing me.'

Shirley almost smiled. Then she sighed. 'No, I'm not using the jack or old generator at present. Go and help yourself. It's in the shed. Hang on, I'll give you the key.'

The old miner looked relieved. 'Gee, thanks, love. Er, when I bring it back can I bring anything up here for you? Toby said you don't get out all that often for supplies.'

'I'm all right, mate.' Then she hesitated. 'Jock, if you wouldn't mind dropping a list into Toby, maybe he could get someone to bring the groceries up when they're coming this way.'

'You bet, Shirley. Happy to help,' said Jock, looking relieved. While his request for the loan of some gear was genuine, he was pleased that he could help Shirley, too.

When Jock told Toby that Shirley did need some groceries, the storekeeper said, 'She should stop locking herself away and moping. She has to get some tucker into herself. I reckon we're going to have to prise her out of that dugout, or keep dropping in to check on her. You know, she needs to get back to doing something proper. Never thought that Stefan would do a runner. He seemed to be a good bloke. You just can't tell.'

And so a routine was established with a regular delivery of supplies sent to Shirley's dugout.

When Jock returned Shirley's equipment he scraped his boots and whipped off his hat as she invited him to come in and sit down.

'You look pleased with yourself, Jock. How'd you go?' asked Shirley.

The normally taciturn Scot gave a broad grin. 'It was there all right. Not much, but it's safely stowed, till them buyers hit town.' He reached into his trouser pocket, pulled out a sock and shook out several pieces of opal onto the table. 'Here, have a look. You're a pretty good judge.'

Shirley studied the stones, admired the colour, congratulated him on his find and spent the next hour talking to him about opals.

Finally, Jock felt comfortable enough to ask, 'You won't be mining no more?'

'Hard work for me on my own,' admitted Shirley. 'But I'm thinking about it.'

'Plenty of fellows would go in with you. In the mine,' he said, looking faintly embarrassed at coming close to what was locally considered the taboo subject of Stefan.

'I'm all right for the moment, Jock. I'll manage. I still have my little nest egg, but when I need to, I'll think about mining again. Plenty of time.'

Jock scratched his head. 'Aye, time, there's the rub, eh? Fellow like me, pushing eighty. I haven't got as long as I'd like. My back gives me trouble. Not as strong as I used to be.'

'So you need to find a young fellow to come in with you. Got any family out here?' asked Shirley.

'No. It's only me. Got a few nephews back in Scotland but they don't fancy this lifestyle. Not that I blame them, it's hard work. And all the new people out here now want the fancy gear. Heavy machinery. They'll be looking for big investors, serious mining people.' He shook his head. 'It's all changing. Don't know how much longer I can keep at it.'

'What else would you do with yourself, Jock?'

'That's a tricky one. Not going back to the city, that's for sure. Reckon I'll be staying in me little camp out in the bush, till the day comes and they find me sleeping the sleep of the dead under a tree.' He smiled. 'Could be worse places. I have a nice bed under the trees and I lie out there under the old net and listen to the leaves rustling and talking. A lot of stories whisper across the opal fields. But one day all those stories will be gone.'

'That's a sad story you're telling me, Jock,' said Shirley, trying to mimic his Scots brogue. 'Don't you know any cheerful ones?'

'Stories! I know stories that will make your toes curl, make you bust a valve laughing, and secrets too. Och, aye, I do.'

Shirley studied him as he reached for his pipe. 'Y'know, Jock, it'd be a shame if those stories were lost. There's a lot of history out here.'

He nodded emphatically. 'Aye. Once people are gone, it's all gone. But what to do, eh?' He shrugged.

'I'll tell you what we do, Jock. We'll write them down. Or I will,' said Shirley suddenly. 'When you're so inclined, come and see me. You tell me those stories and I'll put them down. What do you say?'

He thought about it for a moment. 'That's a grand plan. Will there be biscuits?'

Shirley laughed. 'Indeed there will. Maybe a fruitcake with the tea. I'll look forward to it.'

Jock was pleased to see the light back in Shirley's eyes. He didn't think anyone would be interested in the stories he had to tell, but if it gave Shirley some spark and put the light back in her eyes he'd be sure to come and see her again.

So it began. Jock's visits were augmented by visits from one or two of the other old-timers, who also came to share their stories. At the pub there were jokes about Shirley's old suitors. The men swore they were doing it to help Shirley and give her an interest. But deep down the miners and the loners who'd lost touch with their families long ago saw it as a way to leave their small mark, explaining who they were, what they'd seen and what they'd done.

It was the spark, the lifeline that Shirley needed. Her skills of gentle probing, patient listening and hours transcribing were valuable. She filled notebooks. She dragged out her old typewriter and the tape recorder she'd forgotten why she'd kept, and set them up on her kitchen table.

Gradually she filled the old fruit boxes and cartons that Toby sent up from the store with files and notes and packed them away, clearly labelled.

When she didn't see Jock for a few weeks, she asked if someone could check on him. They found him, as he'd hoped, sleeping on his stretcher bed beneath the sandlewood trees under a shroud of torn netting. The occasional bird call and the soft rustle of the leaves kept him company.

'What a beaut place to sleep through eternity,' muttered one of the men.

They packed up Jock's meagre belongings from his mudbrick shack, pausing to admire the old man's skill in transforming mulga branches into basic furniture as well as the crooked stairway he'd constructed, which led to the flat roof of the dwelling. Amidst the debris of leaves and animal droppings on the roof stood an old tin bathtub with a hose attached to the water tank, where he must have sat and soaked, admiring his view.

Later they delivered a big old rusting biscuit tin to Shirley. She knew that the tin had probably been searched for opals for there was nothing of value in it, only old army medals, yellowing photos and postcards, and a powdery sprig of heather.

Jock was not the last to make Shirley the repository of effects treasured for sentimental reasons rather than their value. Sometimes miners gave her items that were of value with the casual comment, 'If you find something to do with these, then you'll know what to do.'

The miners' stories and their artefacts were carefully documented and stored. Shirley knew that eventually they would be appreciated by a museum or some other archive, for the life of the opal field that they described was fast disappearing. So she kept them safe.

The mantle of keeper of the stories, the one who held remnants of a life that might otherwise be forgotten, settled gently and easily on Shirley's shoulders. She ordered books by mail and wrote copious lengthy letters to academics and specialists to learn more about the detritus of the lives that ended in the pockmarked landscape of unfulfilled dreams and hopes.

More and more people called in to see her, and Shirley always insisted that she was fine, telling them that she was keeping busy, doing the things she'd been planning to do for years. As if to prove it, she even set up a bit of a vegetable garden in a section of galvanised tank, and erected a shade cloth over it to shelter her plants from the sun. Visitors always knew that Shirley kept a pot of tea on the go and homemade biscuits to share. People would check at the store and the post office to see if there was anything for her before they went to see her and sometimes a visit with her could stretch over many hours.

*

285

Shirley looked into the remains of the cold tea in her cup and was silent, remembering. Then she sighed. 'Those old men gave me a reason to be here. So I stayed in Opal Lake, in my dugout, and I tried to forget Stefan and what had happened.'

'What do you think did happen to Stefan?' asked Kerrie.

'I never heard from him again. I blame myself.'

Kerrie waited a moment. 'Do you know if he saw his mother?'

'I don't know but, as I said before, it was hard to find out anything. I tried ringing his cousin Franko again, in desperation, but I got nothing new. I didn't know what else to do.'

'Surely you don't believe there was anything in an old flame or a family marriage setup?' said Kerrie. 'Milton used to always tease me about the girl he knew when he was ten years old who he thought he'd marry. He said that she probably grew up to be hairy and fat.'

'The trouble was that his disappearance seemed so out of character, but I couldn't get any information. I called everyone I could think of at the Ridge in the Yugoslav community and no one was helpful. Even Zoran wouldn't speak to me. They'd closed ranks, you see. I was an outsider.'

'Did you contact the embassy?'

'Yes. They told me the date that Stefan had arrived in Yugoslavia, but said that they had no date for his departure, so he was still in the country.'

'But you believed Stefan never stopped loving you?' said Kerrie, imagining Shirley's pain.

'I was in agony, wondering. But as time went on I began to doubt. I thought that if he had loved me at all, he would have got a message to me to explain what had happened. But nothing.'

Kerrie looked at Shirley sympathetically. 'And you've never stopped hoping, have you.'

'I've never stopped hurting,' Shirley corrected her.

'You didn't want to move from here?'

'Stefan was the love of my life. Yes, I was hurt. I wish I knew what had happened. But he had decided not to come back, for whatever reason. I've done all the rationalising, analysing, blaming and justifying I can. I locked myself away until those old miners rescued me. I was hurt and wounded and embarrassed and I felt foolish, but people treated me with kindness, even though I know some of them speculated about me behind my back. It was only later, when new people moved here who didn't know Stefan, that things became easier. But deep down I never, never forgot.'

'So that's why you're still in Opal Lake?' asked Kerrie softly, deeply touched by this woman's love story.

'I know that he won't come back, but I think I always hoped he would, and I'd be here when he did. He was the love of my life. For better or worse.'

'Oh, Shirley. That's so sad.'

'I've lived with it for a long time, and I've gradually come to terms with how my life turned out. I had a great love. More than I ever dreamed possible. Some people never have that. I've made a life for myself, which I enjoy, in a place that I love.' She smiled. 'Now, Kerrie. Enough about me. I seem to have talked for hours. Tell me, how is your painting coming along?'

'Actually, I think a couple of them are okay. Not sure about some of the others. But I've enjoyed doing them. It's like a light has gone on in my heart and soul and mind.'

'I'm glad. Could I see one?'

'Of course. You've shared so much with me, how could I refuse? And I won't be offended if you don't think much of them,' added Kerrie. 'I'll bring one or two of them to show you. And I'll bring a good bottle of red. I've finally managed to find a half-decent one at the pub, but next time I come to Opal Lake I'll bring my own.'

'That's music to my ears. Next time . . .' Shirley paused. 'It's nice for me that you escaped having Christmas with Milton's girls, but when you go back they'll still be there. You're going to have to sort out your relationship with them.'

'Don't I know it. I love being here without the hassle of dealing with them, but I can't just ignore them. I feel a sense of responsibility towards them because they are Milton's children and I loved Milton more than I ever thought it possible to love anyone. But you know, since Milton's death, I've thought about our marriage and I realise that it was very one-sided.'

Shirley straightened up. Kerrie realised that they had come full circle. Shirley was once again her strong, practical, sensible self. But Kerrie was not prepared for what Shirley had to say.

'Kerrie, we have talked night after night and I know a lot about your marriage and I have come to a conclusion about you. I think that you were a bit of a wimp and you let Milton subsume you! Why didn't you stand up to him? Surely you must have felt and known how he dominated you.'

Kerrie shifted uneasily. 'I guess I did, deep down. But I didn't want to rock the boat. He could be quite volatile. He was much older than me and he frequently made me feel like I was a stupid schoolgirl. I think he knocked my confidence around. Even the girls accused me of being a doormat. But overriding everything was the fact that I was in awe of him! He was so talented and so highly regarded all around the world, and I was in his slipstream. People idolised him and I guess I did, too.'

'There's the public persona and the man at home. You

shouldn't have let him bully you – which, from what you have told me, is what he did. It sounds to me as if Milton was arrogant and selfish. And you let him get away with it. That might be partly why things are so bad with the girls. Why would they respect you, Kerrie, when it seems that you didn't respect yourself?'

'Shirley! You don't understand! I was a very young bride, with very little experience of life, stepping into an established household, with a famous husband and step-daughters not much younger than me. It was hard,' said Kerrie defensively.

'Of course it was. And I understand how you loved Milton, but I think that your relationship with him was at some cost to yourself, I have say,' said Shirley. 'And I can't help but think that he spoilt those girls on a super-ficial level, which didn't really help them, either. The fact that he left the bulk of his estate to you is a thorn between you and the girls, and it's put you in a difficult situation. Now the question is how should you be deal-ing with the present poisonous relationship between you and his daughters?'

'I just haven't known what to do. It all seems too late. I wish that Milton was still here to sort it out.'

'Well, he isn't here and, far from sorting things out, he's left you holding the bag. It's up to you, Kerrie, but I think that you need to decide whether you want to per-severe with your relationship – such as it is – with your stepdaughters or just move on with your life. What do you want to do?'

'Oh, Shirley, what's the point?' sighed Kerrie.

'You haven't answered my question. What do you really feel about those girls?'

Kerrie thought a moment. Shirley was being quite confronting. 'I would like to have an amicable relation-ship with them. They are Milton's children, and I never had children of my own. And, I suppose if I'm truthful, I've always been very fond of Alia, the youngest. I thought that we could be good friends, but her sisters seemed to overrule everything.'

'Aha! There you go then. Concentrate on Alia,' said Shirley.

'That's easier said than done. What do I do?'

'What's she doing now?'

'She dabbles. The girls have always had money so they've been under no pressure to earn a living. But of all of them, Alia has been the most interested in her father's field. She was a fine arts student, and she worked in a studio for a while. Then all the girls opened a trendy fashion boutique, but that didn't last. The best thing she did was work in a friend's art gallery in Paddington, and now she's talking about setting up one of her own.'

'Can't you help her do it?'

'I could but I really don't know if she'd appreciate my involvement. At this stage there's nothing definite about the gallery. It's still all talk.'

Shirley looked thoughtful. 'You said there was a retrospective planned of Milton's sculptures?'

Kerrie rolled her eyes. 'Yes. Wonderful plan, but it's a lot of work.'

'Why don't you get Alia to help you? Get her involved. She'll get experience setting up an exhibition, which, if she wants to open a gallery, she'll need, and it will make her feel that she still has a role in her father's life. And her help will certainly free you up a bit,' said Shirley.

Kerrie thought for a moment and smiled. 'That is a brilliant idea. You are so practical. And smart. I don't know why I didn't think of that. I'm sure that if I approach her carefully and along the lines you've suggested, it might just work. Shirley, you are a gem.'

'Maybe you could take the girls back an opal each.'

'If they wanted jewellery they'd go to Tiffany's in Castlereagh Street,' said Kerrie.

'Okay, not such a good idea, but do approach Alia about the New York retrospective.'

'You're right. I'll give it a try.' She smiled at Shirley. 'You have the knack of making me see things a little differently, a little deeper. You're a good friend, so I guess that's why I worry about you.'

'Nothing will happen to me. My opals and my secrets are safe.'

Nevertheless, Kerrie was still concerned that a physically unfit older woman living in a dugout in a hillside in an isolated spot hoarding valuable opal, which others knew about, could be a sitting duck for a robbery. 'You're so trusting, Shirley.'

There was a noise at the entrance and Davo stomped into the dugout, calling out to Shirley.

'See what I mean? Your open-door policy could get you into trouble,' said Kerrie in a low voice.

'Davo is a mate,' said Shirley and called back, 'In here, Davo.'

'I saw your outside light on. Not like you to leave it on, so I thought I'd check. Hello, again,' he said to Kerrie.

'Hi. Well, Shirley, I'd better go. I'll see you tomorrow, with the promised bottle of red.'

'If I'd known you wanted wine, I'd have brought some up,' said Davo affably.

'It's fine, Davo.'

Kerrie kissed Shirley. 'See you later. And thank you.'

Shirley nodded. 'See you, sweetie. Bye, Davo, thanks for checking up on me.'

On a whim, Kerrie took a drive out to Opal Lake. The shimmering silver sand was, as usual, deserted. Through her dark glasses it glittered like some mirage. She pulled on a hat and walked a little distance, thinking of Shirley as a little girl with her father playing in the waters of the magical lake and, later, Shirley and Stefan camping here under the stars. She paused, shading her eyes to stare at a rusting coil of old barbed wire and a rotten fence post, the last man standing at the end of a hopeless march across the desert.

The beauty of this silent sandy lake now above the ancient inland sea still fascinated her. She planned to come and paint here when she returned in the cooler months. Maybe one day she, too, would see Opal Lake filled with water. She squinted, trying to imagine the surface covered in shining water with flocks of birds dancing upon it.

Maybe it was her specially tinted sunglasses but it suddenly looked as though the endless lake was smeared in muted colours as if a layer of opal lay just beneath the surface. In the sky above the same hot bright colours flashed like a reflection. It must be the glare of the hot sun, she decided, and turned and retraced her steps.

Kerrie left a note for Ingrid, thanking her for allowing her to use her dugout and saying that if she were ever in Sydney she was more than welcome to stay at Rose Bay. Then she propped up the small sketch she'd done as a gift beside it.

She packed the car and drove the few doors to Shirley's dugout. As she looked across the little town and the plains beyond, she committed the primary colours that burned on her retina to memory – deep blue sky and white clouds; russet red rocks; soft, deep green trees; the flash of scarlet flowers; the golden light; the soft-looking, tufted balls of grasses.

'I'll remember all this on a rainy day in Sydney,' she said to Shirley as she came inside.

'My muddle?' said Shirley as she pushed books aside on the kitchen table. 'Time for a cuppa?'

'Thanks, but no. I'll get a coffee in the Hill. I don't want to prolong the agony. I hate saying goodbye.'

'It's *au revoir*. This is your second home. You have unfinished business here.'

'I do?' said Kerrie. 'Perhaps you're right. Anyway, I brought you a parting present. Just a small thing.' Kerrie held out a large flat envelope.

Shirley took it and opened the flap and slid out a sketch beneath a layer of tissue. As she lifted the gauzy paper she found her own face staring back at her. The painting was a double image, one of Shirley throwing her head back with a wide smile and laughter crinkling her eyes, and beside it a profile of a thoughtful, wistful woman, remembering.

Shirley cleared her throat and Kerrie could see she was touched by her efforts.

'This is good, Kerrie. You got me, though I prefer laughing Shirley.' She looked at Kerrie and her pale blue eyes were watery with emotion. 'You see inside people. You have the inner eye good painters have, to be able see a person's soul, not just their skin. You must keep paint-ing, Kerrie.'

'Shirley, you don't know how you've helped me. Not just with boosting my confidence in my art, but helping me be strong and stand up for myself. Might be a bit late, but I'm ready for my life again – dealing with the girls, putting Milton into perspective and getting on with things. I'm going to look up some old friends, have a bit of fun and paint.'

'Sounds like a plan to me,' said Shirley, holding out her arms.

They held each other for a moment and then Shirley patted Kerrie on the shoulder. 'See you when you come back here, girl.'

'I wish . . .' began Kerrie, but Shirley put her finger to her lips.

'No more talking. I'll be here when you turn up again. Drive safely.'

Kerrie nodded and gave a little wave and walked from the cool quiet dugout into the searing summer heat. Whether it was the heat haze or tears, the scenery wavered and danced as she drove slowly away from Opal Lake. The landscape was empty, no breeze, no animal or human moved in the midday sun, but in the cool caverns beneath the surface, in tunnels and shafts and man-made chambers, the search for the elusive opal continued to occupy the hearts and heads of dreamers.

ANNA

10

SHE STOOD BESIDE THE other girls, stretching her legs and flexing her arms, her vision filled with the minutiae of the smooth red track curving away from her and the other poised athletes. She focused on the ribbon of track, screening out the closeness of the other runners either side of her. All of them knew that, in a little more than two minutes, only one of them would be the winner. The sounds of the crowd, the starter and the amplified announcer faded into the background as she waited for the one signal she needed.

The sound of the starter's pistol ripped into her nerve endings and sent her rocketing forward, even before she'd made the conscious decision to move. It had precipitated an instinctive severing of her stationary state. She was instantly in full flight. She'd sometimes wondered if racehorses felt the same. One minute they were at the starter's gate and then they had exploded onto the track at full gallop.

As she ran, Anna kept in her own mental zone. She could see only the two runners whose staggered start had put them ahead of her, and she was oblivious to the others as she ran her own race, against herself, against her pounding chest and straining muscles, hauling deep breaths into her lungs to race her towards her goal, eight hundred metres to the finish. Briefly, her trainer's words came to her about pacing herself, positioning herself, staying with her race strategy, but somehow her mind did not seem able to control the surging energy propelling her forward.

The runners merged into a single lane and jostled for position, passing the finishing line for the first time. Just one more circuit of the track, four hundred metres left to run. Anna overtook the leaders and the exhilaration of seeing the empty track ahead was so great she could hear, as well as feel, her blood pounding, which combined with her panting breath to drown out all other sounds. She knew that she had less than one hundred metres to go but as she neared the finish line she suddenly heard the pounding of feet behind her and, as she lunged for the finish, another girl flashed past her.

Anna doubled over, gasping for air. She shook the hand of the girl who had beaten her, and a slap on the shoulder by the third place getter acknowledged her own achievement. She finally looked around as if seeing the scene for the first time. Then she heard the PA announcements, the shouts, the calls of the crowd. It was all suddenly deafening.

Craddock, who coached her and others in the South Eastern University athletics club, led her away.

'How was my time?'

'Not bad. Could be better, but you can do it.'

'But I came second, didn't I?'

'Yeah. In a pretty mediocre field. Get some of that sports drink into you and I'll see you in twenty minutes on the bus. I want to watch one more race.'

Anna suddenly felt wobbly and lightheaded. She grabbed a bottle of energy drink, pulled on a T-shirt and track pants over her running shorts, picked up her bag and got on the waiting minibus at the rear of the stadium.

'How'd you go, love?' asked the driver. 'No good? Always next time, eh?'

'Yeah, right.' Anna leant against the window and closed her eyes in the winter sun.

She must have dozed. As the other athletes jumped onto the bus chattering animatedly she jerked upright in the seat.

'Listen up,' called out Craddock. 'I want to run through the schedule for next week. We need to put in some serious effort.'

'Isn't that what we've been doing?' called one of the boys, a lanky hurdler.

'You wait. We're all going to have to go up a notch in the countdown to the interstate meet. We need to put in an extra effort, so I'm changing our training schedule, starting next week.'

'We have exams!' wailed one of the girls.

The minibus headed through the sleepy Saturday afternoon streets towards South Adelaide while the group of athletes, most of whom were university students, discussed the rescheduling of their training sessions. It would clash with their studies and their social life, but they were prepared to compromise.

'All right, that seems to suit everyone, then,' said Craddock, looking at his clipboard. 'Anna, you can work in with the others as you're more flexible.'

'I have to work,' she answered. She always had to fit in with the students and the coach seemed to assume that her job came second to running. She knew that the athletics club was funded by the university, so the students' needs took priority, but it annoyed her just the same.

The tall blonde in the seat in front of her turned around. 'You ran a great race today,' said Sonja. 'Have you put in your application to the Track and Field Institute?' When Anna shook her head, Sonja added, 'The numbers are pretty tight. Only a few spots left, we heard.'

'I can't see the point of applying. Unless there's a scholarship, I can't afford to go there fulltime.'

'But, Anna, you're so good. You know Craddock boasts about you being a state champion, or even an Olympic contender.'

'I'm not so sure about that,' said Anna.

'Anna! He's always telling the rest of us that we should be more like you and train more. He goes on and on about us not having your dedication and says that we should put in the hours you do,' said Sonja.

Anna shrugged. Yes, she did a lot of training runs on her own, but it was hard to explain to the others on the team why she did so much more than they did. 'I'll see how I go,' she said.

Sonja lowered her voice. 'Couldn't Craddock give you more one-on-one time?' she asked. 'I mean, he's always boasting about you.'

'I suppose he could, but he has a lot of other runners to think about,' said Anna. 'He seems to like the fact I keep training on my own even when I don't have to and my times are good.'

'You do more than that, Anna. Your times get better and better. I hate the way that at some meets I do well and then at others I drop back. I wish I was more consistent.'

'That's true of everyone and it depends on our state of

mind and fitness on the day of the race,' said Anna as the bus pulled up in the university parking lot. 'See you next week, I guess.'

'Take care, Anna.' Sonja watched Anna sling her bag over her shoulder and walk quickly across the parking lot. It occurred to Sonja that she and her teammates knew little about one of the club's most promising runners. Where did Anna live? What did she do in her spare time? Did she even have her own transport? All they knew was that she worked as a waitress, which was why the coach probably thought she had flexible hours.

Anna wasn't a student at South Eastern University. The athletics club, a member of the University Sports Association, opened its doors to athletes of different disciplines who wanted to compete and improve their standards and move up the competitive ranks, even if they were not studying or working at the university. Sonja knew that Craddock had said Anna could be an elite athlete and that her rising star would cast a little glitter on them all.

For Anna, the contradiction in running for the club and running to satisfy a need in herself was causing her more and more disquiet. She'd had several disagreements with her coach, who constantly criticised her race strategy. He called her a bolter and tried to get her to hold back behind the frontrunners before making the final dash to the line.

'Keep something in reserve! Don't you have any speed other than walking or flat chat? Be a racehorse, not a greyhound. Use your brain!' he admonished her.

'I either win or I don't,' she answered him.

'You won't win if you don't learn to strategise. You're not a sprinter, you're running eight hundred metres. Pace yourself. You don't have to be the frontrunner.'

Again and again she tried: ran and attempted to hold

back. But she found it impossible. She always seemed to want to run as fast as she could from the moment the starter's pistol sounded. Race tactics evaded her.

Craddock was impressed with her speed but exasperated. He tried to explain once again how he wanted her to pace herself throughout the race. 'Too much, too soon. What happens when you're almost at the finish and someone shoots past? You've nothing left in the tank to overtake them.'

Anna irritated him even more by shrugging. 'That's me. I don't know, I can't change the way I am. Something just seems to happen and I can't stop myself.'

'Yeah, right. In the zone, whatever. Don't give me that new-age shit.' When he saw her face close up, he softened. 'Listen, Anna, you're good. You have a lot of potential, but athletics is as much about your mental preparedness as your physical fitness. If you can't keep focused and listen to what I have to say, we have to have a rethink. You have to really want this. You've been given a few opportunities here, so trust me. If you want to go to the institute, we have to know you're going to give it your best shot before we can recommend you.'

'Have I ever not given it my all?' asked Anna evenly.

The coach hesitated before answering, unsure how to read Anna's expression. 'What do your family think? Do they support you in your dream?'

Anna turned away. 'I do my own thing. I'm twenty and I only live at home because it's near the uni track and I don't have to pay rent.'

Craddock spoke more gently. 'Would it help if I spoke to your parents? Let them know that I think you have potential?'

'What for? I make my own decisions.'

'I know that travel to sports meetings and other expenses can add up and funding is sparse and hard to get. What do you want to do, Anna? What makes you happy? How badly do you want to compete in serious competitions?'

'I like running,' she said simply.

'But you need to focus, have a plan. Because if you don't want to dedicate yourself and see how far you can go, you're wasting our time. Mine and yours.'

Anna didn't respond for a moment, then said quietly, 'I'm sorry if I'm wasting your time.'

'It's not wasting my time if you take my advice!' he said. 'You can't do this alone, but you have to choose. Either you dedicate yourself to an athletic career, and that includes your mind not just your body, or you consider it something you just do for pleasure, more a hobby than a career. Then you can have time for fun and boyfriends instead. But if you really want to take athletics seriously, you have to be in the right head space.'

'I know that. I just like to run. But I have to fit running in with my job at the coffee shop. Mum and Dad didn't mind taking me around to Little Athletics meets when I was young but they don't see how it could be a career, you know, how I would make money from it. Maybe I should be doing something for the future, getting a proper job.' This small speech came out in a rush, expelled as if it had been long held inside her.

Craddock lifted his arms in a mildly helpless gesture. 'Then it's up to you to decide. We all come to a fork in the road at some stage of our lives. You'd better do some serious thinking in the next month or so.'

Anna had a lot to think about but no one with whom she could discuss her feelings. What to do with her life? Should she try to pursue a career on the track? Or should she forget that idea and look for something that would make her money? She had fuzzy thoughts but no clear plans. All she knew was that she loved to run. But she needed a job that was flexible enough to allow her time for training. She didn't earn a lot from her job and what she did earn was quickly absorbed by living expenses and travelling costs. She was worried. If she couldn't run the way Craddock wanted, was she just wasting her time?

Anna mulled over these thoughts as she waited on tables at the coffee shop where she worked. She picked up a newspaper along with the empty coffee mugs where two backpackers had been sitting and noticed that a couple of position vacant ads had been circled. As she walked to the kitchen, one in particular seemed to jump out at her.

Find Opals in your Spare Time!
Girl or guy wanted to work in Hotel Bar.
Drinks and Food service. Some cleaning.
Accommodation provided. Opal Lake NSW.
Call Mick.

She tore out the small ad with the phone number even though she had no idea where Opal Lake was. It sounded intriguing and suddenly the idea of going to a remote little town where she knew no one and no one knew her, to work in a pub and maybe scratch around for an opal or two, seemed very attractive. So many thoughts crowded in on her. A bit of a break sounded good, and it would give her time to think and decide about her future. She decided to call this Mick.

'Where's this place? Seems a bit remote just to go to think,' said Craddock. 'How long will you be away?'

'I don't know. I'm not making any plans. I'm looking forward to having no pressure and some freedom.'

'No cranky Craddock, eh?' He grinned. 'Listen,

Anna, if that's going to sort you out, then do it, but don't be away too long. What do your family think?'

'They think I'm crazy. They just want me to settle down in a steady job.'

'Is that what you're going to do?'

'I have to decide. And once I've made up my mind, that's it. I stick to my decision.'

'Good. If you do decide to come back, you'll have to be dedicated and focused, and you'll have to train like never before. Fair enough?'

'I appreciate you letting me have this breathing space,' said Anna meekly. 'And I'll let you know my decision as soon as I've made it.'

'Good, because I think you have the makings of a champion. But just do me a favour and keep fit, eat properly and don't waste yourself on booze or pot or rubbish food. Okay?'

'Of course. Anyway, I won't stop running.'

'I bet this place'll be bloody hot.'

'Then I'll have to get up early to run,' said Anna. And for the first time in a long time she smiled at the coach.

Craddock shook his head. 'I'm taking a punt on you, Anna. I'll be disappointed if you toss me over.' He patted her shoulder and turned away, but at the door he said, 'Be prepared to work bloody hard when you get back. Don't get used to the soft life.'

'I won't,' replied Anna.

It had been a long trip from Adelaide to Broken Hill, but she'd relished the train ride. When she arrived in Broken Hill, she travelled to Opal Lake on Davo's Best Tours bus. She loved the space and emptiness of the landscape and its colours. It was so much bigger, more expansive, than she'd expected. She was absorbed in the country as Davo's little bus rattled along the dirt road, and scarcely listened to the spiel he was delivering to the small group of fellow travellers.

Davo glanced over to her. 'Your first time outback?'

Anna nodded.

'Can seem a bit overwhelming. Where else are you travelling?'

'I'm not. I've got a job in Opal Lake.'

'Fair dinkum?' He gave her an interested stare. 'Opal mining? Nah, you working in the motel?'

'The hotel.'

'Jeez. Mick said he had someone new coming. How come you want to work out here?' His quick glance ran up and down her figure. 'You won't last, love. No offence, but, well, it's a small place. And it's your first time outta the city, right?'

'I'm from Adelaide.'

'I'm sure that's a nice place. But, well, you'll find Opal Lake sorta different. Good little community though. Be careful of some of them blokes out on the diggings. Not a lot of single girls out here.'

'I'm not looking for romance. Just a job.' Anna turned away and looked out the window.

'I wouldn't say the mining blokes were romantic. Them fellas are all in love with opal. She's the queen that steals the hearts of men.'

'That's very poetic, Davo!' called the tourist sitting behind him.

The conversation drifted to opals and Anna tuned out. She had no interest in jewellery or gems. She looked at the unfolding landscape and hoped she would get the chance to explore Opal Lake. Davo had said that the actual lake was some distance away from the little town and rarely had water in it, but it sounded intriguing.

She wasn't expecting much of a township, but she

was slightly taken aback by the flat wilderness intersected by two hills which were dotted with a few buildings and partially buried roofs. The place looked as if a tornado had swept over Opal Lake and scooped its contents up, depositing them randomly over the hillsides.

There was one main street. Davo parked his minibus outside the pub and everyone stepped from the van, glad to stretch their legs, and filed inside.

Davo swung Anna's bag from the roof rack and deposited it on the ground beside her. 'There you go. Hope you settle in all right. I'm over here pretty regular like, so if you want to, you know, get outta Dodge, give me a hoy.'

'Thanks,' said Anna, non-committally.

Mick had insisted on an eight-week trial period, but he'd sounded resigned, as though he knew she'd move on before then. But Anna wasn't going to let Davo know that she might not stay. His familiarity with her had started to irritate her and she hoped that not everyone in this small community would want to know her business. The remoteness of this place had appealed to Anna. She had it in her head that the people who lived here, in the middle of nowhere, and worked down holes in the ground would be self-sufficient, even loners and eccentrics, and pay no attention to her at all. She picked up her bag and headed into the pub.

Two locals were on barstools with schooners of beer in front of them.

'Is the manager here?' asked Anna.

'Out the back.'

'Will I wait?' She put down her bag.

'Better go and get him, love. He's doing his opals.'

Seeing her puzzled expression, the other man added, 'He's rubbing them back, to see what he's got.'

Suddenly Davo was right behind her, calling out loudly, 'Hey, Mick, here's yer new recruit!'

Immediately interested faces turned to look at her and Anna felt herself blushing.

A red-haired man in his forties came to the bar, wiping his hands on a muddy tea towel that was tucked into his waistband. 'Well, good on you, Anna. I'm Mick.'

Anna smiled. 'You look surprised. Didn't you think I'd get here?'

Mick pumped her hand. 'Wouldn't be the first time someone's chickened out. Pleased to meet you. Come on and I'll show you your room. Simple. Basic. Hope it suits. It's not very girly.'

'I'm not really the girly type.' Anna glanced at the old framed photographs lining the walls: people, mines and equipment, ramshackle buildings and faded colour prints of opals that seemed to tell the story of the place.

'Does everybody here dig for opals?' she asked.

'Pretty much. Those that stay. There've been some decent finds out here over the years. But it's kept quiet so as not to start a rush. You know how it is.'

'No. I don't know anything about opals.'

Mick walked down the hallway to a door and pushed it open. 'Is that right? I thought the opal thing might have been what attracted you. What's your interest, then?'

'This sounded an interesting place. I like being on my own. I read a lot,' she added, seeing his faintly puzzled expression.

'That's good. Not much in the way of entertainment out here. Sorry, but the bathroom's down the hall.'

Anna glanced at the spartan room, which at least looked clean. There were French doors with frosted glass and she pushed them open to find an old cane table and chair on a small wooden deck that looked out onto the street.

'It's a bit dusty, no one seems to use them anymore,' apologised Mick. 'Nice in the morning and the evening. Good view of the sunset,' he added.

'This is fine. Thank you.'

'I'll leave you to freshen up. Come in and I'll show you the ropes when you're ready. Thelma, who does the cooking, will be glad to meet you.'

In four days Anna had the pub job down pat. After the busy service of the bustling café in Prospect where she'd worked, the routine of the pub was casual. Customers expected her to linger and chat. It was all pretty laidback.

Outside her working hours, she kept to herself and enjoyed sitting on the little deck, where she could watch the activity, such as it was, in the main street. The early mornings were clear and the evening sunsets that spread across the entire horizon were bold and dramatic. She'd never really watched a sunset before, seeing the colours in the sky change from rose to blue and indigo to greenish black, and the evening star appear. In Adelaide she'd only glimpsed this phenomenon between trees in the park, over rooftops, or behind the stand at the athletics club. It was a backdrop to her activities and the traffic and hectic lifestyle of the city that she'd never had time to admire.

But here the sky, the space, the wavering distant horizon was enveloping. After the night had settled she watched the pale pinpricks of light begin to dot the twin hills and the fluorescent glow from the pub bar shining out onto the road.

Everyone quickly found out her first name and the fact that she was from Adelaide but beyond that no one asked her about herself. Thelma told Anna to keep her business to herself, then asked her if she could cook and looked resigned when the young girl shook her head.

'Mum's a good cook. Ordinary things, nothing modern. If I have to cook for myself it's generally protein,' said Anna.

'Barbecue things? That's not cooking, love. But at

least you're not one of them vegetable people. Don't know how they keep body and soul together living on greens and salads.'

Anna smiled. 'Rabbit food, my mother calls it. No, I like to keep my stamina up with meat and good carb food. I like to exercise a lot,' she added.

'I thought as much, to keep a nice trim figure like yours.' She waved a floury hand at her shapeless bulk. 'Once you let yourself go, that's it. Make the most of it while you can. I used to wear shorts and skin-tight pedal pushers. Can you believe it?' She chortled.

'Actually, I want to get back to my fitness routine pretty soon,' said Anna.

Few noticed that Anna left her room early each morning. Dressed in shorts and running shoes, her favourite baseball cap pulled low on her head and her hair tied back, she jogged quietly down the dirt road in the dawn light, turning onto the dusty track that led arrow straight towards the north. Three kilometres along the track there was a dead mulga tree, branches outstretched, which she used as a marker. Here she would turn and run as hard as she could back to the hotel. Sometimes she glanced at her watch, noting the time she had taken. Other times she just ran as fast as she could with a sense of exhilaration, and whatever time she took was of little consequence.

Mick sometimes heard the rattling of the hot water pipes and wondered why Anna got up so early when she didn't have to, but he quickly went back to sleep. It wasn't his business what she did, just so long as she was on deck when the pub opened.

After a few days of this, Anna decided to vary her routine, settling on a new route. In the pearly new daylight she turned in the opposite direction, circled the two hills, sprinted up the taller one, and did the circuit at the top past the dugouts and the sleeping machinery awaiting the cooler months and the return of their owners. Then she sped back down the hill, sometimes dislodging a small stone that rattled away, breaking the silence. She assumed that by running so early in the day she was unobserved by people living their strange underground existence.

But she was noticed. Once or twice Shirley, who found she needed less and less sleep these days, was up early and sitting at the side of her dugout entrance with her cup of tea to watch the sunrise. The first time she saw the slim shape dash past she was startled. But she quickly saw that the girl was not troubled or distressed. There was an easy fluidity to her movements, the long strides, the firm arms, and a determined thrust to her head. This must be the new young woman working at the pub whom Davo had mentioned.

It was a slow afternoon. Anna was looking for something to do so she started to tidy the fridge in the kitchen that Thelma had hinted needed a good clean-out.

'Anna, if you're looking for work, could you do Marg next door a favour and run Shirley's groceries up to her? The old girl wants some cold drinks too, so I'll sling them in with the food,' Mick called to her.

'I'm happy to help, but when you say run, you don't actually mean carry, do you? Where is this Shirley?'

'Doncha know Shirley yet? Great old bird. Take Marg's car. Greg's away so she can't leave the store.'

'What sort of a car is it? I've passed my driving test, but I've never driven a manual.'

Mick stared at her. 'Cripes, you gotta drive out here, love. I'll see what I can do. Do you want to have a few practice runs in Marg's ute?'

'I'd rather not. Is there an automatic I could use?'

'Let me have a think. We need to get those groceries up to Shirley.'

Anna shrugged and went back to the kitchen.

A few minutes later, Mick called out to her again. 'It's okay. Davo's here. He's going up to see Shirley anyway, so he'll take the stuff up. But he has an idea about getting you driving.'

'Davo? I'm not sure I'm thrilled about that.'

'I don't mean driving his van. Listen, pop up with him and say hello to Shirley and see what he's got in mind.' Seeing Anna's dubious expression, Mick added, 'You'll like Shirley. Been here for years. Knows a lot of local history, where the bones are buried, that sort of thing. I know she's an older lady, but she's special and I think she might be able to help you out.'

'How long have you known Shirley?' asked Anna as Davo's little bus wound up the hill.

'Few years. She gave me a bit of a hand when I started the business, so I like to pop in to keep an eye on her.'

Shirley recognised Anna straight away.

'You're new here. Can you stay for a bit? Sit down. Davo, I think a cuppa would do us all good. Can you put the kettle on?'

'Shirley, how's that old banger of yours doing?'

'Do you mean my ticker or my wheels?' She smiled.

'The car. Anna has no wheels. Thought I'd give her a lesson and then if it's okay with you she could take your car out for a bit of a spin.'

'Really, it's not necessary,' began Anna.

'I'm sure Anna manages to get around on her own two legs quite well,' said Shirley. 'But you're welcome to use the car any time you want. It's going fine. Kerrie used it the first time she was here and Doug still checks it for me.'

'I don't need a car,' said Anna.

'She's only used to fancy automatics,' said Davo. 'Got to teach her how to drive a stick.'

'Actually, that's not true. I've never owned a car, automatic or otherwise,' said Anna. 'And I don't think I need one while I'm here.'

'Davo, could you check the car anyway?' said Shirley. 'Anna, could you help me make the tea?'

Davo went outside and Shirley muttered to Anna, 'You know how men are about cars. Be patient and have a lesson with him.'

'I don't know, and I don't want to give Davo the wrong idea,' said Anna.

Shirley studied Anna as she spooned tea leaves into the teapot. 'Are you planning on staying round here for a bit?' she asked. 'You seem to like the great outdoors.'

'How do you know that? You don't know me,' said Anna lightly.

'I know you like to get out early in the morning for a jog,' said Shirley.

'Run,' Anna corrected her.

Shirley smiled, but didn't probe any further. 'I think you'd find having access to a car out here quite handy. I'm happy to let you borrow my old bomb any time.'

'I thought you had a friend who uses it,' said Anna, as she poured boiling water into the pot.

'Kerrie arrived with Davo the first time she came here. Came on a whim, like I imagine you did. She drove her own car the next time she came.'

'I came for the job.'

'Let Davo give you a lesson. You'll be independent. Besides, I'd like to see more of you.'

Anna looked at Shirley, then eased the tea cosy onto the pot and put it on the table. 'Why do you want to bother with me?'

'Why not? I enjoy the company of interesting, intelligent young women. They are few and far between out here.' She pulled out a chair and reached for the milk jug. 'But suit yourself.'

'Thank you, Shirley. I'd appreciate a loan of the car now and then, if I can drive it.'

When Davo came back inside, Shirley was telling Anna about her days training as a nurse and the fun of living in a nurses' home and how her father had brought her here as a little girl.

'Any tea left? I've checked out the car. It's fine.'

'Thanks, Davo. Sit down.' Shirley poured his tea. 'I was telling Anna about my father being a teacher and how opals were his hobby and passion.'

Davo sipped his tea and half listened while Shirley talked. As soon as they'd finished he carried the pot and his cup to the sink and turned to Anna. 'You ready to go back to work?'

Shirley reached for Anna's hand and squeezed it. 'Thanks for coming to see me. And thank Mick for sending up my goodies. You too, Davo. And Anna, it's been lovely to meet you at last. I'm sure we'll see each other again.'

Anna nodded. 'Thank you for the tea. I've enjoyed your company.'

'She's a good old stick,' said Davo, breaking the silence as he drove Anna back down the hill.

'You seem to be very friendly with her.'

'Yeah. Gotta help out where you can, right?'

'Where do you come from?'

'Mostly Melbourne, but I hardly ever go south. Too cold. What do you reckon about that driving lesson?' He turned to look at her, reaching out to give her a friendly pat on the shoulder.

Anna felt her body stiffen, but if Davo noticed, he didn't show it. 'I'll think about it. Thanks.'

Anna varied her morning run and didn't always go up the hill past Shirley's dugout, instead choosing to run to the outskirts of town where the small cemetery stood in barren isolation.

A couple of days later, as Anna emptied the dishwasher and set out the beer glasses on the bar on a clean towel, Mick commented, 'Pam and Doug are back. You'll like them. They'll pop in some time. They run the Golden Dome B&B. They take a holiday each summer.'

'Do they get someone to run the B&B while they're away?' asked Anna.

'Not worth it. Too damn hot. Not enough tourists to worry about, so they don't take bookings.'

'The miners seem to stay on.'

'Yeah, well, some of them haven't got anywhere else to go or can't afford to leave. When someone takes off on a trip you can bet they've sold some opal. Anyway it's cool working down a mine, better than the pub. You seem to be coping okay. Smart to get out early morning. I wouldn't recommend jogging about the place at night. Could be dangerous in the dark.'

'This place is okay as long as that AC keeps going,' said Anna, pointing to the noisy air conditioner in the bar. She was also grateful for the rusty old air conditioning unit in her room. It might use a lot of power but it made sleeping at night possible. When she asked about her morning shower, he told her that hot water wasn't a problem because he'd installed solar panels years before. Later Anna realised that solar units were fast becoming a fact of life for most of the dugouts and the town's buildings. Those who could afford it had set up portable solar panels to provide their power. Mick told Anna that there had been experimental solar dishes set up at White Cliffs in the 1980s to service the whole town as a test project and even though it had been successful, it was now closed

315

down and White Cliffs ran on individual solar panels like Opal Lake.

As Mick predicted, Pam and Doug came into the pub early that evening. Word must have spread because a lot of locals were there to catch up on their news.

Anna quietly served everyone and in a lull Pam leant across the bar and held out her hand. 'I'm Pam. I'm a friend of Shirley's too. Would you like to come over for a coffee when you can get away?'

'I've just met Shirley. A coffee would be nice. I'll see when it's all right with Mick.'

'Just come over whenever you can. We'll be there, getting ready to open for business. If Mick gives you a hard time, come and see us, we can always do with an extra pair of hands,' she said with a smile.

'Don't try and steal the best asset I've ever had in the bar!' Mick chided Pam.

Anna merely smiled and served a customer.

'How on earth did you find her?' Pam asked the publican.

He shrugged. 'Lucked out, I guess. She answered an ad in the paper. Nice girl. Comes from Adelaide. Quiet. Bit of a loner. Fitness type. She jogs for damn miles, and eats meat like it's going out of style. Never touches a drink. Keeps to herself here, but she might tell you more.'

'I bet business has picked up among the young blokes since she arrived,' said Doug as he joined Pam.

'Word's out she's off limits. Polite but not interested,' said Mick.

'What she does is none of anyone's business,' said Pam.

'Would you like another?' asked Anna, coming over to her.

'No, we'd better be going. Promise you'll come and see us soon,' said Pam. 'Come for a late lunch. We can't offer bright lights and dancing, but we'd enjoy your company.'

Anna gave a rare, big smile. 'Thank you. I'll try to stop by in a day or so.'

Davo spoke briefly to Pam and Doug as they left, then came over and leant on the bar, watching Anna. 'Pam and Doug, lovely people.'

'They seem to be.'

'I'll be heading back to the Hill tomorrow arvo, so you want that driving lesson in the morning?'

Anna busied herself for a moment at the beer taps. 'If it's no trouble, I suppose so.'

'No worries. See you out the front, say nine?'

Anna showered after her run and was ready for her driving lesson when Davo drove Shirley's car down the hill and pulled up outside the pub.

'Hop in.' Davo got out and into the passenger's seat. Mick came onto the verandah and watched with interest.

Davo handed Anna a sheet of paper. 'That's the gears.' He went through his diagram, pointing to it with a grubby finger. He explained about easing out the clutch, and described what to do, but Anna's initial attempt saw the car jerk forward. She stabbed her foot on the brake. 'S'okay, don't panic. Try again,' said Davo.

As Anna tried again, he rested his hand casually on her leg. 'Slow, slow, right. Accelerate . . .'

Anna tried to push his hand off.

He took no notice, and squeezed her leg. 'Now, change down . . .'

Anna angrily flung his hand off her leg. She grabbed the gear stick and pushed it into gear. The car moved forward and picked up speed. As she tried to put the car into second, the gears made the most awful noise.

Davo leant back and chuckled. 'You're grinding the gears.'

'If you don't shut up I'll stop the car right now and we'll forget this,' snapped Anna through gritted teeth.

She looked at Davo's rough diagram again and then braked and started again, working her way through the gears. The car kangaroo hopped a few more times down the main street. Then she suddenly felt her feet co-ordinate and she discovered she could let the clutch in and out smoothly as she changed gears. She turned around at the end of the main street and drove back towards the pub.

'Go up the hill. See if you can do a hill start,' challenged Davo.

Anna found this manoeuvre difficult. She hated the sensation of rolling backwards before she engaged the gears. She raced up the hill towards Shirley's dugout.

'Whoa. Do a turn and go back down the hill,' said Davo.

'I get the general idea. Let's take the car back to Shirley.' She pulled up outside Shirley's place.

Davo leant over and patted her shoulder, idly ruffling her hair. 'Not bad, not bad.'

Anna pushed his hand away. 'I'm not a damned dog! Thanks for the lesson. I'll practise a bit more by myself.'

'Anytime. Give us a yell.'

'Aren't you leaving this afternoon?' She got out of the car.

'I'll be back.' He smiled easily.

Anna didn't answer. She turned to walk back down the hill.

'Hey, aren't you going to say hi to Shirley? I'll give you a lift back in my bus!'

'I have to go to work.' She broke into a jog and headed down the hill.

Davo watched her go as Shirley called out to him. 'How'd she do?'

'Smartarse chick,' he muttered under his breath, then turned to Shirley. 'She'll get the hang of it. Independent little miss.'

'Yes, she is. I'm not sure she's your type, Davo.'

'You're right. She's not,' said Davo. 'Here are your keys. See ya next time.' He headed out to his van. Shirley dropped the keys onto her table and watched him leave.

The bar was unusually crowded for the Opal Lake Hotel. It still amused Anna to compare the pub to the sleek, chic coffee shop where she'd worked in Adelaide. She was intrigued by two men who stood in a corner, close together, their backs to the rest of the room as they looked intently at something one of them held. Anna walked around the room and out onto the footpath, collecting dirty glasses and emptying the makeshift ashtrays Mick had improvised out of earthenware mosquito candle holders. She came close to the two men and they stopped talking and straightened up.

'Can I get you two chaps a refill?' Anna asked as she picked up their schooner glasses.

'Yeah, thanks.' One reached into his pocket and handed her twenty dollars. 'Keep the change, love.'

'Thanks.' She smiled. 'Had a bit of luck, did you?'

She'd seen men be generous with their money once or twice before, and some got drunk before a more sober miner dragged them from the pub, with the whisper 'They're on opal' accompanying their exit.

The other man nodded. 'A bit. Luck's been a long time coming.'

'Well, good on you.' Anna went and got them another drink. No one else appeared to be taking much notice of the men. She brought their beers over and put them on the small table beside them.

'Thanks.' One of the men handed a drink to his friend. 'What's your favourite opal, eh?' he asked Anna.

'Oh, I don't know. I don't know much about them,' said Anna.

The second man rolled his eyes. 'Probably only seen rough opals. Or you're the type who fancies diamonds, are you?'

'Not on what I earn here,' she said with a smile. 'Are you selling opals?'

'Not yet. It's hard to part with a beauty when it comes along. Like women. Go on, Kev, show her.'

'Oh, that's all right, you don't have to,' began Anna, not wanting to be put in a position of trust. She'd heard how secretive miners were about their discoveries. But the men were obviously quite chuffed by their find, and Kev pulled his fist from his pocket and opened his hand.

Anna craned forward and caught her breath as she saw the dazzling stone in Kev's palm.

'Can I touch it?' she asked in a low voice, quite awe-struck. She'd seen rough stones with glimpses of colour in them before and Mick had sawn open a Yowah nut to show her two half centres of intricate earthy-toned patterns shot with pinpricks of gold and red. But this stone, nicely polished, was the size of a bantam's egg. 'That's amazing. It's so big. What will you do with it? It'd be a shame to break it up, wouldn't it.'

'It's up to the jeweller who buys it what he does with it. We just want to enjoy it for as long as we can,' said the other man.

'Have you got more like this?' asked Anna, then realised she'd overstepped the mark.

'Ah, that'd be telling.'

'It's very beautiful. I hope you find more just like it.'

'That's the idea. It's taken us years to find this one.' Kev grinned. 'Gave up good jobs in the city to do this.'

'Are you staying here for long?' asked Anna.

'No, we're heading to Andamooka next.'

'Good luck,' said Anna.

Anna went back to the bar, aware that Mick and several of the men were looking at her with interest.

'So?' asked Mick. 'Any good?'

'I wouldn't know,' said Anna. 'It was pretty but if that's all you find after years of digging I wouldn't be doing it.'

The men turned back to their beer and conversation.

But Anna couldn't stop thinking about the opal she'd just been shown. It was the first really good opal she'd seen and suddenly she understood their attraction. The way the two men gazed at that stone, caressing it, turning it in the light, the fact they'd given up good jobs to find it. Now she saw the hypnotic allure that a beautiful opal could have on some people.

After the pub closed, as Anna emptied the ancient dishwasher, she told Mick that she'd found the opal the two men had shown her to be utterly stunning.

Mick was wiping down the sink. 'Wish I'd seen it. Wonder where they've been digging. Must be some way out, probably at Tango Ridge. Haven't seen them round here before.'

'Where does the opal you're always working on out the back come from?' asked Anna, who'd seen the buckets of potch and rocks in the shed behind the pub.

'My ex missus and me dug a lot. The good stuff she took with her when she left, but I've still got a bit. Some of it's payment for bar bills.' He grinned. 'So far the drinkers are ahead.'

'Seeing that stone tonight, it's got me fascinated,' said Anna.

'Be careful! You'll get bitten by the bug.' Mick laughed.

'I don't think so. I don't want to go and dig it up. I'd just like to see some good stones, all the different varieties,' said Anna.

'I bet Shirley would love to talk to you about opals. She might even show you some of hers. And you should see Ingrid's collection! Some weird jewellery but you're kinda arty, so you might like it.'

'I've never been called arty before,' said Anna.

'Well, you look it. You're different from girls we normally see out here. You keep to yourself, and that's all right,' he added quickly. 'A lot of people out here keep something of themselves to themselves.'

'I've noticed. No last names, huh? Tell me, what do you know about Davo?'

Mick shrugged. 'He's been around for a bit. Built that tour business up a few years back with Shirley's help. Think he said he was from the coast, used to be a surfer.'

'He told me he was from Melbourne.'

'He might have grown up there. Bit of a rough diamond. But he's helpful to Shirley. I guess because she helps him out.'

'Financially? I don't think much of him at all,' said Anna.

'He's not in your league, Anna. But you can't blame a fellow for wanting to chat you up. Anyway, he's harmless I reckon. You just do your own thing.' Mick rinsed the cloth he'd been using and wrung it out. 'D'ya mind if I ask why you spend a lot time out there jogging, running? You don't drink either. You sure are keeping fit and watching your figure, if you don't mind my saying.'

'That's okay, Mick. It's something I've always done and it's part of who I am. Been running since I was little.'

'Is it a hobby or what?'

'Way of life, I guess,' said Anna. 'I don't feel right if

I don't run every day. I used to train really solidly. But everyone needs a break now and then, right?'

'Right. I hope you stick around a bit, Anna. You're a good worker and a real asset here. While you're here, you should get out of town a bit. The area around here can be a pretty magic place. It gets under your skin.'

'Shirley offered me her car. I might go exploring.'

'Good idea. You gotta see the lake.'

Even though it was hot, Anna jogged up the hill to Shirley's dugout.

'You need a cold drink, my girl,' said Shirley, seeing Anna's perspiring face as she entered the dugout.

Anna dropped her cap onto the table and helped herself to the jug of cold water in Shirley's fridge. She had begun to call in on an almost daily basis and Shirley had made her feel that this was her second home.

'Anna, why don't you keep the car down at the pub? Treat it as your own for as long as you want,' suggested Shirley.

'What, and miss out on running up your hill?' said Anna. 'I'll get lazy.'

'Running all the time; just what are you training for?' asked Shirley. 'Can't you put your feet up and read a book?'

'I wish, but we're pretty busy most of the time.'

Shirley watched Anna drink the iced water. 'But you must be training for some event, or why bother keeping to such a schedule?' she asked.

Because Shirley's tone was gently serious and it encroached on the unspoken agreement of not probing her personal life, Anna hesitated before answering.

'I'm trying to train myself. It's a head thing more than a physical thing. I was a serious athlete but it got to a

323

point where my coach and I were clashing because I wasn't doing what he wanted. It was a question of tactics.'

'You mean you didn't agree with his game plan?' asked Shirley.

'I didn't disagree,' said Anna slowly, 'but it's something I have to get my head around. It's about pacing myself, holding back, using judgment to beat the other runners when all I want to do is ignore them and run flat out.'

'You don't strike me as someone who goes flat out, but someone who's more cautious,' said Shirley.

'Except when it comes to running,' said Anna.

'Is that what you were planning to do? To become a serious athlete? What do your coach and your family think about your running away out here?' asked Shirley.

'I told them I was backpacking and doing odd jobs to support myself.' Anna got up to put her glass on the sink.

'Is being here helping you?' asked Shirley.

Anna turned and faced the older woman. 'Yes, in a strange way. I like being by myself and being myself and not having any pressure put on me. But it's not just my running tactics that are the problem. I'm sick of having to take poorly paid jobs, just so that I can train. Sometimes I think it would be nice to earn a decent wage, but if I get a job that doesn't give me flexible hours, I would have to give up running. And I need money to go to the best training schools. So that's another decision I have to make.'

'Yes, you do have a few dilemmas, don't you? We all need time out, as they say, on occasion. But that's all it should be, a space between decisions. It becomes very easy to drift. You see it happen out here and before you know it, you've lost a great chunk of your productive life.'

'Is that what happened to you, Shirley?' asked Anna, hoping she didn't sound rude.

'At my age one can look back with some perspective.

I have no regrets, I had a great career, I found the love of my life. But you're right. I could have made other choices about my life.'

'I understand what you're saying, but I haven't been here very long yet,' Anna replied.

'I know. I have a good friend, Kerrie. I hope you'll meet her one day. She suddenly became widowed at quite a young age, and she ran away out here, just like you have, to avoid making a lot of decisions. But she's now faced her new life and has started to make choices. All I am suggesting is that you don't leave things too late.'

'I won't. Shirley, I value your opinion, and I know you're right. I do have to decide, but not just now,' said Anna.

'And while you're making up your mind, I'm very happy to have your company whenever you feel like hanging out with an old duck like me.'

Anna went to Shirley and leant over her chair, giving her a spontaneous hug. 'I think you're fantastic.'

Shirley patted her hand, knowing this was a deeply felt gesture. Anna was not one for superficial platitudes. 'Where did you want to take the car today?'

'Now that I'm feeling more confident driving a manual, I thought I'd go to the famous lake everyone talks about.'

'And so you should. I suggest you take the car out very early in the morning and go and watch the sunrise. It's very special out there.'

'What a great idea.'

'I'll draw you a mud map. Have you got a camera you can take?'

'No, I don't. I'll photograph it up here.' Anna tapped her head.

'And you said you'd like to see some really good opals after the opal you saw in the bar the other night, so I pulled out a couple of my favourites for you.'

Shirley shuffled over to the desk in her little office and returned with a small toffee tin, which she opened. She lifted out several rolls of tissue paper, which she unrolled and placed on the kitchen table.

Anna gasped at the sparkling opals lying there, their liquid play of colours shifting in the light. 'They're gorgeous! And so many different colours! Did you dig these up? How exciting to unearth something like this,' she exclaimed.

'It certainly is. I remember the first opals my father and I ever found together . . . And you never become immune to the excitement. Every opal captures you, because each one is so individual. These ones have been cut and polished. I've got others that aren't, so they're not as spectacular but they are still beautiful because Australian opals are the best in the world. They don't break so readily when they are being worked and they are easier to find than opals in other countries. These opals are my superannuation.' She smiled.

Anna held one out to admire it. 'What a stunning piece of jewellery this would make. I've always thought of opal as pretty boring, old lady and tourist souvenir stuff.'

'Yes, the old myths still prevail,' sighed Shirley.

'What myths?' asked Anna.

'That opals are unlucky. In the early days a story was put out, here and abroad, about opals being bad luck. It was a deliberately malicious campaign because opals had become as valuable as diamonds. So if someone died in an accident, for instance, it would be said that they were wearing opal jewellery and so on. There's a little novel of Sir Walter Scott's, *Anne of Geierstein*, which I have in my library in there. The story makes it seem as though the heroine dies because of a magic opal. But if you read further it's perfectly clear that it was not the case. She was poisoned. Nevertheless, apparently the idea of an evil magic opal made opal prices plummet.'

'Spin doctors at work,' said Anna. 'But I think that really good opals, like yours, are stunning. I'll start saving for one.'

'Keep your eye open in the pub, there's sure to be some miner who's hard up and who'll sell you one. You just have to recognise what's a good opal.'

'That's the hard part, I s'pose. Thanks for showing me yours.'

Anna took Shirley's advice and told Mick that she was going to drive out early the next day and watch the sunrise over Opal Lake.

The sky was mother of pearl pink and silver as she saw the lake in the distance. In this light it looked like a large expanse of shimmering water and Anna caught her breath. But when she drove through the scrubby hills to its perimeter she saw that it was nothing but windswept sand. Then, as she followed the track marked on Shirley's map, she was dismayed to see flickering lights and a campfire ahead of her. She pulled the car up and saw that pup tents and a trestle table had been set up and people were moving around. It was obviously a group of tourists who'd spent the night.

She was disappointed at having to share what she'd been led to believe was an idyllic isolated spot, but even more so when she recognised Davo's Best Tour bus on the edge of the campsite. She was about to put the car into reverse and find another part of the lake when a figure appeared beside her window and rapped on the roof of the car, making her jump in alarm.

Davo's grinning face looked at her though the car window. 'Surprise, surprise. Are you lost?'

'No, I'm not. I came out to watch the sunrise.'

'So did we. Want to join us? We've got coffee and bacon and toast happening.'

'Thank you. I don't want to interrupt your guests. I really wanted a one-on-one experience.'

'With me?'

'No. The sunrise.'

'You're a weird chick, y'know that?'

'Think what you like.'

Davo remained leaning on the car until Anna began to reverse. Then he stood looking at her but she couldn't read his expression as his back was to the light. She would have liked to ask him which was the best way to go, but she didn't want to have to ask him for any help at all.

She managed to find another way down to the lake and parked so she was facing east. She got out of the car and walked through the soft sand of the dunes and sat at the edge of the strange lake, gazing at the vista that stretched away to the horizon.

'Thank you, Shirley. This was worth the trip,' she said to herself. She was so glad she had found her way here without the annoying Davo and his bunch of tourists that she almost smiled to herself. She realised that she was identifying with the locals as someone who felt protective and appreciative of this special area.

Most tourists who came through Opal Lake rarely stayed more than a day. Sandwiched between White Cliffs and, further afield, Broken Hill there was nothing much to see or do. The place was a breather between stops and its isolation held few attractions for most people.

But Anna was not put off by that or even the lack of basic facilities and entertainment in Opal Lake. Her earlier irritation slipped away as she sat at the edge of the strange, empty lake and watched the great glowing orb rise, red and golden, and light the morning sky. There was magic here and she understood why Shirley had gently pushed her to see it.

She studied Shirley's rough map. She was sitting at one end of the lake but she now understood its topography. She was determined to find the time to explore further, and perhaps find a narrow section where she could cross from one wilder shore to another. It was a large and barren place. It fascinated her, and she had a sense of what drove those early explorers to cross inhospitable landscapes, searching for a mysterious inland sea or places where people could settle, with dreams of prospering, and begin anew.

She drove cautiously back the way she'd come and was pleased to see that Davo's tour group had packed up and moved on. She stopped and walked to where they'd camped. The site was perfect and gave a full view of the lake. The campfire had been doused with sand. The ground was churned from the vehicle and human activity, and there was some rubbish left behind. Anna scooped it up into a large plastic bag and threw it into the back of the car. This was such a pristine place she wanted to obliterate all reminders of Davo and his tour.

When she returned the car to Shirley's, she found that Pam was visiting the dugout. A pot of tea was quickly produced and both women wanted to know what Anna thought of the lake.

'It's hard to explain. I don't think I can put the feeling, or the picture, into words. Anyway, you know it, so I don't have to,' said Anna.

Pam chuckled. 'That's a good cop-out. But you're right. It is hard to describe. It's sort of like a blank canvas, so you can read it lots of ways.'

'I was sorry that Davo and a group were there, because I wanted to have the place to myself,' said Anna. 'And they left some rubbish behind.'

Pam rolled her eyes. 'Typical Davo. He never does things properly. No wonder his business is struggling. Davo doesn't do enough really to enthuse people about this area. I've heard of visitors going out there and coming back complaining, "What is there to see . . . ? Nothing."'

'Which reminds me . . . I have some news for you,

Pam,' announced Shirley. 'It's about Kerrie. You know the sketches she did out at the lake when she was here the first time? When you took her there?'

'I remember. The ones that inspired her to go back and start painting?' said Pam.

Shirley nodded, looking extremely pleased. 'She did finish them. And . . . she's been invited to show them! It's such a feather in her cap and will boost her along no end.'

'Wonderful. At a gallery in Sydney?' asked Pam.

'No! The big art exhibition in Broken Hill next month. It's a huge thing. She's quite knocked out by it.'

'So she'll be up here and come and see us?' said Pam.

'Would she dare not?' laughed Shirley. She turned to Anna. 'You'll love Kerrie. I've told you about her.'

'You know, I think I should go over to the Hill and be there for the opening,' said Pam.

'That's a terrific idea. Take Anna. I'll see Kerrie when she gets here. She's coming to stay for a couple of days. Said she had a surprise,' said Shirley.

'I don't know if I can get time off,' began Anna, but Pam waved her hand.

'We'll sort something out with Mick. You work hard enough for him. If he needs any help, Doug can give him a hand for a few hours. It's settled. You're coming, Anna.'

Anna looked at Shirley, who nodded. 'I agree. And you'll enjoy it. I really want you to meet Kerrie. I'm so thrilled for her.'

'Shirley really encouraged Kerrie to start painting again,' Pam said to Anna.

'Shirley, for someone who doesn't get out much, you wield a lot of influence,' commented Anna drily.

Pam glanced at Anna. 'Yes, she does.'

'Rubbish. I just enjoy having you all around. Pour another cup of tea, Pam,' said Shirley.

11

KERRIE FELT AS THOUGH somewhere between Broken Hill and Opal Lake she had driven across an invisible border. It just felt right and comfortable. She was now in familiar country and heading to a place that had become special to her. The thought amused her slightly. This country, which she knew Milton would consider raw, inhospitable and stark, deeply attracted her and appealed to her soul.

As she drove on she realised that she had missed being out here. She felt that through her sketches and then her paintings, which had grown from rough pencil and charcoal outlines, she had brought this country to life. She wound down the window for a few moments to savour the sensations of the bush, despite the dust and flies that quickly flew into the car. 'Nothing else can recreate the feel of the sun, the air, the smells, and the intensity of the light and colours,' she said. 'You just have to be here.'

'I've so missed all this, especially my friends in Opal Lake. Phone calls to Shirley aren't the same as sitting over a cup of tea in her dugout. Broken Hill was exciting, getting ready for the exhibition, and being part of the outback art scene, but now I feel I'm on the homeward stretch. I'm so glad we have time to make this detour before the exhibition opens.' Kerrie glanced at the young woman beside her. 'I suppose you think I'm a bit crazy.'

'Well, this is pretty wild country, so remote. Not the sort of place I would have thought you'd like, Kerrie. You wouldn't want to actually live out here, would you?'

'Alia, I'm learning that living is a state of mind. I don't think it's the places themselves, but how you react to them.' Kerrie couldn't see Alia's expression because owl-like sunglasses covered so much of her face. 'Thank you again, you did an amazing job helping with your father's retrospective, Alia.'

'Thanks, Kerrie. I think I was a bit overwhelmed by it all at first, but I have to say we had a great time in New York, didn't we? Not that I was entirely at ease with what I did. And I felt as much a fish out of water helping with your paintings in Broken Hill. Maybe I'm still not sure where I belong.'

'I think you've shown that you're a natural curator, Alia. It's obviously something you like and you're good at. And I think you should try to involve yourself with more art shows.'

'Yes. I s'pose so. Being my father's daughter and your offsider helped me get a toe in the door, but I need to get work on my own merits. You're right. I do want to get involved with organising more exhibitions.'

'You're fortunate to know that. Some people never do find their passion.'

Alia glanced at her stepmother. 'You must feel pleased that you're finally doing what you always wanted to do.'

'Yes. I was very happy to put your father first while we were married. When you love someone you don't think that you're making sacrifices, especially as your father was such a formidable talent. But all those years that I didn't paint meant that I lost confidence in my own abilities.'

'He really was quite amazing, wasn't he? I'm sorry I didn't appreciate his work as much as I should have while he was still alive. His retrospective exhibition in New York was quite an eye opener. I used to visit him sometimes in his studio, but it wasn't to watch him work. He was just our dad who was a soft touch,' said Alia. 'And a lot of fun.'

Kerrie was quiet for a moment. Ever since she'd taken Shirley's advice and asked Alia to accompany her to New York to help with the massive job of compiling and exhibiting Milton's key works, Alia had started to change her attitude. At first Kerrie assumed it was the chance for Alia to meet a lot of influential art world heavyweights, but she soon saw that Alia was genuinely keen and interested in her father's work and wanted to make the exhibition a true reflection of his genius. Kerrie found that Alia was proud to be recognised as Milton's daughter.

'I know he was deeply immersed in his work, but never forget he adored you girls,' said Kerrie. 'I think he'd be thrilled to know that you want to enter the art world, too.'

'Are you pleased to be part of it now as an artist in your own right?' asked Alia.

'I'm amazed. I couldn't believe it when Murray Evans showed the bush artists the photos of my paintings I'd sent him, and the Broken Hill Gallery invited me to exhibit. I so love this country. It's really inspired me,' said Kerrie happily.

Alia glanced out the window. 'It's certainly not Europe!'

'I hope you won't be bored in Opal Lake and when you go to the opening. I'm so thrilled you'll be there. It's such a special event in Broken Hill. It's only held every couple of years.'

'Yes, talking to the people at the gallery, I gather it's quite a big deal,' said Alia politely. 'And your work looks terrific.'

'I know it's not New York,' laughed Kerrie, 'but I don't have big ambitions. I think I only want acceptance and acknowledgment by other people that I have some talent. You always wonder what you're capable of doing, which is why I'm so very grateful to my friend Shirley for giving me the encouragement to paint again.'

'She seems to be a pretty special person in your life,' said Alia curiously. 'I've never known you to have many close friends, not counting Tim.'

'You're right. I've never had girlfriends that I hung out with. But Shirley is so warm, smart, funny. It's not surprising that people gravitate to her. I think you'll like her,' said Kerrie, adding, 'Everyone in Opal Lake is nice. Pam and Doug, who run the B&B we're staying in, are lovely too. I think it's something to do with being part of a small, isolated community.'

'It seems unusual that an older woman who lives alone in a cave, whom you met less than eighteen months ago, has had such a big impact on you,' said Alia.

'Yep. But that's about right,' said Kerrie cheerfully. 'Sometimes when you least expect it people come into your life at the right time. I have to say I'm happy that it's going to be reciprocal. She's helped me, so I'm doing something for her in return.' Kerrie looked pleased with herself.

Alia knew that Kerrie was still excited at seeing her

work come together for the exhibition. She had been impressed with the gallery, which had quashed her worries that the Broken Hill show might be a hick country affair, for it contained the work of several well-known Australian painters. Alia had been touched that Kerrie had asked her to come along to Broken Hill to help, and then to join her on her trip out to the opal country.

Since working with Kerrie on her father's retrospective in New York, Alia had a new appreciation of her stepmother. While Kerrie always acknowledged Milton's immense reputation, Alia had also begun to see how important Kerrie had been to furthering his artistic fame. It quickly became obvious to Alia that gallery owners, curators, art writers and academics had known Kerrie for quite some time, as they readily sought her opinion. Now she realised just how much Kerrie had devoted herself to her father's career at the cost of her own. And equally she had a greater awareness of how huge her father's reputation was and what a stunning body of work he'd created.

'Well, you certainly did a lot for my father,' said Alia and added quietly, 'for me, too.'

'Thank you, sweetie,' said Kerrie and left it that. In time, she hoped that Luisa and Renata would also realise that she was not the greedy, self-centred stepmother they'd always assumed her to be. But for now she and Alia at least had created a closer bond through Milton's art.

'We'll be coming into White Cliffs soon. I'm ready for a coffee,' said Kerrie. 'You don't have to drive to Opal Lake this way. You can get there directly from Broken Hill, but I thought you might like to see this little town while you have the chance. And we'll still get to Opal Lake before dark, which is great.'

When Alia glimpsed the distant township she wondered why the town was called white, for, in the afternoon sunlight, she felt as though she was looking at cliffs rolling from the horizon like a red wave. Then she saw what looked like a white crest on top of the cliffs above the stunted trees and scrubby saltbush of the plains.

'Those white lumps are mullock heaps. People have dug holes and shafts and great caverns underground and what comes out of them is piled high beside the mine.'

'The surface looks like a bomb hit it,' commented Alia. 'All those holes.' As they drove into the tiny township she exclaimed, 'It's small!'

'Darling, if you think this is small, wait till you get to Opal Lake. It's a fraction of this size! But it's deceptive because so much of the town is underground.'

'You mean like the shopping malls and football stadium,' joked Alia.

They stopped at the general store where Kerrie chatted with some of the locals, then the two of them headed up the hill to the Opal Delight Café and Gem Shop.

'Pam always says that they have lovely cappuccinos and home-made cake here,' said Kerrie.

While Kerrie ordered, Alia looked at the display case near the counter where local opals and some jewellery were for sale. When the coffee and food was served Alia joined Kerrie, who'd been chatting to the owners.

'Do you know everyone in the district?' asked Alia.

'No, I don't, but they are friends of friends of mine. Like I said, it's a small community out here.'

'There's some amazing jewellery over there in the display cabinet. Very dramatic. Never seen jewellery like that,' said Alia. 'I'm impressed.'

'That'd be some of Ingrid's pieces. She sells a few bits locally. She lives in Opal Lake. In fact I stayed in her place when I came the first Christmas after your father died. I hope she's around, you'd enjoy her company. She might show you some more of her work.'

Another couple came into the café and greeted Kerrie enthusiastically. 'Hi, Kerrie. Gustav and Helen. Remember us? We met at Pam's last year? No, I think it was longer ago than that. We haven't seen you for a while. Are you staying here or going to Opal Lake?'

'I'm on my way there now,' answered Kerrie. 'This is my stepdaughter, Alia. Gustav is a well-known palaeontologist, geologist, fossil specialist and acclaimed academic, and his wife Helen, whom everyone says knows even more,' finished Kerrie with a smile.

Helen laughed as she shook Alia's hand. 'We're still students, too. There's a lot to learn out here. Are you enjoying the opal fields?'

'I haven't been here very long. We've been visiting Broken Hill and now we're going to stay in Opal Lake for a couple of days,' said Alia.

'What are you up to, Kerrie?'

'I have some paintings in the art show at the Hill.'

'Kerrie! That's fantastic! Congratulations,' said Helen.

'Well done.' Gustav pumped her hand. 'Weren't you painting when we first met you?'

'Sketching, and thinking about it. Shirley encouraged me and the lake inspired me. What are you guys up to?'

'We're doing a new book,' said Gustav.

'We've been given access to some specimens in the Natural History Museum and a few private collections, and we'll be identifying them and writing about them. But what we're really trying to do is to get some important sites protected and excavated by scientists,' said Helen. 'Palaeontology is a poor cousin when it comes to funding. Along with finding known species we're sure there's a mother lode of unknown creatures fossilised in the opal dirt from the time an inland sea covered the centre of this continent, anything from small seashells to dinosaurs.'

Alia looked at Kerrie. 'Dinosaur fossils? How amazing.'

'There are a lot being found by miners who now turn them over to people like Helen and Gustav, even though the opalised ones can be very valuable,' said Kerrie, thinking of Shirley's precious Tajna.

'But to us even the tiniest, most insignificant fragment can be a vital clue. The beginnings of life on this planet are recorded in ancient Australian rocks. And a place like Lightning Ridge has lots of fossils like dinosaurs, plants, and even early monotremes. So we've been trying to educate the miners to look for fossils and donate them,' said Gustav, 'and get funding so museums can pay a fair price for them.'

'That's incredible,' said Alia. 'I'd love to come on a dig sometime.'

Kerrie looked surprised. 'Would you really?'

'We now have a little stone cottage on higher ground but our old caravan is parked under the Bimble Box trees as guest quarters, so come over to the Ridge any time,' said Helen.

'You're going to be very busy this season,' said Kerrie.

'We certainly are. But we love the work and this part of the country and most miners are pretty good,' said Helen. 'The opal fields are full of individuals doing their own thing, just pottering away, hoping for that lucky strike. No clocks on an opal field so they can take their time sifting through the dirt.'

'Why do people choose that life? Why do people think they can come out here and find a fortune?' asked Alia.

'Because that's sometimes what happens!' said Kerrie.

'I think it's more the lifestyle and the freedom that people want, whether they find a fortune or not,' said Gustav.

'You should talk to some of the people out here in the opal fields,' Helen told Alia. 'That might help to explain why they want to look for opals.'

'It sounds like a cop-out to me,' said Alia. 'I bet there are a lot of people running away from their responsibilities and opal provides them with a good excuse.'

'You could be right there, Alia,' said Gustav. He smiled. 'We'll probably see you in Opal Lake, Kerrie.'

'Or in Broken Hill. We were thinking of going over to see the exhibition later, and now you've given us a real incentive,' said Helen. 'It's a cracker event. Always impressive.'

When they rolled into Opal Lake, Alia was prepared for anything. 'It's certainly surrounded by a lot of space,' she commented as she looked around. 'Do you feel safe way out here?'

'Totally,' said Kerrie. 'I think it's far safer than in a city. We're staying at Pam and Doug's Golden Dome tonight. See that hill? Shirley lives up there on top of it.'

'You can't wait to see her, can you? Does she know about the exhibition?' asked Alia.

'Yes. I told her as soon as I was invited. See, there's the entrance to the Golden Dome.'

'Those two small pillars have frogs sitting on them.'

'Yes, stone frogs. Pam loves frogs.'

'The Golden Dome made me think that we'd be staying in a Vegas-type casino with flashing neon lights like a spaceship, on top of the hill,' joked Alia.

'Heaven forbid . . .'

Alia was impressed with the style and comfort of the Golden Dome as well as the concept of living underground. 'It's elegant but at the same time really cosy, just like someone's home,' she said to Kerrie after they'd explored. 'I love the atrium with the plants and the hot tub.'

'In the daytime, the sun shines down the overhead shaft. The hot tub's a new addition, but if you want a plunge in it before dinner, go ahead. Take a glass of wine from the fridge with you. Don't hurry, I'm dying to catch up on all the news with Pam.'

'This is all very civilised,' said Alia.

'She's lovely,' Pam said to Kerrie as they sat in the lounge while Doug fussed over the hors d'oeuvres in the kitchen.

'I don't think Alia was expecting a good wine and a hot tub before dinner! This trip has been a bit of an eye opener for her, she's handling it well. I think it's given her a new perspective, that's for sure. Now, Pam, I have something to show you,' said Kerrie handing her a small box.

'Don't tell me this is the ring you found at Opal Lake?' said Pam opening it. 'It's absolutely magnificent.'

'It did scrub up well, didn't it? Roth Cameron tried to find out more about it, but apart from knowing that the stone came from Lightning Ridge and being able to date the setting to the 1920s, he couldn't find out anything else.'

'I don't suppose it matters, although it would have been nice to have learnt more about such a beautiful opal. Isn't Roth a lovely man?'

Kerrie smiled. 'Have you been talking to Shirley?'

Pam waved her hand. 'Absolutely not. You don't have to tell me things if you'd rather not, but I'm curious as to why Shirley might have something to tell me about you and Roth Cameron!' She laughed.

'It's not Roth I've been talking to Shirley about. I told her that I've been seeing quite a lot of Tim Cameron, who runs the business now.'

Pam looked puzzled, then her face cleared and she broke into a large smile. 'Tim? Roth's son? He's lovely. Don't tell me . . . You and he?'

Kerrie tried not to smile. 'Ooh, you're quick, Pam. And you're right, he is lovely. We've just clicked and we've become good friends. Well, maybe a bit more than that. He wanted to come up to the exhibition but he can't get away right now.'

'That's fantastic news. What does Alia think?'

'She likes him. The other two have only met him once or twice. I think that they disapprove of my finding someone else so quickly. I know it's been less than two years since Milton died but to me it doesn't matter. I feel right with Tim.'

'You don't have to apologise, Kerrie. Surely Milton would want you to be happy? No one would wish to see someone they loved unhappy for the rest of their life. Now you've moved into a new phase.'

'I think so. It seems life does go in cycles. I don't regret a moment of the excitement, the passion, the pressure, the merry-go-round that I lived with Milton.' She paused. 'Well, maybe I would have liked some things to have been different, but that's how it was with Milton.'

'For what it's worth, I think that you're still young, so you should move on,' said Pam.

'This exhibition could also be the start of something new,' Kerrie said cautiously.

'I'd definitely say so,' agreed Pam. 'I'll be interested to hear what Shirley has to say about you and Tim.'

'She's happy for me,' said Kerrie.

'I'm sure she is,' said Pam. 'You're doing the right thing. But, you know, I can't help thinking that Shirley should have grabbed the bull by the horns years ago and moved on, too. I've always wondered why she stayed on here. It's not like she was heavily into mining. I suppose it's good that she started recording the history of this place, but, well, it's not much of a life when you think about it. I suppose it's too late for her to change now.'

'You know, I think the same thing,' admitted Kerrie. 'Shirley was the same age as I am now when she met Stefan.

She had almost as long with Stefan as I had with Milton. But I'm prepared to start again and Shirley wasn't. She's like a wounded old bear that refuses to get out of its cave. It's good that she's so caring and wise, so people come to her.'

'Yes, she's been that way as long as I've lived here. Well, dinner is ready. I guess you'll go over to see Shirley first thing in the morning?'

'Yes, of course. I want to show Alia around, too. She's flying straight back to Sydney after the show opens, so this is her only chance to see what's here.'

'We're heading off, too. We'll go to your opening, of course, but then we're going to Dubbo for a big family wedding. Be away a week or so.'

'Is someone coming to look after this place? Do you want a hand here?' offered Kerrie.

'No, thanks, it's all under control. We have friends from Victoria who love coming up here and running the place. They like wandering round the country in their caravan with their old kelpie and they love noodling for opals, so they're happy to fill in when we're away.'

'That's good, because I do plan to stay on for a bit. I have a friend coming to visit.'

Pam smiled. 'Wonderful. Will your friend be staying here?' She wanted to ask more questions, but didn't as Alia joined them for one of Pam and Doug's delicious meals.

Kerrie drove Alia around the top of Old Tom's Hill and stopped the car outside Shirley's dugout. Alia gazed across the town to the emptiness of the surrounding landscape.

'It's a bit like a fort up here.'

'Yes, it would be hard to sneak up here without someone knowing, I suppose. I always felt safe when I stayed here at Ingrid's, but she has very secure locks to protect her jewellery,' said Kerrie. 'Shirley doesn't even lock her door. Mind you, she never leaves the place anyway.'

'I'd like to meet Ingrid and see her jewellery,' said Alia.

'I'm sure you'll get the chance.'

They got out of the car and as they walked to the dugout Kerrie was surprised to see a young woman sweeping the tiny patio by Shirley's entrance.

'Hello. Is Shirley all right?' asked Kerrie, wondering why Shirley needed someone to help. Kerrie was only too aware that Shirley wasn't one to be fussed by domestic appearances.

'She's fine. I just thought I'd help her a bit. You must be Kerrie. She's very excited to see you.'

'Yes, I am. And this is Alia. And you are . . . ?'

'Anna. I'm working down at the hotel. Shirley's inside. I'll go and tell her you're here.'

'Don't worry,' said Kerrie. 'I know my way about, and she's expecting me. It's nice of you to help out.'

Alia smiled at Anna as Kerrie went ahead into the dugout.

'Shirley's a lovely lady,' said Anna.

'Have you been in Opal Lake a long time?' asked Alia.

Anna placed the broom behind a heavy chair and tucked a strand of hair behind her ear. 'No, not long. I'm from Adelaide. I saw a job advertised for bar work here, and I came. It's somewhere different.'

'You can say that again. Do you live in a dugout?'

'No, just at the pub. I'll say goodbye to Shirley.' Anna stuck her head around the doorway of the dugout and called out, 'See you later, Shirley.'

'Aren't you staying for tea, Anna? This is Kerrie I've told you about.'

'No, thanks, Shirley, but you enjoy the visit. Let me

know if you want anything. Bye.' Anna included Kerrie and Alia in her swift farewell and disappeared.

'So you've collected another lost duckling?' said Kerrie lightly. 'Where'd she spring from?'

'Oh, she's been here for about two months, I guess. Taken me a while to tame her, though. Bit of a shy creature. She's a runner. Now, sit down. I'm so pleased to meet you, Alia. Isn't it wonderful news about Kerrie's exhibition?'

'Yes, very exciting.'

'I do wish you could see it, Shirley. Alia helped with the hanging of my paintings and my work is shown off to wonderful advantage.'

'I'm sure they'll all sell in a flash,' said Shirley.

'Oh. I hadn't thought about the selling side of it,' said Kerrie suddenly. 'I'll miss every one of them!'

Alia and Shirley both laughed.

'But that's what you're supposed to do! Paint a picture and sell it, isn't that right?' said Alia. 'Was Dad possessive about his work, too?'

'He was a bit, which is why he kept a lot of them. He called them his heart pieces, as opposed to his commissioned work.'

'If you did decide that you could bear to sell your paintings, is there a special one that you couldn't possibly part with?' asked Shirley.

'Yes, there's one that's definitely not for sale. I didn't even put it in the exhibition.' Kerrie turned to Alia. 'You know the one I mean. Could you get it from the car?'

Alia nodded and rose. 'Oops, I left it at the B&B. I'm so sorry, Kerrie. Shall I go and get it while you two catch up? It won't take me long.'

As she left the room, Shirley turned to Kerrie. 'She's lovely. Not quite as you described her eighteen months ago. So something happened when you two went to New York?'

'Yes, I think so. What was really important was that she came to understand her father's talent and his place in the art world. And it showed her that she has a talent, too. She has a flair for design and she's good at display, and art appreciation. It's given her the idea that she might become a curator, which I'm so happy about. I'm very glad that I took up your suggestion to take Alia with me to help with Milton's retrospective.'

'And the other two girls? How are they these days?'

'Hard to say. I think they are still directionless, though they're no slouches when it comes to shopping and social-ising. I've decided to move out of the Rose Bay house. The girls can either live there, or sell it and divide the pro-ceeds. It's up to them. I hope that then we'll have less of a barrier between us.'

'That seems to be a good idea. Where will you live?' asked Shirley.

'No idea, but I don't need a huge mansion. I want somewhere simpler and easier to manage.'

Shirley leant back and looked at Kerrie. 'Seems to me you're making some smart decisions.'

'Maybe. I'm certainly seeing a way forward through my art.'

'I think there's more than just your art. How's Tim?'

Kerrie smiled at her. 'Couldn't be better.'

Just then Alia came back into the dugout holding a large brown paper parcel, which she handed to Shirley. 'This is for you,' she said. 'From Kerrie.'

Shirley smiled in delight. 'A painting! How wonder-ful. You shouldn't be giving them away, Kerrie.'

Alia helped her to open the brown paper and Shirley gasped as she discovered there were two pictures inside. One was a portrait of Shirley done from the sketches Kerrie had made on her second visit and the other was a small picture of Opal Lake.

Shirley held the portrait at arm's length. 'It's good. You certainly have developed it from those original sketches. You know me very well.' She studied the small painting of the lake. 'Oh, Kerrie, I love this. It's just as I remember it.'

'I'm so glad. You can see that wonderful silvery sandy soil that looks like water in the distance.'

'I like the rusty wire and the old fence post. They are very evocative. I have a lot of memories of that lake,' said Shirley. 'I was there with the two most important men in my life.' She turned to Alia. 'When I was a little girl I saw the lake filled with water and the abundant bird life that was attracted to it, little water birds and great clumsy pelicans. That was a once in a lifetime event.'

Alia glanced at Kerrie, as if expecting her to say something, but Kerrie stood up and hugged Shirley.

'I'm so happy you like the picture.'

That afternoon Kerrie, Pam and Alia went down to the hotel before Pam had to start preparing dinner for her guests, for a drink and a chat with some of the locals. It wasn't very busy and Anna was able to talk with Alia, while Kerrie and Pam took their drinks to one of the small tables.

'Is Anna very friendly with Shirley?' asked Kerrie.

'Isn't everyone? You can't be possessive about the old girl,' said Pam.

'I do feel a bit that way,' admitted Kerrie. 'She's been so supportive and, I don't know, I just feel like she's been in my life forever.'

'She has made a big impression on you, hasn't she?'

'I think she came along at the right time. Murray opened my eyes and inspired me to paint, but Shirley seems to understand me, and talks sense to me.'

'She has that knack,' agreed Pam. 'She never goes anywhere, so the world ends up on her doorstep. She swept Anna into her dugout almost as soon as they met.'

'I worry people might take advantage. Shirley is so good natured,' said Kerrie.

'That's true. She's generous, too. I know of several people she's helped financially but I think she's been good for Anna.'

'How does Anna get on with the other people here?' asked Kerrie.

'Anna is not like most of the other girls who have come out here to work,' said Pam. 'She's a bit of a loner. I worried about her at first, because she's so stand-offish, but when you get to know her, she's just lovely, though she scares most of the blokes away. Nice to see her chatting with Alia.'

'I can't imagine why she's staying out here. It's not really a place for a young woman. Is she interested in opals?'

'You mean coming out here for that opal strike that's your ticket to the future?'

'And then when you've hit opal you stay to look for more and never leave and before you know it, your life is half over,' said Kerrie.

'Yes, how often have we heard that story?' laughed Pam. 'But I doubt that will happen to Anna. I get the feeling that she's waiting for something, but it's not that.'

'Is she waiting for someone?' suggested Kerrie.

Pam shrugged. 'No idea. She never talks about her personal life, but I don't think it's a man. And speaking of men, who's your guest that's coming? Is it a certain jeweller?' she asked.

Kerrie smiled. 'Tim? He's sorry that he'll miss the opening of the art show, but he's going to try to make it before it closes. Maybe there will be time to bring him out to Opal Lake.'

'I hope so,' said Pam, and then changing the subject added, 'Anna would like to see your exhibition. I've

347

spoken to her about it, and since she and Alia seem to be hitting it off, she won't be stuck with us oldies. Mick doesn't mind giving her some time off.'

Kerrie couldn't have dreamed a more perfect evening to show her own paintings than the opening of the Outback Artists' Initiative Exhibition. Although Alia and she had checked the lighting and supervised the display, Kerrie was still amazed by how good her works looked among the other pieces of art on show.

'I never believed I'd have a collection of work to exhibit! I know there are only eight of them, but I'd so given up on my dream of being an artist. It just goes to show, you should never give up on your dreams,' she said quietly to Anna as they looked around the room.

Anna, in a silk jacket borrowed from Alia, stood beside her and nodded in agreement. 'That's what Shirley keeps telling me.'

'It's what she told me too,' said Kerrie.

'Look, Kerrie, there're a couple of red stickers on your paintings already, and the exhibition hasn't even been officially opened yet,' said Alia.

'Ooh, here's Murray! You must meet him. He's my inspiration,' laughed Kerrie, holding out her arms as Murray Evans came striding towards her, a huge grin on his face.

'Look at you! How clever are you!' He hugged her.

'Thanks to you. Oh, Murray. I never thought this would happen. Look what a can of worms you've opened! Oh, this is my stepdaughter, Alia, and Anna, a friend from Opal Lake. Is Fiona with you?'

'Lovely to meet you both. No, Fee is holding the fort back in Lightning Ridge.' He turned to Alia. 'I understand that you helped hang Kerrie's work. It looks great.'

'Thanks. Kerrie tells me that you inspired her to get out the brushes,' said Alia.

'Not me. The landscape. You'll have to come over to the Ridge, have a look around,' said Murray.

'Murray and Fiona have a terrific gallery in Lightning Ridge,' said Kerrie. 'Have you got any paintings here, Murray?'

'I've brought over three or four. They're hanging just around that corner.'

'I can't believe that there's so much artistic talent out here,' said Alia.

'Here comes Ingrid. Have you seen her knockout jewellery, Alia?' asked Murray. 'She puts opals up as *objets d'art* more than jewellery.'

'It's extraordinary. I saw some of her work at White Cliffs. It will be good to see more.'

Ingrid hugged Kerrie, and offered her congratulations. She was wearing one of her designs, a dramatic boulder-opal necklace as well as a snake bracelet studded with opal chips and amethyst eyes that wound up her arm. Both Alia and Anna admired it.

'How productive you've been, Kerrie. I'm telling every-one that the seed for these works began in my studio! You should come and stay every summer when I'm away.'

'Thank you, Ingrid. I agree, Opal Lake is very conducive to being creative.'

Kerrie was delighted to see Jack Absalom again and many other people whom she knew. She reminded Jack of her visit and he was genuinely pleased that it had produced such great results.

'Will you be painting more of the outback?' he asked.

'I certainly will,' replied Kerrie enthusiastically.

Pam and Doug also gave her an excited embrace. 'This is a fantastic show. So many ways of looking at the outback. Your paintings of Opal Lake are wonderful.

I can't believe they are from the sketches you did when we drove out there. We're so proud of you,' said Pam.

Kerrie smiled at Doug looking unfamiliar in his blue shirt and tie, pressed moleskins and shiny RM Williams boots. 'I'm just happy you could make it. I hope you enjoy the family wedding, and I'll see you when you get back from Dubbo.'

'We won't be gone long, but you'll like Liz and Bob who are filling in for us back at the Dome.'

'And Banjo,' added Doug. 'Their dog. We'll see you in a week.'

'That was some night,' said Kerrie as she settled into the back seat of the car while Alia drove to the motel they were staying at in Broken Hill.

'It was lovely. The whole evening was a huge success. Very well organised, too. Music, food, good wine, nice people, intelligent discussions. Better than some of the arty events I've been to in Sydney. This was really about the art and artists, rather than the glitterati,' said Alia.

'It's the first time I've been to an art show, but I enjoyed it,' said Anna.

'You need to get out more,' said Alia. 'What did you do in Adelaide?'

'I worked in a coffee shop, but that wasn't my real life. I'm an athlete with a tough coach. When I wasn't serving coffee, I was training.'

'Are you still in training?' asked Alia.

'I'm trying to decide if I want to continue, and whether I'm capable of doing what my coach wants. But I keep myself in shape and I need to run.'

'What's your sport?'

'Track and field. I'm a middle-distance runner, eight hundred metres.'

'How much time have you got before you have to make a decision? I'm older than you and I'm just working out what I want to do now,' said Alia.

They got out of the car at the motel and Kerrie said, 'Early start for us all in the morning. Planes to catch and driving to do.'

Alia watched Anna go into her room. 'Interesting girl,' she said to Kerrie.

'Hmm. She'd better make up her mind about what she wants to do soon. She can't keep hiding away in Opal Lake forever.'

Alia was tempted to point out that it had taken years for Kerrie to act on her career dream but kept silent.

'If that's what she's doing. She doesn't give much away, but I like her,' said Alia.

'Sleep well. I'll take you to the airport in the morning and then I'll be on my way back to Opal Lake with Anna.' Kerrie yawned. 'I'm fading.'

'It's been a big day for you. Congratulations again.' Alia leant over and kissed Kerrie on the cheek. 'I'm really proud of you,' she added.

Kerrie was surprised and touched by the gesture. 'Thank you for all your help. It's wonderful to know you were part of my exhibition. I think your father would have been pleased.'

'And pleased with you, too, I'm sure. I'll download the photos I took of the night as soon as I get back and send them to you. G'night.'

Kerrie lay on the hard bed in her motel room, pleased that at last she had formed a warm relationship with one of Milton's daughters. With Alia's evolving interest in being a curator, perhaps she would also like to become more involved with Milton's legacy. If so, it would give Kerrie time to paint and travel, and to be with Tim.

'Thanks, Shirley, for your sensible counsel,' she murmured before falling asleep.

After saying goodbye to Alia at the airport the next morning, Kerrie pulled out several CDs and put them within reach to play on the way back to Opal Lake, in case she and Anna ran out of conversation.

They settled in the car with takeaway coffee in paper cups and a donut from the service station where Kerrie had filled up.

'I never normally eat this stuff,' said Anna.

'I feel like a sugar hit when I'm on a long drive,' explained Kerrie. Then she asked, 'I suppose you're a health food fiend because of your running?'

'Partly, but it's also easy to make protein shakes and grill a steak.'

'Don't you cook? Alia and her sisters never learnt to cook because we had a housekeeper who cooked for them. Well, that's their excuse. Mind you, their father was something of a gourmand. We ate out a lot, too.'

'My mum is a plain cook and we rarely go out, though my parents go to the RSL for a feed sometimes,' said Anna.

Kerrie was beginning to realise what a simple, perhaps sheltered and unsophisticated, background Anna came from in the suburbs of Adelaide, somewhat like her own upbringing. How Milton had changed her life. 'Have you ever thought of travelling overseas?'

'I'd like to travel with a team for an overseas meet some time. That would be great.'

Kerrie thought of all the wonderful places she'd been with Milton. 'What about living overseas?'

'Oh, there are sports academies, institutes, universities I could get into, but that all means money, even if I won a scholarship.'

'So your problems are financial ones?'

'There is the money problem, but the rest is hard to explain. Even though I can run fast, I can't run right. My coach says that my race tactics are wrong, and if I can't fix them, I'll never be anything more than a good club runner. I'm not sure that I know how to get them right. If I can't, there is no point in going on.'

'You haven't decided if you're going to pursue an athletic career or not? I don't want to sound like a know-all, but you can't spend the rest of your life just wandering aimlessly, Anna. Don't be like me and put your talent on hold. Make up your mind so if you decide running isn't for you, you can find something else worthwhile to do with your life.'

'That's what Shirley said.' They were both silent for a minute. Then Anna added, 'At least you know you have a talent. You've proved you're good at what you do.'

'Thank you. You mean because of the show last night? That's the icing on the cake. While I'm thrilled that I was considered good enough for an exhibition, and that people liked my paintings, first I had to prove to myself that I was good. I had a lot of help. Murray Evans, you met him last night, started me off by taking me out to the bush and letting me try, and Shirley supported my first attempts at painting. But I also had to find something inside myself.'

'How? What is it?' asked Anna quietly, almost with longing.

'I can't really tell you, Anna. It's a kind of awakening, I suppose. And I also discovered the joy. Being passionate about something is one thing, finding pleasure in it and enjoying what you do is another. And that's not being complacent. I now know I have tons more huge hills to climb. But what's driving me, what makes every day fulfilling, is that I enjoy trying to climb those hills.'

When Anna didn't answer, Kerrie went on, 'Sorry, didn't mean to lecture you. Not my business, of course.'

'I was just thinking. I've never talked about my feelings with anyone before, other than Shirley. Pam is nice, too, but I don't talk to her the same way. Everyone is nice out here,' she said lightly.

'When it's a small community you have to rub along. But I bet there are a lot of people around Opal Lake who suffer their dark nights of the soul.'

'Yes,' said Anna, and Kerrie had the feeling she was about to say something else but she paused, seemed to change her mind, and went on, 'I hear stories in the pub. I sometimes think people aren't so much looking for something out here, pretending it's opals, as hiding or escaping from something. I suppose that applies to me too.'

'Alia thought much the same thing,' said Kerrie. 'But I don't think you are holding a deep dark secret, are you?'

'No. But I bet some people are.'

'Like?'

'Who knows. Like I said, I hear bits of gossip in the bar. No one knows the real story about anyone it seems. And I wonder about Davo.'

'Why Davo?'

'I heard one story that he came from Melbourne, and he told me he was an ex-surfer. I suppose he could have been both. But I don't much like him.'

'It's interesting you say that. I have to say I don't care for him either. He's a bit of a chauvinist. I ended up in Opal Lake because of his attitude. He so didn't want to bring me and that made me determined to come. But it worked out just fine for me.'

'Yes, I suppose it did. But he's so arrogant. Thinks he's God's gift to women, and with no cause. He tried to teach me to drive Shirley's car and he thought that it gave him the right to keep touching me. Yuck. I always feel like he's undressing me when he looks at me with that smirk.'

354

'That's certainly not good. Did you say anything to Shirley?'

'No, he's a friend of hers. He has to be because she keeps giving him money for his business.'

Kerrie, who had not heard this before, was somewhat surprised but said nothing to Anna, instead commenting, 'Well, you are pretty, Anna, I'm sure a lot of men would think so.'

Anna turned and stared at Kerrie. 'Me? I don't think so. I've never been the pretty one in a group.'

'Rubbish, you are pretty. Good hair, beautiful skin, lovely eyes and a great, trim body,' said Kerrie.

The two women continued to chat happily and the drive to Opal Lake seemed to pass quickly. When they arrived back at the pub, Anna grabbed her small bag, thanked Kerrie for the great time she'd had and hurried inside.

Kerrie drove to the Golden Dome and met Bob and Liz and Banjo the kelpie, before turning around and heading straight back out again to go up to Shirley's to tell her all about the successful show. At the entrance to the dugout Kerrie noticed that Shirley's pot plants were looking a little droopy, and she made a mental note to water them.

'Hey, Shirley . . . I'm back. Triumphant!' called Kerrie.

'In here,' called out Shirley.

Immediately Kerrie knew something wasn't right. Shirley was in her bedroom and she didn't sound very well. 'What's up? Why are you in bed?' When Kerrie entered the bedroom, she was shocked to see Shirley not only in bed, but looking pale, dishevelled and, from the expression on her face, in some pain. 'Shirley, what's wrong?'

'I'm a bit crook,' she answered. 'So was the exhibition a sell-out?' she asked, trying to sit up. But as she did so, she winced and caught her breath, clutching a hot water bottle to her side.

Kerrie saw a bowl and towel by the bedside. The bowl had obviously been used and when she touched Shirley's forehead she realised that it was hot.

'Shirley, you've been sick and you have a fever, and also in pain. Do you know what's wrong?'

'I'm having a bit of a bad attack of gallstones and my normal remedies aren't helping.'

'If you're really in pain then you need proper medication. What do you want me to do?' asked Kerrie.

'You could rub my feet and tell me about the show. And bring me some ice. I'm alternating heat and ice. I've tried Epsom salts, cider vinegar, flaxseed . . .'

'Shirley, that doesn't sound like proper treatment to me. We have to get you to a doctor.'

'No. They'll take my gall bladder out and I need it!'

'Shirley, it's a common operation. Can't the stones be zapped and broken up? I hate to see you in such agony. You can't stay here,' exclaimed Kerrie as Shirley doubled over in pain.

Shirley stubbornly shook her head. 'I'm not leaving. I'll be all right. I've had these attacks before and I get over them.'

'Shirley, you can't stay in this dugout in this sort of condition. You need proper medical attention. Let me call someone. What about the Flying Doctor Service? How do you get medical help out here?'

'The sister came to the clinic last week. Kerrie, stop fussing. Make us a cup of tea and sit down and talk to me, distract me.'

Kerrie reluctantly left Shirley to make some tea. The kitchen was messy and she wondered if Shirley had eaten, but realised that she probably had no appetite. Kerrie didn't like the look of her at all, but she didn't know what to do out here, so far from medical help. She wished Pam was still here. She knew that Ingrid was staying a few more days in Broken Hill. Finally, she decided to ring Mick at the pub.

'Crikey, Kerrie, if you think she's really that bad I wouldn't wait. The best thing to do is to drive her over to the hospital in Broken Hill right away.'

Kerrie glanced at her watch. 'If we leave soon we'll get there before dark. I'll call the hospital and let them know that we're on our way.'

'You'll drive Shirley over? I'll come up and help you get her into the car. I doubt if you'll be able to do it by yourself.'

'That's good of you, Mick, but persuading her might be another matter.'

'Well, you call the hospital in the Hill, and help Shirley pack her kit.'

'Mick, how long has it been since she last left here?' asked Kerrie suddenly. 'She won't want to leave.'

'Tell her it's time to go now or else she'll be leaving in a bloody box,' said Mick firmly.

Kerrie was unsure how to broach the idea of hospital with Shirley, but as she went back into the bedroom she caught her breath. Shirley had fallen back on her pillow, gasping in pain, her face ashen, her hands clutching her side.

'Shirley. Shirley. This is no good. We're taking you to hospital. You have no choice,' said Kerrie gently. 'I'll get some things together for you.'

'No!' Shirley managed to say, struggling to sit up. 'I'm not going anywhere.'

'Shirley. Please, be sensible. It'll be fine. Mick is coming to help and I will drive you over. You can't risk staying here. What if it's not gallstones?'

'Well, it is and I won't hear of you driving. You just came back. Get someone to come here,' she finally said.

'Shirley, you need proper medical attention and by

the time the Flying Doctor gets here we could almost be in Broken Hill. They would just take you there, anyway. Have you got some painkillers you can take to get you through the next few hours in the car?'

'A hammer?' said Shirley weakly. 'No. Please, Kerrie. I'm not leaving here. It will pass. It always does.'

'How long have you been having these attacks? For goodness' sake, you're a nurse! You should know better. Where do you keep your nightwear?'

Kerrie began rummaging through a chest of drawers as Shirley was hit by another spasm of pain, which prevented her from arguing.

A soft voice called from outside the bedroom. 'Kerrie? Can I help? Mick sent me up.' Anna came into the room and paled as she saw Shirley.

'Yes, can you go into the pantry? She's got an old suitcase in there. Then help me pack a few things into it.'

'Kerrie . . . no . . . please,' called Shirley weakly from the bed. She was holding a towel to her mouth and sweat had broken out on her forehead.

Kerrie took no notice, headed to the bathroom and began putting toiletries into a small bathroom bag.

'Anna, there's something else you can do for me,' she called. 'Would you mind going to the Golden Dome and getting my bag that's on my bed. I haven't unpacked yet, so it's got everything I'll need. Take it down to the pub and give it to Mick, and tell him to come as soon as he can.'

'He'll be up in a minute. Shirley, don't worry, you'll be right as soon as you get to the hospital. You'll be back here in a flash,' said Anna consolingly, then turned and ran from the dugout.

Shirley lay limply on the bed. She pointed to her pain relief pills and Kerrie refilled a glass of water and handed them to her.

'I'll refill the hot water bottle.'

Mick arrived and without ceremony marched to the bed and scooped up Shirley. Kerrie lifted the cotton bed-cover and a pillow off the bed. Despite her bulk, Mick carried Shirley to the car as Kerrie held open the door to the back seat. They eased Shirley in and Kerrie arranged the pillow and cover to make her as comfortable as possible. Her eyes were closed, and she no longer seemed to be aware of what was happening around her.

But suddenly she opened her eyes. 'What's going on? Take me out of here. I'm not leaving my home!'

Mick firmly closed the car door. 'You sure you don't want me or Anna to go with you?' he asked. 'She's a stubborn old girl.'

'Thanks, no. Just call the hospital and tell them I'm leaving now,' she said, and Mick nodded.

'They won't know what hit them when the old girl gets there. Drive safely, Kerrie.'

'Will you lock up Shirley's dugout?' said Kerrie. It had occurred to her that Shirley not only kept her stash of opals inside but also her valuable fossil.

Mick looked surprised. 'Righto. If you say so. I'll keep the key down at the pub.'

For Kerrie, the trip to Broken Hill in the fast descending light was a blur. She tried to calm and console Shirley, who groaned, complained and then seemed to doze fitfully. Eventually Kerrie put on a soothing classical CD and concentrated on driving.

Once Kerrie thought she heard Shirley whisper 'Stefan', but she couldn't be sure as she was concentrating on the road and keeping an eye open for kangaroos. When she did glance at Shirley in the rear-view mirror, she saw the elderly woman was leaning on her arm, wide awake.

'How're you going, Shirley?'

'As well as can be expected. What about you?'

'Good as gold.'

'Thank you, Kerrie. I'm sorry about this.'

'Oh, Shirley. Don't be silly. We all care about you, and we just want you to get better. Whatever it takes.'

'This is not what I wanted. I just thought that when my time came, I'd slip quietly away and not bother anyone.'

'Shirley! For goodness' sake, you're not damn well going anywhere just yet. We all get little medical hiccups. It's your turn! A little op and in ten days or so you'll be back home receiving visitors as you always do.'

'Hummph. I just want my life back. I still have a lot of writing to do.'

'Then the quicker you get over this, the better,' said Kerrie firmly.

There was silence for a while then Shirley asked, 'Do you ever think about dying, Kerrie? Even though you're so young?'

'I did. After Milton died. I felt very vulnerable. And then my mother's death was so soon after. I felt very alone. I thought my life was over and I didn't have anything to look forward to. But Tim has changed that. No, *you* changed that! We all have to live for each day. I mean, look at Anna, so young and as unsure and confused as I was when Milton died. You think you have a life plan, this is going to happen, you'll do this and that, and then whammo. Everything is turned on its head,' said Kerrie, determined to distract Shirley. 'You and I retreated. Anna runs away. Alia rolls with the punches. Who's right? Maybe we all just deal with things in our own way, no one is to say who's right, who's wrong. But the bottom line is we have to move forward, because that's the key – moving on.'

'You've got Tim. And now you've made peace with Alia. You'll be all right,' muttered Shirley.

'Shirley, so will you! You have a whole town behind you!'

It was a relief to see the lights of the hospital in Broken

Hill. Kerrie pulled into emergency and as soon as she spoke to an attendant, two medics arrived with a trolley. They eased Shirley from the car and wheeled her inside.

In the glare of the lights, Shirley tried to lift her head. She became more querulous and demanding.

'We've been expecting you,' said the triage nurse. 'Are you a relative?' she asked Kerrie.

'Yes, she is!' screeched Shirley. 'And I'm a nurse.'

The nurse sighed. 'The worst kind of patient. If you could come this way and help with the paperwork, please.'

'She's in a lot of pain. Delirious, I think,' said Kerrie anxiously.

'She'll be examined right away.'

Kerrie completed Shirley's paperwork as best she could, before she was taken into the emergency ward where Shirley looked more peaceful.

'She's still in a great deal of pain. The doctor will see you both shortly and let you know what the next step will be.'

The nurse left and Kerrie took Shirley's hand and stroked it. After a few minutes Shirley turned her head and opened her eyes and looked at Kerrie.

'Thank you,' she said softly. She seemed very calm, which Kerrie put down to the painkillers. 'I signed the paper. For the operation.'

'That's if you have to have one.'

'I will,' sighed Shirley. 'I should never have left home. I never wanted to leave, to die somewhere strange away from my dugout.'

'You're not going to die,' said Kerrie firmly. 'And I'm sorry if you think I overstepped the mark, but you were in agony. You couldn't stay there like that.'

'I just never wanted to be carted off to a hospital to die among strangers. I saw it too often. I swore it wouldn't happen to me.'

'It won't. Next time we'll just leave you to it in your bed alone in your bloody cave!' Kerrie suddenly felt close to tears.

'I hate losing control. I want to make my own decisions. I have my reasons for staying put. This is very traumatic. I never thought I'd have anyone looking out for me.'

'Interfering, you mean,' said Kerrie, dabbing at her eyes.

Shirley tried to smile but caught her breath. 'When you've been alone, without family, you come to certain conclusions.'

'Shirley, I felt the same. After Milton died I saw myself dying a lonely old woman under God knows what circumstances. But now I have a great relationship with a man who says he loves me, I've made new friends and I've had an art exhibition. I feel like a whole new chapter of my life is opening up. And it's thanks to you! So I count you as family, too.'

'Oh dear.' Shirley managed a smile. 'So be it, bossy boots.'

Kerrie leant over and kissed Shirley's softly creased cheek. 'Get some rest. I'll stay with you as long as I can, and then I'll check in to a motel.'

'You must be tired, all that driving.' Shirley's eyes drooped and she was quickly asleep.

Kerrie was suddenly exhausted. She was overwhelmed by the long day and the stress of driving back and forth to Broken Hill, tired from the excitement of the previous night and worried about Shirley's health. It staggered her how much this woman meant to her and how much she wanted Shirley to be part of her life. She wished Tim was here so she could talk to him. She just prayed the procedure was straightforward and that Shirley would be all right.

*

362

It felt odd to Anna knowing that Shirley wasn't in her dugout. 'The observer atop the hill' as someone had once called her. The person who kept her finger on the pulse of Opal Lake. Anna slowed to a jog as she wound around the top of Old Tom's Hill. Today Shirley was having her operation. Kerrie had phoned Mick and let them both know that the doctor would be performing keyhole surgery and they didn't think there would be any problems.

The town felt empty. Ingrid was still away, so were Pam and Doug, and the couple looking after the Golden Dome rarely appeared.

Anna turned the corner at the peak, heading towards Shirley's dugout. The dawn was hazy, a diffused light at the hatching of the day. She paused, taking a deep breath, still fascinated by this eerily beautiful landscape. A slight movement down the hill, a lizard, or a small marsupial perhaps, caught her eye in the stillness. Anna always felt she was imposing on this landscape, that she should be tiptoeing and not pounding through it.

But as she was ready to sprint downhill to the main street, a further sound made her pause. She sensed a presence close by. As quietly as she could Anna walked around the circuit to Shirley's dugout, a place now as familiar to her as her own home. She stopped in surprise to see the door ajar, but then noticed the dripping pot plants and realised that someone had come by to care for them.

She was about to call out when she heard a scratching noise in Shirley's office. Her body tensed; something didn't seem right. By the dim light from the skylight Anna quietly padded into the kitchen and reached for the torch that was always on top of the fridge. But she saw that the light was on in Shirley's office and peered in. To her surprise someone, wearing a hooded top against the morning chill, was rifling through Shirley's filing cabinet. A folder of papers was scattered on the floor.

Suddenly she realised who it was.

'What are you doing in here, Davo?' demanded Anna, stepping into the room. 'Why are you going through Shirley's things? They're her private papers. Nothing to do with you.'

'Why are you sneaking around?' Davo demanded, dropping the papers onto the floor.

'What are you doing?' repeated Anna as she stepped closer to him. She saw Shirley's toffee tin on top of the filing cabinet and a package wrapped in a cloth beside it.

'I'm doing some stuff, like Shirley asked me.' He picked up the tin and the parcel.

'When did she ask you? When did you speak to her?'

'Don't be so nosey. What's she to you anyway? You're new here. You don't know Shirley like I do!'

Anna stared at him in shock. This outburst sounded childish, petty, to the point where she almost laughed at him. 'I know she gives you money.'

'None of your business. Anyway, who do you think you bloody well are?' he shouted.

Anna stared at him, now seriously concerned. 'I'm Shirley's friend, that's who.' Then she remembered that the toffee tin held Shirley's opals and she froze. Obviously Davo knew that too. 'What are you doing with Shirley's things?' she asked as calmly as she could.

'Hiding them for Shirley, somewhere safe. Now piss off, or else . . .'

'You don't have to hide them anywhere. They're safe here. She had them hidden . . .' Anna's voice trailed off. Instinctively she made a move towards him to take the toffee tin. 'Are you stealing them?'

Davo reacted swiftly and vigorously, shocking Anna as he lunged at her then grabbed her. Too late she realised it had been a mistake to accuse him.

'What are you doing?' she shouted. She started

squirming from his grasp, but the more she struggled the tighter he gripped her.

Furious, Anna reached out, swung her arm and tried to hit Davo.

This was the wrong move. Enraged, he slapped her face, dropping the toffee tin and wrenching Anna's arms behind her back and twisting them high until she screamed out in pain. Half dragging her, he lurched through the doorway, pulling her along the dark tunnel to a back room Shirley used as a storage room. Anna thought he was going to lock her in there where no one would hear her screaming.

With one hand Davo turned on the light. He held Anna tightly and grabbed a length of rope, swiftly tying her wrists together, looping the rope down to her feet and securing her ankles together so she was hobbled hand and foot.

'What the hell do you think you're doing? C'mon, Davo, what have I done to you? Why are you doing this?'

'Because you came in,' he muttered.

'But you can't steal from Shirley! After all she does for you.'

'Shut up. It's nothing to do with you, bitch.' He ripped an old rag into a strip and leant over Anna.

'What're you doing? Davo! No!' For a moment she thought he was going to strangle her, but he savagely pulled the rag across her face and tightened it over her mouth, gagging her.

Anna was wondering how long she would have to endure being tied like this and left in Shirley's back room before anyone found her. But to her horror Davo picked her up, slung her over his shoulder and hurried through the tunnel to the back entrance where Shirley parked her car. He bundled her into the back seat of an old Land Rover he sometimes drove and then raced back into the dugout.

Anna started throwing herself around in the back seat, banging her feet against the doors.

Davo was back in a few minutes carrying a shopping bag and a roll of wide tape. Her heart sank as he ripped off a length of the tape and stuck it painfully over her eyes.

As he began to drive away with her in the back seat, Anna started to panic. She felt she was suffocating, not just from the claustrophobic tape but from fear. All she could think was, 'Oh, my God, what's going to happen to me?'

12

THE HOSPITAL WINDOW FRAMED a wispy eucalypt. Shirley lay against the pillows staring at the sky, watching the clouds and thinking that the movement of the leaves in the sunlight, looked as though the tree was breathing. The bright airy room was so different from her snug, dim dugout. She felt very exposed. Staff came in and out to monitor her and there was chatter in the hallway. She could hear the passing cars on Thomas Street.

'How do you feel, Shirley?' asked Kerrie, who was sitting by the bed.

Slowly Shirley turned her head from the window and focused on Kerrie. 'I feel like a turtle without its shell.'

'The doctor is pleased with how it all went. He says ten days or so to recuperate and you'll be home, good as new. Better, actually.'

'Why can't I recuperate at home now? I just want to get back to Opal Lake.'

'Shirley, you know you have to be monitored. You can't go home too early, especially to a place where there's no medical backup. It would be dangerous.'

Shirley sighed. 'I know. I just hate being out of my routine. I feel so dependent, and that's making me feel old. I never for one moment saw myself leaving Opal Lake. After all those years in my own space, this is not where I would have chosen to come,' she said tartly.

'You had the Riviera in mind?' asked Kerrie. 'Just be glad that you didn't have to go to Sydney for your operation. Now that would have been a shock to your system!'

'I suppose so. Thank you for looking after me and coming to see me, but please don't feel you have to stay here. How's Tim? When is he coming? You'll want to spend time with him.' Shirley smiled.

'This might work out very well. Tim still wants to come up and see the art show, and I'll be here when he does.'

Shirley reached for Kerrie's hand. 'I'm so glad I sent you to Roth and you met Tim. Has he proposed yet?'

'That's a leading question, Shirley! Yes, he has, though we'd come to the conclusion we'd be together, anyway. We just feel so happy and comfortable with each other. But I loved that he asked me to marry him.'

'Comfortable!' exclaimed Shirley. 'You don't want to be comfortable with a man at your age! You want sexy, exciting, passionate!'

Kerrie laughed. 'That's part of it, as well. He's so attentive and caring.' She didn't want to draw comparisons with Milton but she was finding it very enjoyable to have a man in her life who spoiled and looked after her instead of the other way round. 'I really feel like I'm in my twenties again.'

'But you're still young, Kerrie. Have you thought about having children?'

'Shirley, I'll be forty-three next birthday. I know it's not uncommon for women of my age to have a baby, but I don't think it's going to happen for me. But the fact that he agreed to try is lovely.'

'You regret missing the boat with Milton,' said Shirley gently. 'He was selfish.'

'Well, I went along with what he wanted and any-way, it's all water under the bridge now. I'm getting closer to Alia, and I hope the other girls will see me differently too. Who knows, they'll probably have children one day. I have a pink baby dress put away . . .' Kerrie stopped, recalling how she'd impulsively bought it in Paris. 'Maybe one of them can use it, if I don't need it myself.'

'Get on with your life, Kerrie. Make the most of every day.' Shirley turned back to the window. 'I sometimes wonder what my life might have been like if . . .'

'If Stefan hadn't disappeared?' asked Kerrie gently. 'Shirley, I wanted to . . .'

Their conversation was interrupted by the arrival of the doctor, flanked by a resident and a senior nurse. Before they examined Shirley, Kerrie excused herself to get a cup of coffee. She decided to call Mick to let him know Shirley was doing well and to ask him to let everyone else know, too.

'Hi, Mick, it's Kerrie. Good news, Shirley is doing great. The op went smoothly . . .'

'Great, great. I'm pleased the old girl's fine. But listen, we're a bit worried here. Anna's gone missing.'

'Are you sure? Where would she go? Are her things there?'

'Yes. She seems to have gone for an early morning run, like she always does, but she hasn't come back. We've searched everywhere.'

'She hasn't taken that old car of Shirley's for a drive, has she?' Kerrie asked.

'No, she hasn't, and nothing seems out of the ordinary. I'm a bit concerned that she's gone for a run out of town and had an accident.'

Kerrie glanced at her watch. 'Mid morning, and she hasn't shown up for work? Maybe give it till lunchtime and then what? Who can you call? The police?'

'There's a sergeant in White Cliffs. I'll give him a bell and alert the Broken Hill police as well. Give Shirley our best. Tell her we'll have a party for her when she gets back.'

'Thanks, Mick. Let me know as soon as Anna turns up.'

Anna was terrified. The silence from Davo as he drove was scarier than his ranting. She knew that there was no way anyone would have seen him put her into his old Land Rover or heard the ineffectual banging of her feet on its door. She was so afraid that she started to hyperventilate. She wanted to vomit but she knew that if she did she'd choke, so she calmed herself by trying to work out the direction the car was taking.

She realised that he was driving a long way out of town and thought that he must be heading to his camp, which she'd heard was well out of Opal Lake. Was Davo, whom everyone thought of as the affable tour guide, some weirdo serial killer? Had he decided to steal from Shirley as soon as he'd heard she'd gone to hospital? Or had he gone to water her plants and seen an opportunity? Had he always planned to rob Shirley, or was it just a spur of the moment decision to take the opals? He'd been so aggressive when she'd confronted him. Why hadn't he tried to bluff his way out of trouble when she caught him stealing?

Surely he could have made up some innocuous story to explain what he was doing? He was in and out of Shirley's place all the time. But then, thought Anna, he'd have had to think of something fast, and Davo didn't strike her as being quickwitted.

She had no way of knowing what was behind Davo's actions, but whatever it was, she was in a very dangerous position and no one was coming to rescue her.

Anna was grateful when the car stopped; anything was better than being trussed up in the back seat of the Land Rover and thrown around as it drove over some very rough tracks. She hoped that Davo would see sense. But whatever happened, she knew she would have to stay calm, keep her wits about her and find some way of escaping.

The car door opened and Davo pulled her roughly out. She fell onto the hard earth, cutting her knees on the sharp stones. When Davo went to lift her up, Anna struggled with him and he swore at her. There was a momentary silence and then she felt the rope around her ankles being cut, but then he tightened it around her wrists.

'Walk,' he commanded. Grabbing her shoulder, he propelled her forward.

'I have to get him to take the tape off my eyes and get rid of the gag,' Anna thought to herself. Suddenly she stopped walking and bent over, shaking and gagging. He shoved her forward again and she fell, her shoulders lifting as though she was struggling for breath.

'Okay, then,' said Davo.

She felt the cool smoothness of a knife against her cheek. 'He's going to kill me,' she thought in horror.

Then the knife ripped through the cloth across her mouth. She coughed and gasped, spluttering.

'Please, Davo, get the tape off my eyes.'

'Shut up.'

He pulled her to her feet and pushed her forward

again. She realised that she now felt cooler than before, and guessed that he'd brought her into some sort of building. He pushed her down, onto the floor. She could hear him moving around as she tried to get comfortable. Her arms, still wrenched behind her, were aching and she felt as though they were being pulled from their sockets. She squatted silently, trying to work out where she was. She'd read about people using all their senses to do this, but all she could glean was that she was on a dirt floor. The momentary sensation of coolness had worn off and now it was stifling. Then she smelt petrol. The horror of fire and of being burnt alive in some bush shack flashed into her head.

'Davo, please, my eyes.'

She heard him move closer.

'Why should I do anything for you? Huh? You were never very nice to me. You and that snooty Kerrie bitch.'

'It wasn't like that, Davo. You were chatty and happy and joked with all your tourists but you came on a bit . . . strong, with me. Perhaps we could talk about it. Why are you doing this? What would Shirley say? C'mon, Davo, you just panicked cause I came in on you unexpectedly. I won't say anything. It's not too late. Just take me back, put the opals back, nothing will change. I promise I won't say anything.' Anna tried to lighten her strained voice, 'I mean, who'd believe this? Everyone likes you.'

There was a brief pause and just as she thought her babbling argument might have worked, Davo shouted, 'You'd better believe it!'

Anna felt herself becoming icy calm as her fear was replaced by a strange numbness. The phrase 'Is this all there is?' leapt into her mind. Then, as if another person had joined them, there was a loud scream, '*No!*'

It was her own voice.

Davo hauled her to her feet and wrenched the tape from her eyes, pulling some of her hair out by its roots and taking her eyebrows and skin, too. His red, furious face was pushed close to hers. 'Why'd you have to mess things up, eh?'

Her eyes were streaming from pain, but she could see that they were in a shack with rough walls, a dirt floor and very basic amenities. A piece of hessian hung crookedly from a small window and she saw a flash of daylight outside. Despite the burning pain around her eyes, she tried to focus on the man standing over her.

'What've I messed up, Davo?'

Slowly he leant towards her and, reaching out a hand, squeezed her breast. She wanted to hit him, hard. She wanted to scream at him. But she was numb, frozen. Then she saw a shock of fear in his eyes, as if he couldn't believe what he'd done.

'This is all getting out of control,' thought Anna. 'I don't think he knows what he's going to do with me.'

For an instant he closed his eyes, his face crumpling, but in the next moment he flung a wild punch, an aimless angry gesture as if he could push away all that confronted him and obliterate what was happening. Instinctively Anna ducked and kept silent, hunched and cowering.

Then Davo seemed to change his mind, and he turned and moved away from her, muttering to himself. Whom he was accusing, quarrelling with or justifying his actions to, Anna had no idea. He picked up a jerry can and walked out of the hut, slamming the door behind him. Anna heard the rattle of a bolt being put into place.

She crouched down again, in absolute terror, her head on her knees, her arms twisted behind her. Suddenly she knew that Davo was heading to the dark side. He'd stepped over a line and there was no turning back. He couldn't let her go now.

All was quiet. Where was he? She cocked her head. Was that an engine? A motor? A car?

It was a chainsaw. God, what was he doing? She sat up. How was she to free her hands? She struggled to her feet, in spite of being unbalanced by her restrained arms. This was her moment. She went to the window and saw through the flyscreen covering that he hadn't taken the old Land Rover.

'Maybe he's taken his minibus,' she thought.

Wildly she looked around the room, searching for something to free her hands. She saw the knife Davo had used to cut her gag still lying on a rough wooden table. She leant backwards over the table, managing to grasp the knife in her fingers. But after a few moments she knew that it was hopeless, her hands and arms were bound too tightly.

Exhausted from this futile attempt, she lay back on the floor, smelling the earthy red-caked dirt. Her eyes were still hurting so she closed them to relieve the stinging. When she opened them again she stared at the scene in front of her: dirt floor, the legs of a chair, the base of some kind of cupboard and a rough hearth in front of a wood stove. 'In this heat, who'd need a stove?' she thought. But she realised that winters out here in a leaky shack would be freezing and a fire of any sort would be welcome.

Then she saw it.

Shielding the base of the stove was a narrow length of corrugated iron presumably to stop embers or wood from rolling onto the floor. Anna struggled over and lay across it. She began rocking and wriggling in a sawing motion over its rough surface until Shirley's old rope finally frayed and snapped. She rubbed her cramped, sore arms and looked out the window. She couldn't see Davo but the old Land Rover was close by.

Anna looked around the hut to see if Shirley's opals were somewhere obvious, but there was no sign of them. Then she grabbed the knife from the table and slashed the flyscreen covering the window. Carefully and quietly she eased herself out of the hut and made a dash for the old car. But the keys weren't in the ignition. 'Damn,' she thought. 'Usually everyone in Opal Lake leaves their keys in their cars.'

She could see Davo's tour bus parked some distance from the hut by a shed. Her heart sank. Davo was still around. Then she saw him leave the shed with some tools, walk over to the bus and open its engine cover. Anna flattened herself against the Land Rover. She heard him return to the shed.

Carefully she peeked out from behind the old four-wheel drive. A shovel, a large cooler and coils of rope were scattered on the ground and a rifle leant against the bus. She had to get out of there. It all seemed so surreal. Even the clouds obscuring the sun gave the scene a strange light so that while one part of her was functioning from moment to moment, another side of her felt as though she was looking down on everything.

The air was close, and she had no real sense of time. Walking into Shirley's dugout and finding Davo seemed an eternity ago. From the shelter of the Land Rover, Anna looked around the desolate landscape. Where on earth was she? The drive out here had seemed long, and this place looked like the end of the earth. But she couldn't stay here. She had no idea what Davo planned to do with her and she could not stay to find out.

Anna glanced upwards at the glowering sky, said a swift prayer and, as if hearing the starter's gun, took off in her usual style – running as fast as she could. She tried to fly above the ground, touching it lightly to make no sound. She took heart that the noise from within the shed would mask the sound of her speeding feet.

She headed for a nearby mullock heap, hoping that the white mound would shield her while she got her bearings. When she reached it, she could see that beside it was an old mine shaft. The rusted scrap of iron over the top of the mine shaft was held in place by rocks and a coil of old barbed wire. She had no idea how far down the shaft went but she'd heard stories of bodies being thrown down mine shafts and never found. Was this what Davo had in mind for her?

She crouched behind the hillock and looked around the bleak countryside. She could see that the track Davo had driven along went no further than his shed. Small trees were clustered in the distance, but there was no sign of any kind of road. If she ran along the track leading from Davo's hut, he'd be able to find her. She would have to run across country.

There was no direct sunlight. Everything glinted in an eerie light – the forewarning of a storm. She could see some small bumps on the horizon. Maybe those hazy breaks were dwellings or mining machinery. She decided to head towards them. The empty plain, distantly studded with scrub, stretched in front of her.

While this landscape didn't screen her much, it was flat and she could easily run over it. If she could cover enough ground before Davo knew she was missing, she might stand a chance. Anna took a deep breath and ran with long loping strides – wishing she she could swallow up miles with each one.

The air felt close and there was a strange smell, and not a breath of wind. It occurred to Anna that the changing weather could be an advantage to her. The cloud cover made things much cooler and if it rained, the rain might obscure her from Davo. But she had no idea how far she would have to run before finding help. In this open country where she had no water, could she outrun her pursuer?

Many thoughts passed through her mind, but then came a very familiar voice: 'Pace yourself. This is a long run. Uneven ground. Concentrate on what you're doing. Adjust your stride. Breathe.' Craddock's voice was so clear she almost stumbled. But she kept running.

She focused on a spot ahead and allowed herself to be reeled forward at the end of an invisible line. Keep going, keep going. She kept listening to her coach's advice and found she was pacing herself: slowing down, breathing well and then picking up speed again.

Anna kept running.

Now there was a slight breeze and the hot heavy air was laden with moisture. The day became darker and Anna knew that her prayer had been answered. A storm was coming.

The wind picked up. There was a distant rumble. The sky above the horizon was bruised with large purple and blue thunderclouds. 'Was that thunder,' thought Anna, 'Or the moan of wind?' Then she realised it was the sound of an engine. Her rhythmic pace faltered slightly but Craddock's voice told her to keep calm, not to panic and not to bolt. Her steps remained steady. But between the rising gusts of wind she heard the unmistakable growl of a car getting louder, and she glanced quickly over her shoulder. To her horror she glimpsed the outline of Davo's old Land Rover in the distance.

She pushed down her rising panic as she felt the first drops of rain sting her face.

Anna kept running.

The grey rain began to blur the emptiness around her. Now she felt she was moving through a silver space and she realised that she could end up running in circles if the rain got much heavier. A clap of thunder shuddered high above her.

The sound of the car continued to grow behind her while the horizon wavered faintly ahead of her.

She looked back again. The Land Rover loomed

larger like an animal stalking its prey. She imagined Davo behind the wheel, grinning madly.

She felt the terrain beneath her feet changing; the ground had become softer. She looked down. She was now running on sand!

The engine was louder, nearer, and she knew that the car was gaining on her. Then a flash of lightning whipped across the horizon, lighting up the sky. The large and ominous clouds were speared by shafts of light followed by the roar of thunder.

Soon the storm would be above her on the strange sandy plain.

Anna kept running.

Breathe slow, move forward, speed up.

And then suddenly she knew where she was. She was on Opal Lake, running across its dry bed, being pummelled by soaking rain. She glanced back. The Land Rover didn't seem so close now. It had slowed down. Perhaps Davo couldn't see her in this rain. Perhaps there was a shortcut away from the lake that she didn't know about. Maybe Davo would get out and run after her. She almost laughed aloud. 'Do your damndest, Davo,' she thought.

'Steady, take it easy, take it slow but sure,' came Craddock's calm voice. 'You have a long way to go. This is still dangerous.'

The storm began to whip itself into a crazed whirlpool, stirred by forks of lightning. This scared her. She knew lightning ran to ground through the highest point, travelling along whatever conductor it could, and she imagined being struck at any moment.

Anna kept running.

Then the storm was above her, and she was caught in the middle of a madness of blackened sky, blinding rain clouds threatening to suffocate her, while shards of fiery lightning bounced all around her.

Davo and the Land Rover became remote dangers. She saw a bush bent double in the wind as if cowering against the onslaught of the rain. Crazily her mind spun. 'What to do, what to do? Where was Craddock's voice and advice now? Drowned by this black and blue nightmare,' she answered herself. She stopped running.

She flung herself to the ground and rolled over, squirming and digging herself into the wet sand. Her arms, still stiff from being tied, felt weak, but she scrabbled like a frantic insect, feeling her body being covered by a wet blanket of sand one instant, while the rain washed it away in another. Her hair felt sandy, her mouth gritty. Was she being buried alive?

The crack of powerful lightning hit so close to her that she imagined she felt the ground quiver. Then there was another crack even closer. She had a vision of her body being left a blackened skeleton, never to be found in this vast, arid lake. No one would ever know what had happened to her.

'No!' She scrambled to her feet, shedding wet sand like some primordial creature arising from hibernation. She broke into a shaky sprint, trying to outrun the rain, dodge lightning and evade the dogged pursuit of the now invisible four-wheel drive.

This time she didn't look back. Whatever advice Craddock might have been shouting in her head was deafened by the wind and rain and lightning.

Anna kept running.

It was more than survival that propelled her forward. Now she was being challenged to prove something to herself, to outrun the elements and the man in the Land Rover. She tried to concentrate. She stopped for a minute, drew deep breaths, held her face to the sky and gulped in mouthfuls of rainwater. She slowed her pace, conserving her energy, watching where she went and weaving around the puddles, trying to see what was ahead of her.

She was determined to reach the far side of this lake. A strange calm came over her.

She knew how much those opals meant to Shirley. She wanted to show Kerrie, Pam and Mick that she had purpose and commitment and wasn't just a drifter like some who passed through Opal Lake. She wanted to measure up to Craddock's expectations and belief in her.

But most of all she wanted to prove something to herself. She knew what she wanted to do. 'If I get through this, give me a chance to run seriously,' she prayed aloud to the retreating storm.

The storm passed over her. She adjusted her pace to invigorate herself. Dare she look behind? She couldn't see the Land Rover.

From her only visit and Shirley's mud map, she struggled to remember the layout of the lake. She recalled that there'd been a track at the end of the lake and a small lakeside path. The lake seemed enormous as she looked across to the vast horizon. But it was not the size of it that worried her as much as its remoteness. With no water or food she wondered if she could make it back to town. No one would ever look for her out here.

She shook her head. 'I'm not thinking like that. It's defeatist. I am going to get there. Davo can't win. He mustn't.'

Anna kept running. Steadily. Pacing herself. Pushing forward. Conserving her energy by not allowing herself to feel panicked or stressed. She ran smoothly, in her zone, not thinking, not feeling, ignoring the pain in her body, just breathing as evenly as she could. Every step forward was another bite of the lake swallowed and left behind.

And then she recognised precisely where she was. How long ago it seemed since she'd first come out here to see the lake. There was the old table and seats where people picnicked and there was the track winding down to it. She knew that this was the road into town even though there was still a long way to go.

She left the lake and felt the firm track beneath her feet, knowing that she was heading in the right direction. A renewed burst of energy carried her forward. Scrubby bushes, dripping from the recent rain, and scattered trees lined the track. After the barrenness of the lake, she felt comforted.

Anna put her head down and kept on running.

Ahead of her the track curved, screened by saltbush. In the distance she glimpsed an open patch of ground dotted with mullock heaps.

As she swung around the corner she altered her pace and lifted her head, and then almost stumbled. Parked across the track was the old Land Rover and leaning against its door, with a smirk on his face and his arms folded, was Davo. Without slowing, Anna swerved and headed past the trees towards the open ground, studded with old mine shafts and mullock heaps.

Anna heard Davo shout her name and something else but she took no notice. Her heart was pounding and her breath rasping in her throat.

She zigzagged as fast as she could, racing around the mullock heaps in an attempt to confuse the heavier and out-of-condition Davo, who was now running after her. She was careful to watch her feet, avoiding sheets of rusty iron, rocks and mine shafts. Warnings and tales told by miners about uncovered mine shafts came back to her.

She didn't dare look back to see if he was gaining on her, or if he had his gun with him. All she could hear was her breathing, and blood pounding in her eardrums. She heard Davo shouting after her, but she ignored him. Then she heard a crash. She scrambled behind a large mound of dirt and paused, gasping for breath. She felt as though she was in a scene from a bad western and if she stuck her head up over the mound, she would get shot. Should she stay low and run from mullock heap to mullock heap? Was Davo hiding, waiting for her to make a move? She looked around and waited.

The silence was unnerving.

She couldn't stand the inaction. She would just have to start running again and work her way back to the track and hope that Davo wouldn't pursue her. Standing still in the quiet wet scrub, preparing to make a final dash, Anna heard a yell. Was it a trick?

She waited. The noise became a low growl. A moan. She stepped out from the bushes and looked around. There was no movement. Where was Davo? She moved quietly towards the sounds. Then she knew. He'd gone down a mine shaft. But which one? She had no idea. She could hear him, so he was still alive. She broke into a run and headed back down the track. She looked in the old Land Rover and to her great relief saw that the keys were still dangling from the ignition. The rifle was on the back seat. She leapt in and started the motor, flung it into first gear and pushed her foot down onto the accelerator.

'Thanks for the driving lesson, Davo!' she shouted.

Anna sped along the track. She felt rejuvenated knowing that she wouldn't have to run all those final kilometres back into town.

Suddenly she braked and stopped the car. 'I can't leave him without finding out what he's done with Shirley's opals,' she said aloud. She turned the car around and drove cautiously back, half expecting to see Davo limping along the track towards her. Thank goodness his rifle was still in the Land Rover. She stopped at the mine site, and got out and looked around.

All was quiet.

'Davo? You out there, Davo?'

Was this a trick? Maybe she should just go. But she wanted to get Shirley's opals. She knew how important they were to her friend. She had to try to find out where Davo had hidden them.

Anna picked her way across the no man's land of mullock heaps and mining detritus. Here and there were scattered slabs of iron, which had escaped the anchors of old tyres and stones, leaving dark holes exposed.

This was hopeless. There could be hundreds of places he might have fallen. She shouted, 'Davo! If you can hear me, make some noise!'

Anna strained to listen, aware of every sound – the faint sticky rustle of wet leaves from a small wattle, the distant croak of a frog. What if he was dead? If he'd hidden Shirley's opals they'd never be found. She turned back to the car. And then she heard it. It was small, but too regular to be an incidental noise. She hurried towards it.

The sound came from a shaft where a sheet of iron looked to have been recently disturbed. She looked down into the darkness but couldn't see much.

'Is that you?' asked a faint voice from the bottom of the shaft.

'Yes,' called Anna.

'I've broken me leg.'

'I can't get you up, but Davo, I'd like to help you. First you have to tell me where Shirley's opals are.'

There was no answer for a moment, then, 'Don't know what you're talking about. Just go and get help.'

'Sorry, Davo. Don't think I can do that if you won't tell me where the opals are. You'll be right down there. At least for a day or so. Someone might come by and find you.'

'You wouldn't leave me here? I'm in a bad way.'

Anna didn't answer.

'Okay! They're at the camp. In the water tank. Now will you get me some help?'

'Yeah, Davo. I'll get back with someone as soon as I can.' She dusted the dirt from her clothes and jogged back to the Land Rover.

Mick hung up the phone. He was worried by Anna's disappearance. The police sergeant at White Cliffs had reassured him that young people did take off occasionally, so they'd wait twenty-four hours before sending out search parties. Mick was not happy with this response. Anna had been missing since dawn. What if something serious had happened? He went into the cubicle that served as his office to ring the police again when he heard someone come into the bar.

He called out, 'Be right with you,' and hurried back into the bar. 'What can I . . . Holy cow! Shit, Anna!'

Anna was clutching a glass of water and leaning her head on the bar. She suddenly slid onto the floor and started shaking.

'Jesus, Anna, where've you been and what happened to your face?' He rushed over to her.

'Now that I'm here, everything's all right.' She tried to smile. 'I just have to have some water.'

He waited while she gulped the glass of water, then he helped her to her feet.

'What happened?'

'I caught Davo taking Shirley's opals and so he took me too.'

'He abducted you? Are you okay? Did he hurt you?' Mick asked. 'How did you get away?'

'I'm all right now, Mick. He took me out to his camp, but I got away. I've been running for hours. I came across the lake.'

'Geez. That's miles. Did you come through that storm out there?'

Anna nodded.

Mick stared at her. 'You sure you're okay? Do you want something stronger than water? Do you want to tell me what happened?'

'I'll be fine. I was pretty scared, but he didn't rape me or anything. I feel safe, now I'm back in town.' She paused and then told Mick what had happened. 'I went into Shirley's dugout and there he was. Taking Shirley's opals. When I surprised him, he tied me up, gagged me and put me in the back of his Land Rover.'

'Geez. Davo did that? We'd better call the cops.'

'He's not far away. I ran across the lake and he drove around it to wait for me on the road into town. He fell down one of the shafts at the old mine site there and I think he's broken his leg. I made him tell me where he'd hidden the opals. They're in the water tank back in his camp. Then I took his car and drove back here.'

Mick looked grim. 'I'll call Broken Hill now.'

'Will I have to take the police out to find him?'

'Shouldn't think so. You're clear about where he went down the mine shaft, so they'll find him. I expect they'll drive out to his camp and get Shirley's opals, too. Don't you worry about Davo. Go and have a lie down and leave everything to me.'

Mick dialled the number. 'Why would he steal from Shirley? She gave him money . . .' he muttered to himself.

'Hello, Broken Hill cop shop? I'm reporting a crime.'

As Mick talked to the police, Anna went slowly to her room. She could barely put one foot in the front of the other and she fell onto her bed. When she woke up, it was dark and she was ravenous. She had a quick shower and was about to return to the bar when there was a tap on her door. She opened it, and when she saw Mick she asked, 'What's happening?'

'The police've got him. Found the opals, too.

Someone'll come out tomorrow and get a statement from you. I said you should have a rest and I told them I'd keep an eye on you.'

'Thanks, Mick. You've been so kind.'

Anna turned and went outside and sat on her little patio in the crisp night air. The sky was clear and the evening stars glimmered in the deep lilac sky. She started to shake again and tears ran down her face.

Mick joined her. 'Anna, love, what can we do?' He sounded concerned. 'Have you spoken to your family?'

'Not yet,' said Anna. 'I don't want to worry them. I'm fine. No, I'm not. I'm tired, I'm hungry. I'm upset.'

'You should talk to your mum and dad.' He patted her hand. 'Never thought Davo'd do the dirty on Shirley, after all she did for him.' He shook his head.

'Is Shirley all right?' asked Anna. It felt like she'd been away for weeks.

'Yeah. Kerrie is with her. You should speak to Kerrie. Perhaps it might be better if she tells Shirley what's happened.'

Anna shrugged. 'Maybe it was all a spur of the moment thing with Davo. He went into Shirley's and she wasn't around. He knew where she kept her opals so he took them.'

'You're being too kind, Anna. He didn't have to take you, too. Why don't you go into the kitchen and get Thelma to give you a big feed? Then when you're ready, call your parents and Kerrie, too, if you want to.'

'Kerrie, it's me, Anna. How's Shirley?'

'Shirley is doing just fine. Doesn't want to be here, of course. Thinks she can have an operation and go straight back to her dugout. I can't believe she was a nurse. What've you been up to? Mick said you'd gone walkabout.'

'Yeah, you could say that,' said Anna drily. 'There's been a problem at Shirley's dugout but it's sorted. She doesn't have to worry.'

'What's up? What happened?'

'I found Davo inside her place stealing her opals.'

'What? You're kidding!'

'He'd been there watering the plants, I think. I went into the dugout to see who was there.'

'The dugout was locked. Mick had the key! I s'pose Davo could have taken it from the pub. He was in and out of Shirley's place all the time.'

'When he saw me and I accused him of taking Shirley's opals, I think he panicked. He went nuts, grabbed me, tied me up and threw me in the back of his old Land Rover.'

There was a momentary silence at the end of the phone. 'Are you okay?' asked Kerrie. 'Can you talk about it?'

Briefly Anna told Kerrie the details.

'Anna, you have been so brave. Poor Shirley . . . Was it just the opals he took?' asked Kerrie.

'I think so . . . and a sort of package as well,' said Anna. 'I made Davo tell me where he'd hidden them, and the police have been to his camp and got them back.'

'Of course, of course. I'm so glad you're all right, Anna, and the police have retrieved the opals but I need you to go and look for something important in Shirley's dugout.'

Anna listened as Kerrie explained.

'I want to make sure that Davo has told the police about all of the opals he took and not just some of them. Call me back as soon as you can.'

Kerrie paced around the hospital wondering how she'd tell Shirley the news. Maybe she could wait until she'd heard what the police had recovered. What a terrible thing Davo had done to Anna. Kerrie had found him an unpleasant, arrogant man. He probably was not that bright and she'd been told he had a quick temper, but she would never have guessed that he would do something as frightening as this. And what a thing to do to Shirley, especially after she had helped him by putting money into his tour business. What a way to repay her kindness! How stupid.

Her mobile rang. It was Anna.

'It's not there. I found the hole behind the light but it's empty.'

'Oh no.'

'What was it?' asked Anna.

'Opalised fossil. Very valuable. But more importantly it had an incredibly high sentimental value to Shirley. We have to make sure that the police get it back to her.'

Kerrie sat down by Shirley's bed. 'There's been a bit of drama over at your place, but things seem to be under control. Anna is the heroine of the day.'

Shirley didn't like the anxious tone of Kerrie's voice. 'What do you mean, at my place?'

'It's Davo. Anna caught him red-handed going through things in your office and he took your opals.'

'What? How dare he? What did he say to Anna when she caught him?'

'Actually Shirley, he panicked and grabbed her as well as your opals and took off.'

'The opals?'

'And Anna.'

Shirley gasped and laid her head on the pillow. 'Is she all right?'

'Yes. But he got a bit nasty. It must have been terrifying. Luckily she got away.'

'Are you sure she's not hurt? Did they find the opals? Oh, Kerrie, what about Tajna? He knew where I kept it.' She threw a stricken look at Kerrie. 'Poor Anna. Where is she now?'

'Back at the pub. Davo took her out to his camp, but she escaped. He chased her in his Land Rover, but she ran right across the lake. He caught up with her on the road into town. Evidently he got out of his car and went after her but fell down one of the shafts at an old mining site and broke his leg. The police found him and they went to his camp to retrieve your things.'

Shirley had paled. She shook her head. 'I can't believe Davo did that. After all I've done for him. He's nothing but a low-life ratter. Davo, a ratter. Of course, I should believe it. There are always ratters on the opal fields and they often think that violence is okay. I just can't believe that Davo would be one.'

Shirley straightened up in her bed. 'What about Tajna?' You know how much it means to me . . .'

'Shirley, calm down. I've checked on Tajna. Davo had taken it, but I rang the police and they assured me that it was safe with the rest of your opals. It's fine and you'll get it back, but perhaps this has been a good warning. Maybe it's time you put it somewhere more secure than your dugout or gave it to a museum. Why don't you talk to Gustav and Helen about it?'

Shirley shook her head. 'I can't. It's my only link with Stefan.'

Kerrie's heart lurched. Suddenly Shirley looked older than her years. 'I understand, Shirley, I really do.'

'What will happen to Davo now?' asked Shirley. 'No one will want to have anything to do with him. Don't know how his business will survive.'

'More than that, Shirley. He'll be charged with theft, kidnapping and assault!' exclaimed Kerrie.

'I suppose he will. Hard to believe that he could have done this. Is Anna very upset?'

'I've been talking to both Anna and Mick and I don't think you have to worry about her. She seems pretty resilient.'

'I'll be so pleased to see her. I can thank her for looking after my opals. She's been amazing,' said Shirley. 'I just want my life back the way it was. Knowing I have my opals to cash in if I need to and knowing that Stefan's fossil is close by. Dear Kerrie, let me rest a little. Hearing all this has worn me out.'

'Of course, Shirley. But I'll be back later. I want you to meet someone.'

'I'm not up to visitors,' Shirley said weakly, but then curiosity seemed to get the better of her. 'Is this person a friend of yours?'

'I asked him to come and see you, yes.'

Shirley closed her eyes and sighed. 'I trust you, Kerrie. Whatever.'

'I'll see you later,' said Kerrie gently, and left the room. She grabbed a takeaway coffee from the little coffee shop in the hospital grounds.

'No muffin today? How's your friend?' asked the girl behind the counter.

'Doing fine. No time for a muffin. I'm on my way to the airport to collect someone.'

Shirley was dozing when Kerrie re-entered the room. But she opened her eyes and smiled when she saw Kerrie. Then she looked at the man beside her. He looked to be in his fifties, good looking and definitely Slavic. He was smiling hesitantly at her.

'Who is this? Where's your Tim?' asked Shirley bluntly.

'Tim is coming up soon. He's going to take you

dancing,' joked Kerrie. 'This is Goran Zilich. He's visiting Australia from Croatia.'

'Oh.' Shirley looked momentarily blank, then gathered herself, sat upright, adjusted the folded sheet and studied the visitor. 'You have family here?'

'Not in Broken Hill. My relations are in Sydney. We haven't seen each other for a very long time, except for a cousin who came to Dubrovnik for a holiday. Tourism is very big there now. When you're recovered you should visit Dubrovnik. It is a beautiful place.'

Shirley shook her head. 'Too late, although I did once dream of going there. What are you doing here? How do you know Kerrie?'

'I had some people do some investigating for me, or rather for you, Shirley, and that's how I met Goran,' explained Kerrie.

'What do you mean, Kerrie?'

Goran leant towards Shirley. 'May I call you Shirley? I feel I know you. I also knew Stefan.'

Shirley caught her breath and grasped his hand. 'How do you know him? Where is he?'

Goran swiftly took her hand in his, shaking his head. 'I didn't mean to raise your hopes. Sadly, sadly, he is no longer alive.'

'Then why are you here?' demanded Shirley.

'Shirley, it's a long story,' interrupted Kerrie. 'After our last visit, when you told me all about Stefan, I just knew that I had to find out what had happened to him, so at least you would have some peace. Not knowing what happened to the man you love seemed so strange as well as terribly sad. So I decided to try and make some enquiries on your behalf. Through his art, Milton knew many important people, including a dear friend of his from Croatia. I contacted him and he referred me to a man who was experienced in finding out what happened to people who disappeared in Yugoslavia during the communist regime. So an investigation began. This man not only found out what had happened to Stefan, but he found someone who was with him when he died.'

'That was me,' said Goran. 'Kerrie asked me if she could fly me to Australia so that I could personally tell you what I know about Stefan. So here I am. I met Stefan when I was still young. He was wonderful to me. We became friends.'

'Where was this? In Yugoslavia?' whispered Shirley, tightening her hold slightly on Goran's hand.

'Yes, in Goli Otok,' he replied, giving a little shudder. But the name meant nothing to Shirley so he continued. 'It was a terrible place, an island, a lump of rock, in the Adriatic Sea, not far from the Croatian coast. Goli Otok means naked island and it is isolated and the vegetation sparse. Tito turned it into a political prison, to house those people who were still Stalinists, or who might have had pro-Soviet ideas. Later, when Serbian, Croatian, Macedonian or Albanian nationalists tried to make their voices heard, they were also sent there, as well as common criminals. I was imprisoned there with Stefan.'

'Stefan in prison? Why was Stefan in prison?' Shirley's eyes blazed, demanding answers.

'Shirley, wait. Goran will tell you the whole story,' said Kerrie gently.

'I can't believe it . . . after all this time. If only I'd known before . . .' Shirley sighed.

Goran shook his head. 'You could have done nothing. It was a very difficult time. Most Yugoslavs never knew of the existence of Goli Otok. A few tourists go there today. It is all just rotting away as it was left.'

'Why was Stefan in a political prison? He was only interested in becoming a good Australian. He didn't have any political or nationalistic ideas,' said Shirley.

'Yes, I know. He didn't but I did. I was young, passionate and reckless, and I protested and was arrested and ended up on that fortress island. That's where I met Stefan. Sometimes I think it was meeting him that saved me. We shared a cell for a brief time and laboured together in the stone quarry. It was such heavy work, but Stefan was used to hard labour and he would do his work and then help me.'

Goran turned to Kerrie. 'It was hellish on that island. The winters were freezing, the wind like cutting ice, and the summers hot, like a fire. There was no shade and when we looked to the sea we wanted to jump from the cliff just to cool ourselves. How I longed to see a forest or a lake. The prison was a whole township where we were forced to work in the quarry and workshops. There was a section where the solitary confinement cells were that had a chamber where . . .' He glanced at Shirley and lowered his voice, 'where unspeakable acts happened.'

'But I don't understand. Why, why was Stefan in that terrible place?' asked Shirley. 'He had only gone back to Yugoslavia to see his dying mother.' Tears welled up in her eyes.

Kerrie began to wonder if bringing Goran to meet Shirley had been such a good idea. His words were like a scalpel opening up an old wound.

'Stefan told me that he was arrested at the airport as soon as he left the plane. He was told by the authorities that they knew he was a subversive who had been plotting against the regime. It all happened so quickly that he had no chance to contact anyone, family or friend.'

Shirley shook her head vehemently. 'There's no way that Stefan could be involved in that sort of thing. He was honest and he despised the others in Lightning Ridge who were hanging on to the old battles and ancient prejudices instead of getting on with their lives in their new country. Stefan was a good man.'

Goran nodded. 'Yes, he was a decent man. I liked him very much.'

'Please, go on with your story, Goran,' said Kerrie.

'Stefan had a trial, of sorts. The authorities presented their case and he had no way of defending himself, so he was convicted. That was not unusual. Anyone who was thought to be opposed to the regime could be imprisoned with very little chance of justice.' His expression softened. 'We talked about many things. Our homes and our family and how we hoped that things would change. He told me about Australia, that it was a good place. He talked about his Shirley, and how living with you was the happiest time of his life. He told me how he met you, and the fun you both had camping in the bush and living in a cave. I found this last part very strange, but Stefan said it was true. I liked to listen to his stories. You both seemed to be so free and independent, living the life you truly wanted.'

Shirley closed her eyes and a tear slowly slid down her aged cheek. Kerrie reached out and gently touched her shoulder.

Goran went on in a quiet, steady voice. 'We both talked about our dreams, and how we hoped our lives would turn out. One's life can change so quickly and for unexpected reasons. That prison was a horrible place. But Stefan was always sure that one day he would get back to Australia and to you, Shirley.'

'What happened to him?' asked Shirley flatly, her eyes still closed.

'I'm sorry, Shirley. He had been away from Yugoslavia so long that he was no longer used to the harsh winters. One winter he became ill, but the prison authorities ignored him. He was forced to continue the back-breaking work in the quarry, although he was not fit to do so. He collapsed and although he was taken to the prison hospital, he died of complications from pneumonia.'

Shirley took this in, then shifted in the bed. She folded her hands on top of the sheet, tears streaming down her cheeks. 'My poor, poor Stefan. How could I have ever doubted him? I can't believe that anything so terrible could have happened. My poor darling man.'

Kerrie smiled at her. 'Now you know that Stefan never stopped loving you.'

Shirley nodded. 'I suppose so, but when I think that I didn't trust him. How could I have had such thoughts? Kerrie, I don't understand, Bosko told me that Stefan had got married. How could he be so cruel as to say that?' Shirley's eyes narrowed. She suddenly understood. 'Stefan was set up, wasn't he?'

'Yes, he was, and by that man Bosko,' replied Kerrie. 'The man I hired to trace Stefan's records was very lucky. Many files had disappeared, but he found Stefan's papers and it was clear that the person who had falsely accused Stefan and alerted the Yugoslav authorities of his arrival in Yugoslavia was Bosko. It seems that Bosko was really an agent provocateur. While he was supposedly recruiting Croats, Serbs and Albanians in Australia to work against the communist regime in Yugoslavia, he was really working for the UDBa, the Yugoslav secret police. So far from supporting these nationalist groups, he was making sure that the Australian authorities thought they were terrorists. At the same time, the money he extorted from the opal miners went to the communist regime, and not to the people that the miners really meant to support. He was a very busy man.'

'I suppose he hated Stefan for not buying into his lies,' said Shirley.

'And from what you've told me, Shirley, Bosko might also have been worried that Stefan could have gone to the Australian authorities over his extortionist activities. I suppose that when he knew that Stefan was going back to Yugoslavia to see his mother, it was a good opportunity to get him out of the way. I'm so sorry, Shirley,' said Kerrie.

Shirley turned to Goran. 'And you flew out to Australia to tell me all this. Thank you very much. What happened to you, Goran?'

'I survived my sentence and things began to change in Yugoslavia. The prison closed down entirely in the late eighties.'

'So if my Stefan hadn't died from pneumonia, he would have been released eventually? It's so hard to believe that such a terrible thing happened, but at least now I know. And you found this out for me, Kerrie. How can I ever thank you?'

'Shirley, you've been such a good friend to me, it was the least I could do. If the same thing had happened to me, and the love of my life just disappeared into thin air, I would always wonder what happened, just as you did. I had the means to hire someone to do the search and then to fly Goran out here, and I am so pleased that I could,' said Kerrie. She leant over to hug Shirley.

Shirley looked at Goran. 'Thank you for being a friend to Stefan. See what good friends I have, too.'

'If there is anything else I can do to help you, please let me know. I was in bad shape when I came out of Goli Otok. I was sad that Stefan had died. Perhaps I should have tried to find you, but I wanted to pick up the threads of my life again. Australia is such a long way away and there were too many Shirleys to look up.'

'Please, it's all right. I'm so grateful to you. All those years I spent wondering and now I know. I wish I could thank you properly. If I was home in my dugout I could. I loathe being in here,' she said crossly, sounding more like the Shirley of old.

Kerrie smiled. 'Goran is happy to stay a few days,

seeing as he's come all this way and you're in hospital. We'll take him out to Opal Lake. Then he can see the "cave" you live in. Now, Shirley, do you want to rest? I'll pop back this afternoon and we can talk if you like,' said Kerrie, standing up. 'Goran, let me buy you lunch.'

*

Shirley walked stiffly, using a stick, but she was already feeling better and had renewed energy, so she decided to take a few slow laps around the hospital corridors. It was days since the visit from Goran, which she sometimes felt she'd dreamed, but her general sense of peace and well-being reminded her that the encounter was real.

She thought she'd like to look at the orthopaedic section of the surgical ward because it was where she used to work all those decades ago.

A passing nurse paused and asked, 'Can I help you?'

'Now that I can walk, I know that I have to keep exercising. I used to be a ward sister in an orthopaedics unit years ago, in Sydney. I bet things have changed since my day.'

The nurse smiled. 'Yes. We try not to immobilise people for weeks on end these days. We've only got a few orthopaedic patients in at the moment, mostly knee and hip replacements.'

They chatted as they walked.

'You look like you're recovering well,' said the nurse.

'Gallbladder. Glad it's over. Everyone has been very kind and efficient here and looked after me really well, but I don't plan to come back any time soon. Any patients here with broken bones that I could have a look at?'

They moved further along the corridor until they came to a private room where a bored-looking policeman was sitting outside a closed door reading a newspaper.

'The patient in here is under arrest. I don't know why they bother with security,' the nurse said to Shirley in a low voice. 'He's got broken legs. He's not going to run anywhere.'

Shirley stopped. 'Could I look in on him? I'd like to see how you treat such patients now. No more high traction you said?'

The nurse spoke to the policeman who stood up and folded his newspaper before nodding. The nurse opened the door to the room. Shirley paused in the doorway.

'You have a visitor. A former sister who knows all about broken bones,' said the nurse to the patient.

Shirley ignored the modern equipment. She was staring at the occupant of the bed. Calmly she said, 'Good morning, Davo.' He turned his head away from the window and his eyes widened. Swiftly he brought his one good arm up to shield his face.

'You know him?' asked the nurse quietly.

Shirley walked slowly to the bed and stared down at Davo.

'Why'd you do it, Davo? Why? What were you thinking of when you took off, not just with my opals, but with Anna?'

'Dunno.' Then he mumbled, 'Sorry, Shirley.'

'You stole my opals, went through my things and hurt that girl,' she said angrily.

'I don't think that we should be talking to him,' said the nurse in a worried voice.

'I dunno what happened. Everything was going bad. I thought the business would fold and then what would I do?'

'You could've just asked me to help you. You were supposed to be my friend,' snapped Shirley. 'Now look at the trouble you're in. You're a big disappointment to me.'

'What's going on in here? Do you know this man?' The policeman bustled into the room.

'We're just going,' said the nurse. She took Shirley's arm.

'Am I going to jail? What'll happen to me, Shirley?' Davo whined.

'Do you expect me to care, after what you did?' Shirley turned away.

'Are you the woman he robbed?' asked the nurse, looking incredulous, as they headed back down the corridor.

'I thought he was just a bit stupid, but he was a ratter, and ratters can be very violent when they're after opal,' said Shirley. 'He took my opals, but he did more than that. He took a young girl against her will. Now he wonders why he's in hot water.'

'I thought you were very decent, under the circumstances,' commented the nurse.

'He'll have plenty of time to think about what he's done. I'd better go back to my room. I have a friend coming to visit any time now. Thanks for the tour.'

*

The hotel was closed. Anna finished cleaning and wandered into the sunshine out the back where Mick was busy with his buckets of rough opals. Anna sat in a chair and stretched her legs as Mick stepped away from his wheel and studied the opal he was holding for a minute before sitting beside her.

'It's got some nice colour but patchy.' He handed it to her.

'Yes, blue and green stripes.' She gave it back to him.

'Ribbon, with a bit of pinfire. I'm trying to collect examples of all the different opal patterns.' He turned the stone in the sunlight, enjoying the flashes of colour.

'Why don't you mine fulltime, Mick?' asked Anna. 'Digging out opal yourself must be more exciting than buying it from a miner.'

He nodded. 'Sure is. I used to love mining. Now you need money to buy dozers and heavy equipment. Price of diesel has gone through the roof, times are tight and people aren't paying the good prices for opal, not like they used to. Lot of miners who have the good stuff are sitting on it, waiting for times to change. Too many restrictions from the mines department now. So little blokes like me, retired people working up here in the winters, are finding that mining is too expensive. We're being pushed out by the big boys who are after the gas below the opal level, and whatever else they're finding down there. Nah, I'm happy being in town now. Let the others do the mining, while they still can.'

'I've been happy here too, Mick. But it's time I went.'

'I understand that, love. Been a terrible thing, this Davo business.'

Anna paused a moment. 'It was scary at the time. But when I think about it now, somehow it's made me stronger because I came through it. I'm not going to let it affect me negatively. In fact, in a way, it's proved something to me.'

'What's that?'

Anna almost smiled. 'Having to pace myself out there, at the lake, because I knew I had such a long way to run showed me that my head can control my feet. I used to be a mad bolter, but now I know I can stop that. I really understand what my coach was trying to tell me. When I start running competitively again, I'll be able to run a tactical race.' She added, 'I need to get some money together somehow and I'll be right. I'm raring to go and give running my best shot. So Mick, I'm going back to Adelaide to find my coach.'

'Well, I'm blowed. All of us felt real bad about Davo.

Never would have thought that he would grab you like that. But, as everyone says, ratters can be dangerous. In a way it was my fault, too. Everyone knew Shirley's key was hanging in the bar, so I guess he just helped himself. I s'pose he thought he could get away with it. Would have too, if you hadn't surprised him. You pressing charges?'

'I can't pretend it didn't happen, but I just want to move on now. I've told my parents and they want me home for my twenty-first birthday.'

'That'll be a big day. When is it?'

'Quite soon, actually.'

'You know what would be nice? How about we give you a send-off party and make it an early twenty-first bash as well!' exclaimed Mick enthusiastically. 'Y'know, Shirley will be home in a day or so, and we might be able to get her to come down to the pub, now that she's been to Broken Hill. Kerrie's bringing her back. Kerrie's bloke, Tim, is bringing some Yugo friend. Pam and Doug are back. Ingrid's here. Yep. Sounds like a party.'

'I don't want any fuss,' began Anna.

'Thelma can make a cake, we'll have a barbie out here. Give you a right old send-off, Anna.'

Mick phoned Kerrie who agreed that it was an excellent plan.

'We'll be back in a couple of days,' she told Mick. 'Tim has taken our friend Goran to Lightning Ridge for a bit of a look-see while I'm here keeping Shirley company in the hospital. Tim's father Roth is on the valuing committee over at the Ridge.'

'So he's one of the experts who values stones anonymously for miners unsure about their value. Been a good system that,' said Mick.

'Yes. Roth wants to bring more jewellers and marketing people from all around Australia to learn more about opals. He says people don't know enough about them to appreciate the fabulous stones. I told Tim that every Aussie girl should get an opal when she turns twenty-one!'

'That's it! That's what we can give Anna! She needs money so she can go on training or something.'

'I'm one step ahead of you, Mick!'

There was a shout from the front of the pub and everyone moved outside as a great cheer went up. Kerrie and Tim were on either side of Shirley, supporting her as she gingerly walked from the car, while a smiling Goran walked behind her. Spontaneously everyone broke into applause as Shirley was helped inside and settled into a chair.

Pam and Ingrid looked at each other, their eyes filled with tears of delight. Kerrie sat beside Shirley, who gazed around, taking in the scene.

'Never thought I'd be down here again,' she said softly to herself.

'Gin and tonic, wine or . . . ?' Mick asked Shirley.

'This is an occasion. We thought champagne!' said Tim. 'Mick, bring out your best bubbly.'

'This is an amazing place,' said Goran. 'I see why it meant so much to Stefan. And Shirley is very special. But that place she lives in. It is a cave! I could hardly believe it when she showed me. I always thought that Stefan had exaggerated.'

'It's different,' agreed Tim. 'Some dugouts are very luxurious. But Shirley seems to have all she wants around her and even if she is nearly eighty, she manages quite well.'

'There are good people here, too,' said Goran. 'It is a friendly community. My relatives have never left Sydney. They have never seen places like this, which are nearly on their doorstep, while I have flown nearly halfway around the world to be part of this.'

'We haven't had a big bash in Opal Lake for some time, so this has turned out to be the perfect opportunity,' said Pam as she surveyed the room from the other end of the bar.

Anna laughed. 'This is such fun, I can't thank everyone enough.'

'I'm glad that we could get here, too,' said Helen. 'Who's that with Kerrie and Tim?'

'It's quite a story. That fellow – Goran – met Shirley's Stefan in Yugoslavia. Bit of a tragic tale as it turns out,' said Mick. 'I'm sure we'll get the details eventually.'

'I believe it's made a big difference to Shirley,' said Anna quietly. 'I'm so happy for her.'

'We're just glad to have her back at the Lake, safe and well,' said Mick.

'How is the fossil research going?' Tim asked Helen and Gustav as they came over to join him, Kerrie and Shirley.

'It's so exciting. Our dream of establishing the Australian Opal Centre is becoming a reality. Soon we will be able to exhibit properly the greatest collection of opal, opalised fossils, and heritage and stories that have come from the opal fields,' said Gustav. 'Glenn Murcutt and his wife, Wendy Lewin, have designed a groundbreaking building out near the Three Mile open-cut at the Ridge, so it's in situ so to speak.'

'It's an amazing building,' enthused Helen. 'It will draw visitors from all over the world – a global centre of research to promote everything to do with our national gemstone. There's nothing like it anywhere else in the world!'

'Sounds fantastic,' said Kerrie. 'Tim and his father have some novel ideas for ways to promote opal. How about in the Sydney to Hobart, one of the maxi yachts used a spinnaker made of opal print material? And at the Sydney Festival opal-patterned lights could be projected onto the sails of the Opera House!'

Shirley listened to this exchange and said to Helen and Gustav, 'I have something I'd like to donate to this Opal Centre, but there is one proviso.'

Kerrie stared at her, guessing what Shirley was about to say.

'It's a rather lovely opalised fossil and I'd like it to be displayed as a gift from Stefan Doric.'

Kerrie touched Shirley's arm and said softly, 'That's a lovely idea. Very appropriate.'

Shirley turned to Anna. 'And for you, young lady. I want to help you. You were very brave and I want to thank you for retrieving my opals. Over the years old miners have bequeathed me their opals on the understanding that, when the time came, I would know what to do with them. I think that time is now.'

Anna looked stunned and began to shake her head, but Shirley took her hand.

'It's time those stones were put to good use. I'm sure Roth can organise a good price for them and you can use that money to get to wherever it is you need to help you become a great runner.'

'Shirley, I couldn't possibly accept . . .' began Anna, her eyes brimming with tears. 'Just offering them is so wonderful of you . . .'

'I'm not just offering them, I mean it. And I hope I get to see you on a podium winning some medal, if that's what you're aiming for.'

Anna was speechless, embarrassed and shocked. She turned and flung her arms around Shirley, hiding her face.

'This calls for a toast,' said Tim. 'Everybody, gather round.'

With their champagne glasses raised, everyone in the pub grouped together, some even spilling out the front of the little hotel onto the footpath.

'To the doyenne of Opal Lake, Shirley! We're glad

you are healthy, happy and back home. To Goran, thank you for making the journey to bring Shirley the truth. And to Anna, who is our hope for the future not only as an athlete but as a young woman we all admire.'

'And the best barmaid this pub ever had,' interjected Mick.

'And . . .' Tim continued with a smile, 'to Kerrie, whose generosity has brought so much of this about, and to your own future, your own dreams and your own happiness. May they be mine, as well. I love you.' He leant forward and kissed her.

Cheers, laughter and shouts followed, and people gradually moved to the barbecue and its tantalising smells.

Kerrie reached for Anna's hand. 'A small birthday gift from me. For you to keep and remember Opal Lake.'

'I don't need anything to remember, this has been . . .' Words failed Anna. 'I'll come back and visit, may I, Shirley?'

'Of course, dear. I'd be upset if you didn't. Open your present.'

Pam and Ingrid came forward to watch as Anna opened the little bag Kerrie handed her.

Anna simply stared, speechless, at the shining, glittering gem in the palm of her hand.

'It's the ring from Opal Lake!' exclaimed Pam. 'What a wonderful idea, Kerrie.'

'I found it there when I first went to the lake,' said Kerrie. 'It had been there a long time, waiting for the right person to claim it. You conquered that lake, Anna, so I think you are the right person. I hope you enjoy it.'

'I can't accept it, it's too much,' said Anna, but she couldn't take her eyes off the magnificent ring.

'Wear it for Australia,' said Tim firmly. Kerrie slipped it onto Anna's finger, where it sat snugly. Kerrie and Shirley exchanged a smile.

'I will,' said Anna simply. 'Thank you.'

Shirley turned to Kerrie and took her hand. 'I was resigned to the fact that my days would fade quietly to black in my special hole in the ground. But knowing Stefan is never coming back has freed me to step outside into the world again. Thanks to you we have formed a bond, learnt from each other and our friendship will stay as bright as that opal ring.' Shirley's eyes looked as blue as the sky above, giving a sudden flash of the young girl she'd been.

'Yes, Shirley, you're right,' said Kerrie. 'Women friends are special. They can shape who we are and who we want to be. They support and nurture us and give us strength and comfort. Out here we've helped each other but let's not wonder why it happened but just enjoy being the friends we are.'